Arula Books by Karen Michalson

Enemy Glory
Hecate's Glory
The King's Glory

Enemy Glory and *Hecate's Glory* were originally
published by
Tom Doherty Associates
175 Fifth Avenue
New York, NY 10010

The King's Glory

Praise for the Enemy Glory series

"Brilliant. Unforgettable. Poetic. *Hecate's Glory* — like *Enemy Glory*, the first book in Karen Michalson's proposed trilogy — is a masterpiece of fantasy. You don't read these books: you experience them. It's like listening to beautiful alien music whose slow, hypnotizing melodies could either originate from an ancient, long-forgotten race or some madwoman's dreams. The lyrical narrative is equally fascinating and disturbing. . . . If you're looking for a light read, stay away from these novels. Michalson's series is heavy in every sense of the word. If you enjoy stories that are complex and intellectually as well as morally challenging, I highly recommend *Enemy Glory* and *Hecate's Glory* — dark, cerebral fantasy with enough treachery and revenge to satisfy even the blackest heart."

— Paul Goat Allen, Barnes & Noble

"Here's a little something for *Enemy Glory* fans who've been wondering whatever happened to Karen Michalson's luckless Llewelyn. *Hecate's Glory* will fill you in on the whole gory, blasting, twisted, dark deal that Michalson's devilish imagination has rendered in ink — maybe it was blood. If you like your fantasy dark, depressing, and a little disturbing then *Hecate's Glory* won't disappoint. . . . Frankly, I'm wondering how many mediocre, pulp churning, New York Times List-making successful writers could meet Michalson's well-crafted writing quality, or even read well enough to clue into her devastating deconstruction of the literary world."

— Eva Wojcik-Obert, *Fantastica Daily*

"Llewelyn might say he serves evil – and, in truth, he's no saint – but he remains a truly likable and, oddly enough, decent person. Michalson's study of the darkness and light in every soul has created a powerful and memorable character."

— Penny Kenny, *Starlog*

The King's Glory

Karen Michalson

Arula Books

THE KING'S GLORY

Edited by Donald Weise

Cover art by Dave Laabs

Arula Books

For information visit:
www.karenmichalson.com

First mass market edition: August 2019

ISBN of this book is 0-9853522-4-8
978-0-9853522-4-0

Printed in the United States of America

For Bill
For patience

Acknowledgements

Grateful acknowledgment is made to:

Donald Weise for agreeing to read *Enemy Glory* and *Hecate's Glory*, and to take on the editing of this final third of the trilogy. Mr. Weise's suggestions were consistently meticulous, astute, and utterly pitch perfect. Also, working with him was an absolute pleasure.

Ryan DesRoches of Massachusetts Web Designs for creating, maintaining, and beautifully redesigning my website at karenmichalson.com. And for coming on this journey through all three books. And for drumming.

Dave Laabs of The Airbrush Shack for creating the covers for each of the books in the trilogy. And for working something close to magic by manifesting the heart of each book in a single image.

Namukulwa Nakazwe, for book promotion. And for her consummate skill with social media marketing and graphic design. And for her kindness, sensitivity, professionalism, and energy.

My spouse, Bill, for beta reading and book design. And for guitar playing. But mostly for his ongoing support of the trilogy, and for simply being there and welcoming my characters into our lives.

My readers who, having twice entered Threle, have asked to go back. Third time's a charm

One

I do not know how long I remained outside the hovel. I stood lightly on cold sand and watched a star fall into oblivion. Then I waited for the rest of my life to begin, holding myself open to whatever would come. But nothing came except unsteady pulses of North Country sun and the sound of Isulde's scarefisher.

I felt nothing. I knew less. And then I crashed.

I know I crashed because my palms stung with the impact. And then the chill of the wet sand slammed and spread through my body. But it was hard knowing anything, except that I hurt, and that hurting meant I was alive.

I painfully pushed my palms against the packed sand, carefully lifting my body until I could sit, then stand, then find my way to sit again, resting on a rock. I wanted to think, but my thoughts were like scattered shadows. They softly sharpened and dispersed as I idly watched a water dragon moving on the lake's surface. Then the dragon submerged and the lake went still. That was all I knew. Until finally, out of the stillness, my thoughts returned in slow, slippery surges of self-awareness.

My first thought was that I died at dawn. Walworth, my one-time friend and the new King of Threle, had satisfied his sense of law and judgment by converting the hovel into a makeshift Threlan courtroom and finding me guilty of murdering his cousin, Lord Cathe. Which I suppose was fair. But you'd think Walworth would account his cousin's death as something of a favor to Threle, considering Cathe's own personal roster of treasonable acts. However, I had killed Cathe without bringing him to a proper trial and all that. And since Walworth has always been mad for proper trials, there we were.

Then, instead of killing me himself, he sentenced me to die from exposure to the North Country. Which I did, briefly, before Isulde tripped into the hovel and, for reasons I couldn't begin to parse, interfered by singing fairy songs that pulled my spirit back into my body.

So here I was.

My second thought was that, if I wasn't careful, I might sit on this North Country shore until I sickened and grew dead again, for I could feel the hollow Northern drag against my rising life force. In remembering my death, my body told me the North Country was still bane, but told me instinctively, in the dream way a dying animal's hunger-ridden stomach still tells it to avoid a deadly herb. I knew that my death had dissipated my ban, the wizard-curse that insured I would die if I came here, because I now felt a strange blankness where my ban used to be. But feeling that blankness meant that I was still magically sensitive, just as feeling pain meant that I was still alive. And so I understood that even though my ban was gone, the Northern energies would sicken and kill me again, like any other magic user, if I stayed too long. But how long was too long was the gods' own guess.

You see, in some ways, the North Country has no time. In other ways, time makes occasional stops here, but it is always the sort of time that doesn't really happen and that you can't really know about. A wide, buzzing planet may send her image here to skim the sky and dimly mark what passes for seasons, or the seasons may sometimes curl round themselves in the semblance of the cycles you think you know, but mostly seasons just happen in different places, at random, whenever they feel like happening. Weeks speed and slow and chase each other by the tail for sport or spite. You'll sometimes sense hours or minutes, but only as spurious outlines of experience. Young ghosts fighting to be seen in a soft, blinking wind.

North Country time is all ghosts and semblance. You are to believe none of what passes for change. Besides, whatever you do notice is usually irrelevant to whatever is happening. Study the dawn and it vanishes like a bleak moony charm. Measure the hours and they laugh at you and disappear. Trace the sun and your skull freezes.

Which makes it damnably difficult to make plans.

It took an afternoon's forever to know my thoughts again. But as I kept encountering my bodily echoes as memory, I began to remember why I had come here, what I had told Walworth about that decision, and why, contrary to all the laws of magic, I was alive again.

I had come here to sacrifice myself for Gondal, the country that Emperor Roguehan had strategically made me king of shortly before I murdered him. Roguehan, who had mysteriously emerged out of the remote southwest kingdom of Furnesse and fought a protracted war with Threle for the aesthetic pleasure of watching the Threlan people, inspired by his propaganda, destroy themselves. He particularly enjoyed watching them kill each other. He found it exquisite when they burned their own towns.

But even though his alignment to evil infused his artistic tastes, Roguehan loved elvish beauty. So much so that he lusted after Arula, Gondal's oldest city, because it held the only elvish art remaining in the world. And so he needed a Gondish king to kill so he could embody Arula by taking the king's power. Which is where I came in.

I killed him with an elvish arrow as he stood, at my invitation, heart-struck before the unspeakable glory of an ancient elvish painting, after he failed to kill me and claim his prize.

But as to my sacrifice. Almost immediately after I killed Roguehan, Hecate, my goddess, commanded me in a divine vision to make a horrific choice. I was to either destroy Gondal, whose elvish beauty I also loved and whose power I embodied as king, or enter the North Country and die there in a state of eternal damnation. That was Her judgment on me for murdering two evil high priests. One of whom, ironically, was Walworth's cousin, Lord Cathe.

For reasons I still could not explain to myself, I chose eternal damnation, throwing my newly-acquired crown into the unwilling keeping of my friend Aeren, a lonely, sharp-tongued storyteller who had her own claims to the Gondish throne and little interest in asserting them. Then I resolutely rode here to die, expecting that my ban would kill me. Of course, I had no idea that Walworth was also riding here.

Roguehan was fascinated by self-destruction in all its forms, and surely would have cheered my own foray into same had I let him live to know about it. Walworth, on the other hand, had merely respected it. "I would like to think I would have had the strength of heart to risk as much for Threle," he said before sentencing me to death by exposure to the North Country, in what was possibly the most redundant act of his reign, considering I was already dying from my ban to satisfy Hecate's judgment for killing Cathe.

Ironically, I *had* once had the strength of heart to risk as much for Threle. That's sort of why we were here, and Walworth knew this better than anyone, although I still had no idea if he saw it that way. Before he became king, I had risked my life and more to gather evidence at Kursen Monastery to save him from being executed on a false treason charge that arose from his secret attempts to defend Threle. He rewarded me with abandonment to spiritual torture in that same monastery, where I rashly chose to become a priest of Hecate. If not for Hecate's judgment on my crimes against Her, I'd still be in Arula.

I also had no idea if Hecate had accepted my sacrifice; my choice to die in the North Country in place of destroying Gondal and its elvish art. Hecate was a goddess who destroyed through excessive order, who strangled lives through rigid application of oppressive law and pedantic scholarship. The North Country was pure chaos and therefore anathema to Her. Any attempt to communicate with Her from here would fail. The problem was, I did die. But then I didn't. And so it was possible that my sacrifice wasn't completed. But if she had accepted my sacrifice, I was now irrevocably damned to Her.

That meant I saved Gondal, but could now look forward to eternal torture upon my next death.

El, my master at Kursen, would have considered that justice. He happened to be the other high priest I murdered. He cheerfully dedicated his life to evil. I convinced him to commit suicide, to sacrifice himself to save Kursen Monastery by embracing goodness. I did this knowing it was pure torture for an evil high priest to wrench his spirit into an opposing alignment. And El, unlike me, loved evil. I felt sympathy as I watched him suffer.

As part of my monastic training, I had been forced to memorize the sort of punishments Mother Hecate could mete out to wayward priests. One of them came to me now, vivid as a waking dream.

I envisioned Hecate making me into a ball of flesh so I would sicken on myself as my long years in Her servitude had led me to sicken on meat. In this form, I felt myself endlessly dissipating in the lower belly of one of Her dogs, all of my senses heightened and howling. The dog kept digesting me in the dark of its stomach. I writhed as the acid seared me but I never dissolved. I kept believing that I would remain in that quivering form, suffering for eternity. And then for mercy, if that's the right word, evil old Mother Hecate removed me from Her dog and shaped me into my body again. She then, with a hellish maternal delight, squeezed all my long, low evil back into my terrifyingly open heart; dirty black ink forever staining an empty scroll. Then She flattened my body into the form of an old toad, which She slowly crushed in a volume of dead learning until the pages ran cold with my poison. And then I dried between the pages, the way a dead flower does, my wet toad-guts staining the paper and turning to powder. My only companion was the horror of knowing that my punishment was to be so undisturbed forever.

Even as the waking dream vanished, I could feel myself imprisoned in a slow rotting silence under the deadening North Country sun. The ball of endlessly-digested flesh and the eternally book-flattened toad were two of my best guesses for punishment. But there were no limits here. Hecate was capable of torturing well over anyone's best guess.

I pulled my robe around me and endured the memory of how closely I had come to eternal damnation, of how I had come within mere words of Hecate's torments before Isulde sang me back me into life. My failure to die—or to die for long—meant I both failed to sacrifice myself and failed to destroy Gondal.

I watched the hard waves dash and dance out of the strange lake and knew once more that I had to be careful not to sit here too long and die again.

If Hecate hadn't accepted my sacrifice, I would not be damned to Her, because the eternal damnation was contingent on self-sacrifice; that was the price for saving Gondal. But I might be helplessly bound to work Gondal's destruction, whether I willed to or no. I had no idea if Hecate still found me an acceptable priest, but I knew She didn't release Her clerics lightly. If Walworth and Isulde had somehow botched my sacrifice, then my true spiritual alignment, if I still had an alignment, was really anybody's guess. Including mine.

Ah well, no life should be without excitement.

I again considered Walworth and his motives. Walworth had prevented me from dying in the North Country, that is, before he coolly sentenced me to death there and just as coolly pronounced all debts paid when I unexpectedly returned to life, because from his perspective, my brief death paid for the murder of Cathe. Which was a decent thing for him to do, considering that he knew I had been a spy for Roguehan and that I had been planning to kill him and destroy his household. That was mostly Cathe's idea, but wreaking revenge on Walworth for having left me to suffer in Kursen had its charms at the time.

Not that Walworth's decency made sense, but, under the circumstances, if the King of Threle was pleased to prolong my life, I was more than pleased not to argue sense. And besides, we had once been friends. Although that hadn't been obvious for a few years. Not since I joined his cause as a youth, apprenticed with his wizard, Mirand, and pledged my loyalty to him and Threle.

I then considered Walworth and how little of himself and his motivations he ever revealed.

What business did Walworth, the self-proclaimed new King of Threle, have up here if Mirand really had defeated Roguehan by using the Wand of Surprises I had once unwittingly brought them to "reverse the order of things"? Those were Walworth's words, but what did they even mean? When I asked Walworth about that, he responded with a complicated, mysterious word game involving mystical power transfers between himself, his twin sister Caethne, Mirand, and the forces of history. "Defeat became victory," Walworth said, explaining that Mirand had wrenched the energy of Roguehan's victory and somehow shifted it to Walworth. And that hole in time, in the worlds, in the All—whatever cosmic mess Mirand had created with that desperate maneuver with the Wand of Surprises—was the strange bend and flow of time and elements that I experienced when I escaped from Walworth's castle.

In other words, Walworth cheated. He and Mirand created a Threlan victory where none existed by using magic to change history. Roguehan had won, and Mirand had trespassed on the gods' prerogative by re-arranging time.

So I wasn't the only one with potential problems with my deity. Mirand was now anathema to his goddess, Athena, and Walworth had admitted as much when he confessed that he "did not know if it should have been within our power to change history. It was an act for the gods, not us, and Mirand fears he lost Athena's favor through his action."

What could I say to it? I didn't have a run of sympathy on that score.

Curiously, Walworth didn't object or appear surprised when Isulde restored me to life. Instead, he indicated that he wanted me cleared of my crimes should I ever work for him. So something in my life was valuable to him.

I knew I could be a great asset to Walworth if I chose, despite our colorful past. For one thing, as a priest of Hecate, I knew all about evil. And I was beyond intimate with the uses of clerisy, although I had no intention of doing anything practical with Hecate's force for a while. I also had a fair deal of wizardry at my disposal, having learned much from Mirand. Also, I was fluent in three mundane languages and devastatingly proficient in several magical ones. The new king would be hard pressed to find another advisor with the same curious educational background and experience as myself. If I worked it right, I could probably command a fair sum.

But I refused his implied offer of work. I had once loved Threle as much anyone could, but Threle, or Walworth, had nearly destroyed me by leaving me in Kursen.

I then considered all that Walworth had transcribed during our trial. When he returned to Threle, my role in the destruction of the Threlan border town in the Duchy of Helas would be public knowledge. And not just the border town. It would also be known that I had caused the destruction of one of Roguehan's military camps in the recent war, which had also been located in Helas. Some Threlans might account that reasonable work because Roguehan was in the process of invading and destroying Threle. But I deliberately caused the deaths of hundreds of Helan soldiers, Threlan ex-patriots who had gone loyal to Roguehan out of anger with King Thoren, Threle's previous king, for executing their duke. And given that their duke was executed as a result of my exposing him as the real traitor at Walworth's treason trial, I decided that I could do better than return to Helas.

Also, because I had murdered Roguehan shortly before coming here, and had a hand in destroying his chief wizard, Zelar, I didn't care to try my fortune in Sunna, Sevalas, or any of the southwest kingdoms recently under Roguehan's influence.

Biding my time in a monastery, among other evil clerics, was not an option. Given that business of leading El to destroy himself by wrenching his evil to goodness, and my well-earned conviction for killing Cathe, I knew I needed to avoid my own kind. Whatever my current relationship was with Hecate, I was now a fair mark for other evil clerics.

That was a bit of charm to break into my expanding self-awareness. A horrible feeling like a tight cloud of panic accompanied this insight as I suddenly realized again how close to a horrible damnation I had come. I briefly wondered if Threle ever hired assassins. Seemed to me I might make a go in that line. Not everyone can destroy two evil high priests and live, or live again, as the case might be.

Something like a hermit crab made a jumpy movement in the distance. The lake was now a shuddery storm, the way North Country things suddenly turn into other things. I shivered and the lake was a lake again, snarling and gray and crashing bitter against the scarefisher's creaky weave.

I had been made King of Gondal and now the world and I were dark to each other. Perhaps that was some ancient elvish joke. I thought again of Roguehan, who tortured men for pleasure and died for love of elvish beauty. Hadn't he and the world also been dark to each other? And then of Walworth, who lived by reason's light, by Mirand's teachings. Was he any less dark? Hadn't he conspired with Mirand to torture the fabric of the world by changing history to his liking? Hadn't he been willing to damn the gods for love of Threle?

My thoughts were now starkly complete and stunningly useless. And for all I knew, so was I.

I walked slowly toward the hovel. I had no idea of what else to do. I knew I needed to return to the world, but I could not guess what that would mean, or even know how much time had passed there while I was in the North Country. Months? Years?

When I passed the scarefisher, he was weaving a bowl of water in his lap. I paused and watched. And then, without intending to, I drank. The water tasted clean.

Inside, the hovel was warm and smoky. Isulde was still there, tending a fire, and her foster-father, the fisherman, was sitting where my body had lain. He was eagerly banging one of his bowls with a stick. I didn't see Walworth, which was just as well. "Hey, evil one, I'm sitting where you died." The old man looked up at me and smacked his tongue in his lips. "I'm sitting where my fairy daughter put me. To stand in for you."

I leaned in the doorway and watched Isulde, wondering what sort of fairy game she was playing by making the fisherman a proxy for me, or for my corpse. My tongue was too heavy to speak but my desire to say something was making my head feel lighter than a morning wish, so I knew the words would come. I noticed my old black riding cloak draped over one of the old man's storage chests, so I donned it and watched the fire. The cloak felt familiar and evil to me, and then the evil felt strangely comforting, because it grounded me into my past and so made my life feel firm and real.

Isulde was making merry with the fire. In a kind of fairy play—because what isn't play to a fairy?—she made the flames pop rough stones across the sandy floor. The stones kept sprouting into fresh grass and the grass kept withering into mice. The mice kept squealing and running back into the flames. And then the mice stiffened and became stones, starting the life cycle again. Stone to plant to animal to stone. Isulde played with nature's universal transitions the way she had played with my particular transition from death to life. And so her magic meddled with the remains of the fire, by which I had stood trial, just as her magic had meddled with the trial's outcome.

Then I didn't think of the fire. Or the old man. Then I just didn't think.

"Did you have a good death, Llewelyn?" Isulde turned from the hearth to greet me with one of her long, hard Isulde-kisses while the fisherman held his bowl out toward us and smacked his lips. When she left off kissing, my throat felt bruised and cold. She took my hands in hers.

"Where's Walworth?" I felt awkward asking, but worse than awkward not knowing.

She giggled. "Gone." Then she smiled. I smiled back. My new life didn't matter, come what will. It was good and lovely to be here with her again, as temporary as being here was.

"And now it's over." She dismissed all my being dead as a minor irrelevancy. "And now you can eat up all the mice before they die. Like bread. Here." She picked up a gold and white mouse and it did stretch along her palm into a piece of rye bread. "For eating and new strength."

I did eat, hesitantly, because my throat was still too bruised from her kiss to swallow anything solid. The bread wriggled horribly in my empty stomach, as if it had transformed back into a mouse. When the wriggling stopped, I did feel full. And then dully sick. The bread was now a mouse again and my body wouldn't take meat. Perhaps I was still bound to Hecate.

"So come." She brought me to a pile of blankets. "And tell me stories. Or wishes. Or whatever you like." She lay beside me and threw her arms around my waist, vanishing my confusion into . . . if not comfort, something like it.

"No, no, no," crowed the old man in strange, playful admonishment. "Tell *us* stories. About you."

"He already has," remonstrated Isulde.

"Then make him go dead again, the nasty thing. Then you can turn his bones to porridge. For the fish." He held out his bowl and stick.

"Shush. I shall turn your bones soon. Into fish. For it is nearly your time." Isulde was now speaking to both of us. Something in her tone caused me to tremble a little, as I imagined my body being fed to fish and my spirit rising to Hecate for torture.

The old man gasped and blubbered. "Please do not put me away like an old toy."

Isulde ignored him. She turned and spoke directly to me, grasping my hands and pulling me from the blankets. I stood unsteadily, unsure of what she wanted. "Kiss me your death." I tried to oblige, to send my experience of death into her through my kiss, but she pulled back laughing and stroked the waning moon—Hecate's mark—that scarred my palm. The old man hooted and sobbed. "Such an old kiss to know you by in your new life." Isulde was referring to Hecate's mark as a kiss, but she was also teasing me about my failed attempt to kiss her. "Watch. This is you."

Isulde took the old man's face in her hands and gazed intently into his eyes. He squeaked in terror as she began to squeeze and pinch his cracked skin. The skin softened and stretched and molded like watery clay and the fisherman squeaked once more before he shrunk to the size of a toad and she flattened him in her palms. And then there was nothing left of him but powder. I watched, horrified, as Isulde carefully swept the powder with a thorny broom into the bowl he had been banging. Then she threw in his stick and fastened a piece of slate over the bowl with twine. A shape like a spiny water dragon formed in the stone, with a face that resembled the old man's. She closed and locked it in a storage chest.

"What did you just do?" Even though I had spent my life studying magic, fairy magic was beyond my understanding. It was serious and playful and violent and gentle and dark and light at once; it was a power that flowed from another world, like the North Country did, and only occasionally brushed against this one. There's a reason that simple farmers, with no experience of fairies, nevertheless associate them with chaos, proclaiming candidly: "If fresh milk spoils, the fairies played a trick. If you find a coin in your boot, the fairies played another."

It's best not to argue. Especially since like all proverbs, that one has a thread of truth.

Isulde replied to my question in typical fairy manner, by answering and not answering. "His powder is porridge in the bowl. And now my poor old foster-father is a water dragon playing with the fish he used to catch. But I can use his powder to bring him back again, like I used songs to bring you back. You see?"

"No."

"Whatever Hecate does, I can do better."

Fairies are older than the gods; they care nothing for them. I now sensed that Isulde was able to read my fears and had transformed the old fisherman to comfort me, to show that if she could bring me back from death she could bring me back from torture, just as she could mold her foster-father into the toad I feared becoming, turn him to a playful dragon, and still bring him back to his North Country hovel when she pleased.

But I had learned a long time ago to take fairy magic as it comes. Analysis is useless and fairy explanations aren't much better. Besides, like the North Country, fairy magic lies among so many energy paths and worlds and realities that there's no other way to take it. And Isulde, as a North Country fairy, was equally enigmatic. The world was her plaything. And its elements—good, evil, life, death—were elements of one great game to her, pieces she shuffled into whatever amused her. It wasn't even clear whether Isulde loved the world or anyone in it, although some loved her, including Walworth and Roguehan; enemies as opposed to each other as the oppositions with which she played.

She handed me something warm to drink out of the fire. I tried to swallow but the heat went all stiff and solid in my mouth and so I spit it up. "Still a little dead, then?"

"Just a little, I suppose. It will pass when I leave the North Country."

Isulde studied me gravely. "Welcome back to the world you know."

The way she said it sounded almost like a joke, and I laughed a little, but the laughing hurt and I stopped. "How goes the world I know? The world beyond the North Country."

"Silly Llewelyn. How goes any world? It goes. So. What would you like for a homecoming gift?"

I couldn't answer.

"Would you like to play in the chest with my father's dreams before I bring him back?"

"No."

"Would you like to die all over again here and be happy?"

"No."

"What then?"

"To have our dreams again. The ones we had in the world I knew."

"We always have our dreams. Tell me what else you should like."

"I should like to return to Gondal. To what remains of my life."

"So make your wish and go."

"I can't. I have nothing to wish on and I don't know the way out of your Northern chaos."

"So stay," she said simply. "And when you die again here from all the Northern chaos, I will keep you like my foster-father."

"I don't want to die again. Ever. Can you help me?"

She opened a chest and a small black horse with a white face climbed out. "Your horse ate fairy thistles and turned into sea foam." That was the horse I rode here originally. "This horse is a wish." She led him outside. I followed.

"Yes, and what shall I call this horse, this wish?"

"Call him Shadow. He will take you anywhere you want to go. Once."

"And then?"

"And then he dies."

I mounted quickly.

"You need not mount so sudden. He won't die here. He'll come back here after he dies. Shadow isn't a magic user so, unlike you, he can stay here forever." She stroked the horse's neck and fed him a mouse.

"But I can't. Already I feel your energies pulling me back toward the sky, the way I felt my spirit rise."

"Then take this agate to ground you as you need. And to dream of me in words." She poured sand through my fingers and rubbed grains into my palm. "The sand will be an agate when you leave." The grains made cuts all through Hecate's scar that marked me as evil. "But if you must leave, I charge you with the dream."

"Which dream?"

"The dream that is your own. To serve all beauty, day and night."

"I will. I do." As I said this, Isulde softly kissed my scar and smiled. Then she was no longer there.

The North Country chaos rose and swirled and Shadow rose to meet it like an old friend made of the same stuff. "Shadow." I whispered his name in Botha, the tongue of my childhood, but he appeared to know what I meant. "Take me back."

And so I rode. Or rather, Shadow carried me. He plodded steadily through the North Country as if he didn't know or didn't care that the land spread around us like a cruelly distorted vision. Sometimes it rose and fell and bent back on itself in random waves that crashed and roared as Shadow ambled through the chaos. Sometimes those land-waves would crest, go still, and burst into mountains that we suddenly found ourselves climbing. But when Shadow patiently made his way to the highest point, the mountains dispersed and we found ourselves back on land that tilted and swayed. Sometimes he trampled on fairy flowers that shuddered with pain. Then the land went still and we rode through storms; dark winds that stained the ground in foreign colors I had no name for.

I had no name for anything. Our trail was a lucid dream lurching out of a dull sky.

I didn't experience leaving the North Country, but at one point I realized that my legs were sinking into something cold and wet and gray, and Shadow was suddenly slipping and unsure of himself. And then I understood that we had left the Northern chaos and were crossing a forest stream, and Shadow, being a fairy horse, was having difficulty traversing the normal world. I held his mane because he had no bridle, and when I looked into the bright sky through a rush of leaves, I could see we had barely left the North, for the Drumun Mountains that marked where the chaos began were still visible. That meant that the forest stream was part of the River Kretch, that bordered the North.

As skittish as Shadow was getting, there was nothing for it but to trust the horse to get me to Gondal. I closed my eyes and the sand that Isulde had rubbed into my palm hardened into a sharp agate. The agate did ground me, as she promised, but it grounded me to the North Country, and so I felt such a rush of sickness that I threw it away. And the instant the agate hit the river, Shadow lurched and we were flying together into the world. I kept my eyes closed because the moment I opened them, I knew I would be starting my life again and I wanted to pause and feel exactly what that meant.

What that meant was that Shadow became all dust and death in the sunshine of a bright field of wildflowers. But I saw the field as if I were coming at it from a dream, for my eyes weren't open yet. I remember falling through the quickly dissolving cloud that Shadow became when he died. I remember wildflowers that whispered and twisted into rushed explanations of color. But then the flowers went dark and I knew that whatever fairy path Shadow had brought me on had closed.

The fall stung and slapped my back, but at least it was a healthy hurt in contrast to the North Country's low crush of sickness. I opened my eyes.

I was alone and back in my life, in my rooms, in my castle, in Arula, in Gondal, and for all I knew, in the crush of Hecate's mind. In the world, anyway, and open as an empty grave.

Two

The rooms I once occupied as Gondal's king held only failing sunlight. There was nothing else.

When I told Shadow to take me back, I understood that "back" might be unrecognizable, depending on how much time had passed during my absence. But somehow I didn't anticipate that my royal chambers would be as bereft of their former glory as I was.

The elvish paintings that once graced my walls, weeping beauty like a failed god disbelieving eternity?

Gone.

The elvish statues that once graced my rooms, capturing the fall of divine energy as it lapses into mortal form?

Gone.

Rectangles of setting sun marked exposed floor and walls. The only furnishing was a pile of torn and bloodied clothes where my sumptuous bed used to be. I knew I was still sensitive because the dried blood caused my senses to creep a bit when I examined the clothes. They were Roguehan's. He was wearing them when I killed him.

There was no way to determine how long ago anybody had been here, or how much time had passed while I was in the North Country. The door was locked. This was so cleverly pointless, considering there was no longer anything here to protect, that I decided Aeren must have moved everything in one of her fine rants. She wasn't enthusiastic about me breaking our contract by tossing Gondal at her to run, so vacating the royal chambers and tossing Roguehan's death clothes here as some kind of obscure statement could easily have been her way of showing appreciation. But before entering the rest of the castle, the rest of my life, and an unpleasant disputation with Gondal's unwilling queen, I had more pressing concerns.

Here, in these rooms, Hecate had commanded me to destroy Gondal and purge the world of elvish beauty, or experience eternal damnation. And here, I would know from Her if my choice mattered. If I was ever to know anything again, I would know that. Was I still clean for Her? Damned to eternal torture upon my next death? And if I were so damned, what did my life now mean?

I retreated to a deeper part of my rooms to avoid the minor distraction of the blood. My cache of weapons, the scrolls I had taken from Zelar's cave, the shards from the Mirror of Transformations, were also gone. And then I remembered that I had unshielded and unlocked these rooms before I left, not expecting to return. Of course the weapons were useless, as I alone could call down the power words from Hecate to activate them. That is, if Hecate was still for me to call. The shards retained considerable power, enough to have caused Aeren to assume dragon form during the elven battle. They were worth much. As to the scrolls, I had no idea who might want them as, except for the two in Botha detailing the weapons' uses, I had no idea how to read them.

I stood in the innermost section of my chambers, waiting for what remained of the sunlight to die. Not because it was strictly necessary, but because I was trembling so violently that useful prayer was impossible. I clumsily removed my cloak, spread it on the marble floor, and sat lightly as the sun slowly faded. If I were damned, did I want to know about it? How to live knowing that, on any blessed day, death might come and gift me with unspeakable suffering? And yet how to live, how to practice magic, without knowing where I stood with my deity? Could I still practice magic? Was I still a priest? A king? Bound to evil? Would Hecate hear my prayer?

The light withered into a mere suggestion of light, as if it needed to deny its own nature to satisfy the Gondish night. That was my only answer.

To still my thoughts, to prepare myself for the awful prayer I needed to make, I focused on what was around me, needing to know intimately this fragment of world Isulde's fairy horse had brought me to before knowing anything else. And in doing so, I began, instinctively, to read the energy around me, using the wizardry Mirand had once taught me. Not just to read these rooms, but to take their energy into myself and make its acquaintance before facing the horror of knowing myself again as Hecate now knew me.

What came back was emptiness and anger. There are many kinds of emptiness, just as there are many kinds of anger. The emptiness was the sort of emotional hole in which some people hide their damaged hearts. But whether this hole was protection, a vantage point to spit at the world, or both wasn't clear from my reading. The anger was violence-laden frustration. I sensed that it concerned an argument that somebody desperately wanted but was unable to have. I also sensed that if it were possible, this person would earnestly commit ten thousand atrocities just to make that argument happen. But I also sensed that whoever had been been here cared more about making some obscure point than about whatever the point was.

It had to be Aeren.

Be that as it may, there were clearly no impediments to drawing upon Hecate here. Emptiness would work. In fact, emptiness is one of the best conduits of Her force.

So in this oddly furious nothingness, I opened myself in prayer and willed myself into trance, hurling everything I was—mind, life, energy—into Hecate's keeping or that of whatever deity would have me.

What came back was dirty, broken, and silent. That is all.

I stopped my prayer.

I considered my past, my destruction of El and Cathe, and how I was now anathema to my own kind. My willing self-sacrifice, or my willing destruction of Gondal, was to have paid for those acts. But Gondal was still here. And I was still here. And so my "sacrifice" felt as undefined as the emptiness through which I now called to Her and as open and indecipherable as what came back.

I prayed again, hesitantly.

Nothing.

That is, nothing but reverberations in the dark. I knew those reverberations. Some say they emanate from a fit of anger that happened shortly after the world began, that the energy from that anger still ripples through time. Aeren once told me a tale about that anger. Her tale concerned a fighter who lost the world for sulking in his tent over some imagined slight. Except the way she told it, the slight, imagined or not, was of a nature to justify such a loss. You almost admired the fighter for sticking to his fit despite the cost, thinking a mere world is worth such stunning discipline.

Anyway, it was that kind of silence that my prayer brought back. Reverberations I could read old tales into but take no meaning from. So I sat there, heavy with my thoughts in the Gondish night, unsure how to proceed, unsure if I should proceed. And then, somewhere in my maze of distraction, or in the emptiness of these rooms that was all I had left of my former kingship, Mother Hecate took me into Her keeping.

Again I am croaking and wordless. I know myself as a shuddery bird in the nasty nest of Mother Hecate's heart, trembling and terrified. Hecate tightens Her cold fist around my wings, pressing them flat into uselessness. The pressing hurts my narrow bones, which break and crack into whistles of pain. I also know that the frightened bird is merely a form that contains my being, and that my being is only a streak of excess energy, constantly seeking to be contained in matter.

She offers me a dirty choice: to exist in physical form as Her priest, for Her evil and from Her evil, or to become pure formless energy again and dissipate into oblivion. Exist in Her evil or don't exist.

And then, before I can make my choice, She snaps my bird-neck and drops my now limp bird-form into Her energy stream.

It is timeless here, in Hecate's energy, and so I am dying forever, dying eternally, in a moment that never begins or ends, touching but never reaching death. My bird-neck hangs loose where She twisted it; it mirrors Her symbol, the waning moon.

And here, between bare flutters of existence and nonexistence, is my divine Mother's voice, harsh and glittering with poisoned light.

"I know your life. I was there when you cried for the flowers to love you. I was there when you played your childhood witch-games with Grana. It was me lurking in her heart. I also lurk in yours.

"I loved you in your evil. I found you beautiful with transgressions. Each time you destroyed something you loved, I sickened your heart for solace. I gave you my tears for strength. I alone keep you while the world condemns you.

"You chose not to destroy Gondal, your pretty toy. And so you rejected the cleansing I required for your murder of two high priests of Habundia Christus, my highest form. For elvish Beauty you chose to die damned to me forever in the North Country, and through no fault of your own, failed in your choice. However, your capacity for sacrifice attracts my mercy.

"And so you shall feel me in your flesh, as a promise of what is to come to you forever when you die again. But, for mercy, you may void this promise if you perform two sacrifices in my honor.

"One. You once caused my beloved child El to turn to good. You shall balance that loss by causing your former master, Mirand, to embrace evil.

"Two. Mirand marred the world to save Threle. You will heal that wound by destroying Threle, which you once loved.

Should you die before you accomplish this mandate, you will spend eternity as you spend this night."

Hecate fled my cracked mind.

I was in human form again, but I had scarcely breathed before something cut my body, carving a line of blood that curved around my back and stomach. The cut was made so swiftly that I didn't feel pain until after the cutting stopped. And then—how do I describe this torture from Mother? She carefully, slowly, almost tenderly, pulled my skin from my chest and arms and over my screaming face the way one removes a soggy shirt from a child. As I lay in an agony that quivered through exposed flesh, veins, and muscles, Hecate's words caught me like thorns:

"I don't want you to die. I want you to understand."

And then, to peak the excruciating pain dancing through my mess of half-skinless body that should have died for mercy, Mother cleansed me. With salt. Her pale fist rained salt against my exposed flesh. Over and over. Without end.

Except sometimes the salt paused. And then I was Her toad, eternally existing in the excruciating moment when my cold life matter spurts irretrievably out of my flattening body. There would never be anything but this experience of horror, this eternal moment of terror. Except sometimes I was a screaming bird forever in the maw of that damned orange cat I once loved in the Helan border town. As the beast ripped and tore me, fluttering and raw, I returned to myself in my empty chambers and experienced my open body burning. Every nerve an enemy. Everything I might have loved—language, learning, music, Threle, that damned cat—resolved into waves of smashing pain. And then my language, what words I could hold onto, swarmed out of the salt like confused insects, stinging my vulnerable flesh out of all experience, I mean all ties to existence—and into a terrifying dissolution. The word-insects gnawed me backward into wordless elements. My mind dried into dead stars. And then I hung, a graceless pulse of pain, a nasty tangle in Her womb. But there was no respite there, for I knew that every month, when the moon went dark, Mother would make me grow back just enough to again be birthed into torture.

When dawn became morning, the torture stopped. In a breath, a thought, Hecate replaced my flesh, with only a light line of scar to motivate me. And around my neck was Her mark, a silver chain bearing a waning moon that I knew instinctively I could never remove. And then there was a cold maternal kiss on my face and I was back. Too terrified to *be* back, too terrified to *be*. I lay clutching the silver moon for hours, maybe days, holding to Her energy, waiting to feel like I could even begin to know how to live again.

Welcome home, I thought ruefully. *Welcome back to the world I know.* Turn Mirand. Who, for all I knew, was halfway there anyway. Destroy Threle as payment for Gondal. Finish the vengeance I no longer had enthusiasm for, and the torture of that night would pass me over when I died. If I would risk eternal damnation to save elvish Beauty, would I do the same for Threle?

There is a kind of freedom in only having one goal, in not being distracted with what-ifs. Mirand had spat at the gods and torn history to save Threle. In justice, there was no cosmic reason not to turn him, save sentiment, and the knowledge of the torture I'd be suffering even now if Walworth had not kept my death at bay. And yet Walworth had appeared to know that Isulde would be able to bring me back, that his death sentence would have no power. And for such hidden mercies I should work to destroy Mirand? Yes, I had done the same for El, absolutely, but Mirand would be difficult in ways I didn't care to admit to myself—and I was not somebody he had reason to trust. What to do? Ride to Threle with no real plan, take Walworth up on his implied offer of work, and steal his country?

There was nothing for it but to enter the world, so I unlocked and opened the door. The castle was as empty as my chambers. I was still shaking so badly I stumbled through the hallways, staggered into the rooms. There was nothing here now but nothing. I could feel pockets of the same anger I felt in my rooms when I opened myself. But mostly there was only silence. And empty space. The elvish art, the stunning emotional tones, the energy I had been willing to damn myself to save had all evaporated.

I faltered onto the balcony where I had witnessed the elvish battle. And there, I saw that my city, Arula, had been razed. I mean, as far as I could see were sunshine and ruins. If I had some kind of holy mandate to destroy Arula, then somebody had clearly done my job for me.

I don't know how long I stood in front of that terrible void, helplessly staring at the wasteland, grieving for a history that wasn't even mine. At some point, I remembered that I needed a plan, a goal, a damned understanding of what I was supposed to do next, but the wreckage before me revealed nothing, and I wasn't eager to follow my thoughts. I tried to command the power of the land to surge through me but drew only a gust of emptiness. And then another. I was a king of air and shadows, nothing more. Or else I was still King of Gondal, but the land had gone to death, and so death is all I felt.

I conjured a stone in my palm. A small dull rock appeared, slowly, to match the one in my heart. I still had wizardry. I tossed the rock and stood for a long time after it fell, remembering the elves, remembering that Arula was once their city, created as a repository for their art. I'm sure I mourned. I sent a wizard call to Aeren but my call felt weak and insincere. I received no response. I didn't expect to.

Eventually, I made my way through the city's remains. There was nothing else for it. There was silence here—charred and unreadable as Arula now was. The earth was dead and scarce before me. A desolation without apparent cause. That is the only way I knew that day. That is the only way I knew myself on that day. That is all I knew as I stood sickened by this sad strange stain on the world.

Later, as the moon set, I called down Hecate's power, screaming for an explanation. For a word. For anything. A broken old horse came straggling through the ruins. That was Her only answer. Using wizardry, I changed my clerical garments to those of Athena. That was mine.

I rode the broken horse. We kept a broken pace. I thought if I could get to Anda, Gondal's other city, I might learn what happened to Arula. Of course there was nobody on the road to ask. There being no towns between the cities, and no actual city left of Arula, there was no reason for anybody else to travel along this path. I rode three days in solitude.

As I neared Anda, I started to pass the farm that belonged to Relyr Ean Gransag, the reticent farmer that had supported my bid for the throne. I saw him working outside so I dismounted and approached. "Relyr! Ean! Gransag! Old friend. How long has it been?" I admit the greeting was pure show, but I was also genuinely relieved to see him. He was someone familiar. Also, I felt reassured that he and his farm were as I remembered them. Perhaps I hadn't lost a lot of time in the North Country.

Relyr was highly annoyed by my presence. "Aren't you the so-called 'king' that Ygresan D'an Fen said was going to restore the monarchy?" He kicked the fence post he had just shoved in the ground with a little more aggression than necessary, appeared satisfied, picked up a bucket of farming tools, and headed across his hay field toward the barn that had once been my command quarters. He had no use for me. I kept pace with him anyway, leaving my tired horse to rest.

Relyr had once placed himself—or rather, allowed his farmstead to be placed—in the center of Ygresan D'an Fen's various political schemes. Not that he ever had any confidence in Ygresan or in his schemes, but, being Andan, he liked feeling important too much to forgo being in the center of something. I was certain that, because of his prior political involvement, Relyr would know what happened to Arula.

I was wrong. Probing Relyr's mind as we crossed the field yielded nothing of interest. The old farmer had grown isolated and ignorant. He liked it that way. He'd been disappointed by his fellow Andans as often as he'd trusted them. Relyr was, at base, intensely angry over having been wrong in his support of Ygresan and myself. Publicly wrong. Being Andan, that was intolerable. And since the world clearly lacked the ability to appreciate how intolerable, he had no more traffic with the world. He had his farm. He was all set.

Relyr made a show of ignoring me, as if further comment would have indicated that he cared enough to notice. When he stopped to repair the gate to the pasture where his animals were grazing, I retrieved my poor old horse and let her into the pasture without being asked, to see if that would elicit a response. It didn't. Relyr was not going to be manipulated into speaking again. My probe told me that he was annoyed, but that he could not let on that he was annoyed because he wanted to impress me with his silence. He wasn't supposed to care about anything anymore, and chiding me about letting my horse into his field would have marred the game.

As to Arula, I couldn't find anything in Relyr's thoughts, not even an indication of how much time had passed since I left the throne.

"How many coins will it take to let me stay here a few days?" I still had some conjured coins from my last visit to Anda.

"You can't count that high."

"Will you sell me a better horse?"

He helplessly ruminated for longer than the question merited. He would have liked my gold, but he wasn't *sure* he wanted my gold, which would have been too much like admitting he wanted anything. Also, he might regret having sold me a better horse than the sorry one I had, which was too much like doing me a good turn.

"No." His thoughts conveyed unease. Maybe he was passing up a good deal on the gold, but as he couldn't be sure, and he distrusted everything, "no" was safe.

So I attempted to lead him to think about Arula. "What's the news out of Anda's sister city?"

He looked at me incredulously. "You mean you don't know?" He rubbed his chin and stared at the ripples the breeze made in the growing hay. His exaggerated tone and gesture was meant to mock my ignorance. "It got wrecked. I hear." It was not a loss that made much of an impression on the old fellow at this point in his life. "Not my concern." I probed his mind again, but he really didn't know anything else about it. I sensed that he was happy to have something awful to tell me, to impress upon me how miserable the outside world is, and how justified he was in his isolation.

Relyr's snit annoyed, but his braggy reticence suited me. I could do worse than take lodging with someone who chose to isolate himself in ignorance and didn't talk to anyone. At least until I could discretely educate myself on recent events.

I showed him some gold. "Horse and a few days lodging?"

"Seen Ygresan?" His sudden curiosity surprised me.

"No, actually I haven't."

"Neither have I." He said this like an oblique condemnation that carried a hint of us now having something in common. He meant it as a rebuke to me for having been fooled by Ygresan, and as a way to draw attention to his own discernment. I used it like an opening line.

"Relyr—the world is a broken deal. I haven't seen Ygresan or anybody else from Anda in a long time." I emphasized this as if I, too, felt betrayed. "But I know you for a plain dealing, dependable sort." I said the latter like I was complimenting him, and I sensed from his slight shrug that he took it that way. "You I always trusted far more than Ygresan and his associates." I suddenly sensed Relyr pulling back. He didn't want to be trusted. He feared entanglements. I backed off. "I'm not here for any other reason than I remember you kindly, and I'd rather give my coin to you than to the innkeeper in town. To make up for past inconveniences, including Ygresan's."

He considered, squinting at the sun so he wouldn't have to look at me, and said in spite of himself, "You can take that horse." He indicated a dull brown mare. "And keep the barn for a week."

"Come home, then." I gave him a fistful of gold, which he managed to look both eager and confused about because he didn't have a handy place to put it. He poured the coins into his tool bucket. "That's what they say in Threle—in the old Duchy of Helas—when someone's made a good bargain."

Relyr had no more interest in Threle than in Arula. He was done.

I wasn't. As Relyr turned his attention back to his tasks, I used wizardry to cause him to trip and spill the bucket. As he crawled over the ground to retrieve his tools and gold, I knelt near him, reached my arms under his shoulders as if to help him up, and set a binding spell on his tongue as a precaution. "You may not speak of me or of my presence here save to me alone. The word 'gold' renews the spell should the binding fade." The spell held fast, and Relyr was none the wiser. He really thought I was just being a good guest, helping him.

In what appeared to be an attempt to simultaneously reciprocate my gesture and ignore my presence, he ambled over to the gate on the opposite side of the pasture, called the mare, and walked her toward my new lodgings.

And then, as he set off across the field, something blasted him and the horse into a pile of death and bones.

It wasn't me.

The blast was so pure and clean that I instinctively thought it was clerical. The aftershock knocked me to the ground. I lay there shuddering with the terror of how close I had come to returning to Hecate before I realized that the blast was wizardry, for its energy still hung lightly in the air. But I was too dazed and scared to focus enough to read the energy before it dispersed, and putting up a wizard shield seemed like a better choice. That, and throwing a clerical shield around my wizard shield. Not that a clerical shield would necessarily protect me against a wizard blast at close range, but I had no idea what I was going to encounter.

I had no shortage of enemies, but I also knew that if the blast was meant for me, it wouldn't have missed. A wizard powerful enough to raise that amount of energy wouldn't miss. So why was an obscure Andan farmer like Relyr marked for special attention?

There was nothing for it but to stay hidden in the hay, cursing the fact that my shields prevented me from reading my surroundings. But I wasn't about to make myself known to whatever wandering wizard had decided to blast Relyr. So I waited as the day crawled into dusk, waited as the dusk slowly collapsed into darkness, waited as the moon set in the early evening and night collapsed around me.

Uncomfortable from having lain so long on the earth, I dragged myself through the dew-soaked hay until I could feel the edge of the blast's bare circle. The suddenness of the scalded soil startled, not because I wasn't expecting it, but because I was.

Still I waited, listening. Only the peculiar silence of the newly dead tinged the hardened ground. The thick growth surrounding the blast area would block any light on the ground, so I risked conjuring a candle. I did the working inside my shield to prevent my spell from being sensed, and I kept the flame so weak it barely traced an area the size of my hand before sputtering into the near-total darkness.

That's why it took several minutes to explore the dead earth. As I suspected, there wasn't enough left of the farmer and the horse to sicken on, even if I hadn't been shielded. But something glinted near a piece of the mare's skull.

I recognized it as a death charm. Somebody had tricked up the horse with this thing, and Relyr had taken the blast after reluctantly selling me that particular animal. The charm was spent and cold and therefore as impossible to read as Relyr's now dead thoughts. I placed it in my pocket, extinguished the candle, strengthened my shields, and slowly stood up in the darkness.

Not a star, not a guide. I cautiously made my way to Relyr's dimly lit farmhouse.

And there, through a faintly illuminated window, I observed a young man in a slightly overwrought wizard robe. The kind of robe a new wizard might wear if he wasn't sure how to show acceptable ambition without annoying his superiors. He was sitting at Relyr's coarsely-hewn supper table, utterly focused on whatever he was writing, except when he looked over at the fireplace wall, which was often. Then his expression conveyed something approaching mortification. Then he would read, look vexed, write intensely, stare back at the shadows on the wall, and nervously rub his palm over his mouth.

He clearly lacked the casualness that accompanies experience. But he also had none of the blaring self-consciousness that burdens novices. His carefully muted eagerness revealed unease. I decided he was new, but not green. Much as I wanted to probe his mind, or conjure some parchment and manifest his words, dropping my wizard shield and exposing myself to a blast wasn't an option, even if it were possible to work a manifestation without him sensing it. Also, I had to assume he was shielded, although my own shields prevented me from knowing for sure.

Obviously, I needed to render him useless for magical workings. Just as obviously, I needed to keep up my shields. That left one option. Wizard shields being cobwebs to clerisy, I brought down Hecate's force against the fellow. That is, I called down Hecate's energy with the will to cause this wizard extreme pain. He was writhing across the floor like a piece of just-shredded snake when I entered the farmhouse. Nothing incapacitates wizardly focus like a generous serving of divine agony.

"Who are you and why did you set up Relyr Ean Gransag to kill me?"

My would-be assassin began to vomit a little, so I helped him out by kicking him in the stomach. He vomited again. Hard. Then he stopped and hunched and lurched like he wanted to heave his scathing insides into eternity. I knew from my clerical training that Hecate had stirred acid in his vomit. He made awful choking noises because the more he heaved, the more his insides boiled in pain. "Wizardry is no match for clerisy. Drop your shield and I might show mercy."

"I have . . . done it so." He gagged the words in horribly stilted, academic Sarana. Given that my shields were up, I had no way of knowing whether he actually had dropped his. Not that it mattered now, but I wanted him to feel as vulnerable as possible.

I stuffed his writing in my cloak without reading it. That was hard, because I was intensely curious, but I had to focus on keeping him so distracted with pain that he couldn't concentrate his power against me.

"Answer my question, Wizard. Who are you?"

He refused to answer so I called upon Hecate to increase his suffering. I willed Her force to scathe his flesh and eyes in addition to his gut, but only to the point of agony, not death. I let him scream and crawl and roll around until he simply couldn't scream anymore. Then I let up enough for him to speak.

"I call myself Beotun. I have . . . I am . . . to travel . . . I do travel the way from Sunna."

This time I could make out that his accent was Helan, and that his command of Sarana was not simply academic but sketchy.

I responded in Botha, using the Sunnan cadences I grew up with. "So you are Helan and you come from Threle." I increased his pain again to show I wasn't pleased with his lie. He nodded slightly, almost involuntarily, but he mostly just suffered. I wouldn't let him do anything else. "What's a Helan wizard doing in my country? Who sent you?"

Beotun scrunched his eyes and prepared himself for another onslaught of torture. "Take it from my mind," he responded in perfect Botha. This wasn't exactly an honest challenge, although he probably wanted me to think that it was. It sounded more like a response he had been taught to say in such a circumstance. When caught in a lie, scoundrels rely on policy. Particularly new scoundrels.

"I've no intention of dropping either of my shields, Wizard. And I've no intention of ending your current . . . *religious experience*, shall we call it . . . until you answer me." I increased his torment as far as I dared without killing him. After a minute or two, I eased off, but not by much. The real problem was that if I let him reach a comfort point, or even a point of stasis he could adapt to even briefly, he'd be able to focus his power enough to blast me. He might do damage at such close range despite my shields. So I had to keep unexpectedly changing the intensity of the suffering I was sending him. "Proposal. I blast you out of your miserable Helan life just as you sought to blast me." He cried and twitched. "Or you tell me your story—as they say in Threlan courts—and I might reconsider my death sentence on you for attempting to murder Gondal's king."

Beotun chuckled and coughed at my referring to myself as Gondal's king. That, of course, piqued my interest. "A murderous tyrant of a 'king' that can't keep his throne. Or will you keep torturing me for speaking truth?"

So now the guy fancied himself a political martyr? "Gondal values free speech as much as Threle does. Say whatever you like about me." I didn't give a damn about his speech rights; I just wanted him to keep talking.

"You're no more Gondish than my grandam's goat. You're a Sunnan commoner that destroyed the Helan border camp and all that was in it. And our border town. That one's out now, too."

"So you're here on behalf of the Duchy of South Walworth?" I asked coolly.

"*Helas*," he corrected. "I've got a charter from the king to kill you."

"The King of Threle?" I was nonplussed.

"No, may Walworth rot with the grain. The King of Helas."

Damn, I had much to learn about the state of the world. "So Helas is a kingdom now, is it?" I managed to say this with a hint of sarcasm I didn't feel, as if to convey that Helas's affairs weren't worthy of my consideration.

"*Helas* took its rightful independence." He emphasized the traditional name again. "Or haven't you heard, King?"

"Against the rest of Threle?" This time I tried to provoke more information by sounding like I didn't believe him, or didn't believe in Helan independence, or something.

"The 'rest of Threle's' king hasn't been particularly present for the last two years."

So that's how long we were in the North Country. I considered asking who destroyed Arula, but decided it was not strategic to show my ignorance by asking my would-be assassin to educate me on my own country's recent history. I tried to get at it another way. "How did you know I'd be visiting Relyr Ean Gransag's farm, Wizard?"

Beotun stiffened. Despite my considerable attempts to ruin his evening, he clearly didn't want to say more and lose his job. I increased his torment into chaotic pulses of pain cracking through his bones. That got him talking. That is, when he finished screaming. "Crystal. Pouch." I picked up a small cloth purse from the table. Inside the purse was a tracking crystal that my shields had prevented me from sensing.

"This? How were you able to track me since I've nothing for the crystal to detect?" Beotun shuddered, his limbs trembling like the remnants of an old storm. He spat pain. He dreamed pain. He shimmered with anguish. If I let up now, I knew he'd kill me. He gagged, jerked, and forced his face into an odd half-grimace. "We apprenticed with the same master." He spoke with as much embarrassment as it is possible to have while being tortured. "We're bonded, damn the gods. If you dropped your bloody wizard shield, you'd know that." He gasped and gagged. "You sent out a wizard call days ago."

I had called Aeren in Arula and Beotun picked it up. We had a wizard bond. Something in me went breathless. Then I did. "Mirand sent you?" I asked thinly.

Beotun winced and nodded. The next hit of pain I sent him had nothing to do with interrogation strategy. It was helplessly personal. Then I kicked him again. In the head. "That's for your . . . *our* . . . master."

He moaned uncontrollably, in long low violent sobs that didn't stop for a long time. Then, appearing to make peace with the unfairness of the situation, he groaned until he could form something resembling words again. "He made a death charm . . . set to your wizardry. I placed it in a horse's mane . . . paid Relyr to be certain you took that animal." *Meaning my binding spell set off the charm when Relyr led the horse, because the charm sensed my wizardry.*

"How needlessly complicated."

"It was my idea."

"Obviously." I could tell he resented the implied insult. "You're new at this sort of thing. You'll improve." I said this without emotion. Emotion was a deadly distraction. "What did Relyr know?"

"Nothing. I told him nothing. He was the perfect front. I used the circumstance." *That's why I didn't catch this in Relyr's mind.*

"Why does Mirand believe I'm a threat to Threle?"

Beotun laughed at me like he thought the question was a joke.

I tried again. "The only time Mirand ever consented to the death of a fellow wizard—let alone a former apprentice—was when he believed—no, knew—that wizard was a threat to Threle. So why does Mirand want to kill me?"

"Take it from my mind." It was another invitation by rote. But if Beotun thought I was dropping my wizard shield, then Mirand never taught him how to think.

"Mirand didn't send a Helan rebel to Gondal with assassination orders against the king."

"Former king," he struggled to remind me, which made the rebuke worse because he had to work so hard through his considerable suffering to speak. "Mirand and I play the same coin on that one."

"Call him then." I threw the crystal at his chest. Beotun groaned and shook. "Send Mirand a call through the crystal, give him my love, and I'll let you live. How's that?"

Beotun cried, grasped the crystal, tried to focus through the chaotic throbbing of his pain-riddled mind, and failed. I knew he would.

"Well. As they say in Helas, 'Coming home is always an act of belief.' Isn't it? Here. Take this message to our beloved master." I blasted him into eternity along with the damn tracking crystal. If Mirand was on the other end, he'd know what happened. Besides, Mirand appreciated elegance in intellectual arguments. So maybe he'd give this one a pass. Me? I simply appreciated the elegance of expediency.

Then, spent from the energy I'd used on magic all day, I fell exhausted into the chair, propped my feet on the table, and wearily renewed my shields. Somewhere the night was a comfort of clouds, but I was too confused to know this more than distantly. I shakily took Beotun's parchment bundle out of my cloak and began to read. The writing was in Botha—no surprise—and appeared to be notes and commentary on an academic paper. Then I tiredly realized that it was commentary on one of *my* academic papers.

Beotun was carrying one of the essays I'd written on Habundia-Ceres as a propaganda piece for Cathe to disseminate after El died. It was one of the pieces Cathe told me to target for Mirand. Beotun's intended rebuttal was competent. I'll give him that. Not that I cared. I was mostly amused that he was doing me the honor of taking my phony argument seriously after he believed he had just killed me. Then I sobered with the realization that a true student of Mirand's would not see that as funny but as a mark of professionalism. Then I looked at the back of the parchment and laughed a little, because Beotun had written that he had "problems with the sincerity of these arguments." He figured that out, did he? But I immediately went cold and strange when I read Mirand's response. "Study the process, not the mask."

Of course Mirand knew I was evil, but how could he know about my mandate from Hecate to destroy Threle? He couldn't. But if he didn't know, why then did he send Beotun to kill me? And provide him with the means to study how I think? And what, if anything, did Walworth know about this little adventure?

I manifested the words "no defenses" next to Mirand's writing. Then I magically erased them. Staring tiredly at the darkening fire, I contemplated the twisted implications of my next move.

Three

I am the enemy of Threle. I am the enemy of the world. Bless me, Mother, for I am damned.

The more I considered Beotun's story, the less sense it gave. Or my mind was too cracked to understand any sense it might have hidden. It was a reasonable guess on Mirand's part that I'd return to Gondal, and a reasonable guess on mine that Walworth had returned to Threle. I had no idea how much world-time Shadow's fairy journey had consumed. But if Beotun had arrived in Arula when I did—and even that wasn't obvious—he would have had to leave Loudes months ago. Maybe weeks if he left from Helas. Hecate spoke to me three days before I arrived at Relyr's farm. So if Mirand believed I was Threle's enemy, he was deriving that from something else, although the gods knew what. The trial record? Walworth transcribed the trial, so surely Mirand would have now had an opportunity to read it. My refusal to return to Threle and work under Walworth's "protection"? My unfortunate alignment to Hecate?

If I hadn't been so focused on torturing Beotun, I would have asked better questions and gotten better answers. But isn't that always true? Beotun was able to track me. He heard my call to Aeren. That made it believable that we did have a wizard bond, and his apprenticing with Mirand was the only practical explanation. Also, the death charm was set to my wizardry, something only my former master could have worked. As to my propaganda piece—a well-read wizard could have gotten a copy anywhere. Cathe had distributed those things all over Threle. But then there were Mirand's handwritten comments. Beotun had no reason to forge them. What would be the point if he thought I was dead? "Study the process, not the mask." Well, I was doing my best, but the process wasn't pulling any answers.

To the mask. I couldn't understand why Mirand would hire a Helan loyalist to kill me, even if, as Beotun claimed, they "did play the same coin on that one." That, and the amateurish, messy nature of the plot. Hiding the charm in a horse's mane and passing some coins to Relyr with vague instructions to sell me that particular horse? What? Not that anything could possibly go amiss there. Beotun said he used the circumstance, but given his ill proficiency in Sarana and Relyr's self-conscious isolation, I couldn't begin to parse how that exchange could have happened, let alone worked to his goals. Why didn't Mirand send someone to kill me who was fluent in the local language? Like himself?

I mean—if he felt that strongly about it?

Dawn was pale light and confusion. Or else that was just my way of seeing. Mirand taught me that belief is not a choice. You take the facts as they lay. But what of *these* facts? I had to choose to believe them. I had to act as if Mirand was fully informed of my divine mandate, incredible as that seemed—and as if he were a more than worthy opponent, which of course he was.

And I had to investigate Beotun's story.

I searched the farmhouse when there was enough light, but found nothing that appeared to be Beotun's. Interesting. So he had taken other lodgings, presumably in the city and possibly in Anda's only inn, where I had once stayed. But that didn't explain why he remained here after my supposed death, scribbling his commentary on my forced propaganda.

There was nothing for it. To town I must. I chose a piebald mare from Relyr's field. Her colors, a chaos of black against white, mirrored my newfound enmity with Mirand. They also matched the turmoil in my heart.

Anda infuriated me. Not because it was unchanged but because it was untouched. I rode past the same plain, perfectly-fitted doors; the same clean, interchangeable roofs; the same flat, one-windowed shop fronts showing different goods in nearly-identical displays. The city was still impeccably dull.

I wasn't going to drop my shields to read random strangers on the street, but my best guess, given my experience with Andan attitudes, was that whatever had happened in Arula was at best an annoyance and at worst an unforgivable insult. Whoever had destroyed Arula hadn't found Anda worth destroying, despite the Andans generally high opinion of themselves. That had to cause wide offense in the narrow hearts of this little city. Then I wondered if that was the perpetrator's point.

I didn't see the stable boy at the inn so I tied my horse and entered. I also didn't see the dour-faced innkeeper. The place felt emptier than I remembered it, although little else had changed. The walls held the dense quiet that sticks in unused places. But the inn didn't appear abandoned, just temporarily vacant. I decided it was open to anyone who happened to enter because nobody cared enough to actually be there. It annoyed like the rest of Anda. What kind of innkeeper leaves the door open to absence? An Andan innkeeper who was probably too self-important to work. I went carefully up to the rooms.

The upper floor was silent, save for muffled morning sounds making an occasional entrance from the street. I stared at the spot where Aeren had killed Zelar, felt an involuntary clutch in my chest as I remembered that Zelar had taught wizardry to Mirand, and tried the door of the rooms in which we once stayed.

There was a wizard lock on the latch.

I leaned against the door, bringing the wizard lock inside my shields. The lock's energy was so close to my own that I opened it without much effort. That told me it was Beotun's. More evidence that he'd apprenticed with Mirand. I entered, restored the lock, and stood warily in the place where I had once plotted my ascent to king-ship.

The room was exactly how I remembered it. Still gracious. Still exceptionally well-maintained, capturing rivers of clear morning light as if the light were just tangible enough to get entangled in the air. In that moment, the room conveyed a dim suggestion of Arula's glory. Which was still pretty damn fine, albeit a sad reminder of how far Anda had fallen from Gondal's dazzling past. If not for Beotun's wizard lock, I would have assumed that the room had been unoccu-pied for a long time, because it was a shade too orderly for anything but light to live in. But reading the energy meant dropping my shields. So I did the next best thing. I searched it. That is, I system-atically destroyed the place.

I tore apart the bed, and when that yielded nothing, I conjured a dagger and shredded what was left. I did the same with the furnish-ings, rugs, and curtains, but found nothing except neatly folded clothes and empty traveling pouches, which had to be Beotun's. What the hell was that wizard lock guarding? I thought again about dropping my shields to get a read on any small magical items that might be hidden here, remembered the torture that awaited me should I die without accomplishing my mandate, and decided that continuing my methodical physical search was the best option. My best option yielded nothing.

When I entered the adjoining room, where Aeren had stayed, I went numb in the Gondish light. I had to remind myself to move. And then to keep searching. Because there, sitting in a corner of floor that the sunlight cheerfully ignored, was a small wooden chest that I recognized as Mirand's. I had sometimes kept papers in it when I apprenticed with him, and I had practiced word manifesta-tions by magically carving and erasing Sarana text in the wood. Some of my clumsy early carvings were still there. Either Mirand was here or he had given the chest to Beotun.

I uneasily approached the corner. It took minutes to clear enough space in my thoughts to simply pick up the chest and bring it inside my shields. It took minutes more to sit stiffly with the light on my back and with the chest in my lap. It took even longer to be able to focus enough to—I don't know—sense for traps and death charms, remove the damn wizard lock, which felt like the one I had opened on the door—and prepare myself for what I would find.

What I found were the seven scrolls I had taken from Zelar's underground workshop when I freed Aeren from her dragon form. I immediately recognized the two that were written in Botha, in a hand that differed from the others and which contained the now useless notes on the specific uses of Zelar's crystals and wands. I burned those notes with a dash of wizard fire and a smile, remembering how I had rendered Zelar's wands useless to anybody save myself, and how even I couldn't activate them without calling down their power words from Hecate. Whoever had taken those wands from Arula was in for a time of it getting them to work.

I took the three scrolls that were written in a language I didn't recognize, along with the two that constituted a single map of an area I also didn't recognize, and stuffed them in my cloak for later study. Whatever Zelar had written on these scrolls would be worth knowing, seeing as they found their way into Mirand's chest. And then, as I continued to search—I mean methodically destroy—I heard somebody enter the other room. Somebody who knew how to open my wizard lock. Somebody who wasn't Beotun and who let out an angry indeterminate low-pitched cry at the wreckage I had caused. There was no place for me to hide, so I kept still, waiting, trusting to my shields and praying that it wasn't Mirand on the other side of the wall.

Then I heard the person stomping and throwing and slamming and smashing heavy objects, which told me that he was more angry than frightened at my intrusion. Taking advantage of the commotion, I quickly and quietly stalked to the door, managed to open it during the sound of a heavy object smashing on the floor, and exited into the hall. And there, as I glanced through the open door of the first room, I saw the back of a dark-haired young man, who was now stomping into the room I had just left. It was obvious when the guy found the chest I'd raided, because I heard him smash it on the floor and swear an epic in perfect Sarana as he threw other things against the wall.

The swearing helped. I could now tell from the voice, distorted by anger though it was, that the "guy" was Aeren. So the wizard lock matched my energy because it was hers, not Beotun's, and the male clothes I'd found were also hers. And she'd somehow gotten possession of a chest that had once belonged to Mirand. I needed that story. Badly.

So I entered the first room, quietly closed the door, and waited for the rant to end. It was a long wait, and between the sobs, cries, stomping, smashing, and loudly executed dismay, I assumed her rage was causing her to wreak at least as much destruction on her room as I had on mine.

When she finally heaved herself back into my former room in a mess of anger, I took two scrolls out of my cloak and asked earnestly, "Missing something, Stormdragon?" Then I smiled and spread my arms like I wanted to embrace an old friend.

Aeren went as still as the sunlight clinging to the wall. Maybe stiller. I kept smiling for what felt like a length of morning, maybe several. Aeren kept staring. An eternally angry sun blackening an impossibly scorched earth. Then she went to fire with fury. Which should have been predictable.

"What the scorch are you doing here? Those are mine!"

I respectfully inclined my head, thinking that by politely indulging her rage I could make it dissipate faster. I was wrong. She grabbed the scrolls, kicked me in the shin for thanks, and cried, "There's still five missing! *Where are they?"*

I recovered balance, shrugged, and pretended to ignore the thump of pain in my lower leg, which infuriated her. She threw the scrolls on the wreckage that used to be a bed. "What are you doing here *again* and what the scorch do you want and *where are the rest of my god-be-damned scrolls?"*

"I wanted to see Gondal again." I said this with a touch of self-mocking irony, which Aeren was too trammeled up in anger to acknowledge.

"To see *what?* Do you *see* this room?"

I made a show of glancing around the room as if nothing was amiss.

"Do you *see* that somebody broke into this room and wrecked it? Do you have anything to say about that?"

I tried to look concerned and sympathetic. I needn't have bothered.

"Oh, I forgot. You don't have much to say about anything unless it involves scorching up somebody else's life, and after two god-damned years I see you're ready to scorch up mine. *Again."* She was no doubt referring to my abdication.

"At your service." I tried to say this like a friendly tease.

"You're supposed to be dead!" She shrieked this with all the righteous disappointment of a wounded stormdragon denied the last bag of golden mice that would ever exist in the world. "So why don't you have the decency to stay that way?" I had no answer for that one. "Oh, of course. If you bothered to die in the North Country on your scorch-be-damned 'spiritual pilgrimage' you wouldn't be able to wander back into Gondal waving *my scrolls* around and annoying me with a self-satisfied theatrical greeting as if I'm supposed to be awestruck

at your goddess-be-damned presence. Which of course just pays for all."

"I'm sorry to disappoint you, Queen," I said quietly. *How did she know I should have died in the North Country?* I never told her that. What did Walworth tell her when they met?

"I am not the scorch-be-damned queen. *That's your fault!* You gave up the throne and threw the queenship on me so you could cultivate some grand air of mystery slouching it up to the North Country. I never wanted it. Go to hell. Nobody cares."

"I am in hell." She didn't respond, which was just as well. "Anyway, I thought you might care."

"What? I care? *I want you dead.* Do you understand that? *So why aren't you dead?* Is that because when it comes to following through on your pathetic attempts at self-promotion, you haven't got the courage to actually ride North and make it happen?"

"Why do *you* want me dead?" I managed to laugh a little, to pretend to take her outburst in good humor.

She stared at me again like she couldn't decide if I was playing with her or if she should return the favor by playing as if she took me seriously. "You don't know? Really?"

"Educate me." I tried to sound naturally curious.

Her anger flowered into hopelessness, embarrassment, contempt, and back to pure rage. She was completely the Aeren I remembered. She hated having to respond but she was too angry with me to hold back. "I was supposed to be your royal bard. We had a blood contract, making *me* your chief storyteller, your 'jewel' as you once put it, finally guaranteeing me an audience. That's *why* I helped you become king. But like most Threlans, you couldn't 'come home' to a bargain if you sat in it. Educate you? You're a bigger fraud than Zelar ever was. Study that."

I kept smiling, kept veiling my well-earned chagrin. Of course she was right. It disturbed me that "come home" was a local Helan expression rarely heard in the rest of Threle, and not an expression I'd ever heard Aeren use. She'd said it in sarcastic, badly-pronounced Botha, which stung, but which meant that she'd learned the phrase from somebody. Beotun? Mirand? Also, I couldn't recall ever discussing Helas or my early life in Sunna with her, and she had once complained about my speaking Sarana with a northern Threlan accent. I'd never spoken Botha in front of her. If she was angrily throwing Bothan phrases at me, somebody had told her about my past.

"So what do you do?" She continued berating me by imitating my voice and mocking my northern Threlan accent. "Oh, Aeren?

You manage Gondal. Go to it without benefit of friends or allies. But I'll give you a stunningly limited knowledge of wizardry to make the whole bloody game worth the broken candle. Maybe you can tell a tale or two in your spare time—*like a scorch-be-damned hobby*—I'm off to king it around elsewhere."

"Aeren—"

"Go to hell. You broke the law—you broke our law—you *should* die for it. That's my judgment if you care to know it. But wait—I don't get to make judgments because I'm not even the queen any-more, just an innkeeper's scorch-be-damned serving girl who can't even get a place on the Assembly after being on the throne. So once again you win. *Scorch you!*"

"What law?"

"You broke our contract. Last time I heard, that's a breach."

"You mean the Assembly imposes the death penalty for breach of contract?" Despite the sting in my leg, I couldn't help but laugh, and then I couldn't help but be aware of how helplessly hollow my laughter sounded.

"No. But I would. I happen to respect tradition." The weight of her anger had now crushed all emotion out of her voice.

"*What?*" I was used to Aeren's non sequiturs, but I couldn't navigate this one. My shields made reading her thoughts impossible.

"Oh, I'm sorry, *King*. I forgot. You never bothered to learn Gondish law."

"You mean Gondal has laws? Other than the Assembly making ad hoc decisions on the dispute of the day? Aeren, Gondal has less organization than a nameless Helan border town, and that's going a ways."

"We have stories. We have traditions. And one of them is that if you break a blood-contract, it's blood that's owed. You signed in blood. You made your life surety to our agreement. You said I would be your royal bard if I gave you my claim to the throne. I kept my promise, you breached yours." So that was why she was so shriekingly happy when I made a show out of signing that damn thing in blood. "So die!"

"Aeren. My abdication made you Queen of Gondal. Surely that paid for all. Couldn't you use that as a platform to bard it around from?"

"*No, I couldn't.* That doesn't work if you don't have friends. Something you wouldn't know about. If you had bothered to stay on as king, with me as king's bard, people would have had to accept me. I would have been able to tell tales at royal celebrations, epic stories of our foreign savior who killed Roguehan, even though you had nothing to do with the elves' surprise victory over him. As it stood, you left, and I got to be—let me see—the unknown girl from the empty taverns who couldn't get a following in the first place—who nobody really knew—who had no friends or supporters—who nobody really believed had a hand in that victory—but somehow got Gondal thrown into her lap to run. So of course people just saw me as someone they could push around and belittle and try to jostle the throne from."

"I gave you everything. Why couldn't you keep it?"

"Keep it with what? My tales? My exceptionally limited knowledge of wizardry? Llewelyn, without your power behind me, I had no way to keep a scorch-be-damned throne. I can't make people respect me or see me as the legitimate monarch, particularly when every second person in Gondal fancies themselves as such and resents me for having a claim. How do you get to be queen of a country and still manage to get ignored? I can manage it. When the Assembly shamed me by sending people to force me out, I grabbed what elvish gold I could, which of course melted to mist in my hands, came back to Anda, and took the only work I could find—assisting the innkeeper in exchange for room, board, and coins when I can get them."

"When did—"

Aeren ranted my question into oblivion. "And of course it wasn't just the throne. I had to hear my scorching 'escort' berate me all the way back to Anda. They were desperate to make me agree that I was unworthy of the honor I'd received, that I should have had a more honest sense of myself than to accept an elvish throne, that no one was good enough for that throne and that's why it must stay empty— never mind my saving Arula—that I might have believed I turned dragon but that couldn't really happen to somebody like me, even though everybody saw it happen. And of course since I can't just do it at will that means I never did it. So now no one acknowledges that I was once queen or saved the land or that the land ever needed saving. Naturally, no one listens to my tales. It's like I'm dead." She paused. My heart broke for her during that pause. It was awful. So awful I felt something dark creeping though the sunlight, despite my shields. "I hate them all. Almost as much as I hate you. Maybe not even almost. I hope Anda gets scathed like Arula and you burn with it."

"Aeren—I'm your supporter—I'm your friend—"

"You're my *what*?"

"There's a lot you don't know. There's a lot I don't know."

"You destroyed my chance to get an audience for my tales. That's all I know and all I need to know. If I had a wand and the ability to use it without guidance I'd blast you like I blasted Zelar. He also falsely promised me an audience."

"What happened to Arula? Who burned it?"

She stared at me for a long time, unhappy at the change in subject, measuring her words. "I did."

"What?"

"Or maybe I didn't. Maybe I only helped. Maybe I only wish I did. Maybe I'm telling you a tale that never happened. What do you care? You left the city unprotected."

"Why don't you tell me a tale of what *did* happen?" I thought she was going to cry. Then I thought she was going to kick me again. "Who destroyed the city?"

"Why should I tell you? What are you going to do about it, King? Break another bloody contract and pretend you've come to heal us with your kingly powers and make us whole again? Restore elvish Beauty to the world when, of course, you couldn't be bothered to promote my poor tales?" She waited for an answer that wasn't forthcoming. "Here's one for you." She studied me like the hardened dragon she was. "It was the elves."

"Please go on." My voice was thin. I didn't care to disguise it.

"They took their work back, they buried Arula into the ground of history, and they retreated to the wasteland of Gondal with their treasures. Some of the Arulan people made it to Anda. Some didn't. Some stayed in this inn for the sole purpose of making me feel bad about myself. For weeks I heard dripping comments about how 'safe' I must have felt being in Anda when it happened, which was really intended to mean that I couldn't have saved Arula even if the Assembly hadn't removed me and how it was just as well there was no queen when the elves came. I swear most of the people who discussed it with me cared more for making me feel bad about myself than for Arula's demise."

"Why?" I heard myself ask as if I were somebody else.

"Who the scorch knows why? Does it matter?" She was offended that I was asking about the elves' motivation rather than commenting on her hurt. I decided that her unspoken need for sympathy meant that she was softening a little toward me, although nothing else about her indicated so. "Maybe they didn't want some unknown would-be bard from Anda without any friends sitting on their precious abandoned throne. Maybe they just wanted their stuff back."

Aeren sounded like a dying soldier learning that his country had betrayed him. "They didn't want me. My stories didn't merit any kind of invitation to join them. That was obvious."

I wanted to hold her, to hold her hurt in my heart, but good sense prevented me fom bringing a woman who wanted me dead inside my shields, limited as her wizardry was. For all I knew, she had magical items on her person or in the other room where I'd found Mirand's chest. And she clearly had some contact with Helas, possibly with Beotun. "When did all this happen?"

"After you abdicated. Obviously. Again, does it matter?"

"Did you get any other visitors after I left?" I was thinking of Walworth telling me that he learned from Aeren that I'd gone to the North Country.

"Visitors?" She smiled wryly at my referring to the elves that way. "No." But she sounded hesitant, like people do when they can't decide whether it's in their interest to lie. "Why would I?"

"Aeren, I need your help. I need to understand the state of the world."

"I need to understand the state of my rooms. My wizardry isn't that advanced because there's nobody in Anda to study magic with, and you and Zelar didn't teach me more wizardry than necessary to establish a bond." I grimaced at being linked again with Zelar, but couldn't deny that our motives were similar, in that we both exercised caution against teaching Aeren enough wizardry to be magically dangerous. "So I've got an idea," she mocked, "why don't you use your bloody skill and read the energy here and tell me what happened? And then why don't you go to the Assembly with me, contract in hand, because you're such a 'good friend' and everything, and admit you breached your promise, and throw yourself on my mercy to not ask for blood? And, now that you're back, just to see Gondal as you say, why don't you use your wizardly power to promote me without running away to the North Country again?"

"Whatever it takes." I knew she was too angry at Anda to be serious about the Assembly part.

"Here's the state of the world, Llewelyn. The elves hate us. The Andans prefer it that way. I get to be a servant. My rooms are destroyed. You show up."

"What about Threle?" I asked too quickly.

"Who gives a scorch about Threle?" She sounded angrier than I expected her to, almost as if she was now forcing her anger on top of another emotion, but I wasn't going to drop my shields to read her. "How the scorch should I know about Threle?"

"What have you got against Threle?"

"You."

That was a rare piece of brevity.

"Their king. All of it. He came to Arula looking for you. When I told him you went to the North Country, he rode off so fast he probably thinks the elves razed Arula to celebrate his birth. Oh, but he did promise he would ever be at my service. So that's something."

"But not in blood, I suppose," I said lightly.

Aeren glowered. "No, but I believed him. I'm stupid. After Arula fell, I sent him a request for bard work. With samples. Heard from some official or somebody that I wasn't needed, because I don't have a following, and actually reading my samples and using his own judgment was apparently beyond his skill. So here's Arula in ruins, Threle unable or unwilling to do anything about it, and I still can't find bard work. Scorch Threle too."

"Because you didn't get bard work or because King Walworth ignored your request for help?"

"Scorch Walworth. I don't need his scorched-be-damned help. He came without warning, and when I greatly inconvenienced myself to accommodate the King of Threle, to show him honor, he left to find you. Hey—glad he found Gondal useful as far as it went. So I'm now a servant in a bloody inn. How's this? Because I'm getting older and I never get bard work. Because my tales are as good as anybody's and better than most. I can turn dragon, save Arula, become the scorch-be-damned queen, and nobody notices or cares to admit to noticing because, well . . . you tell me. Because I've always been a loner. Because no matter what I do to gain friends, people either have no interest in storytelling and are too threatened by mine to associate with me, or pretend to have no interest so they don't have to hurt themselves by acknowledging my one poor gift, or they're 'fellow' bards who resent the competition. And scorch me for daring to complain about it, right? Because that just makes people act nasty at me for daring to say that my heart hurts. So I'm silenced."

"Not with me. I'll be your audience. I've never judged your stories by how many people listen to them."

She wasn't listening. "Because I work for a scorch-be-damned innkeeper who also refuses to let me tell tales to the few visitors we get, mostly because she's terrified I might earn attention. Because it's torture to make stories for myself and the moon. Because I hate the goddamned world more than the elves do, if that's possible."

"Sisterkin."

"What do you want, Llewelyn? Why are you really here?" She sat on the wrecked bed and looked hard at me. She studied me for so long I thought she might never stop.

"I have no idea." I knew how inadequate that sounded. "Perhaps I thought we could be friends again."

"I felt your wizard-shield when I kicked you." She sounded less angry now, but only because she was suddenly more focused and analytical. "So you're obviously protecting yourself against magical attacks. Which means you're expecting problems, which is beyond strange in a wizardless city like Anda. Also, you had no problem breaking into my chest and stealing my scrolls. What's your story?"

"Where did you get that chest?" I asked this like I'd just thought of it.

She ignored my question. "What's your story?"

"I don't have one." I shrugged. "You tell me, Aeren. You're the storyteller." Her silence felt like the dead sky I'd found kissing Arula's ruins. "You want a story?" I adopted a vaguely hopeless tone. "Will you settle for the truth?"

She nodded slightly, suspiciously. "Why did you steal my scrolls?"

I gave her a story. "I met King Walworth in the North Country." I stared dolefully at the light slowly coloring the wall, deciding how much fiction was needed to clearly obscure the sad facts. "Time runs differently there. Reality bends."

"I know. I've heard." She was offended by my stating the obvious.

"Of course, Aeren," I gently acknowledged. "I'm not at liberty to tell you why we met there or what we discussed. But I can tell you I've missed two years out of the world."

"So what?"

"So . . . I returned to Gondal with the intent of . . . meeting up with an acquaintance from Threle, from the Duchy—I mean the *Kingdom*—of Helas. A truly lovely area that I always think of fondly—"

"Who is this acquaintance?"

"A fellow wizard. Part of our magical family, Aeren. His name is Beotun, and he studied with my old master, who happens to be King Walworth's chief wizard and former tutor." I succeeded in sounding almost nonchalant. Aeren succeeded in looking like a stone version of herself. "He sent a message from Threle, from Walworth's old duchy, to meet him in Gondal, at Relyr's farm." Aeren looked like she didn't believe me. I kept dissembling. "You see,

Beotun has studied Sarana, but it got decided that I would come here to serve as a translator for him. I grew up in Sunna. Botha was my first language."

"Is that why you speak Sarana with a northern Threlan accent? You learned it up there, but you're not from there?"

"Yes. Sure." That was close enough to be true. "As to Beotun—I tell you this in confidence—" I made myself look pained and uncertain, which was easy under the circumstances. "Can I trust you, Aeren?"

"*I* don't go around breaking blood-promises."

"Beotun was posing as a Helan loyalist, spying on Helas for Threle. We had planned to meet here, on neutral territory, as part of . . . what I'm not free to discuss. I planned, with your consent, to resume my kingship, with you as bard, of course, only to find Arula destroyed, and, well—" I stared helplessly at the floor for effect and then at her. "The short of it is that Beotun's dead." Aeren gasped. I could tell she didn't want to react, but that she couldn't help it. "Relyr's dead, too." I watched her emotions confuse themselves into something I couldn't read. "Somebody almost killed me, but I managed to get here, hoping, well, to find you, knowing I could trust you to be truthful with me—are you all right?"

She was trying not to tremble. It wasn't working. "I'm just concerned for Relyr."

"Since when?" I said this with sudden harshness to throw her off-balance, hoping to get through her defenses with emotion because magic wasn't an option without dropping my shields. "Your face changed when I mentioned Beotun. What do you know about him, Aeren? I've trusted you with more than I should. Now trust me. Did he give you that chest?"

She hesitated. "Yes. A Helan wizard called Beotun stayed here, in this room. But his Sarana wasn't as bad as you describe it. I mean, he wasn't as fluent as you and his accent was terrible, but I could understand him."

It was possible that Beotun's Sarana was better when he wasn't being tortured. "What did you really know about him?"

"What does that mean? What was I supposed to 'really' know about him?" She was angry again. "You make it sound like he conned me for a fool. I only knew him enough to tend to his rooms, exchange pleasantries—"

"Accept gifts. Aeren, I've never known you to 'exchange pleasantries' with anybody. You shared adjoining rooms. Beotun was on essential government business and he's dead. Relyr's dead. Someone tried to blast me, and until I know who, I'm staying shielded. I'm taking a risk to say this, but you're now in line for some of the same. Whatever you think of my jaunt to the North Country, maybe you ought to tell me what you know about Beotun."

It took her a long time to respond. It wasn't clear she believed me. It wasn't clear she didn't. "Here's what I know, Llewelyn. Beotun was some sort of traveling scholar. He knew I'd been queen. Unlike everybody else in Anda, he treated me with respect and deference." I now understood the relationship was calculated on Beotun's part. Threlans, even former Threlan Helan separatists, are too egalitarian to show much deference to a fallen queen, or to anybody. Beotun was putting it on for her. "He was looking for me, looking for those scrolls. I never understood how he knew I had them and I don't even remember who mentioned them first. He never spoke of you, or of coming here to meet you, or of Relyr, or of trying to pass one over on Helas for Threle. If anything, he hated Threle."

"He was paid to say it." I waited, hoping my tale would elicit more information. She waited a long time before speaking.

"He was translating the scrolls into Botha. He respected that they belonged to me. He paid me for access."

"That's a Threlan trait."

She considered. "Two are in Botha, but three are in some ancient elvish language that Beotun studied, and there's a map on two other scrolls that shows the way to an elf colony in the wasteland."

Interesting. Beotun was a competent wizard. He could have manifested copies of the text on a scroll and brought them back to Threle or Helas to translate. Why spend so much time here?

"Why were the scrolls important to him?"

"I never asked him." She sounded defensive. "I'm just a humble servant."

"Then why are you angry about me having the scrolls?"

She had no answer.

"Where are his translations?"

"They wouldn't mean anything to you."

"I can read Botha."

"Of course." She gestured sarcastically, unhappy with my claimed proficiency and unhappy with her implied limitation, but she retrieved the translations from her room.

"Thank you." I put the scrolls in my cloak and retrieved the two she had thrown on the bed. "Why did Beotun keep his important work in your room?"

Aeren chafed. "What do you want, Llewelyn?"

"To offer you protection. On behalf of Threle. Aeren, I don't know who destroyed Beotun's room. The chest was open so I took the scrolls for safekeeping. You aren't safe."

"I know. You're here."

"So I'm proposing that we leave the city. That we . . . pay a visit to the elves." I wasn't enthusiastic about traveling with Aeren, but I was less enthusiastic about leaving her behind to talk about my visit. "We've got a map."

"Scorch the elves."

"Scorch the inn, Aeren. Scorch the servant work. Scorch the awfulness of Andan pride that prevents you from getting the recognition you deserve. Scorch the world. We're going to the source."

"Do you speak elvish?"

"No."

"Neither do I."

"Elves are known for speaking many languages. We'll be understood." I was thinking of all the languages Ellisand knew, but wasn't about to prick Aeren's sensibilities by mentioning him. "There's nothing but death and obscurity for you here."

"Death. Obscurity. That's all there is anywhere." Her agreement was riddled with the hard silence of futile objection. "That is the state of the world."

"Then we understand each other." I extended my hand as if she had offered cheerful assent. "Come, bard, let's finish our game."

Four

To our game. So we began our journey to the source of the world's Beauty, the elf colony hidden in the Gondish wasteland, by lying to each other. I'd call it creating mutually convenient fictions, except neither of us was willing to suspend disbelief. I believed part of what Aeren told me, but I had no idea which part. And of course I had no idea what she thought of my tale.

I had the added difficulty of keeping shielded, but that would be necessary with or without Aeren's company. Of course, I could keep my clerical shield up indefinitely with nothing more than an occasional prayer, barring interference from another cleric, which would take a higher level of skill than I cared to think about. But given my clerical transgressions, I had to assume that level of skill would be no impediment to an ambitious Brother seeking honor. My wizard shield needed occasional renewal from my own energy. Not that wizardry should defeat my clerical shield any more than applied magic should defeat theory, but Beotun was a wizard and he was sent to kill me. I had to assume he knew my background. I also had to assume he learned it from Mirand, because the chest I'd found in Aeren's room now made it difficult to doubt that Mirand was involved.

So I renewed my wizard shield while Aeren was out of the room gathering supplies. *Necessities from emptiness.* Perfect as a poisoned metaphor. I considered the line, which came from a petition to Hecate that we chanted at Kursen to thank Her for providing us what El called "life joyless, life without more." And didn't Aeren also have this "life joyless" without the burden of asking? I had pretty much earned it through hard work and harder choices. Only the gods could decide which of us shined a finer tragedy.

Traveling with her would be challenging, but there might be advantages to approaching the elves with Gondal's rightful queen. Leaving her behind could be fatal if she talked of our meeting. Even a binding spell would fade in time. And desperately heartless as I now was, I couldn't bring myself to kill her. Once you understand someone, there's an oddness that happens. Either you can't kill them or you can do so with impunity. Aeren was in the first column. Mirand? I couldn't begin to answer that.

Then, while I heard Aeren stomping about the inn, I looked at the translations she had thrown at me. They were senseless. Bothan gibberish. They consisted of long, unbroken, unpunctuated text comprised of random Bothan words. I couldn't even make out if it was some excruciatingly literal translation in which the word order was pristinely perfect to elvish and therefore a mess in Botha, because I couldn't construe any meaning from the slippery chaos on the page.

That, too, is my life.

Aeren disrupted my thoughts by trudging into the room and hurling saddlebags of food packets onto the bed. I put the scrolls in my cloak as she grabbed clothes and stuffed them into an empty saddlebag. Then there was nothing left to do but stand awkwardly together in the quiet Gondish sunlight. A dragon and her prey? A friendless, bitter bard and the ruined magician who once freed her? Gondal's rightful queen and king?

We left in silence. It's all we took of Anda—along with inn food meant for passing strangers, scrolls bearing language of unknown meaning, and our ragged, disbelieving selves.

We rode for days through the formless desolation of Gondal's wasteland. The moon kept spitting pale dreams. At least, that's how the moon's reflections across the sweep of featureless land appeared. The reflections formed indistinct images of rivers and towns that disappeared as we approached. Somehow, I knew that meant we were getting closer to the elves. The map was unhelpful and odd. There were faint markings in Sarana that indicated physical distances, but it was scarce on noting landmarks. And what it noted, it failed to define. Like a song. "Storms run here . . . land appears as east wind rises . . . dead meadow, three decades . . ." was as clear as it got. Some of this was the poetic nature of Sarana. Some of this was the map-maker's personal insanity. So I had to guess by madness where I was in the world.

"Hey, Aeren—bard—what do you suppose 'three decades' means? Thirty years of wandering? Three groups of 'ten beggars stout'?" I jokingly sang the line from an old north Threlan folk song. Aeren sincerely ignored me. "Or maybe that Sarana verse form— the one with three stanzas of ten lines each?"

I tried to show her the map but she wouldn't look at it. Instead, she glowered dully at the trackless land.

Not that it mattered. Aeren's anger at the world and everything in it was palpable and would have been visible to my magical senses had I dropped my shields. On the rare occasions she bothered to notice me, she stared so long and hard that she could have been focusing on the next world. I knew she was angry at the deliberate lack of recognition afforded by her fellow Andans, but whatever she carried wasn't as simple as resentment or as pure as the anger extracted from deep, justified disappointment. It had a dangerous, quasi-philosophical edge that carried those qualities into something—well, almost clerical. She would have done brilliantly at Kursen.

She no longer felt compelled to browbeat her once splendid misanthropy into me. Not because she was at peace with herself, but because she no longer cared to engage the world. Like Relyr, she was "all set" and had become a hermit in her own way. This fascinated me, and I wondered if everyone in Anda had gone this way, becoming a more extreme version of the prickly personal isolation that so many Gondish carried as a defense against being found ordinary. I mean, if the world fails to recognize you, simple self-preservation demands that you return the favor.

Then, out of the dark, on a night so silent that even the waxing moon was a noisy distraction, she threw an unexpected question at me. "What do you think the elves are going to do for us?" I had just magically induced the end of a log to burn within my shields before tossing it to ground, where we both added more wood to increase the blaze. It was the first time in our journey that Aeren decided to work with me on anything.

"Accept us as Gondal's rightful rulers." I didn't believe this, but unsupported confidence was a better option than unsupported truth. "Do us the courtesy of explaining why they destroyed our city. Wouldn't that be worth knowing?" Actually, that was part of the truth. The rest was that whatever impulse moved the elves to break from isolation and behave so uncharacteristically had larger—perhaps worldwide—significance. If I were to somehow destroy Threle, I needed to know what was infusing the world. Also, although the elves had razed Arula, I had no reason to think that they wanted or needed to destroy me, and I didn't have a multitude of choices right now as to where I could settle and plan. Not even Anda was safe. "Besides, Aeren, you have elvish ancestors. Maybe they'll welcome you as a long lost daughter—or son—embracing the tragic bard-queen who comes disguised as a prince in exile. You could end up in an elvish legend."

"They'll probably just kill us." She didn't appear to care.

I couldn't tell whether she was being candid. "Why?"

"Had either of us been on the throne when they invaded, do you think we would have been spared? Or given the 'courtesy' of an explanation?"

"Aeren. They saved Arula before they destroyed it—they appeared in Arula to fight off Roguehan before I killed him—and you were part of that plan. Something happened, something so awful I can't imagine what it could be, that made them decide to return and take Arula from the world. We had nothing to do with that, but we do have a certain standing to approach them about it."

"No, we don't. Besides, what makes you think the Assembly hasn't approached them?"

"The Assembly traveled the wasteland?"

"I don't know." She sounded disgusted. "Maybe. Supposedly. A lot of members pushed their way into this grand plan to cross the wasteland and contact the elves because nobody could tolerate somebody else being chosen for the honor. When they failed to return, another large party set out to get talked about by finding them."

"And?"

"They found them. Dead."

"You mean the first party got lost in the wasteland?"

"They got massacred by elvish arrows. Just so you know. As you say, 'death and obscurity.'" I waited, watching the bulging moon start its slow slip to the ground. "Well," she continued with a just a glint of bright sarcasm, "maybe the elves just don't like Andans, either."

"Then you'll have something in common." I tried to make this sound like a joke. Aeren hooked a stick and drew nervous patterns with it into the soft ground. Then she threw it into the fire I had created, and stared so intently at its ashy demise I wondered if I was missing something.

"I'm going to tell you the truth, Llewelyn. You can do whatever you want with it, I don't care."

"Speak, bard."

The fire's sparks whirred and died. She watched the sparks, and then she waited for a long time before she spoke. Apparently, she did care about whatever she was going to say, because she clearly needed to work up the courage to say it. "There's nothing for me in Anda." Her tone was curiously irresolute.

"No." This time I sounded sarcastic.

"I don't expect we'll get to the elf colony alive. I don't expect we'll even find the colony, or that we even know where the scorch we are. So—uh . . . thank you." She hesitated. "Thank you for your promise to make me your bard. It made me happy for a little while. Thank you for freeing me from the dragon form that Zelar trapped me in when he forced me to guard his secret wizard lair, and for helping me to kill him later."

"Noted."

She stopped speaking for another long time. Kept focusing on the sparks and fluttering ashes to avoid looking at me. "Here's what I know about Beotun." She stared at the firelight lapping the crazy patterns she had drawn with the stick she had thrown in the flames, and then she stared into the space where night had obliterated the horizon. "He did mention you. He was aware that we had known each other, that you abdicated. He also said that you were responsible for the destruction of a Helan border camp during Threle's war with Roguehan. Were you?"

"Yes."

She raised her eyebrows a little in mock surprise and consideration. "Helas, the former duchy, went independent after you killed Roguehan. There's a bounty on your life. Beotun thought I might like a cut of the coin."

"And why would he think that?" I tried to sound more genial and amused than accusatory.

"Because when he mentioned you I told him about your breach."

Naturally. And of course Aeren would have put as much anger into her telling as possible. "So. You really did want me dead." I didn't know what else to say.

She nodded so slightly it was only half an admission. I genuinely felt badly for her. "Like I wanted Zelar dead. He trapped me as a dragon by promising me bard work. You trapped me as a queen. At least the dragon had a limited amount of power and training for the job."

I waited. She waited. "I expected no less." I said this generously to break the silence. I didn't mean this, but thought it might reassure Aeren. She poked at the ground with another stick.

"So, if . . . if Threle sent you to meet him, if he . . . ."

"Go on, buddy. Say what you think." I spoke softly, a trained cleric using mundane means to elicit confidence.

"Then Threle . . . or whoever sent you from Threle . . . had no idea that Beotun wasn't just pretending to be a Helan loyalist, that in some respects . . . at least where you're concerned . . . he really was acting for Helas."

"So it seems." I managed to sound light, surprised, and angry. "Threle thought him loyal. We were fooled."

"Beotun never said that Threle was sending you here to translate for him. He said he was here to research elvish. He said he had reason to think you were back in Gondal, but he never told me why." That could only mean he had some contact with Walworth or the trial records, and that Shadow's fairy journey had consumed enough time for him to arrive here before I did. "Then I heard your wizard call and guessed that you'd go to Relyr's, if anywhere. I mean, where else would you go?" She waited an excruciatingly long time, long enough for me to notice fuzzy stars sweeping across the sky. "It's odd that he supposedly sent you a message to meet at Relyr's, because he seemed so interested when I suggested you might be there, as if he had no idea. It's odder still that you apprenticed with the same master wizard and couldn't track each other."

"We travel shielded. And it would be past odd if Beotun had seen fit to confide Threle's business in you—in anyone. It seems he wasn't even completely honest with Threle."

Aeren considered for a long time. "Your wizardry has the same source. Even I know your shields wouldn't block each other."

"My clerical shield—"

"Scorch your clerical shield, Llewelyn! Your story makes less sense than his. You're both lying. And your concern that I'm not safe in Anda and in need of Threle's protection is mouse feathers and wind. Threle doesn't care. I'm not important enough to be in danger. So, you know, here's a spot of truth for variation. It was my idea to hide a charm in a horse's mane and blast you."

Beotun told me that Mirand made the charm and that it was his own idea to hide it. I didn't believe somebody with Beotun's background would take advice from Aeren, but the amateurish nature of the plot didn't make sense, either. And Aeren had no reason to lie.

"Who taught you to weave death charms?" I tried to make this sound like an understated compliment.

"Beotun made the charm."

"You saw him do this?"

Aeren looked down and shrugged. "No."

I was silent a long time. "Disappointed?"

"You have to ask?"

I thought she was going to cry. I was wrong. "Sure." I said this with a hint of understanding, but I sort of meant it. "What else do you want to tell me? Accuse me of? Before the elves kill us, I mean?"

"Nothing."

"Was Beotun alone?"

"Yes. But he wasn't acting alone. He said the Kingdom of Helas would reward him. Also, you're not too popular in certain quarters in Threle."

"Did he ever mention a wizard named Mirand?"

"Is that King Walworth's chief wizard? The one you both apprenticed with?"

"Yes."

She pointedly avoided the question by asking in a strangely emaciated voice, "What's your relationship to King Walworth?"

"I worked for him once. Why?"

"Did he find whatever he was looking for?"

"I doubt it. He isn't the sort who would."

She broke her stick into pieces and hurled them at the fire. My response annoyed her. "Does he ever hire foreign bards?"

"I don't know, Aeren. Pretty much everyone in his old duchy is sort of a bard. His sister is quite a storyteller—but not like you," I added quickly. "I'm sure it's different in Loudes. The royal court attracts folks from all over the kingdom."

She nodded and turned to hide her face in the night, making it difficult to hear what she said next. "Llewelyn—what do you think King Walworth would do if he knew that Beotun came here at Threle's expense, harboring his own plans to kill you for Helas coin? I mean, *if* that's what happened."

"I have no idea. Most Threlans respect a good business decision."

She ignored my attempt at humor but continued to speak away from me, as if she both did and didn't want to be heard. "I mean, if the king, or his advisors, could misread Beotun that badly, what else have they misread? Do you suppose that somebody close to the king is sympathetic to Helas and was protecting Beotun?"

"I thought you didn't care about Threle's affairs."

"I don't. But *if* we are to be allies again—let's understand each other." This was hard for her to say, but at least she was facing in my direction again, so I wouldn't miss a syllable of her anger.

"I thought we were. Understanding each other."

"*You thought what?* Helas hates Threle. It isn't clear from your story what Threle thinks of Helas right now or that you even know. But the king is concerned enough to send you and Beotun to Gondal to restore your kingship, even though I'm already here and available. Not that I care about resuming the throne, but how the scorch would Threle know that? Beotun never once offered the subject of whether I'd like to be reinstated."

"He had a mission, and you made it clear how you felt when you told him about my breach."

"Yes, but according to you, he came here for you before he ever met me, and he knew our history, knew I'd be here. So I wasn't Threle's first choice. Oh, and Beotun is—was—some kind of scholar of ancient elvish. Maybe he really was—government is where lots of scholars find work, I hear—willing to reveal his true clothes to Threle by killing you. I mean, Threle would surely learn what happened and want Beotun executed, so he must have been extraordinarily motivated."

"I suppose."

"And now you tell me Beotun—and Relyr—are dead. So, obviously, Threle was protecting you, although you also said somebody tried to kill you."

"Somebody did, Aeren." She went still with embarrassment. "But your plot failed and all is forgiven."

"Won't your Threlan protectors wonder where you are?" Her voice was quietly fearful.

This was a damn good question. "Uh, sure. But I had orders to leave Anda immediately if there should be trouble, and my 'protectors' are aware of that. In fact, they told me to get out. It's understood I'll travel the wasteland and get back to Threle eventually. Visiting the elves is my own idea."

"Is that why it's not safe for me in Anda? They suspect me?"

"I don't know. Possibly they do. But, Aeren—should anything come of that potential suspicion—I swear by my life—your secret is safe with me. I *would* make your innocence obvious." I stared as hard at her as she had sometimes stared at me these past few days. This time she did cry, but just a little. "You see, buddy, we do understand each other." I said this as gently as I could. I hated the implied threat, but short of constantly dropping my shields to work magic on her, the unstated implication would effectively spin loyalty out of my bard's uncertainty. "And now—no more of Threle, Helas, or Anda. We're alone in the wasteland and should be friends again. To the elves."

"To the elves," Aeren mumbled.

Aeren's silence returned with the morning, but it was now more soberly hesitant than angry. I kept a cheerful mask as we rode. She no longer ignored my attempts to jolly her so much as willfully shut them out. I marked that as an improvement.

And then, sometime around noon, the sky went black. Not like a storm, but like we had crossed a secret border and suddenly lost an afternoon into night, except there was no moon or stars. Had we been in the North Country this would have made sense, but that was impossible as we hadn't crossed the River Kretch. Our horses stopped instinctively. The dark was too thorough to see through. I renewed my shields.

"Looks like we found the colony," I said with an exuberance I didn't feel. I had no idea of sudden darkness guiding the way to the elves, but I had no other explanation.

"Prepared to die?" Aeren asked absently.

I softly pressed my heels into my horse's sides to encourage her to keep walking. She took a few reluctant steps, turned in a half circle, and walked back out into full noon light. Aeren's horse followed. It wasn't as if there was a line here where you could see light end and darkness begin. It was stranger. You either saw everything in the plain light of day or took a few steps and suddenly experienced a night-soaked world.

"Well, Wizard?"

"Wait here."

Aeren remained stiffly on her horse as I rode forward again, found the world shrouded in silence and darkness, and then rode back into sunlight.

"You disappeared when you crossed over. You and your horse. I couldn't even hear you. And yet the sun remained."

"That's useful to know," I said, although it really wasn't, because I had no idea what was happening. "It went dark for me again." I dismounted. She did the same and held both horses like a fort around her. "I'm going in alone. I'm going to mark the exact spot of change, and you're going to mark carefully what happens."

She nodded.

I manifested a rope from my saddle bag. "Hold this end and tell me what happens when I cross over holding the other end."

"I can't. I'm holding the horses."

"Then stop holding the horses and belt the end of the rope around your waist." She did so, clumsily, and immediately grabbed the horses again for protection. Poor Aeren. Zelar and I had taught her some simple wizardry, but she had no idea what to do here, and the horses were her only comfort right now. "Aeren, can you get a clear view through the horses?" She had sort of buried herself back in the middle of them. "It really would be best if you dropped them and stood forward to better observe."

She glared at my suggestion, but she let the horses go.

I conjured a candle inside my shields and touched it with wizard fire. "I'll mark the border with this candle. Tell me what you see."

Then, pacing slowly through the blatant Gondish sunlight, aware of the wasteland stretching and falling all around me, I followed the mark of our horses' hooves until everything disappeared into world-blackness. I was curious to know whether the rope connecting us would remain tangible to one or both of us from our respective sides of the border, although I wasn't sure yet what that might mean. Carefully stepping backward and forward, from darkness to light and back again, I found what I thought to be the exact point of change and placed the candle on it. Half of the candle disappeared, but I was able to move the entire candle just inside the dark side of the border, where it became entirely visible. As to the rope, it was visible by candlelight to the point of change, and then it wasn't. I pulled gently at it and could see some slack. Then the rope suddenly tensed and pulled back into complete invisibility, so I assumed that Aeren had angrily tugged it back over to her side.

So I took up the candle and stood alone, listening, trying to see through the endless night, and deliberating on how to proceed. The map indicated, as much as it indicated anything, that we were close to the colony but marked nothing of this darkness. What little the candlelight revealed looked like more Gondish wasteland. There was nothing for it but to return to the light.

Except I couldn't. No matter how carefully I retraced my steps, slowly following the hoof marks by candle, the silence and darkness remained with me. Even after the marks disappeared as if crossing back into sunlight, the blackness remained when I crossed the same spot.

I called to Aeren before remembering that she said she couldn't hear me after I crossed the border. I then considered a wizard call, which should reach her through my wizard shield because we had a bond, but decided against dropping my clerical shield. I imagined her alone in the wasteland with the horses and tried again to trace my steps to cross over to her, but was unsuccessful. As the candlelight didn't illuminate much and the melting wax was distracting me from thinking, I magically obliterated the candle. As soon as the light went out, the world filled with sunlight again and I found myself almost tripping over Aeren.

"What the scorch are you doing?" She pulled back. I noticed she had unbelted the rope and thrown it on the ground. The horses were placidly eating weeds.

"I wish I knew, bard. Why did you pull the rope?"

"Because you did. I almost fell." She hesitated, then asked sullenly, not caring to admit ignorance, "What do you think?"

"Whatever it is can sense my magic, my wizard fire, through my shields. As long as that candle burned, I couldn't get back to you."

"I saw the candle disappear."

"I think the elves are in it somehow. I think we should go back in."

"And do what?"

"Call your ancestors. The way you did the evening before we marched on Arula, and they responded by saving the city from Roguehan. Perhaps they'll respond now."

Aeren focused her attention on a piece of brilliant sky that framed her wandering horse. "I already did, Wizard." Then she crossed her arms and squinted at me. "Or didn't you notice the patterns I drew in the ground?" Her voice was accusatory. "But then why would you? Notice, that is. Those were elvish sigils that Beotun showed me. Not that I expected they would actually do anything. I drew them, I sent a call—" she made a sarcastic gesture like she was tossing invisible coins "—and now it goes dark."

"I'm impressed." Actually, it wasn't obvious that Aeren had accomplished anything. Maybe she inadvertently made it go dark, maybe she accidentally drew us to this strange border, or maybe her call had nothing to do with what we were encountering. But I knew my tone of respect for her efforts was necessary. "Can you call from the darkness? I mean, if I provide some light?" She ignored rather than missed the irony of my question. Then she made another sarcastic hand gesture, which I took as assent. I conjured two burning candles and gave her one. "Come then, prince, let's enter the dark."

We crossed the border again and placed the candles in the ground. Their light covered a large enough area to scratch patterns by. I respectfully inclined my head to Aeren, who self-consciously traced inscrutable lines in the dull ground. Then we waited.

The only thing that changed was everything.

Blackness dried into sallow sky. It was still wasteland around us, but its features were no longer what we knew, and the light was now heavy with gray. Soft mountains we hadn't seen before showed dull blue against the distance. The sun was smaller and less insistent than it should have been. A bird laughed out of a gnarled tree that wasn't there before and flew into the gray, skimming over a rough stone wall that straggled into the rising land. The wall was flanked by occasional thin wooden poles that glistened from a recent rain. The candles had disappeared. "Well?"

"Uh, good job, bard."

"I wasn't asking you." She was looking past me. I turned and saw a large, broad-faced fellow in a thick blouse, woolen mantle, woolen trousers, and oversized but well-made boots. He smiled at Aeren, doffed his shapeless cap, and made an ingratiatingly confident bow that was so overwrought it contrasted with his peasant attire. I renewed my shields.

"Gentlemen. You come here seeking elves, is it?" He spoke in passable Sarana. Then he repeated the question in flawless Botha, which appeared to be for my benefit, or to show that he spoke my language or something, although with heavy southern inflections. I didn't respond. I was busy trying to determine how he knew I spoke Botha and whether he could read me through my shields. "Unfortunately, you've missed them." He repeated this in Sarana, seemingly for Aeren's benefit but mostly to let us know how adept he was with our languages.

"Where did they go?" Aeren's tone indicated she thought far less of this stranger than she did of the elves, and that his only use to her was as a pointer to somewhere else.

The stranger smiled again, but it was a smile that conveyed that he considered himself superior enough to let the insult pass. "They left the world, sir. And now they live among the clouds. And the starlight. And the moon on the wane." He spoke grandly, in Sarana again, as if he were gracing us with the stunning conclusion to an opaque argument that only he understood. "But, as king of this . . . formerly elvish realm" —he made a wide, ostentatious arc with his cap— "I bid you welcome to stay. As my guests."

"You mean there's another king in it?" groused Aeren, with all the fine social grace I remembered she liked to display when meeting strangers that annoyed her.

"At your service. And the service of the world." He said this without his previous sense of grandiosity. He was now speaking plainly, as if serving the world was all a matter of course for him. "I am *another* king," he mused. "I like that. King Furna. Of Furnesse. And lately it seems of everywhere else."

So this was the mysterious King Furna who sent Roguehan to destroy the world? I hadn't heard his name in years, not since Caethne mentioned him back in Helas when she brought me to eavesdrop on Walworth. Caethne told me then that nobody knew much about Furna. He was an old story; I'd forgotten he was ever supposed to exist.

"We don't know where we are," Aeren remarked sullenly.

"That's obvious." He smiled generously. "Right now you're with me, my friends. In the after rain. In the garnished fields. In the moment after taking. It's a late—very late—harvest. And today, this thick hour—I am the spirit of same." He bowed ostentatiously again. Furna wasn't exactly pretentious, but he clearly enjoyed pretending that he was by throwing around stock Sarana phrases. "My poor kingdom" —his tone suggested that he meant anything but poor— "they say it lies so far west it touches the end of the world. But really I like to think it only touches the end. Yet . . . here you are."

"Until we crossed the dark, I was sure we were traveling east. At least, that's what I was told." Aeren looked at me while she spoke.

"You were."

"It was barely past midsummer last week."

"Yes." Furna's attention was on me while speaking, so he could respond to Aeren while appearing to ignore her. Then he spoke in Botha to underscore that he was now deliberately disregarding her. "As a cleric," he nodded slightly at my Athenic robes and made an almost imperceptible gesture like an edgy compliment, "*you* are of course aware of the state of things."

"No."

He ignored my response, and continued speaking in a flatly evaluative tone. "Well then, luck's a blessing that you're here, Brother. And more that you're under my protection. So come, we'll feast and drink the harvest time, where I play peasant king of plenty and then we'll go to work."

"Go to work at what?"

"Justice. In the pure sense of setting things right." His tone was now, if not exactly serious, devoid of play. "So now the elves are gone, and the world has places where light and dark, east and west, merge and scream. As if the North Country were colonizing corners of mundane reality, or the two Habundias are confusing up the universe into themselves at random. Surely you've noticed." He drew a small wooden flute from his belt, played a few desultory notes, and nodded. "And so. Here comes the party." He swept his arm in a wide semicircle, and maybe a dozen soldiers, weapons drawn, emerged from scattered clumps of trees and bushes and quickly flanked their king. Their weapons weren't focused on me or Aeren, but the unstated implication was that they could be. A seriously expressionless wizard and a high priest of Habundia-Christus, both in full garb, were also on hand.

"My friends." Furna wasn't boasting, just commenting on practicalities. Of course my shields offered no protection against physical attack, blasting through them was useless and dropping them was not an option.

"What did you say to him?" Aeren whispered harshly at me.

I ignored her, as did Furna. "My friends," Furna repeated, still speaking in Botha but playacting at joviality. "Know that I have granted these humble travelers, the rightful rulers of Gondal" —so he knew who we were— "my royal protection." He spoke directly at the high priest when he said this. "They are my guests, and should any harm befall them, thrice harm shall return for violating my promise of hospitality. By Zeus All-Giver and all the gods."

I quietly translated for Aeren. Her only response was an angry shrug, which I took to mean she either disliked not knowing the language or was annoyed by the reference to the gods.

"And so we shall feast to our new alliance. Dance. Come all— to the great hall, where I, your good plain fellow of the fields, shall happily serve with my land's abundance." Furna half sang this, and everyone shouted enthusiasm for the coming celebration, without, I noticed, lowering their weapons.

Everyone, that is, except the wizard and the cleric. They were blandly nonresponsive. Furna didn't seem to care.

"Come, my guests. To our feast. To the sun. To our days of enjoyment. To the blessed broken world."

Five

To the blessed broken world.

Furna's feast was hollow in its generosity, like a dying man desperate to be remembered.

The king was keen to impress with his land's abundance. But nothing else was clear. The affair was as difficult to read as the notion that we were feasting in the far southwest kingdom of Furnesse after traveling east across the Gondish wasteland. That we'd somehow jumped a world.

I couldn't answer how we got here or where "here" actually was. For all I knew, we had stumbled through an elvish fracture into an area of Gondal that Furna was now claiming as his own. That made some sense as a working guess. But those dull distant mountains differed so much from the wasteland that I wasn't convinced.

Even the language wasn't what I knew. I easily understood the king's southern-inflected Botha, but his people's tongue came smeared with slurry pronunciations and stinging idioms that felt like senseless foreign intrusions, even though they slouched and slithered from forgotten corners of my first language. Botha isn't as beautiful or layered as Sarana, but it can be aesthetically pleasing, particularly the way it's spoken in Helas. Here it careened between graceless and ugly. Every phrase was punctured with garbled half-words. And the half-words had missing syllables. Sloppy tonalities made it hard to determine if someone was flattering you, insulting you, or both.

The large hall was mostly empty, and many of the guests appeared equally so, as if they weren't sure why they were there or how much appreciation their king wanted them to show for the relentless stream of food and drink he kept commanding. The soldiers' enthusiasm was more palpable than anything else in the room, but it was clearly well-practiced and exquisitely meted out to the extent necessary to please the king. The guests modeled their own responses after the soldiers' fist thumps and cries of approval. If Furna was bothered by the acting, he didn't show it.

I looked around for my buddy the high priest, who appeared properly and ostentatiously respectful whenever Furna looked in his direction, and more humorless than a dead cat when he studied me.

As to the king. He grinned. He bowed. He half-danced in his heavy boots as he poured heaps of fruit and grain at the head of each table, making certain that nobody could miss the point that he was the land. The proud, demanding happy land. He produced vats of boiled corn and nuts and carrots bleeding with dull glazes, pots of stew, slabs of thick meats and cheeses, pies and breads, and more ale than a gnomish tea party. It was almost Threlan in its abundance. And I noticed he was so meticulous in his show of hospitality that he avoided serving the meat stew or the slabs of meat anywhere near the end of the large table we were seated at. I wondered how much he did know about me. Aeren noticed this, too, and so of course remarked on it.

"Why do you think we're the only ones restricted to bread and vegetables?"

"Perhaps the harvest king is respecting us with a show of scarcity," I joked, not caring to explain what Furna's behavior implied. "Enjoy your peas and porridge, guy." A hurried servant brought us more dishes.

"Is that what he said? That we should enjoy his scarcity?"

I shrugged a little as one of the guests at the table interrupted to ask, in a querulous tone that bounced between nervousness and rudeness, if we spoke Botha. He spread his arms and waved his open palms at us in a gesture of slight aggression that was mostly intended to impress the other guests.

"Of course, friend," I replied easily in my native tongue, and, because his southwest provincialism annoyed me, continued in a deliberately overwrought manner, "I was merely congratulating my companion on how delightful it is to partake of the good king's harvest feast. Now consider this excellent porridge, these exquisitely spiced peas—"

"Eh . . . you are from Sunnashiven, then, Brother?" My interlocutor relaxed a little. Another guest nodded agreement with the question. Because, of course, when speaking my native language, I naturally fell to my native accent. The fellow was both remarking on my Sunnan accent and on my extended appreciation for the feast, because of course anybody from Sunnashiven was presumed to have intimate relations with the famine that had threaded its scrawny fingers through the city for decades.

"Yes."

"And how goes the city?" He was now a bit fearful of asking but mostly curious. Three or four other guests looked at me expectantly—none of them willing to ask, but all of them wanting news of Sunnashiven.

"Sunnashiven? Yes. Well, it's—"

"It's a rum deal what happened to Sunnashiven," half-whispered an anxious woman, trying to impress by putting on a show of sympathy for me, as if we two alone could appreciate whatever had happened there. "No one expected Helas to turn aggressor." Thank the gods! There's always one person in every group that has to know more than everybody else, and I was eager to indulge her. So I looked glum and nodded, as if it were difficult for me to speak.

"Well, no one's expected a lot of things out of Threle lately," said somebody else. "It's not even clear who runs the country since their king went missing."

"Nobody runs the country. Ever been to Helas?" another guest tried to joke. "Besides, I heard the king came back."

The anxious woman lectured. "Helas isn't Threle anymore."

"That's obvious," the first guest hastily corrected himself, "but I was saying—"

Furna strategically approached the table, singing a loud folk song and waving his hands around to indicate that everybody had to join in. Which everybody immediately did, except Aeren, of course. I made sure to sing more loudly than the others to deflect attention away from questions to which I had no idea how to respond. The version I knew was different than theirs, but that was helpful as it only added to the distraction and earned polite laughter at the difference. Also, our fellow guests enjoyed a shallow kind of relief that there was something everybody could force laughter about. Aeren smiled awkwardly because she understood neither Botha nor the Bothan folk song. Then she quickly decided not to bother smiling.

Furna noticed her expression and playfully caught her hand, deliberately raising her from our table to dance a bit with him to the rhythm of our singing, which she barely did, and did clumsily at that. "Lady. Prince," he said in Sarana when they had finished. "Speak to us in your beautiful language. Tell us a tale."

"Nobody in the world should understand my tales."

Furna appeared to miss the Sarana implications of Aeren's use of the word "should" —that it was both apology and warning, but a few nearby guests winced at her harsh tone, which needed no translation. "Then come for it. It is a fair response," Furna announced in Botha, to cover up the sudden awkwardness. "The Brother shall serve as translator, and this fair gentleman shall entertain us."

I guessed that Furna's intent was to prevent me from revealing my ignorance of Sunnashiven by breaking up our fascinating conversation, so I enthusiastically agreed to make myself useful. I made a Sunnan style bow, to scattered cheers of approval, and whispered to Aeren, "Go on, bard, turn a phrase. I've got your tongue."

Aeren looked doubtful, then she seized the moment. "To the king." She bowed slightly in his direction. He acknowledged her gesture with a broad smile and a deeper bow. She then told a story about an elven princess who painted the sun on her wall, over and over, in various shades, until the real sun turned gold in defiance of the rainbow that strangled it. It wasn't brilliant, she had better stories, but it was a much better story in Sarana than in Botha. Also, my out of the air translation was too literal, so much of the depth and color was lost. And so, of course, was her delivery. When people quickly lost interest and started chatting among themselves, Aeren stopped the story and dejectedly returned to our table.

Furna applauded like he had drums for hands, the guests mindlessly followed by pounding the tables, the soldiers shouted, and the feast moved on. I dropped some bread on her plate in a weak attempt to console.

Poor Aeren sat stiffly with hard pointed shoulders and sweaty face, trying not to breathe, trying not to show she needed anything, including the blessed air, while our table companions continued chatting without making a single reference to her abbreviated tale. Which was rude, although Aeren couldn't possibly know this from the fake smiles and nods they tossed at her when Furna approached our table again. He was carrying a serving tray of harvest food.

"I am the servant of the earth. My fruit swells with the world's blood. My grapes groan, my corn cries, my blackening berries swell and burst with seeds of violence. Come, Brother, taste the trash that trails between lives, between the surety of decay and the fragile impudence of sprout." Furna kept half singing these lines in his southern-inflected Botha, which were a version, or translation, of an old Kantish invocation to Habundia-Christus. But he made the words sound darkly humorous, so the guests laughed and helped themselves to the fruit like they thought they were supposed to. I glanced at the high priest, who grimaced and stared sullenly at the king's back.

"And now, Brother, I have something beautiful to show you and your charming companion."

Furna and two soldiers led us outside, where the sun was setting behind the hills.

"Everyone who matters knows you are under my protection now." He wasn't smiling like a cheerful peasant king anymore, but he wasn't merely stating a fact. He was maybe slightly self-congratulatory, if anything, like he'd just pulled an incomprehensible trick. "Tomorrow I put the harvest mask aside, and we meet in private." He was speaking Botha, to exclude Aeren. "She need not know about that, or about anything we discuss."

"Understood."

"Tell her whatever you need to. Tell her—for now—that Furnesse shall provide for her happiness."

"That's a job no one can win." I said this simply, sadly, thoughtlessly.

He laughed in appreciation, then smiled and nodded in her direction. Aeren was leaning against a large rock and watching the last glint of sun as it disappeared into dusk. I didn't need to drop my shields to know that she was mourning her disrupted story and her life. "Painting, my lord?" Furna called genially and playfully in Sarana, referring to the elven princess who painted the suns in Aeren's tale. "What color do *you* call the sun?" Even though that was a line from her tale, she didn't respond. She was too absorbed in watching the dusk become night to care.

"Tomorrow, Brother," he turned back to me and spoke earnestly in Botha. "Pray for my poor kingdom tonight. Pray for what remains of the world."

"As I can. As you will."

Sparse candlelight stung the walls of the plainly furnished room in which Furna's soldiers left us.

The moon was visible in the window, but it's light barely penetrated the room. Like this strange new world, it revealed nothing but itself.

I sat on a hard bed and watched the weak light trace Aeren's hair and shoulders. That was all I could see of her as she stood in the window ignoring me, the world, and eternity. We were alone with the moon and alone with ourselves, but not with each other. Then I understood that Aeren was too detached to be alone with anybody.

"Bard." I waited for a response. There wasn't any. "I loved your tale. So did the king. I'm afraid my translation wasn't adequate—"

"Is anybody's translation ever adequate?"

"I guess not."

She turned to face me in the semi-darkness. "I don't just mean stories. I mean how we translate, understand everything."

"I know," I said testily. "I know what you mean."

"No, you don't. That's my point. Nobody knows what anybody means. That's the world." She left the window, sat on the opposite bed, and stared at me through the shadows for a long time. "So where are we, Llewelyn, and what happens next? What does Furna want? What did the other guests tell you? Are we guests? Prisoners?"

"A little of both, I suspect. The king does like you. He wanted me to tell you that Furnesse will provide for your happiness."

"What does that mean?"

"Point taken, Aeren. I don't know. In Threle—in Helas, but really throughout Threle's southern duchies, it's considered a form of courtesy to greet strangers by asking them what they want. The practice probably originated with Helan merchants, because in Botha the question implies that the speaker is capable of providing, for a price, whatever the stranger asks for." Aeren kept staring through the shadows, her face inscrutable in the dim light. "So what do you want?"

"You mean I'm a stranger to you?" She sounded annoyed.

"Well, as you say. We're all strangers to each other."

"I want . . . to destroy Anda. The way I wanted to kill Raen for assuming the Gondish throne with nothing to commend him but his unearned self-belief. And Zelar."

"So you want to finish what the elves started when they destroyed Arula?"

"I suppose." She didn't like the question. She turned her face toward the floor and spoke without emotion. "I want to feel and know this room, this moment, without impediments."

"Uh . . . I want that too." There were so many times I *really* didn't understand Aeren.

"But I can't ever know anything. I mean—I *could* know things— I could sit here and pay strict attention to what's around me, embrace whatever is next, explore and experience this new living story I've been thrown into. A lot of people would."

"But of course *you* can't." I was tired and my voice was suddenly harsh.

"No, I can't." Her voice got harsher, then plaintive. "I can't help feeling that any focus, any attention I give to anything is illicit because I should be off by myself creating a new tale, even if nobody will ever hear me tell it. I can't tell you—*translate* for you—how difficult that is."

"Please try. I want to understand." Actually, I just wanted to keep peace.

"If I never set out to be a bard, that's fine. Nobody holds a life against someone simply because they never pursued the arts. Most are glad to hear it. But if you start out pursuing the arts and fail, people consider you a failure forever, no matter what else you accomplish. They decide without any other information that you lacked ability at the one thing that mattered to you, and so anything else you ever do is considered second rate. So you have to keep creating in spite of the world's indifference because then you haven't failed yet. Sort of. Although the older you get, the more ridiculous it feels. It's cosmically unfair and really hard to translate. I'd like to have adventures, destroy Anda, learn new languages—but how do you do that if you've got to isolate yourself like a monk every day to create stories? And when nobody hears those stories, is the sacrifice of your life worth it?"

"I don't know. Probably. It depends. Most experiences aren't worth the candle, either, Aeren, when you truly focus on what's happening around you. And if you find one that is, you'll know if it's worth a new tale."

She ranted over my response. "I can't even try to understand this new experience because I feel that I have to waste my life instead."

"You should really study clerisy."

"I'd rather study the scorch-be-damned moon."

I renewed my wizard shield, prayed again to renew my clerical shield, threw several magical locks on the door, and allowed myself into an uneasy stupor that lasted until dawn crawled over the bare floor.

Once I was fully awake and surrounded by light, I prayed Hecate for guidance, got none, and renewed my shields again. Aeren was back in the window. It looked like she'd been there all night.

"Planten srina vocamen baurra," I said with a lightness I didn't feel, translating the phrase in my head to Botha: *May you call yourself blessed before the dawn sun.* That was the first phrase I ever spoke in Sarana, when I tried to ingratiate myself with Walworth by offering him a simple morning greeting in his native tongue. It felt odd and off to be here in this unknown part of our lives, saying those same words to Aeren.

"No, I don't. I don't call myself blessed before the dawn sun. There are no gods, Llewelyn. Nothing is blessed. There's only energy patterns that certain magic users learn to manipulate, and some of those patterns are so powerful they manifest as images and abstractions—so people confuse some mindless random energy surge with some notion of Justice, or an aspect of Apollo. Admit it. The Habundias are as fictional as my tales."

"Good morning, buddy." It was too early to argue with Aeren and I really wanted to think about Furna.

"Is that your only response?"

"We're just random energy clusters, Aeren. Yet we manifest as . . . ourselves. I can assure you that the energy clusters people 'confuse' with a god are as real as we are, by any name. Yes, we—they—everything is 'just' energy. But some of us random energy patterns are horribly self-aware."

"You can't prove that."

"That we're self-aware?"

"Well, Beotun said the gods don't exist."

Interesting. Mirand didn't teach him that. "Beotun was flattering your Andan sensibilities."

"I don't have sensibilities."

"I didn't think so," I responded agreeably. "Aeren. I'm going to find the king. Why don't you stay here until we understand what's happening?"

"Where do you think I'm going to go? Home?"

F urna was no longer playing peasant. He was dressed as a merchant, in vaguely Helan style, his cap displaying the blue and brown colors of the Helan flag. He greeted me like we were two seasoned traders.

"Gold, sir. Hulla, my friend, and what's your pleasure? What do you want this fair morning?" He was seated at a counting table and had several bags of coins in front of him. There were flowers scattered among the bags, as if nature were being put to use to call attention to his new artifice. They were late harvest flowers, common to the southwest and bright and huge with impending death. I thought briefly of Caethne, of our early relationship in Helas before everything went awful, and then felt sad to look at them.

"Yes, King, what's the play today?" I decided cheerful, noncommittal banter was my best opening.

"Ah, still robed as Athena's votary, are ye? If you need the disguise, I won't insist on honest presentation, but really it's not necessary between us. Sit, sit. You are among friends in Furnesse."

"No, I'm not, King. You obviously know who I am."

"But, of course." He grinned. "I know who everyone is. Sit down anyway."

I sat warily and focused on Furna's unreadable cheerfulness. "Then you know friendship is not in the interest of your magicians?"

"Certainly. But you are going to be working together, so it's time to put factional differences aside." I must have looked incredulous. "Yes, well, they both stand to gain from killing you, but why let that destroy a productive working relationship? Besides, they have much incentive to protect you from . . . shall we say . . . random unpleasantries? They know that should anything . . . *untoward* . . . happen to you, I will assume it came from one of them, whatever the truth may be, and respond in kind. So they *shall* be careful of you and for you."

That's a small mercy. "Why?"

"Because you and milady the prince are the rightful rulers of Gondal. It's not clear at this point which of you has more right, so I need you both. More than I need any given magician." His voice assumed a solemn casualness. "More than I needed Roguehan. Or should I say, Emperor Roguehan, as he liked to style himself?" He bounced a bag of coins in his palm. He was playing merchant, but I couldn't make out what he was pretending to sell. Damn my need for the shields. "So here's what you need to know, my lord. In the two years—is it?—that you wasted in some trumped up trial with Walworth—"

"About that—"

Furna waved a hand to silence me. "The verdict was wrong, by the way. I would have acquitted you. On *all* counts."

"Thanks." I managed to sound like I appreciated his high-handed assessment of Walworth's legal reasoning, even though I didn't share it.

"But I'm burning the tale before lighting the torch." He shifted a little in his chair and looked steadily at me with an expression of blank honesty. "For two years, nobody knew what happened to Threle's king, or if anybody did know, it wasn't obvious. Maybe you're aware that he left letters making his chief wizard regent during his unexplained absence?"

"No."

"Well, Master Mirand kept the details of that decision close to his cloak, as well as everything else, including his brief jaunt as a self-styled King of Helas, in the hope of swimming the distance between Threlan loyalists and Helan independents while 'ruling' from Loudes. For all I know he's still claiming the title."

So is this why Mirand wanted me dead? Perhaps Mirand played up the Helan independence part, particularly in Walworth's absence, which is why Beotun said they "played the same coin." That would make sense. A friendly Helas independent of southwest influence would enjoy the freedom to make its own decisions, something Mirand valued to a fault. And a free Helas would be a viable trading partner, something Walworth would likely welcome. And should Helas freely decide to become a Threlan duchy again, Threle would certainly embrace it. *But why would Mirand send an assassin after me and what did Walworth know about it?*

Furna continued. "When the King of Threle quietly returned, my associates in Loudes, of course, obtained a copy of the scrolls he brought with him, his notes on your trial."

"When was that?"

"Seven or eight months ago." So that was the length of Shadow's journey, aside from my brief time in Gondal. More than enough time for Beotun to arrive in Anda before me. "The world knows you, my friend." He grinned. "No secrets."

"I am encouraged that we can be open with each other, my lord."

"As open as the blessed gods." Furna half-sang these words and waved a broad hand in a wide arc in a show of high good cheer. Then his expression went serious, suddenly thoughtful, and slightly tense. "That's the difficulty. The world's gone open, and wrong. Worse than the famines. Worse than whatever 'inconveniences' came with the war I started. Not that I would expect the good people of self-isolated Gondal to know that."

"They know the elves destroyed Arula."

"They know their world's gone wrong. They just don't care to admit it." Furna said this quickly, threw some coins on the table as if pretending to wager, and quickly changed the horse's color, as they say in Botha when someone abruptly changes the topic of conversation. "You know, I once considered becoming a cleric, aligning myself with Zeus All-Giver. I once thought that such was the way to experience the world, to know all. I also thought if Zeus wouldn't have me I could try to become the greatest witch-king to rule nature. Now, I suppose, I shall merely be the savior of the world. My world."

"About my city, King—"

"I don't know why the elves destroyed your city. That's for you to discover."

I didn't believe him, but it wasn't in my interest to be disagreeable, so I said lightly, "And yet you called yourself the king of that 'formerly elvish realm' when we met. Surely—"

"Ah, surely I know what happened? Know why my poor kingdom now kisses theirs at the world's end? Ask your former master if you get the chance. I'd love to know."

The slight tease in his voice told me he knew. He just wasn't going to tell me. I knew it was useless to press.

"So here's the tale, Brother. When your former master used the dirty weapon you once bestowed on him, that Wand of Surprises, to cage an unearned victory for Threle, he interfered with the fabric of the universe. He broke time, which caused the world energies to bend back on themselves and sicken into something unspeakable."

"Isn't that what wizards are supposed to do? Bend the world?"

Furna smiled and shrugged. "A little. As we all do. Some say the world is for play. But to rewrite history like a clumsy redactor rewriting a sacred text that doesn't dress him? It's an insult to the gods. A clever, brilliant, strategic insult, but an insult."

"Perhaps that's what the gods intended? An unexpected plot twist in the sacred text of the world?"

Furna didn't like the question. He slapped the counting table with his heavy hand, threw back his shoulders, and jerked his head in annoyance. "Victory should have been mine, Brother! And *was* mine!" Then his fit suddenly dissipated into a quasi-genial harshness. "Divine plot twist? Well, here's another. I still rule the southwest— Sevalas, Sunna—Helas has a new king now but . . . we're friendly. I helped him to the throne."

I decided not to mention last night's chatter about Helas turning aggressor, or my recent history with the previous Helan king's assassin. Better to compare whatever version of truth Furna wanted me to have. "I'm not in a mood to wield aesthetics like a weapon—like Roguehan insisted on doing—when the messy world is my birthright. Nature, commerce, art, politics, justice, poverty, wealth—should we—should I—know such limits? I'm a king. I refuse to be kept. And so should you."

I thought of Aeren's complaint that barding kept her from life and of my years in Kursen Monastery. Furna continued lecturing. "Do you know what makes a king and a beggar kin? Freedom. Unfettered, at the extremes, we become like gods, spending our days into eternity as we choose, becoming whatever we like."

"Cleric or no, my lord, you clearly are a son of Zeus."

He accepted my strategic compliment with a solemn nod. "Brother. We are going to heal the world by reclaiming our victory. We will do justice. We will set all right."

I remembered Hecate's words: *Mirand marred the world to save Threle. You will heal that wound by destroying Threle, which you once loved.*

Furna continued speaking, his voice taking on the bright cadence of breathy merchants' banter. "So, as the trial record notes —King Walworth and Master Mirand colluded in a cosmic word game of energy transfer. Master Mirand set himself up as 'lady' of the land in the same way a male high priest takes on the power of his goddess. He then blasted Roguehan, in the moment of his victory as 'lord' of the land, into a life that never should have existed—prison, that unfortunate business in Gondal that I had nothing to do with—and all the rest." Something in Furna's cheery gaze collapsed into focused sadness.

"We can't begin to name the changes that Mirand's act caused in the past, although my clerics assure me those disruptions in time were confined to whatever was minimally necessary to create Threle's 'victory.' But we now have a world where midsummer wears the harvest, the elves make a guest appearance in history to destroy Arula, Furnesse and Gondal meet in light and dark, and evil clerics who have spent their lives training to destroy beauty for Hecate's glory become Gondal's putative king in Arula."

"Enemy glory." The speaker's voice was nearly emotionless, containing only the barest suggestion of greeting as he entered the room. It was Furna's high priest. Furna motioned him to sit, but the cleric chose to remain standing to the side. We deliberately ignored each other.

"I suppose." Furna sounded mildly agreeable. "Also, here and there, once-dead warriors walk as if their lost battles were victories." The cleric faintly nodded in my direction. "Not that anybody remembers differently. For the most part, for most people, the cracks aren't noticeable. Life runs along, and it's only at the edges that things get frayed. Again, it's only beggars and kings and the occasional philosopher who notices. We outcasts" —Furna included both of us in his gaze— "we catch it." He smiled. "Except in Gondal. Nobody notices anything in Gondal."

Neither myself nor my colleague indicated amusement at Furna's sally.

"So. Here's what's needful. We have invented—well, let's say reverse engineered—our own Wand of Surprises. You, Brother, as a priest of Hecate or Athena, I don't much care, will return to Threle in the company of Brother Stomr here, and my chief wizard Zyren, who also graced us with his presence last night. You will ingratiate yourself with Walworth, who is now lord of the land, and with your old master, if necessary. My . . . *friends*" —he waved cheerily at the high priest and at Zyren, who had just rather breathlessly entered the room— "will of course assist you in any way you desire, as well as milady the lost prince, who will also accompany you. You will execute Walworth with the Wand for his crime against the world and the gods, and in so doing, restore the world to the state the gods intended. You will do the same for his wizard."

Everyone waited, whether for me to respond or for Furna to continue wasn't clear. This opportunity aligned so well with what Hecate required I could only assume that She arranged it. Walworth had sentenced me to death . . . spiritually and physically . . . sort of. Mirand was doing his best to make that stick. But something in me blanched, a ghost in my heart that no longer belonged to me but had somehow never left. Out of my incomplete thoughts I heard myself asking, "Perhaps changing Master Mirand's alignment would be just as effective?"

Stomr looked deeply surprised, then briefly impressed, then thoroughly dour. The high priest didn't want to jeopardize his relationship to his deity by changing somebody's alignment. Also, he had to know from the trial records that I had destroyed El, the high priest that trained me, by persuading El to change his. Working with an outcast cleric like me to perform a spiritually dangerous act was giving him pause.

Furna shrugged. "Whatever works."

"Why do you ask me to . . . perform such justice? And Aeren? Surely there are better qualified magicians?"

"Well, surely there aren't." Furna turned affable. "You see, one of you—perhaps both of you—embody Gondal as Walworth embodies Threle. Gondal has always been isolated, empty, neutral. Even Arula's former elvish beauty was resentfully ignored by the locals, as if it never existed. And Anda, while free, ran along in splendid unconcern with the rest of the world. It's neutral absence that's needed. You, as the embodiment of the unyielding empty Gondish wasteland, are perfect because by blasting Walworth with the Wand of Surprises, your combined force of neutrality will send Threle's stolen victory back to the cosmic wasteland of nonexistence and set the world right. Also, I was impressed with your description in the trial record of Aeren's cool assassination of Zelar. She has the heart for it."

Something in Furna's tone suggested he had less confidence in my heart than hers, despite my earlier suggestion concerning Mirand. I tested him. "What if I respectfully refuse this honor, King? I mean, of course, only in theory."

"Then—and only then—my friends here will respectfully kill you. I mean, of course, in theory. We'd still have Aeren, who would indisputably embody the land. And without Aeren, well, we'd eventually find whoever's next."

"Done. A fair deal to come home to, my lord. But surely we should get Aeren's consent?"

"You get her consent if it matters to you. I don't consider it necessary." He said this like he wanted to imply an admirable informality in his affairs, but then turned serious. "To be clear, Brother, I don't consider it necessary that she know anything about the purpose of your pending journey until it *is* necessary."

"Understood." Actually, it wasn't, but I supposed Furna considered the mechanics of Threle's victory more trouble than it was worth explaining to Aeren, who only had a minimal knowledge of magic. I know I felt guiltily relieved at not having to explain everything to her.

Furna played with his gold to indicate that our meeting was over. Stomr and Zyren left immediately, as if they had separate concerns to attend to. I awkwardly made my way back through the castle of an unfamiliar king who donned familiar images, a follower of Zeus who wanted to remake history in the gods' own image in order to remake the world in his own.

Hecate's will be done.

Six

Aeren was sitting on the floor when I entered the room, watching the door but focusing on the air around it. I thought of a broken old dragon pointlessly guarding a broken old tower from the ruin that would always keep happening. Then I sat on my bed, tried to look nonchalant, reached under my robe to conjure a gilt black rose, and prepared myself for the gathering storm.

"For you, my queen. A token of the good king's very high regard."

She stared at the rose, or maybe somewhere past it. A vacant sunbeam fell between us, like the border between our hearts, the world, and each other. Even if I wasn't lying, I knew she had no reason to trust me or the king.

I pressed the flower into her hand, taking the risk of briefly breaking through my shields to do so. "King Furna spent the night thinking about your tale. He regrets that Sarana is not his first language, so impressed was he with what he heard."

She looked up at me through dead, dragonish eyes.

"He would very much like you to honor him by representing his interests." She slightly bent her head as I slid onto the floor to better converse with her. "You see, the king was aggrieved by what's happened in Gondal, and he was indignant to hear that you lost the throne. He told me this morning that when the elves left the world, they created that dark-light passage between the Gondish wasteland and Furnesse, but that nobody knows why. Furna believes that the passage is a sign that the elves have designated Furnesse to be a kind of successor to Arula, and he's convinced that's why you're here."

"He said this?" Aeren didn't believe me.

"Yes. Would I lie?"

"If you're not lying, Furna is. *I* drew the sigils. *I* called on my elvish ancestors. *Then* the passage happened."

Damn! I needed to be careful. "Furna couldn't know this. He is aware of the passage, but he did say something drew him there when we showed up. Perhaps that was you."

She stared into the corner. "So the passage had been there. The elves didn't hear me."

"Except it appears they did. Aeren. You are a queen. Considering your ancestry, you are also an elvish bard. And a prince by choice." I smiled generously. "Furna also said that he would be 'running over with happiness' if you—and I—but mostly he's interested in you—would agree to go on a journey to Threle on his behalf. To impress upon Threle the high level of culture that Furnesse enjoys. And as a show of friendship between two countries with a difficult past."

"What do I know of their difficult past? I've got my own."

"Surely Beotun told you of the recent misunderstandings—let's call them poor translations—between Helas, Threle, and the southwest?"

She shrugged noncommittally. It was hard to read her. "Why doesn't Furna send his own people to Threle? Doesn't anybody like him?"

"Well, he is sending his own people. We'll be traveling with his own people. You'll like them, Aeren. They seem really nice."

"I don't like anybody."

"Which is why you'll be an excellent ambassador." I smiled enthusiastically. Then I kissed her rose. "And I shall be at your service. The service of King Furna's royal traveling bard, who gets to have a royal adventure in Threle because of her undeserved obscurity in Gondal."

Aeren dropped the rose onto the cold floor, as if it were suddenly too heavy to hold, and then studied the floor to avoid responding to me. She wanted to believe me. She was still wary. "So we travel to Threle," she said dully. "Under King Furna's protection?"

"Sure."

"Does that mean your 'protectors'—the ones who told you to leave Anda after . . . after . . . ." Her voice trailed off. But I now knew what she feared, so I now knew how to proceed.

"After you tried to kill me?" I laughed, took up the rose, and pressed it back into her hand. "My Threlan contacts—should we even encounter them—would welcome you as my friend and ally. As to whatever happened in Anda, they would only know what I tell them, and I can assure you I've quite forgotten what happened in Anda."

Aeren shifted a little. "How can you represent King Furna, who's had a number of 'recent misunderstandings' with Threle, when last I heard Threle was supporting your return as King of Gondal? Isn't that a sort of treason?"

This time I hesitated. "Uh . . . well, Threle *was* supporting my return. But I wasn't working for Threle. I mean there *were* other things at play. But I've always been friendly toward the country, toward King Walworth, and so Furna sees me as useful, as a putative head of a foreign state with a good relationship with Threle. He thinks I can help balance things between them in a way a purely Furnessian party couldn't." Well, that last line was sort of true. "The same can be said of you, with the added interest of your considerable storytelling ability." She didn't move. "Aeren . . . this isn't just politics for me. It would make me very happy to see you happy. Whether you choose to believe it or not, Prince, one of those mindless energy clusters that we clerics call gods has seen fit to bless you with everything you want."

Aeren graced the silly rose with a tight, enigmatic smile that conveyed more pain than pleasure. I knew that pain. Hadn't Zelar trapped her in a dragon form with a promise of bard work? Hadn't I reneged on my promise to make her my royal bard? Hadn't some Threlan official from Walworth's court rejected her tales?

I regretted my lie, but quickly put regrets aside by telling myself that once we set the world right, as Furna put it, one or both of us would take back the Gondish throne and I would make sure that Aeren got recognized as a bard.

Aeren spoke. "I'll *choose* to believe it, then." Her dead eyes livened a bit, or maybe that was just the morning light. "For bardic purposes. May the gods save King Furna. And Threle!" Her voice was less confident than her words.

I respected her effort. Mostly because effort was all she had right now.

"You have said it, bard. May the gods save Threle."

Since Stomr didn't care to disguise his alignment, it was pointless for me to disguise mine. That is why at some point over the next few days, while Furna's servants made travel preparations for our merry little party, I quietly transformed my Athenic clerical garments to Hecate's. I hated how comfortable I felt in Her robes, how necessary to my psychic health it was. I would always be Mother's bruised and bastard child. Nobody remarked on the change except Aeren. She glanced dourly at my simple dark robe and stared a little longer at the now visible waning moon that Hecate had chained around my neck. "Would you like me to conjure new traveling clothes for you? Something befitting a bardic prince?" I was trying to jolly her, to set her at ease concerning my display of my evil alignment.

"No. I like my garb. I wish to remain as I am."

"We must be as we are," I said absently. "It's like a dirty god-given secret that no one can keep."

"And you're Hecate's dirty secret?"

"At your service."

Whenever I encountered Zyren and Stormr in the castle's halls, they spoke to me in Botha. That is, when they spoke to me at all, which was seldom and mostly in mutters. I had no idea whether they understood Sarana, although it would be poor game on Furna's part if they didn't. So I tried Zyren by casually approaching and asking him in Sarana about testing the wands we were bringing.

He turned, huffed impatiently, and responded dismissively in Botha. "My wands work, Wizard. Do yours?" Then he yelled at a hapless servant before returning to his preparations, ending our pleasant exchange.

Stormr was even less affable. I happened to cross his way in an otherwise empty hall, so I cheerfully greeted him with dark blessings in both Sarana and Botha.

He kept walking.

I kept telling Aeren what a fun journey this was going be. She kept pretending she believed me.

After these interesting encounters, our freedom to go about was suddenly skimmed by three ragged courtiers, sent by Furna to "accompany" us wherever we wanted to go. "As a show of the king's hospitality," said a straw-bearded, shabby-genteel fellow. His voice was soaked in apathy. He was a stranger to hospitality and wished to keep it that way. The others had his back.

Another courtier in a painfully ostentatious cap kept tilting his head toward the third, rolling his eyes at Strawbeard's back, and pushing loud, impatient breaths through tightly pursed lips. He appeared to be mocking something in Strawbeard's appearance for the other courtier's benefit, although it wasn't clear what. His face was an unhealthy white, mottled with darker creases like a parsnip, which made an awful contrast with the brightly hued eyesore falling from his head. His sallow expression announced that he disliked Strawbeard, disliked us, and probably disliked the other fellow, but found him a convenient audience for his annoyance.

The other fellow wasn't impressed by Parsnip's antics. He stared at the back of Parsnip's magnificent cap as if it were a dirty plate he wanted somebody to clear. Then he shrugged contemptuously, stared at the ceiling, and shifted impatiently from foot to foot. He was desperate to show off his boredom. He was peeved that nobody cared.

Eventually Strawbeard caught the general enthusiasm and outdid the others by screwing up his face in a dramatic display of vexation while shaking his head like a wounded cow. Having established primacy, he ordered us to wait, as if we were now imposing on him. I started to leave, just to make him order us again. Which he did, but with less gust and more irritation. He then indulged in high-handed bellowing about "the *important* matters begging, pleading, and screaming like starved chickens" for his precious attention elsewhere, managing to both belittle us and assert his considerable self-regard over the other two. It was a masterstroke of efficiency.

Parsnip, however, refused to yield ground. He glanced balefully at Strawbeard, loudly clicked his tongue, and slowly removed his cap. The cap was besieged with tarnished metal, a mess of cock feathers, and a muddle of confused embroidery that was supposed to represent "the king's gardens kissing the dawn." He pointed out every dull decoration, boasting of the many illustrious personages who gave him such fine trinkets. Furna himself contributed the cluster of cracked opals. Strawbeard loudly whined that the opals weren't from Furna. The third fellow stopped shifting back and forth long enough to goad Strawbeard by insisting that they "had to be." Parsnip recited each bauble's tedious backstory, making everyone wait upon *his* pleasure while Strawbeard fumed.

It was an exceptional show of southwestern civility. I'd decorate them all.

When Strawbeard had enough of being upstaged by Parsnip's cap, he decided to terminate the "make them wait" game he had imposed on us by declaring victory. "You people know you don't *need* an escort? It's not like you're sitting heads of state of a real country or anything, right?" The questions were thrown in a quick, too-casual, take-it-for-granted way that left no room for argument. A way of making sure we understood that, despite the king's desire to show hospitality, we shouldn't consider ourselves important enough to merit any, because really we were just a couple of fobs who happened in by mistake, right?

Aeren took in their aggressive disinterest like a dead tree takes in sun. She stared questioningly at me when I dutifully translated, impassively at our hosts, and then mostly at the floor. She didn't even bother to look up to admire Parsnip's splendid cap.

"They don't want to." She spoke with uneasy simplicity, each Sarana word stark with sadness between us. Her face and shoulders stiffened like the quiet that shrouded her voice.

It didn't seem politic to translate her remark. "They want what the king wants." I knew this wasn't necessarily true, but hoped it would mollify.

"No. They resent us. They wish they were important enough to be watched. That's why they are working so hard at snubbing us, and snubbing each other. It's Anda all over again."

"So what?"

"I'm sorry for them."

"I didn't think you were sorry for anybody."

"I'm sorry for them."

"Get on one side or the other, bard. Recognition brings resentment."

"I can't. I know what it's like." She awkwardly faced the courtiers. They were smiling with barely disguised relief, clearly enjoying the strident undertone of our exchange even though they didn't understand a word. Aeren then spoke her thanks for much longer than necessary, including weirdly ornate expressions of appreciation for the king's choice of hosts that were a bit much even for the southwest. She went on for so long that I found myself toning down my translations of her gratitude so she wouldn't sound quite so overwrought to southwestern ears. Her speech was received with nervous, uncomprehending glances in my direction. Parsnip and the third fellow looked as if they wanted my assurance of her sincerity, or thought I was putting it on. Strawbeard appeared heftily satisfied, as if he had every reason to believe her but was too great a personage to take her praise as anything but his due.

Aeren concluded her speech by bowing to each of them in perfect imitation of the bow I had made at the feast. Then she kissed their hands in greeting, and looked briefly into each one's eyes before slightly inclining her head. The effect was that she was naturally too overwhelmed with their presence to speak further, yet bravely determined to let them all know in what high esteem she held them, despite the untranslated spat we'd just had.

Being the southwest, it worked. Like a damn love spell. Despite her male attire, which now only increased our reluctant minders' sudden curiosity. They stepped back. They exchanged confused smiles. Strawbeard and Parsnip made excitable hand gestures, caught each other, then pretended they hadn't. The third fellow forgot to look bored.

But she didn't stop there.

For once, Aeren was charmingly, excruciatingly polite. Breathtakingly considerate. Witty in a way that made our "hosts" feel clever simply for being in her presence, even through my bewildered translations.

Aeren's new admirers threw off their sudden daze long enough to usher us—or rather her, I simply followed like a forgotten servant—into a courtyard. The point was to show off one of Furna's royal gardens. The garden was a panoply of bright disorder. Given the state of the world, it could have been a piece of high summer that lurched out of time and landed here after harvest. Parsnip constantly commented on the confused runs of roses, dragonroods, gnomestockings, and other patches of "desperate flowers fierce with color" as he put it, misquoting an old Helan folk song, which was interesting. Much of those "desperate patches" happened to be mirrored in his cap. But whenever I translated for Aeren the writing on an occasional stone marker proclaiming a rose bower a "royal gift" to some favored noble, Parsnip would rush us past, cloaked in the awkwardly obvious silence of envy.

Aeren noticed his silences, and made gold out of them. "You are so sensitive to color it hurts my eyes, Master. When I hear—I mean *see* your words—it's as if you understand flowers like flowers understand earth and water laughing through them. I don't mean to embarrass you," she added softly, "but, it is quite beautiful to know this."

Sweet gods on a broken world! Where the hell did "Master" come from? I dutifully translated what she meant to be taken as a high compliment. Parsnip beamed.

"No artist in all the worlds could overcome your description of these flowers." Then Aeren—how can I put this—skillfully pressed her back against a marker as if its inscribed praise held no interest for her. "When I remember this place, it will be through your words."

She looked at the ground and then back at Parsnip. If she didn't sound so helplessly diffident, she would have been cloying.

The courtier laughed in earnest, something he clearly wasn't used to.

Strawbeard cut off Parsnip's laughter to insist we visit the king's stables. In the middle of a row of the finest stallions I'd ever seen, or possibly anybody has ever seen, Strawbeard, who naturally resented the attention Parsnip had scored, breathlessly expounded on the excellence of Furna's steeds. The length of his praise was an obvious rebuke to Parsnip's enthusiasm for the garden. But his voice also carried a tone of harsh wistfulness that Aeren made more gold with.

"Didn't I see you riding one of these yesterday? You looked as though you and your stallion were one."

"No, milady . . . I mean milord, I'm afraid you did not." Strawbeard hated saying this. Almost as much as he hated Parsnip's self-satisfied tongue-clicking when he said it.

"Oh." Aeren managed to sound broken-heartedly chagrined. "I'm sure I dreamed it then. I get these prophetic dreams sometimes. I make stories out of them. I kept seeing you riding something graceful and swift. Like a wish. Or one of these horses."

My bard kept it up all afternoon. Which meant I had to translate her nonsense all afternoon. All. Damned. Afternoon. Which didn't even cover the sensitive, aren't-we-friends glances she kept throwing at the third gentleman, who was tongue-strapped by her sudden cloud of charm.

Later, in the privacy of our room, I remarked on her sudden change of demeanor. "You had those court spies practically on the floor to you."

"It isn't a change. It's a reversion." Aeren sounded cold, hopeless, and angry. That is, more like herself. "That is how I used to be."

"It is?"

The dragon glare returned. For long uncomfortable seconds. Then the expected rant. "There was a time, before Zelar turned me into a dragon, when I . . . when I knew myself as courteous, charming, understated . . . even if nobody else did . . . I wanted to be that kind of person . . . a prince, I suppose. One of those colorful, charismatic male bards. But without the awful vanity that attends that sort of thing. A quiet mirror to the world."

"So?"

"*So?* So I wear the clothes—my own self-chosen turning. So I play the polite, arch gentleman. So, in Anda, my persona gets mocked and my studied courtesy gets taken for weakness, or strangeness, or affectation, or all three at once. Which maybe it is, but other bards are worse, and they get an audience for being worse. So, of course, I get figuratively backstabbed out of storytelling, and later my so-called throne, and constantly told that I haven't earned the right to act that way, and all sorts of ugly things that leave scars on the heart. So I turn quiet. Destroy that part of myself. But then I'm 'too quiet' to attract notice. Or 'too intellectual' for anybody to bother with. Or, laughably, 'too nice.' Because of course simpletons mistake quietness for niceness and niceness for not having anything insightful to say—"

"Obviously."

"Well, certain things, certain types of lives, put one in a permanently foul mood."

"I guess I can respect that."

"*Respect that?* I want to be a mercurial, clever, fey, attractive young male with an audience for my tales. If I *was* that man, that princely bard, I would have that audience, I'm sure of it, because young men with those qualities do attract. But whatever 'energy cluster' flowered into me, if that's how you clerics put it, cursed me with a womb. Which means fey doesn't work. It reads as female foolishness, not insight. Something to mock. Mercurial, witty adventurer doesn't work, either. It reads as pretentious. Who I am doesn't function well in the body I was born with, so most days are a kind of torture, and the stories get more difficult as the days go on."

"Not today, bard. Your stories came thick and fine."

"You know what? I could be myself today only because Furna gave me the power to be. There's a difference between the king's bard playing 'thick and fine' and the Andan innkeeper's servant doing the same. Or even Anda's queen. Even if they *are* doing the same. One is charming, the other is annoyingly pretentious, the third gets mocked and dethroned because she's friendless and in possession of something everyone else covets. And that's a deadly coupling. Maybe, just maybe, King Furna values who I am."

"I know he does. The king highly values who you are. That's why he's sending you to Threle." I had no intention of telling her I made up the bard story.

"I shall be ever at his service, the good King Furna." Aeren's smile was broad and possibly even genuine, but it was hard to tell. "The king of disguises. We know each other."

I knew in that moment that if Aeren should ever learn that I lied to her, that she would kill me. Just as she killed Zelar. I also knew that despite the terribleness of what I would experience after death, I wouldn't blame her.

That night, in the moon's cold reach, I saw Aeren scribbling. She said it was a new tale. She was calling it "Hecate's Grace."

I strengthened my shields.

I don't remember when we left Furnesse. Perhaps it was a day or two later that Furna met us in the gray before dawn, dressed as "night's servant" in tattered pieces of dirty robe, like a beggar. I remembered what he said about kings and beggars being kin.

Aeren and I waited outside his stables as Furna insisted on leading out five choice stallions packed with supplies and weapons. "I am your servant until dawn," he said mysteriously. Aeren bowed low to him, reacting to his playful tone because she couldn't understand his language. "And . . . ah, here are my masters Zyren and Stormr. Good day, sirs." The wizard and the cleric approached from opposite points. They were clearly determined to arrive no sooner than necessary. Whether to avoid each other, me, or the king was anybody's guess.

"Five stallions," said Zyren, a bit too loudly to emphasize his surprise without also conveying his annoyance.

"And three mares, sir," wheedled Furna in his best beggar's voice. "And then, sir, you shall of course ride with honors, with a few . . . mundane sentinels, royal servants shall we say . . ." The king's voice became a whisper. "Who know nothing of your quest." He then shouted playfully, "Sentinels who will help with whatever is needful on your travels. They ride at your convenience. Lord Graen, second son of Count Lianon, who keeps my royal armory—"

Somewhere out of the stables a thin, stringy-haired gentleman emerged with three young and somewhat fearful servants. It took perhaps half a minute in the semi-darkness for me to recognize Parsnip without his cap.

"My lord," I called sociably.

Zyren glanced at him, groaned in annoyance at the unexpected addition to our party, and mounted his steed. Stormr bowed slightly to Furna, and mounted his. So I mounted mine. Stormr and Zyren waited impatiently while Parsnip—I mean Lord Graen—and his servants got ready on their horses. Aeren was the last to mount, because she once again bowed to Furna. The king grinned, placed his hands on her shoulders, lightly kissed her cheeks, and indicated it was time for her to ride, by waving the back of his hand at her horse. She clumsily climbed and pulled herself onto her stallion, with Furna's enthusiastic assistance. Then she caught her breath and confidently tossed back her hair and cloak, ready to ride.

I conjured a gold coin and tossed it to the beggar-king. For his luck or mine, I couldn't say. And then we rode.

Stormr would, of course, be reading me, but that was a mutual problem. My wizard shield was clouds to clerisy, and our clerical shields were practically open doors in regard to our thoughts, even though my clerical shield prevented me from reading others. That is because evil clerisy crawls from the same source, and it's through that source, Habundia-Christus and her lower manifestations, like Hecate, that evil clerics can read each other. Our thoughts travel through our deities like prayers. That is also why our shields would only dampen each other in a blast, at best. And yet, Stormr gave no indication that he knew my thoughts or that he cared when I occasionally read his. Not that I found anything there that I didn't observe through non-magical means. Or, strangely, anything regarding the logistics of our quest.

Stormr embodied intense confidence. Not intense in the sense of fraught nervousness focused on fear of failure, but in the sense of having passed that point in his life and come into a hard-won high-status position. I learned through my reading that he was fiercely protective of this position, because it allowed him to display a quiet grandiosity that shouted how little he cared for the world. He was devoted to Habundia-Christus in a distant, perfectionistic kind of way, but he mostly enjoyed impressing with his cultivated sense of being devoted. It was an odd combination of working hard to present an image of something he had worked hard to make real anyway. The image mattered. He was human. He needed to impress. I wasn't surprised to find that he understood Sarana, but his exposure to the language was purely academic. That was why he chose not to speak it. He feared revealing imperfection.

When I edged my horse between Zyren's and Stormr's, so the three of us would ride abreast in front of the others, like equals, Zyren called out to no one in particular, "Rides the Beloved of Hecate." His tone begged notice as mocking himself, our quest, myself, the king, and possibly the life that brought him to this point.

"It is an honor to ride with the king's chief wizard." I spoke carefully, attempting to mollify.

Zyren made a sound that was part forced-laugh, part grumble, and entirely dismissive. Stormr lightly grimaced. When his grimace had no effect on me, he rebuked me in casually superior tones meant to impress Zyren by discrediting me. "You may be *styled* the 'Beloved of Hecate,' but you never had to work to gain that status. I have as much difficulty thinking you a peer as I do thinking you a king."

"Then don't think, Brother," I responded cheerily. "It isn't worth the game."

"I don't care enough to game." Stormr kicked his stallion and rode ahead. Having established his preferred hierarchy—which meant more to him as a southwesterner than my former clerical crimes against El and Cathe, which he never mentioned or even appeared to think about—he continued to behave as if I didn't rate notice.

Zyren also mostly ignored me but with less punch. He didn't make a deal of it like Stormr did. He didn't appear to care for anything. My presence wasn't special.

I knew our companions would be reading Aeren, if they hadn't already. Shielding her was impractical. A wizard shield would drain energy I didn't have to spare, require me to occasionally drop my shields to maintain hers, and it would do nothing to block Stormr. A clerical shield from Hecate would be equally useless because Stormr would read through that. The only "revelations" they would get from reading her thoughts were my lies in King Furna's service, her belief that Threle had been supporting my return to the throne before a turn-cloak wizard named Beotun tried to kill me for Helas, and that I still had Threlan "protectors" out there somewhere. That would be problematic, except that Stormr would, of course, be reading me, too. He'd know I lied. He'd also know there was a possibility that Mirand had sent Beotun to kill me, but the gods knew how that would play. Probably in my favor.

Despite Zyren's strategic apathy and the uselessness of my shields against Stormr, I still kept them up for protection against strangers on the road. They both had to know this, but neither remarked on it.

Although they weren't engaging me in conversation, they weren't making an effort to exclude me from their occasional exchanges as we rode. But they said little to each other. It wasn't even clear that they liked each other so much as tolerated the fact that they shared a long working history.

Zyren appeared to resent Stormr because Stormr liked throwing his status around, but he also appeared to resent everyone, mostly on principle. He liked to sigh and bark pointless anecdotes at whoever would listen whenever Stormr made a public show of prayer, like a child competing for attention. Sometimes he could get Graen and his servants to listen, but that wasn't exactly what he was after. It was a kind of victory over Stormr for Zyren to get me, the other cleric in the party, to notice him without the wizard appearing to notice me in return. Sometimes he would accomplish this by throwing obscure wizard jokes at an uncomfortably servile Graen, knowing that Graen wouldn't understand them. But even his flashes of aimless jollity were a thin cover for his weary resentment. I would say that Zyren was terminally bored, but he was also somewhere beyond boredom. It was almost spiritual.

One of Zyren's jokes involved crystals. "So here's the deal," he announced during one of our rides. "Three crystals harmonically clash, and you need to spin gold."

"Uh . . . sure," Graen hesitantly agreed, calling from his place behind the rest of the party, where he led the servants.

"So you get fire. So you say, 'Hey, I thought you wanted gold.'"

The joke involved what happens when too many energy streams run in alternating directions, overwhelm the crystals, and cause a small fire. Spinning a story to your patron was like spinning gold out of the fire or something. It wasn't that funny. Except that it possibly once really happened to Zyren, and he was using a joke to illustrate his own cleverness.

"What would *you* do?" Zyren apparently mistook my failure to laugh as ignorance and wanted to underscore it for Stormr, who, from the arch of his back, didn't appear to be listening.

"Realign the crystals to spin gold out of a linear arrangement, like you spin thread. Why would you even let energy flash back and forth, which is sure to end up fighting itself and immolating one or more crystals? Or, if you had to do it that way, I suppose you could shield or replace the discordant crystals with something more compatible. Better than exhausting your own energy to smooth everything into something workable."

Zyren nodded and huffed.

I had no idea of his magical lineage or whether he had a personal stake in avenging Zelar or had even known Zelar. It was possible he would have resented Zelar, too, had they known each other. He mostly struck me as someone who had lived long enough, and practiced wizardry long enough, to be experienced enough to do great work but was now tired enough to not care anymore. Barn weary, as they say of old horses. When I did initiate conversation with him, I was always interrupting—even when he was silent, or just fussing with his own stuff. His favorite response was "What what wha . . ." in a voice of gruff irritation that meant "get on with it and leave me be."

So I let him be. Which piqued my curiosity, because of course at some point we would have to strategize, even if my companions did resent my inclusion in the quest and possibly also their own. They needed me more than I needed them, so I decided it was strategic to hide the weakness of too much curiosity.

Surprisingly, Aeren accepted her linguistic exclusion with something close to equanimity. She listened to my occasional translations of the servants' talk with an air of focused utility that I'd never seen in her before. Sometimes she called snatches of Botha phrases to Zyren's back. Zyren would laugh harshly and respond in a torrent of words she couldn't possibly understand.

"*My* horse?" Aeren repeated to me in Botha, trying her pronunciation before shouting playfully at Zyren. "My horse . . . it wants . . . a drink."

"Ah, give it a bottle of Krygon. Fit for horses and fools!" shouted Zyren.

Aeren looked at me for help. "He says to give it bad ale," I explained in Sarana. "You meant to say '*to* drink.' '*A* drink' implies that your horse wants something more fun than water."

She smiled mischievously at Zyren's back, and shouted in barely passable Botha. "*A* drink! My horse . . . it wants and likes! A lot!"

Zyren conjured an empty ale bottle and made it appear in front of Aeren's saddle, growling, "He drank it!"

Aeren smiled and tossed the bottle to Graen, who clumsily caught it, looked briefly confused, and passed it to his servants.

Aeren and Zyren sometimes shared dried fruit and bread, and although he never appeared to completely warm to her, he did flash occasional smiles of pale generosity as he'd carve pieces of dried apples and drop them in her lap. Those smiles told me that there had been a time in his life when he enjoyed having younger people look up to him. He was bored and cynical now, but here and there he forgot himself when he could play the Great Man. He spoke Sarana with some difficulty, but chafed with bruised pride when I offered to translate, so I left him on his own.

Lord Graen, second son of whatever, was mostly cowed. He kept back, unwilling to initiate conversation with the rest of the higher-ranked party and risk getting rebuffed in front of his men. Aeren took advantage by occasionally hanging back and riding with him. Sometimes she'd try to start trouble by sharing Zyren's fruit with him.

We rode southeasterly through Furnesse for maybe a week, staying at the houses of various put-upon gentry who reluctantly gave us shelter when Stormr, buoyant with seriousness, showed the king's orders. Then, if Stormr was feeling particularly pretentious, he would make a show of blessing the domicile "for Habundia" without actually troubling himself to bring down energy. That was the extent of our party's direct communication with our inconvenienced hosts. Everything else was handled through Graen and his men.

Until we got to Sunnashiven.

We didn't enter the city. We passed by its brooding bones in the distance. I knew from Stormr's thoughts that we were avoiding Habundia's temple, or rather, the nest of clerics it housed, solely because he feared that my presence would compromise his safety. Naturally, he did not say this. But he rode from the northern edge of Sunna at a furious pace as he sought to put distance between himself, Sunnashiven, and me.

So I rode at his heels for fun.

When our horses tired, the rest of the party was so far behind that we were alone on the trade road that connected Sunnashiven to the nameless Helan border towns, surrounded by the same forest on whose hidden paths I'd first entered Threle. I remembered following Baniff, the gnome-illusionist who worked for Walworth, out of Sunnashiven, along those paths and into Walworth's household, my apprenticeship with Mirand, and everything that happened after. I decided not to think about that, so as not to make it more Stormr's business than it needed to be. Or mine.

"What's to come, Brother?" I asked Stormr to distract him from trying to read me. Also, it was odder than monk's chatter that I still couldn't read our strategy in him. "We're traveling to restore the world, but nobody ever feels up to discussing it."

"Ask Zyren."

"Don't you know?"

"The world concerns me not."

"There's a lot of that about," I agreed before adding, "Must make adventuring for the king a chore."

Stormr halted his horse as I was speaking, so I did the same. The wind was tinged with black, like poisoned sunlight. I dismounted. Uncharacteristically, Stormr followed. The sky's colors were suddenly too sharp; blues and violets and reds blazed without fading into each other. Then I felt a thrust of sickness in my blood. That was Stormr, who had suddenly slammed us both to ground as a fireball scathed the forest around us into oblivion. It took less than a minute, while Stormr grasped me within my unsteady shields, for the swathe of land around us to burn.

"Somebody missed." I spoke with more coolness than I felt, surveying the devastation, the gusts of ash that used to be horses, the sky that was still wrong but fading now into patches of normalcy. Stormr, breathless and shaken, had pushed himself away from me. He was retching. Violently. I could see green down the road, the graceful shimmer of oak trees beyond the line of devastation. Our party should be somewhere beyond that line, but if they had somehow caught up to us and crossed it, they now were dead. But I couldn't let my concern for Aeren distract me.

I waited for Stormr to finish. He gagged, coughed, and warily dragged himself into a half-sitting position on the still-smoking ground.

I spoke with casual courtesy, as if we weren't sickened embodiments of opposing forces surviving to chat on a newly opened void.

"So, how long have you been a high priest of Habundia Ceres?"

Seven

"I suppose that's personal." Stormr glanced at me. His usually expressionless face was distorted with revulsion. But whether his disgust was for me, the recent blast, or both wasn't clear. He was still shaking as he leaned on his arms and surveyed the smoldering land encircling us. And then he was silent. He wasn't exactly waiting for me to speak so much as simply not saying anything.

"That's unfortunate," I remarked sourly.

"My being aligned to Habundia Ceres?" His condescension annoyed me.

"No. You fooling yourself that it's personal."

Stormr wanted to argue. "Yours was personal. Unless you lied in the trial records. You dedicated yourself to Hecate because you felt betrayed."

"I was betrayed. What of it?"

"Then it's personal for you, too."

"Well, not so much anymore. Now it's just there." We didn't speak for several minutes. There was no sign of the rest of our party. Either they were dead or staying well behind the blast line while Zyren huffed around deciding how to proceed. The sky had recovered its normal soft shades of blues and violets fading into each other, and the sunshine was filling the air as if nothing had happened. There was nothing to cast shadows on the newly opened ground, which was still trembling softly under my hands. Or else that was me, still sickened by a high priest of opposing alignment entering my shields, still tremoring from coming so close to eternal torture. "So, why do you wear Christus's robes? Does the king—and the rest of the party—know you belong to Ceres?" I didn't expect a response. It was something to say to the emptiness.

Stormr grimaced. He didn't like answering, but he liked letting my question hang like an unanswered rebuke even less. "King's orders, not mine." He looked past me as he spoke. "Furna thought you would more likely survive the journey if other evil clerics saw you in the company of one of their own."

"Then why not send one of their own?"

"You wouldn't have lived two heartbeats out of the king's presence, if so long. Despite Furna's threats." Stormr was nettled. There is something unavoidably personal in guarding another's life. This is particularly grating on somebody as heavy with self-importance as this high priest. Stormr stretched, groaned, and contorted his face again, making a grand performance out of slowly standing and focusing his attention away from me.

"I'm sorry you got the jackdaw's job." I spoke with only a hint of sarcasm.

It was enough to elicit a flash of cranky resentment, which Stormr immediately masked with an overwrought blandness meant to signal his indifference. "No one, including you, was supposed to know. So no one, including you, could reveal my spiritual loyalties and compromise the king's quest."

"Including Zyren?" I forced myself to sound mostly disinterested and slightly accusatory. It worked. Stormr continued talking in spite of himself.

"He knows. That was unavoidable. But Zyren has no personal quarrel with you and no interest in dying for disobeying the king."

"He might have died notwithstanding his obedience to the king." I stood, swaying slightly in the awful starkness as I thought of poor Aeren, comforting myself that if she had died, she died believing she was a royal bard. At least I had given her that. "And where does that leave us?" I asked reasonably.

"There is no 'us.'" Stormr spat out the words like he'd just taken a mouthful of warm bread and suddenly discovered that the bread was laced with bones. "We're not equals. I'm here because I'm the best cleric Furna's got. Of any alignment. I've spent years perfecting my ability to reverse the current of Ceres's energy as it runs through me. I can hold out for an hour without sustaining damage. I can fool your brethren. I fooled you when you thought you were reading me. That's why you only got an echo of what you expected when you tried. Crafted thoughts thrown outside my shield."

That explained why I never felt him reading me. He couldn't get through my clerical shield because his clerisy came from the other side of things. "I'm impressed," I said dryly but sincerely. "That's twice as long as—"

"No, it's four times as long as what you claimed at your trial you learned from Cathe when he was teaching you how to pass as an Athenic priest to gain Mirand's trust and destroy Walworth's household."

"You're better at lying than me. Congratulations."

Stormr scowled. "Cathe did you no favors by forcing you into a direct initiation with Hecate without appropriate training. You may be a natural priest as a result of his efforts, but, thanks to the trial records, we both know that it wasn't as a result of your own."

He might have been a votary of goodness, but Stormr was also an insufferable crow. I wondered how he'd fare in Threle, where those who aligned themselves to Ceres saw no need for high priests. "If you're so skilled at shield work and everything, why did you throw me to the ground and use my shields for your protection?" I knew he wouldn't let that pass. I wasn't disappointed.

"I didn't. You know your shields are useless against that kind of blast. The gods know why you bother with them." His rebuke was odd. It was steeped with resentment, possibly envy.

"Stormr . . . I don't understand you." He managed to look both incredulous and disgusted. "I'm not playing with you. I respect your position, your path, and your obviously hard-earned skill too much for that—"

"No, you don't. You can't respect what you don't understand." Stormr turned away and strode angrily in the direction of the blast line, ending our conversation. I renewed my "useless" shields, desperately trying to parse what he meant as he disappeared into the distant trees, leaving me alone with the devastation. I performed a purification spell to ease my sickness. Then I prayed. Then I sank back again to hard ground and watched the tree tops moving against the sky beyond the blast line. They mimicked a wind I couldn't feel.

I remained seated on the dead earth for possibly an hour before Stormr emerged from the trees. He was riding Aeren's stallion. Zyren was close behind him, and Lord Graen and his hapless servants were close behind Zyren.

"There's Hecate!" Zyren barked this at me as I stood to greet them. "We've got a problem." The wizard dismounted. He seemed vaguely pleased at having a problem. It was a new reason to bolster his terminal annoyance, goad me, and justify the cynicism he wore like a second shield.

"Where's Aeren?"

"The 'queen' is gone," proclaimed Zyren in a tone of self-satisfied ridicule for our quest. Lord Graen looked around at the damage from the blast and then stared between his horse's ears at nothing. His servants glanced back and forth between him and Zyren, unsure of what they were supposed to do. "So you don't have a horse and we're down fire power."

I wasn't sure what to do, either. "What do you mean, Aeren's gone? Was she frightened by the blast?"

"I offended her royal humor, so she showed her high displeasure by stalking off into the woods. No one can find her, so we presume the blast did."

Graen spoke up, somewhat timidly because he was outranked, but also somewhat angrily over Zyren's cavalier description of Aeren's potential loss. "I saw her leave, Master Wizard. She didn't look angry or 'royally offended' and I didn't see her putting on any 'queen' about it." He then addressed me in a slightly less angry tone. "She was weeping. Weeping so hard she could barely see to walk, so she blundered into the woods and fell. I went to help her, but before I could reach her she rose and disappeared into the brush, like a mortally wounded animal."

Stormr showed a shade of interest while Graen spoke, but then quickly pretended to boredom. He wasn't going to compromise his dignity by crediting a social inferior with contributing anything useful to the discussion. Zyren huffed and waved his arms, tried several times to interject, and finally managed to deflect the implied blame from himself. "She was crying because her ally in endless trouble" —he swept an arm in my direction— "told her some half-truths and spider tales and . . . ." His voice trailed off with the realization that he was about to say more than he was authorized to in front of Graen.

Graen looked down at me like he wanted to trample me with his horse and order his servants to do the same with theirs. "What did you say to her?"

I turned to Zyren and asked in simple slow Sarana, to be sure he would understand, "What did *you* say to her?"

"The truth." He didn't like responding to me in Sarana. It was all fine to chat with Aeren in her native language, but speaking with me invited unflattering comparisons from Stormr regarding our relative proficiency in an acquired tongue. That's probably why he reluctantly dismounted and urged in equally simple Sarana, "Come with me. We need to talk."

I wasn't in a mood to save his southwestern pride. "Then talk," I responded in Sarana. "Or talk," I repeated in Botha, before reverting again to Sarana, this time speaking rapidly. "I don't much care what you say in front of Graen. That's ultimately a problem between you and King Furna." I made sure to say "Graen" and "Furna" loudly and clearly to catch Graen's curiosity. Zyren obviously didn't want Graen to hear his version of the facts, so naturally I wanted to force Zyren to tell me what happened in front of Graen by refusing to move and making it difficult for him to keep up with my speech.

My ploy failed. Zyren looked balefully at Graen, and spoke carefully and quietly in Sarana. "She learned you lied to her."

This time I acceded. "All right, tell me privately in Botha." I wanted Zyren to be able to tell me all the details without language constraints. Stormr dismounted from Aeren's horse and grudgingly accompanied us for a distance across the burnt expanse, unwilling to appear as if his presence wasn't needed for this important conversation. Graen remained on his horse, taking in our movements like he was born to do nothing else.

But he must have gotten bored watching a conversation he couldn't hear, because at one point he rode off to join his servants beyond the blast line. Zyren and Aeren's horses followed his.

Once we were well out of earshot, Zyren spoke defiantly in Botha, as if he dared anyone to hold him accountable for what happened. "She thought she was going to glorify King Furna by barding it around Threle. That's your fault. I was translating for the lord there when he sought to curry favor with milady" —he made Graen's poor infatuation sound like a moral failing— "by asking what she intended to do with herself in Threle."

"So you weren't thinking."

"No, Wizard, it didn't occur to me, in the heat of translation, that you had given her some strange image of herself at odds with our purpose."

"In the heat of *what?* You mean your Sarana wasn't up to reading her, Wizard?"

Zyren's anger was harder than the blasted ground. "Of course I read her! Of course I knew you had her convinced that she was some kind of royal bard—"

"And *of course* you couldn't damage your pride by pretending that you didn't understand how to translate the question, and *of course*, being a highly educated, experienced wizard and everything, you *knew* from your readings that she was staking her entire personality—her way of being in the world—on that fiction, on that story—"

"It was *your* story. What do I have to say to it?"

"The damage is done," said Stormr unhelpfully.

I ignored him. "What happened when you translated Graen's question?"

"She told him—through me—that she would be performing to honor the king, and then Graen looked confused and said nobody told him, that he had no idea she was a bard, and—"

"*And you of course translated this?*"

"Well, maybe the 'queen' needs to live with the truth. Nobody cares about her damned tales." He nervously fingered his robe and looked around at the blasted ground. "We need to reassess our strategy."

"How's this for strategy, Wizard? You killed my friend."

"Zyren couldn't know that Aeren would wander into a blast." Stormr wasn't defending Zyren so much as castigating me, which only made me want to kill both of them. But the consequences of losing a clerical battle with Stormr kept me from blasting Zyren. And Stormr didn't deserve death. I caught myself thinking like I was still Mirand's student, and stopped.

I faced down Zyren, who was doing his best to show more interest in the emptiness around us than in discussing what happened to Aeren. "When I gave my poor queen a spot of cheer, I didn't count on you poisoning the pot. But then, you're too much the coward to openly destroy whatever self-regard rubs against yours, particularly if you should gain the king's disfavor by doing so. But if you can passively pierce a hole in somebody's heart and disclaim responsibility, that's all to your ease. The gods know why you're on this journey, why you've been entrusted to set the world right."

"You're not so suited for the job yourself," retorted Zyren.

"Without Aeren I'm the only one suited for the job. I'm the god-be-damned King of Gondal. When *you* embody a country—a region—whatever it is—let me know."

"A wasteland," said Zyren with simple rancor. "When I stumble into embodying a wasteland, I'll let you know."

"You just did." The intensity of my anger surprised me. Despite our having gone strange with each other, Aeren was my only connection to my life before the trial. While Mirand was changing history with the Wand of Surprises to steal a victory for Threle, I escaped from Threle to take my chances elsewhere. Then I found Aeren, freed her from Zelar's imposed dragon form, and adventured with her all to the way to Gondal and its precarious throne. Without her I had no past, and the world had shifted in such a way that I had no world. For me there was now only Hecate, Her horrific mandate, the trial records, and the scrolls in my cloak that I couldn't read. Even the forest waving in the newly created distance, which hid the paths I took out of Sunnashiven so many years ago, had taken a blast.

Stormr graced us with the obvious. "We lost two horses and our magical weapons except for what Chief Wizard Zyren is carrying." Zyren looked inexplicably proud, as if luck should be a credit to him having one over on us. "You two need to determine whether it's viable to continue."

Zyren spoke confidently. "I've still got the Wand of Surprises. That's what matters."

"I had three or four untested wands." I didn't really care about the wands. "And you still killed my friend. That's what matters."

"I carried six, if I recall," said Stormr breezily, not to be outdone. "But wizardry isn't my concern." He didn't need to say this. He just liked reminding us, and himself, that he was a cleric.

"As nobody's been particularly eager to discuss tactics," I spoke coldly, "and we're down weapons, we should return to Furnesse and sort this all out before continuing to Helas." I wanted to give King Furna my assessment of Zyren's role in Aeren's loss. Most likely, Furna wouldn't hold Zyren accountable for the blast, but I might be able to shame the chief wizard where it counted. Also, I wanted to gain a little time before entering Threle. Not because of the blast, which strangely, nobody was discussing, but because I still hadn't "sorted out" my charge to destroy Walworth. Such an act still felt necessary without feeling right. "I'm assuming the blast was a welcome from Threle, which means that Walworth's advisors know our purpose." Actually, I wasn't sure of this at all. It wouldn't be Threlan to destroy anybody outside their border, no matter how sure they were of the threat. A blast from Threle was more likely to happen crossing from Helas into Kant, which was still part of Threle proper, as far as I knew.

"Helas is friendly to the southwest, and closer. We'll lodge with the king in Hala, which is still Helas's capital city, no more than two or three days' ride, and then 'sort this all out.'" Stormr was his usual condescending self when he mocked my words back at me. Zyren nodded in vigorous agreement. He clearly wasn't eager for Furna to learn of our latest mishap. "It's the king who has Furna's orders. Furna thought it better to keep all of us ignorant of those details while we traveled to Threle."

"About that. I heard Helas turned aggressor against Sunnashiven not long ago."

"When did you hear it?" grumbled Zyren, implying it was old gossip.

"It was remarked upon at Furna's feast."

"One hears a lot of things at feasts." Stormr didn't care to be distracted with politics.

"On to Helas!" shouted Zyren. "Gondal's 'king' can share a horse with our loyal lord, or a servant, or . . . ." He ambled away before I could argue, and Stormr quickly followed.

And then, just as they strode into the center of the blasted area . . . there was another shadow, a screech against the wind like a storm skidding across a suddenly icy sky and bruising itself in airy pitches and falls. The wind and sky disappeared into an explosion of light and the blasted ground crumpled and charred from gray glass to black dust. At first there was the terror of Nothingness, the sickening expectation that I had failed Hecate and would forever face the consequences. Then, as my body stopped vibrating against the pulsing devastation, I sensed that my hands were deep into something soft and scratchy, and that I was choking on the dust-devoured air. I slowly understood that I was still alive and lying face down in ashes, my back exposed to the killing sky.

At some point I heard a thin voice vibrating like a dull bee through the awful silence, words buzzing and folding into each other and forming sentences I couldn't understand. I sluggishly pushed myself up into a low crouch. I waited while I slowly stopped gagging, my body finally achieved something that resembled breathing, and my eyes stopped burning so I could see again.

The voice stopped, disappeared into hazy light, and then rapidly shouted. ". . . You are alive? . . . can you sit? . . . stand? . . . here." I began to realize it was Graen's voice, although I couldn't hear all his words through my awful gasps.

I forced myself to kneel. Graen's voice kept drifting in the thick air as I shakily surveyed a perfect circle of twice-blasted land. This twice-blasted circle was inside the larger circle formed by the original blast. The second blast area being smaller than the first, I had to assume it was more focused on its intended target. But that told me nothing.

The sky was clear now, pale blue and quiet. All I understood in my still terrified state was that pale sky, and its horrifying depth from which the blasts came.

" . . . Stand. Wizard . . . cleric . . . King." Graen's voice trembled as badly as the hand he was stretching out to me. He was almost begging; he needed to assure himself that I could offer some protection against another blast. His horror had overpowered his anger over Zyren's claim that I had upset Aeren into running to her death. But he was still the southwestern courtier, quick to flatter with honorifics when he found it in his interest.

I refused his help. I wanted to think, and Graen was a distraction. I slowly stood, still dazed. I prayed. I renewed my shields.

Graen stepped back and pointed hesitantly in the direction Zyren and Stormr had gone, toward the new blast's center. Something white glinted like death in the sunlight. Bones. Charred shadows of flesh. Then I noticed Graen's servants sitting on their mares, just outside the blast line, along with the three stallions that Aeren, Zyren, and Graen had ridden on our journey. One of the servants appeared to be shaking and crying, although it was difficult to tell from a distance. The horses were stiff with fear.

I nodded briefly at Graen to acknowledge the carnage. He waited for me to speak. I had nothing to say. So to get some reassurance from me, Graen tilted his face upward at the steady aftermath of blue. He rocked uneasily. "Do you think it will return?"

"Do I think what will return?"

He narrowed his eyes into slits of desperation and disbelief. His words ran unhindered; fear made him speak like a wreckage of his formerly politic courtier self. "Didn't you see? It was dancing in the sky. Before the second blast. Like a cloudy snake that nodded and slithered in shapes and arcs. It wasn't so much dark as carrying the dark around it. Bringing the dark in a basket, as they say in old tales. Nodding like . . . the way an old horse nods when it's pleased."

So Aeren had gone dragon! And of course my wizard shield was proof against her blasts! Bloody damn Aeren! I was so angry I wanted to turn dragon myself and have it out with her. But I forced myself to appear neutral. "Did your servants also see this . . . thing in the sky?" Graen gestured helplessly, as if to say he didn't know. I wordlessly started toward the servants. He followed in silence, both of us avoiding the awful pile of death.

Ashes sucked my footsteps into the dead ground, slowing my pace as we made our way and giving me time to consider this new situation. Stormr had said my shields were useless against "that kind of blast" when I asked him about the first explosion. But Stormr knew from the trial records that my magical lineage to Zelar informed my shield and protected me against Aeren's dragon fire. Surely he would have mentioned the dragon if he'd seen her, would have suspected from the trial records that Aeren had transformed. So Stormr had assumed the first blast had a different source that he didn't find convenient to tell me about. Was he guessing Mirand? What had he known?

As far as I knew, Aeren could not control her transformations. They were as chaotic as she was, driven by extreme circumstances like Roguehan invading Arula and by the residual energy of Zelar's spell. Zelar originally cast that spell to make her a guardian of his name stone, so of course it made sense that her dragon form would emerge to protect her own "name stone"—her fragile bardic identity. And if she was angry enough to unintentionally turn dragon, she was angry enough to forget that my shield was proof against her blasts, or angry enough to not care so long as she could seize the moment and scorch the earth.

The servants stared hard at me. Like their master, they wanted an assurance of safety. The one servant was still trembling. He leaned over and vomited to the side of his poor horse.

"I'm taking Zyren's horse and continuing to Hala." I actually had no idea where I was going, but I had decided that traveling alone would give me time to consider my next move. Taking Zyren's steed would grace me with the Wand of Surprises. I wanted to find the hidden forest paths and pray in solitude. I also wanted to send a wizard call to Aeren, if I could somehow learn when she shed her dragon form again, but I wasn't going to risk another wizard hearing it. I wanted her to know that I believed in her, that my strategic lie was a poor trick of fiction illuminating a truth so sacred that only we could see it. That I didn't want her to stop hurting because I knew that such a wish was an insult to her pain, and I respected her anger and isolation from the world too much for that.

The servants looked incredulous and angry, pointedly turning to Graen and waiting for his orders. I mounted Zyren's stallion to indicate that I was serious. Graen glanced at me and sadly placed his hand on Aeren's horse. Then he briefly pressed his face against the horse's side and softly wept. Graen's grief was genuine, which is why it was annoying. He barely knew Aeren, and what he knew of her wasn't exactly her. And yet he was acting as if he had a better right to mourn than anybody. I truly needed to leave. "You will all return to Furnesse and tell the king what happened."

"No." Graen spoke unexpectedly, his thin voice uneasy with determination. He looked up at his mounted servants. "You will return to Furnesse." The servants murmured surprise and relief. "*I'm* riding with Gondal."

I knew he meant Aeren, Gondal's putative queen, although he appeared to intend the servants to understand that he meant me, to assert that he was of a status to ride with a putative king. He mounted Aeren's stallion, patted its neck, and imperiously and somewhat self-consciously waved his arm, describing a half-circle in the general direction of his previous horse. The oldest servant shakily dismounted from his mare and rapidly tethered Graen's riderless steed to Aeren's, as Graen stared sadly at a distant cloud. Then the servant exchanged the horses' saddlebags, so Graen had his own weapons and supplies at hand, and Aeren's supplies were attached to the horse that Graen had ridden until now. The servant remounted his mare without daring to look at his master or his fellows.

"Go. Tell King Furna what happened. That I risked my life for him and will continue to do so at his pleasure." Graen still sounded more tentative than his words, but that didn't inspire the servants to wait around for clarification. They were gone before he finished speaking.

And then, a boiling silence of awkwardness. It mocked us as we rode. Our pace felt oddly fearless, and then simply odd, as if we were taking a lazy pleasure ride across the burnt expanse and then north along the trade road. As for me, I was too distracted to argue with my plodding, blast-weary horse. I saw no reason to hurry now that I knew my shield was proof against Aeren's strikes and would therefore protect my horse. Graen kept insistently to my side.

Sending his servants back to shape the tale, while proceeding with me on a journey he didn't know the purpose of, showed a surprising sense of courage I hadn't looked for in a social striver like Graen. Aeren's put-upon persona had created this quality. Which was sort of sad and sort of discomfiting, but I decided not to interfere with her work. I'd already interfered enough.

The forest was punctuated by sounds that should have been familiar but had somehow gone hollow and strange. Hidden animals softly wailed like they were in mourning. Birds sang sweetly and then they sang brokenly, as if they couldn't recall the songs that nature gave them. And then it sounded like the birds weren't there anymore, but that they had somehow left their voices behind to whistle aimlessly through the foliage. It was like meeting somebody you hadn't seen in years and now didn't recognize through the obscurity of old age. And then it was like slowly realizing that yes, that person still existed, but that you no longer knew each other.

"So enlighten me." Without Zyren and Stormr to status-slap him into silent subservience, Graen seized the opportunity to status-slap me. "Your history with . . . milady Aeren. You both ruled Gondal, but isn't Gondal something of a joke? A fake kingdom?"

"Aren't you something of a joke? A fake courtier? The *second* son of some count who keeps King Furna's armory?" I regretted my outburst, but I also regretted his showy mourning for Aeren and his forcing his company on me.

"I do the actual armory keeping. My brother is dead. My father is often unwell." His tone managed to be both haughty and muted. He still wasn't sure of our relative status. I wasn't going to help him out. That's why it was a long time before he spoke again, this time in a tone of quietly unwilling exasperation. "How did you and Aeren come to rule Gondal together? Based on your resemblance, were you siblings? Cousins?"

"She was a friend to whom I happened to give my kingdom."

Graen looked unhappily confused. "Why?"

"Because I was her friend and she had originally given her kingdom to me."

"Then . . . so . . . who does Gondal belong to?"

"Nobody knows. That's part of its charm."

Confusion silenced him again, but not for as long as I would have liked. "His glorious highness King Furna" —Graen went slightly hesitant— "he chose me to accompany the party for my well-known discretion, and sword skill, and—"

"And he respected you so much that he decided not to tell you why he was sending us to Threle."

"An affair of state, I presume. I know not to ask."

"You just did." That is, his tone conveyed an expectation that I would tell him our business in Threle. "What do you know about Helas's king?"

"Not much. His name is Hathe. He's from Furnesse and a distant cousin to King Furna. Furna sent him to Helas to keep it loyal and himself safe from Hathe's ambition. I've met him."

"Interesting." Our horses stopped to drink at a shallow stream. Graen fidgeted his preference to be out of the clearing and back under cover of trees. "Where's your other horse, milord? The one carrying Aeren's supplies?"

"It's . . . ." He turned, panicked. Somehow his second horse had slipped its tether and wandered away unnoticed.

"Gone to wind," I remarked with mock cheer. "Shall we turn around?"

Graen glanced at the sky, breathed sharply, waivered. "How far is Helas?"

"If we hasten, without a tethered horse, several hours. A day, perhaps."

"Helas, then."

"Naturally."

The Kingdom of Helas was sadly inscrutable. The former duchy had a border now, but nobody was there when we crossed. The border towns had names, but nobody liked using them. Every commons and marketplace had signs proclaiming these names—Rogueton, Furnahaven, and others it pains me to credit—but the signs were often bashed and broken and the letters defaced. I kept hooded and shielded, speaking to no one. Graen took my reticence as an opportunity to assert his standing by speaking for both of us. Which meant he kept falling in it with the locals.

"Give me your best room for the night. And food. For two royal stallions." He held up two fingers to emphasize the number of horses and his growing impatience with the innkeeper, who was ignoring him in favor of sweeping the floor. Graen shook his two fingers in the air and smiled so stiffly that he half-grimaced.

The innkeeper looked him over, taking in his southwestern accent and clothes. "Go to hell, Furnie."

"I represent his Highness, the Most Royal Majesty King Furna."

"Exactly."

And so it went pretty much everywhere. The Helas I remembered had no use for shows of self-importance; and on that score it didn't disappoint. Also, nobody we encountered appeared to have much love for King Furna and the southwest empire, despite or because their new king was Furna's man. Which is why we spent the first night in a field on the road between two towns, to Graen's loud chagrin and therefore to mine. We found lodging near the end of our second day in the kingdom, about a half day's ride from Hala, but only after offering three times as much gold as the room in the derelict outbuilding was worth. And we had to carry in our own supplies from the stables at the far end of the walled area that enclosed the back of the outbuilding from the street. That was fine with me as I didn't care to leave my magical weapons unguarded. Graen grumbled as if it were his patriotic duty to complain. "Helans are more provincial than anyone knew and far more ignorant. They don't appear to recognize their own allegiances."

"Maybe it's your accent."

"You could speak." Graen made this sound like he was being generous. Sadly enough, he probably was.

"Why? It's more fun watching you." The clang of quarreling street merchants broke through the cramped space in our meager room, a peculiar cadence that left me feeling both vaguely comforted and unexpectedly desolate. The nameless Helan town I had loved and destroyed still lived in those cadences. Hearing them again made me think of my time in Walworth's household, and how the Helan marketplaces and their merchants' banter once made me fall in love with Threle. "We'll be in Hala tomorrow, milord, where I'm certain the king will receive you with all honors."

"You sound as if you find such respect distasteful." Graen wasn't being critical. He sounded mildly astonished and somewhat curious. "As a king, as a cleric, as an emissary of King Furna, don't you think your status should be respected?"

"Respected for what?"

Graen half-shrugged, waved his palms, and glanced briefly around the room.

The merchant patter swelled and faded. "Friends, taste my nutmeg. My cinnamon jumps like dreams. Burning pleasure on the tongue. Sample here."

And the response, "His spices are older than your grandmother's dreams, friends. Mine were birthed here, from the sun's own purity. Fresh they are and sharp. Sharp as a fox's tooth on honey apples. Taste mine."

Maybe I smiled a little. I know I closed my eyes and covered my face with my robe, to better listen, to remember my past encounters with Helan merchants, when Walworth's sister Caethne would send me out to buy supplies for our secret household. I also wanted to privately suffer the wash of emotions those memories unleashed.

"What are you doing?"

"Praying."

Graen huffed and left. He returned within a quarter hour, or maybe when the warm Helan darkness fell. But I didn't know the passage of time. I had gone halfway into a trance, helplessly singing the merchant patter I could no longer hear and had no right to because I had a hand in killing it when I was involved in destroying the border town. I was playing the weight of that awful night in my heart. Knowing that even though Mirand wreaked the actual destruction, it was my idea that got us there.

Graen entered the room while I was chanting. His face went rigid with disbelief at encountering my odd solitary performance.

"Wine for cider; hearts grow wider." I murmured the line that I had heard many so times.

"They want to kill us."

"Who? The local merchants?"

"The local everybody. What is wrong with these people and why don't they like us?" A rock crashed through a window, followed by a burning torch and the sounds of a mob.

"Kill the Furnie! Burn the overking's man! And the overking, too!"

I grabbed the torch, killed the flame, and renewed my shields. "Can we get to the horses?"

"Yes, yes." Graen waved his arms in exasperated circles. "I prepared the horses when I saw the crowd forming, while you were selling cider to the air."

"I'm impressed." Actually, I was.

"An apple merchant started havoc in the marketplace when I—"

"Showed up and tried to impress. Tell me later." I magically reworked my robes to look Athenic. "Now you."

"What?"

"We're going disguised." I moved beside him so I wouldn't have to drop my shields for the working. He backed off, distrustful. "You take the clothes I give you or you take on the mob yourself. Milord."

Another rock came through the window. This one burned and exploded in the corner. Somebody inexperienced at drawing power had made a clumsy attempt at wizard fire.

While Graen's attention was distracted, I snatched a fistful of his cloak and made his clothes over into a monastic servant's. Then I threw a silencing spell on him. "That will take care of your southwestern accent." Graen clenched his fists, screwed his mouth around like he'd just swallowed poison, and jerked his body like clumsy acrobat drunk on anger. "You're my servant or the mob's. Choose wisely. I'm riding to Hala." I grabbed my wands.

Graen made the right choice. He took his weapons and followed, kicking the floor in anger.

Getting to the horses was easy, because Graen had the good sense to leave them in the walled yard behind our building. Feeling my wizard shield shudder as the building and part of the wall exploded in wizard fire moments after we mounted was less easy. I managed to ride through the darkness made darker by the dying flames and into the confusion of the now dispersing crowd. Even better, whether through fear or fury, Graen managed to stay close.

It appeared that some of the locals weren't happy with Graen, but that they also weren't happy with each other. So I got a quick lesson in current affairs from the voices of the Helan people that, moments ago, had inspired my trance.

"Kill the Furnie! Burn the god-be-damned overking's man!"

"Kill yourself, friend. All allegiance to King Furna." *So some Helans supported Furna?*

"Furna's a thief. Thieves die."

"So was Walworth. He stole the duchy." *No, Threle's previous king, Thoren, gave him the duchy when he learned at Walworth's treason trial that Walworth had worked in secret to defend it because the previous duke was a traitor. I thought everyone knew that!*

"Then Walworth should die, now that we've stolen it back." *This was either another Furna loyalist or somebody loyal to the previous duke.*

"King Furna stole it back."

"And sent his man to destroy an inn yard." *Didn't anybody recognize the inn got hit by wizard fire out of the crowd?*

"Or somebody as didn't like the Furnie played 'ruse the chicken' to start trouble."

"I'll ruse your chicken. And your hens and cows, sir." The speaker brandished a cudgel.

"The gods bless the Kingdom of Helas. *And* the overking, good Furna." Somebody kicked Master Cudgel in the back, causing him to drop his weapon.

"There is no Kingdom of Helas. There never was. Helas belongs to Threle."

"Helas doesn't exist."

"Threle shouldn't exist."

Scuffles scattered through clutches of crowds as they ran from another blast of wizard fire, bashing each other with words, sticks, empty buckets, torches, fists, and feet. It was extraordinarily helpful for getting out of town with the minimum of fuss, particularly since the disturbances were confined to a few streets near the inn.

Graen remained close, and sensible enough to ignore the chaos, even when a passerby, who'd clearly had too much ale, pushed another fellow almost under Graen's horse, promptly forgot he had just started a fight, and shouted, "Hey—hey, Brother—give us a bless— for our poor *nameless* trading town."

Graen glanced at the fellow he'd just missed trampling, who had tumbled himself off to the side of the street and was now sitting breathless and stunned. He then stopped his horse and gestured helplessly in my direction.

"Hey—a bless, a bless—for old Athena, is it? Pray for us. By your robes, Brother."

I made a meaningless gesture and kept riding. Graen took the hint and followed.

"Thank you. Thank you. Bless you too, Brother. May your goddess save Threle. Save Threle."

The words "save Threle" in a loud, Helan-accented drunken slur, repeating like a bad folk song, faded long before I stopped hearing them.

We were several miles on the trade road to Hala, in the relative comfort of moonlight and quiet, before I allowed Graen to speak again. My shields made it awkward to stop the spell, because I had forgotten in all the excitement to charge a word to kill the silence. So I told him to dismount, enclosed him in my shields, removed the silencing spell, but left him dressed in servant's clothes.

"Why don't you restore my proper attire?" Graen protested as we continued riding.

"Because your proper attire nearly got us killed. What happened in the marketplace?"

"I tried to buy apples."

"And?" I waited. Graen waited back. "What the hell did you do?"

"I didn't do anything."

"Then since you have nothing to say, maybe I should silence you again."

"The apples were multi-colored. Like flowers. Like the flowers Queen Aeren told me I understood in the same way the flowers themselves understand 'earth and water laughing through them.'" Graen choked a little but bravely continued speaking. "I went to the marketplace to find flowers to remember her by, and instead I found those apples. Clion apples, they were called. I tasted one—glorious, like tasting and knowing the essence of the color it wore. Green melted over my tongue."

"You started a riot over Clion apples?"

"I told the merchant, in a regrettable pass of enthusiasm, that I wanted a dozen apples to honor the dead. She was greatly offended. 'My apples are for the living, sir. Every one of them carries life from County Clio. Why would you offer them to the dead? Is that a southwestern practice?'"

Graen's voice strained as he mocked the merchant's indignation. It was an uncharacteristic display of genuine anger and regret on his part, and he had to catch himself before continuing. "No. It's mine. I wish to honor the former ruler of Gondal, who brought such joy before leaving the world, to whom I forever owe fealty in life and death."

I interrupted his telling. "You said *what?* You called Aeren a *former ruler* of Gondal? *Not queen?*"

"Out of respect. Milady is merely queen of my heart. But Gondal," he added pointedly, "was entirely hers to rule."

So much for his well-known discretion. "So when you stood in the marketplace dressed like a southwestern courtier, insulting imported goods from Clio, and declaring your loyalty to Gondal's former ruler, who also happens to be me—"

"Things quickly went to chaos. The locals don't like you, either. The apple merchant drew a sword."

"The apple merchant. From what you tell me it sounds like she was from County Clio."

"She had a slight accent. Possibly." Graen shifted. "So what does County Clio have against you?"

"Nothing it can justify." I remained silent for a long time, riding until the sky lightened and we could see Hala catching the dawn in its white towers. I renewed my shields. And then, exhausted and still wordless, I entered the city to see the king who would save the world by destroying Threle.

Eight

The city wore daylight like an ill-fitting disguise. Hala's roofs didn't reflect the sun so much as refuse it, shedding sunbeams in random corners like one sheds embarrassing clothes. Speckled sunshine made the red and orange roof tiles look like decaying gourds. Broken eaves threw hard-angled shadows that partially masked bolted doors and untended gardens.

I saw no street merchants. Of course, I was too tired after riding all night to see much that mattered. The few open shops offered candles or cloth or shoes, but their stock looked more like samples of desolation than honest goods. Shopkeepers peered through doorways and retreated, offering wariness where Helan merchants once offered welcome. The few locals we did encounter ignored us, looking away as we passed. Whether from shame, defensiveness, or both, I wasn't going to drop my shields to read.

Hala, the once-bright mercantile capital of Helas, still existed, but you had to work to recognize it. It was hard work and hard pay, because what you earned was a mere suggestion of what the city used to be. Gone was the vibrancy of trade and good fellowship. The city was now a huddle of unwashed trash-filled streets, shops gone dark or shabby, and a pervading sense of chaos, only without signs of actual chaos. Meaning Hala now appeared to be a pointless city with no real identity or purpose, but lacked the energy to disperse into complete disorder. What remained was something like a postscript to history.

When we reached the king's residence, a pair of servants hastily led our grateful horses to much needed rest and food while a pair of guards separated me from Graen. Graen, who was still wearing the fine servant garb I'd conjured for him, naturally assumed he was being taken for an inferior. He tilted his head and screwed his mouth into a grimace to get my attention, and, when that didn't work, he awkwardly beat the air with his arms. But as I wasn't eager to share quarters with him, I pretended not to notice.

"King's preference," my guard explained as we began to walk away. His ready friendliness was so characteristic of the Threle I once knew, that I fell into an equally amiable well-met lock-step with him before I noticed how easy that felt.

We stopped our stride when the other fellow loudly elaborated over Graen's tired protests. "King Hathe extends his high respect to his cousin the overking through the *hospitality* he offers to *all* who travel from Furnesse." He slightly emphasized the word "hospitality" as if he was merely humoring the king's conceit, and heavily emphasized the word "all" as if to finish with some opaquely egalitarian political statement. Knowing Helas, I understood this as a veiled criticism of both the king's motives in entertaining us and of his ties to Furnesse.

Graen, however, understood this as criticism of his attire. "I'm not *all*. I didn't blow in here on a southwest wind. Despite appearances" —he glared at me— "I'm here on the overking's business."

"You're here to get cleaned up first, sir. The overking's business can wait."

I didn't hear the rest of this diplomatic exchange because my fellow unceremoniously brought me to a room attached to the king's apartments and left. A waiting servant immediately fetched food, bathing water, and other necessaries, which she quickly placed around my room.

"The king will see you at your pleasure, sir." The servant spoke with the jaunty cheerfulness that once defined the Helan people, as if she had somehow survived the recent troubles with Threle and Furnesse with her heart intact. I gave her a gold piece, sent her away, and threw a wizard lock on the door. Then I renewed my shields and threw myself on the bed to sleep. The king could wait.

And then, at some point, the servant returned. A shade of power crept through my wizard lock and smiled through my shields. Then I slowly understood that the servant was Isulde, or rather, that Isulde had taken the Helan servant's form and dress to visit me in a dream.

"What to buy and sell, Athena?" Isulde laughed, played with my robe. "So now you wear the other side's colors to make your own colors invisible. But what colors do you hide in your heart?" She plunged her hand inside my robe and placed her palm against my chest, pressing the waning moon that Hecate had chained around my neck. "Your heart has no colors. Not even Hecate's. Does it hurt to be bound to your goddess without being able to truly honor Her?"

"You tell me. You're doing the reading."

"Don't you know?"

"I honor Hecate by keeping the poor tattered world in my heart, Isulde. That's enough."

She withdrew her hand, giggling. Still laughing, she offered me a battered bowl, like the one her foster father used in their North Country hovel. "A fairy gift. Drink." The bowl contained blood. But because the blood had a fairy origin, it did not sicken me, so I drank.

Then she placed her head against my chest and crossed her arms against my back, and as her fairy magic entered my body through the fairy blood, she cajoled me. "Come, then. Let's play. Let's know ourselves as we were before there were gods or a poor tattered world to contain us, when we only existed as pure energy, without form."

The spell began to work before she finished speaking. And so I learned that what we were, before we had material forms, before Hecate even came to be, was cold. Through Isulde's fairy magic, we knew ourselves as the motion that informs river eddies, and the wind that made us spin in the primeval water was our ancient mother. The wind was insensible, just a difference in potential, before it began to know itself as the two Habundias, the two primal goddesses from which all eternal oppositions spring. Then an agony of friction from opposing currents, the dance of the Habundias, chafed us into solid existence. Water, breath, blood, bones. And then we were here in the present again, laughing, in our dream, in our bodies, in Helas.

The battered bowl from which I drank was now a bird, preening itself in Isulde's hands. Owl or raven, Athena's bird or Hecate's, I couldn't tell. Probably a little of both. And then the bird was gone. "What did you see when we swirled in the river, Isulde?"

"Reality before it comes here to play. Before All That Is disguises itself as everything we see." She reached back inside my robe and gently withdrew my moon, balanced on her fist. She gazed at it for a long time, scrying its secrets. "But now I can see what Mother Hecate gave you. This charm that no one can remove." She dropped it against my chest and stepped back, giggling again. "Hecate didn't tell you as much as I know. She keeps Herself close."

"So do I, Isulde. What do you know that Hecate keeps secret?"

"You."

Didn't Aeren ask if I was Hecate's dirty secret? "What do you mean, fairy?" I knew it was futile to make sense out of fairy nonsense, but I had to ask.

"Hecate keeps you secret from yourself. She doesn't let you see your own heart. But now I can see it and see through it. Now I know you as the river eddy, as the first manifestation of the energy you came from." She clapped her hands and danced a little, her body imitating a swirling river. "Water fairies know water. I know you."

"Then tell me what Hecate keeps secret."

"Your moon, your mark. The secret is that it protects you from the world. Go unshielded, Beloved of Hecate. Not even a dragon can kill you. Nor any blast or weapon. So long as the world is dirty, this charm is your shield."

Roguehan also said the world was dirty. Just before I killed him. "How do you know this?"

"From your moon and our play, I see how things really are. I also see your torture. I see the toad Hecate made you experience. And I see that you clutched your moon after all your suffering, but that you never studied it as a priest-scholar should. You merely assumed it was to mark your mandate."

"What else would it be?"

"A physical manifestation of a poem—a poem written by the gods. The material form of the divine energy that made this poem. A poem you can't read, but fairies can."

"If what you say is true, fairy, why wouldn't I already know that?"

Isulde laughed. "Silly priest. You can't know a poem you can't read."

"Then you read it."

"To read it is to perform it." The strange bird, that was neither owl nor raven, reappeared in her hands. And then the bird was a dagger. "Cut yourself." I sensed no magic in the weapon, but like the odd hybrid bird Isulde wove it from, it fused the symbols of Hecate and Athena. Images of waning and waxing moons glinted along the blade, and on the handle was an image of an owl and a raven tearing at each other's heart. "I made this from universal oppositions. I sang divine energies into physical form." I thought of the elvish art in Arula and briefly wondered if Isulde had copied an elvish design. Then I took the dagger, lightly cut the waning moon scar on my palm, and offered my blood to Hecate.

Isulde held my bleeding hand.

"Poem. That physical line you cut was, on a deeper level, the first line of the poem. In the poem it's a line about Threle killing your spirit in Kursen and how I came in dreams to remind you of who you should have been. The line you cut bleeds on your scar, your mark of evil, just as my visits made your years in Kursen bearable."

I made another cut. "And this physical line? Does this fresh cut stand in for another line of divine poetry that I can't read and you can?"

"Yes. The line that describes your other death. When Threle, that is, Walworth, let you die in the North Country and I brought you back."

Isulde took the dagger from me and charged it with a song, invoking power into it as my blood pooled into a sticky mess in my palm. Then, before I could stop her, she "performed the poem" by trying to kill me. There was a jerky tension in my chest where the now magical weapon went in, painless as an aging shadow and fading so quickly it felt ancient before it was gone. Traces of fairy magic inside my shields rained poison before turning to remnants of river rain. My moon felt warm. And at my feet was the dagger, blade bent harmlessly away like a watery reflection of itself before it disappeared. "See? You can only hurt yourself. Until you make the world go right, nothing else can hurt you."

I mourned the fairy magic dying out of the weapon. I did not understand why.

"Why couldn't I know this before? Why didn't Hecate reveal this to me?"

"Because now you are in Helas."

"So?"

"Helas is another unreadable poem. It isn't itself anymore, but it tries to be all things—former Threlan duchy, southwest acquisition, independent kingdom, loose association of trading towns. Here, you, who have no colors and all colors, no loyalty to Hecate and complete enforced loyalty to Hecate, are a mirror of Helas. You're both borderless; neither of you know yourselves. That is why only in Helas can you know that Threle can no longer kill you, that almost nothing can, whether through mundane or magical means." She smiled like we were co-conspirators. "You see? Coming home to Helas is on one level like coming home to yourself." If Isulde knew that in Helas, to "come home" was to arrive at a mutually satisfactory bargain, it wasn't clear. "But that's all poem again. Another line. Anyway, I came here in play, in dream, to tell you."

I gratefully released my shields. And as I did so, I suddenly emerged from the dream.

I was alone in my room with the necessaries the servant left me. I heard nothing but a distant footstep. A Helan voice that swelled and faded. There was still blood in my mouth and stomach from the fairy bowl. It sickened now upon waking, because the dream had fled and so had the fairy magic. I prayed until the nausea stopped, willing the blood into water. Then I cleansed myself. *Why do you write me poems I can't read, Mother? What else can't I read?*

So I could only hurt myself. A metaphor for Kursen, for my path to Hecate. I couldn't be killed by magical or mundane weapons. A metaphor for my execution, which was death by exposure to the North Country when Walworth withdrew the protection of his sword, which was both a magical and mundane weapon, and let things take their course. Only Hecate can kill me. Only Hecate can take me back.

And I could only know this when I came to be both in Threle and not in Threle, that is, in Helas. Hecate's protection was a riddle written between worlds, an unknown poem that Her priest couldn't read and only a fairy could discern.

Divinity is unreadable. But so is the world and its disguises.

I then remembered what Stormr said after we survived that first blast. "Your shields are useless against that kind of blast. The gods know why you bother with them." And this coming from a high priest so skilled with shield work that he fooled me as to his alignment. How did he, a votary of Habundia Ceres, know how to read Hecate's moon, know that it would protect him if he lurched upon my body as if we were one? He also said that "you can't respect what you don't understand." Sure, and you can't know a poem you can't read.

I ate some hard bread that turned soft and sweet on the tongue. And then I drank a confusion of spices disguised as a dull beet broth. Nothing in Helas was as it seemed. Nor was anything in me.

"Servant!" I called into the silence, hoping the woman who had fetched me food and water when I arrived, whose voice and demeanor was so characteristic of the Helas I remembered, would return.

But a different servant came this time, an older man, world-weary and illegible. "Yes, Brother. What is your will?"

I had no answer.

W hen I entered the king's apartments, I found the end of the poem. Or least an unexpected stopping point, like a turnaround that sheds and changes meaning with each repetition. Like an eternal, divine snake. I went breathless trying to read what was in front of me, my mind went useless trying to understand.

"Sweet coz! And so we meet again!" The King of Helas embraced my shoulders and lightly stepped back. His smile froze when he saw my moon, but only for a heartbeat. "Happier than a plague it is to see you, blowing as I am like a blasted weed filling its shriveled maw with filth. And *you*, Beloved of Hecate, to come so late on the overking's business. Come, coz, let us know each other again."

This time I stepped back, my mind too disordered by reality in its latest disguise to let me say anything except, "Aren't you supposed to be dead, Cathe?"

"Aren't you? The world is deliciously dizzy with cracks and surprises, courtesy of Threle's poorly-won victory. But you're here to set it straight, praise Hecate and" —he glanced up and down at my Athenic robe— "Everybody else. Welcome to Helas."

I kept staring. Kept trying to understand. Kept considering how to begin to understand how the man I had killed, and was sentenced to death for killing, was now Helas's king. Gave up.

"Charmed. Sit, sit." Cathe dropped to the floor and sat with his left foot wedged against his right knee, balancing his upper body on his spidery hands, which he held flat against the floor. It was a show of informality, and I sensed he was making himself as comfortable as he was capable of being. I sat warily across from him, aware that we were now positioned to raise a cone of prayer together and undecided as to whether I would cooperate. Two dead and resurrected priest-kings of uncertain countries calling on the gods for blessing felt vaguely embarrassing. But that was another poem.

I spoke. "No prayers, Brother."

"No prayers, no poems," Cathe answered agreeably. "So what *do* you want now, I wonder?"

"Plain history." It was the only thing I could think to ask for.

"Ah. I suppose you *would* want my story. Well, you see it's like this." Cathe sniffed noisily and stared dramatically at a blank wall that glistened with emptiness. Then he focused his attention back on me. "We're both victims of Threle."

"We're not both anything."

"I speak truth, coz. The plainest history. Threle avenged me by killing you—or should I say, fulfilled its law by playing justice like a bad theater piece—but you performed a service to Threle by killing me. We're even as goats now and just as sacrificial. Really, we should have just openly supported Roguehan and taken the crown from him."

"At one time that was the plan."

"Yes, well." Cathe grasped my hands, puffed his cheeks like an old fish, and immediately dropped them. "The world changes. But here's where we are. Besides this halfway version of Helas, I mean." His voice suddenly colored itself in thick shades of calculated misery. "When you and my lady Caethne murdered me, Caethne had just taken on Walworth's power as lord of the land. Well, of the duchy anyway." He contemptuously flipped his hand.

"And?"

"And nothing, except that means that I really was betrayed by the Duchy of Walworth, the last remnant of Threle at that sad time. *That* makes us a 'both.'" Cathe studied me and quickly looked away when he saw I wasn't convinced. "So here's the spiny point of it. Caethne, poor lady, who was once my wife, and once my crone leading me to death, is now my mother. Just like a triple manifestation of either Habundia."

"*What?*"

"Well, what else was for it? When you destroyed my body instead of conveying the immortality that was promised, I begged Habundia-Christus for divine justice, howled to Her to let me live again. And so She did, as Caethne's son. Mirand's, too, if you want my full credentials. So you see we *are* brothers. You draw some magical lineage from Mirand, and I come by way of flesh."

"And Mirand . . . Caethne—"

"Oh, no, I'm sure they don't speak of me at all. They certainly don't speak to me. I aged so quickly in the womb that Caethne barely had time to know about it before I ripped my way out. And I've continued to age more quickly this time, too—much more quickly than when dear Grana birthed me. Although Habundia Herself has now paused the inevitable."

"And suffered you to become Helas's king?"

Cathe sighed. "You see, it's like this. Furna helped me to the throne, much to Mirand's chagrin, as he was pretending to the same from his perch in Loudes. Habundia will suffer me to become a god. But I must make the world right, which of course means destroying Threle. I can't fail there, or I'll age and die into a rainbow, or a perfect rose, or something else flawlessly loathsome. I'm sure you understand."

The heat in my thoughts seared my words into silence. I needed distance, possibly more distance than the entire world afforded. I stood up and started to leave.

Cathe spoke to my back. "We *are* honored. We are chosen for sacred work. And really, we do work well together when there's need."

I kept walking.

"There's much I could tell you. Would you like to know why the elves destroyed Arula? How you came to Furnesse from Gondal?"

I stopped and turned. "*If* you know, tell me now. If you're pretending, I walk alone with Hecate."

"Me, pretend? My dear coz, I'm a materialist! Besides, I would open my mind to you to verify anything you wish." He spread his arms in what was supposed to be a gesture of openness.

"I wouldn't read your mind through twelve levels of divinity, let alone two."

"Then I'll give it to you. Come."

He watched me eagerly as I sat down again across from him. "No poems."

"Of course there's poems, Brother. But here's plain speaking. Days after Threle destroyed the world, my dear mother Caethne awoke from a punch of sunshine to her face, blood between her legs, and me yowling like the twice-born puddle of flesh I now was. She knew me before I remembered myself. She named me Hathe, so to mingle my previous name with Habundia's, and wove me clothes of ashes and weeds. Then she brought me to Furnesse, to the world's end, as far from Threle as possible, where Furna's clerics oversaw my divinely rapid growth and education and Furna himself gave me Helas to run."

"Did those clerics include Stormr?"

Cathe . . . or Hathe . . . looked confused. "Well, his evil clerics, of course."

"So what happened to Arula?"

"The elves destroyed it after your stand-in had been pulled from the throne. But that's entirely on Walworth."

"Aeren losing the throne?"

"No, your losing Arula." Cathe looked mildly annoyed by my incomprehension. "Well, the short of it, Brother, is that's the sort of thing that happens when one abdicates." Cathe's annoyance at my silence turned to impatience. "I mean your responsibility to Hecate, not the Gondish throne. No priest of Hecate, let alone yourself, has any business ruling Gondal, save to blight the land in Her honor. Which you . . . regrettably . . . sought to avoid through some misplaced affection for elvish trinkets. Unless I misread the record."

"Hecate gave me that choice. What does Walworth have to do with it?"

"Walworth? Everything. You chose to die damned to Hecate in the North Country, to accept an eternity of torture to save elvish Beauty rather than destroy Arula yourself" —he waved his hand dismissively— "but Walworth passively executed you in a fairy hovel he claimed for Threle. Condolences, Brother, you failed through no fault of your own. Just as I died through no fault of my own. Now we exist in a state of grace, where we may yet avoid divine torture by saving the world from its own mistakes."

"And again, what does Walworth have to do with Arula's fall?"

"By interfering in matters he knew nothing about, everything. By letting you die, he unwittingly prevented you from saving elvish Beauty from Hecate's destruction. But seeing as your motives were pure—so to speak—I have it on divine authority from Habundia-Christus Herself that the gods unleashed a half-destruction, opening the door for the bless-be-damned elves to take back their works and destroy your city. But really that's the least part of the fun."

"I'd like to know the elves' version."

"They aren't likely to bother themselves with telling you. They kicked you into Furnesse when you and Aeren went in search of them."

"How do you know this?"

"I don't actually. But I do know from King Furna, who styles himself a 'friend of the elves' and everything else, that something like that happened. Does it matter? You're here now. And we need each other."

"No, we don't." I stood and turned to leave again. Made it almost to the doorway before reality bent and broke once more. Stormr, in the plain spun clothes of a simple Helan farmer, slid lightly into the room, leaned against a graceful pillar, and stared at me with more than his usual haughtiness. Which I supposed was a backhanded compliment, given that he utterly ignored Cathe. Most likely because Cathe was a high priest of opposing alignment, and a king.

"Ah." Cathe gamely bounced to his feet and clapped his hands. "And here's our good Brother Stormr also taking a second suck at the worm-ridden apple of life, praise All."

Stormr continued ignoring Cathe. But he couldn't resist needling him and me by intoning, "Hail Habundia-Ceres."

"Hail." I spoke with a hint of sarcasm and a dollop of confusion. "I see you're back, too."

"I never left." Stormr didn't care to explain himself.

"Last I heard you got kissed by a dragon."

"Why don't you tell Llewelyn what happened?" Cathe was suddenly the genial host asking for an amusing anecdote. I seriously thought he was going to offer tea.

"Yes—I mean—I'd like to know why you're not dead." Somehow I made this request sound light and jovial, too.

Stormr restored the mood with his usual efficiency. "Because I understand shield work." He still managed to ignore Cathe, who was looking so self-consciously politesse that I had to ignore him, too, so I wouldn't laugh. "Having been inside your shield once, I was able to mimic it to protect myself against the dragon. Had you traveled nearer the point where her blast 'kissed' ground, you would have observed that only Zyren took the hit. I hid under tree cover while you were still stunned, holding out the shield until I sickened of the reverse energy. Then I caused the horse carrying the dragon's supplies to slip its tether and come to me, and so I followed the king's orders by following you."

"Why didn't you join the party?

"I prefer to work alone."

"That makes three of us. If you count Aeren."

"The gods have a wonderful sense of humor," remarked Cathe, playfully clapping his hands and desperately trying to pretend we weren't excluding him.

"You said that it wasn't my shield you needed for that first blast." It was worth knowing where Stormr thought that blast came from, as he had clearly accepted Zyren's account of Aeren wandering into that blast. "You stole protection from my charm."

"At least one of us understood what it's for."

I don't know what annoyed me more, the belittling blandness of his tone or just him in general. "So why doesn't your understanding put you out of a job? I mean, if you know my charm protects me, why did Furna hire you to do the same?"

"Because the king trusts me. He merely *has* to work with you."

And so. But whatever his attitude, I still needed to settle my curiosity concerning his thoughts on the first blast. Unfortunately, attempting to read a cleric of good alignment through his shield was useless, particularly with a cleric as skilled in shield work as Stormr. So I asked. "Where did that first blast come from?"

Stormr widened his eyes and smiled as if he meant to mock innocence from winter's dew. "Damned if I know. Maybe you've got enemies?"

Cathe couldn't take being the unwanted shadow in his own kingdom anymore. "Brothers. Brothers." He caught himself, glanced at Stormr, and corrected himself. "Or . . . perhaps I should say 'distant cousin' as we're *all* children of the Habundias. Come now. And ah yes, here is my lord Graen."

Graen hesitantly stepped through the doorway trailing two Helan servants and showing fine in new courtly attire. As the servants retired, closing the door behind them, Graen slowly bowed to Cathe with more unremitting formality than an apprentice wizard's first mathematical proof. Then he noticed Stormr in his peasant garb, looked questioningly at me, and gathered enough composure to recite, "The great Overking Furna sends his glorious greetings to his dear friend and cousin King Hathe, with whom—"

"And of course the same." Cathe stopped Graen's coming speech with a raised hand. "The King of Helas welcomes the esteemed emissary of the King of Furnesse. Now it's time to discuss your mission." Cathe saw that Graen was focused on pretending he wasn't completely disquieted by Stormr's presence, and therefore a bit too distracted for a strategy discussion. "And of course we are *all* delighted that Brother Stormr survived the dangers of your journey through his impressive use of clerisy. Something he must tell you all about later."

Stormr glowered. He didn't take to Cathe volunteering him to tell tales to Graen, for whom he never had any use.

"But now to our work. My most highly honored Lord Graen, because you have also survived the journey due to *your* considerable skill" —Graen looked briefly confused, but recovered brilliantly— "I am authorized to tell you why you are here. You have been chosen to help these fine clerics, and my humble self, restore the world . . . ." As Cathe relayed the gist of our quest, Graen went so blank with honest self-regard that he forgot to breathe. "King Furna regards you as the greatest swordsman in his kingdom."

"Nice job on starting that riot," said Stormr.

Graen didn't exactly ignore Stormr's mockery, but he managed to pretend that he did by making another showy bow to Cathe and using the opportunity to mask himself with a ridiculous expression of extreme humility.

"And so, my friend, the overking has authorized me to give you this." Cathe pulled a faded cloth that was covering a small chest in the corner, eagerly threw the chest open, and produced a large sword. Cathe staggered a bit and quickly pressed the sword in Graen's hands to relieve himself of the weight. "I hear you've some experience with magical weapons."

"Yes, King, some." Graen spoke with self-conscious diffidence, but there was an unexpected strain of natural confidence in his bearing that he failed to suppress. It slightly increased my opinion of him. He cut a flourish in the air, making the heavy sword look like more air. "I feel its pull." He spoke directly to Cathe, smiling as if he expected they both understood something about the sword that the rest of us didn't. "May I?" He glanced at the cloth that Cathe had tossed on the floor.

"Yes, of course." Cathe playfully gave the cloth to Graen, who set the sword on the chest and deftly tied the cloth to the pillar next to Stormr, who stepped back to watch with some interest.

"And those nearly dead blooms on that table? May I?"

"Yes, yes, of course, my lord," said Cathe affably, while Graen tied some dead roses and once-green flora in the cloth. The decaying flowers hung like an executed criminal that no one cared enough about to bury.

Graen studied his strange makeshift target as if it were a rival for royal favor. "I need something with more life in it." He glanced around, his excitement obliterating his southwestern sense of status. "Do you see that log of living oak on the hearth that still has a spot of green growing from the end?"

"Of course, my lord." Cathe gestured toward the hearth. "Take it."

Graen was so entangled in his enthusiasm that he was at the hearth before Cathe granted permission. This fascinated me enough to attempt to help him tie the log in the cloth, but Graen waved me away. This was his show.

Graen tied the log a little lower than the death bouquet, with the living green protruding into space around the pillar. Then he took up the sword again, and stared hard at Stormr. "Stand back, Brother."

Stormr did so, but slowly and reluctantly, like an unhappy cat. He didn't like taking orders from Graen, but he understood the value of keeping clear of this enigmatic new weapon that twisted an unremarkable courtier into a potentially valuable warrior, or rather, allowed the warrior to show himself.

Graen held the hilt with both hands, keeping the point toward the ceiling. He closed his eyes, felt for the pulse of energy the way a wizard might sense current running through a new wand, listened for the sword to speak its secret martial language. I watched him become one with the sword the way a skilled rider becomes one with a difficult horse, not so much controlling the power but translating it into use. The only other person I'd ever known with comparable skill was Walworth. I now understood the real reason Furna had placed Graen in our party.

And then . . . Graen slashed the sword point like a dragon's tongue through the hapless cloth in a rapidly figured performance that dizzied everyone in the room and left the dead and living targets scattered on the floor. Sort of. The cloth went bright, as if it were new again, and formed itself into an elaborate dress. The log split open and spilled something like dark blood at the pillar's foot before going soft and melting into the mush of slow rot. The flowers were now exploding with light and crawling and leaping along the cold marble floor, blooming and singing and green. Cathe watched them with horror, Stormr and I with curiosity. Then Stormr noticed our similar reaction and pretended he wasn't impressed.

Graen grinned at all of us. "It's a truthfinder." He looked admiringly at the blade, and then proudly at us, clearly enjoying the attention. "I practiced with one once. It kills to bring forth what should exist. That old cloth was torn from a discarded dress. That log should have been dead in the earth to spurt new growth. And those flowers" —sadness sparked through his voice and breath, but he caught himself— "were meant to live and dance. Something killed them too soon."

Cathe coughed. "Yes. Brilliantly done. King Furna considers you the only swordfighter in the kingdom, save himself of course, who can wield this kind of weapon, which has obvious advantages for your world-saving mission."

Graen spoke carefully. His voice was weighted with an odd mix of uncharacteristic humility and southwestern self-regard. "My most esteemed overking does me great honor. This sword requires intense focus. There can be no duplicity in the one who wields it, lest he destroy himself."

"Then you need to keep your heart pure." I was half-teasing and half-respectful. Graen laughed at my sally. He wasn't used to honest camaraderie, but he appeared to appreciate it.

Stormr glanced dourly at my Athenic robes. "What's *your* weapon of choice?"

I glanced dourly back. "Myself."

Graen laughed like he thought I was joking.

Nine

I don't remember how long we stayed in Hala. Long enough for me to practice destroying whatever I liked with the wands I had carried on Zyren's horse. Long enough to learn to modify their particular forms of death into whatever results might be strategically useful. Strategically useful for what wasn't obvious. Each choice, each foray into creative destruction, was pain-ridden and pointless.

Pain-ridden because I now knew that the wands were intended as teaching devices for Aeren, which is why we never practiced with them on our journey. Once we got to Hala, I was supposed to have taught her wand work through our wizard bond. This would be a foundation for learning to use the Wand of Surprises together, to focus all the verve and thrust of the Gondish wasteland that one or both of us embodied. It wasn't clear when Aeren was to learn that the reason for her training was to execute the King of Threle, to please gods she didn't believe in. It also wasn't clear what stories I was supposed to tell her while teaching her how to kill my former friend. Or tell myself.

Pointless because keeping a cache of small, defensive wands in my cloak and under my shirt was a magical nuisance at best and an unnecessary liability at worse due to the constant energy drag. It was quite enough to keep the Wand of Surprises close and shielded. But as Cathe didn't have a suitable wizard to provide us with, he insisted that I carry Zyren's wands in case I somehow found myself in a spiritual place where I couldn't draw on Hecate's force, or blast through another wizard's shield with wizard fire. "Skilled as you are, Hecate's force will weaken should you find yourself having to . . . ." His voice trailed into a hand wave.

"Having to what? Pretend to measured cheer among Athena's favorites?"

"Well, pretend to anything, which I assume you'll be doing a lot of if all goes well."

What I did a lot of was destruction. Mostly to the local landscape outside the city, where my blasts would not attract notice, or if they did, could be explained as the "king's private pleasure, his solitary games to relieve the burdens of state." Cathe would sometimes accompany me, as if to make good the tale.

"You *might* practice destroying living creatures instead of rocks and ridges. I will provide you with servants and animals. A condemned prisoner or two."

"I'll be all right."

"Keep your distance and keep shielded and you won't sicken," he helpfully advised. Cathe couldn't read me through my moon, so he compensated by making bad guesses about my motives. I *had* to kill Walworth. I didn't have to kill random Helans, his former people.

"I'll be all right," I repeated, trying to end our discussion.

Graen was to kill Mirand. My wands and blasts would get through Mirand's defenses, and Graen's new sword would find its home. Truthfinder would destroy Mirand by returning my old master into what "should exist" —that is, death and defeat. This meant that if I was going to fulfill Hecate's mandate by changing Mirand's alignment to evil, I needed to destroy Truthfinder. Preferably without anybody noticing. Which meant waiting until we got to Loudes. Because even though Furna hadn't opposed the idea of effecting an alignment change, it was sure as sunlight and sickness that Stormr wasn't going to risk his status with his deity by supporting that. Death for the greater good of making the world right, sure, just as Mirand once agreed to kill a fellow wizard to protect Threle. Risking Habundia-Ceres's displeasure by wrenching a high-powered wizard from Athena to Hecate? I was on my own there.

Graen would vie with me in what we called our "death games." I would destroy small objects or deconstruct rock piles with the Wand. I learned to melt hardness into gray slop, which I came to think of as a running metaphor for my general state of mind. Graen would restore the rocks to their previous glory, or rather, their true versions of themselves. One time he confused himself by slamming Truthfinder on a stone wall and producing a pile of salt. He looked to me for an explanation.

"You found their tears." I don't know why I said that. "Even dull rocks weep for the stars they used to be if you know how to listen."

"Is that the essence of magic, to listen for what's really there?"

"No. I mean it can be for some. For others it's a sad result."

Graen managed to look vaguely sympathetic without having any idea of what he was supposed to be sympathizing with. "Lew." Now that he understood himself as valuable to our party, the world, the gods, and King Furna, he had taken to using the familiar form of my name. "What would I find if I struck you with Truthfinder?" His voice was a tease and a friendly challenge. It was also a kind of affirmation of our newly-equivalent status. Graen was not the sort to waste banter; in his world of backstabbing decorum, studied familiarity was another weapon for advancement at court, one to be used sparingly. So I was mildly bemused and somewhat intrigued by the simple sincerity under his words. So much so that I responded in the same tone.

"Nothing. You'd destroy it." I explained my moon charm without explaining my mandate. "And Furna would be angry. That's an expensive weapon." I smiled and nodded to show appreciation of his skill.

"I suppose so." Graen sighed, sat on the ground, and leaned against a stump. He tossed a few rough stones at the salt pile he'd created. The stones formed random patterns as they skidded and fell across the salt, like empty rivulets. "I like this. I like being here."

"Better than guarding yourself against court intrigue?"

"Yes." Graen looked pleasantly surprised that I understood him, that I understood his attraction to this new life that he had no name for. "Actually, it's cleaner."

This time, I didn't respond. I sat on the ground, leaned on my arms, and studied the silent sky.

"Don't you think so?"

"I think you're becoming one with your weapon, my lord. I think you're becoming who you're meant to be." I spoke with friendly nonchalance, as if I had known his truth all along and approved.

Graen smiled with a sincerity he was powerless to restrain. He considered us friends. Although, given his political background, friendship was probably a new experience he wasn't sure he should be having. He glanced at the sky, then at me. "See any dragons?"

"No."

He tossed another stone and watched the salt swallow it. "King Hathe said that he's heard from sources close to King Furna that, should we be successful, I am to get a small kingdom. That Furna will carve a place for me to rule absolutely, save, of course, keeping loyalty to his royal self." Graen's tone was now self-consciously uncertain. He wanted to know what I thought, wanted me to say something confirming Cathe's words. "We should both be kings then."

I shrugged and smiled. "It appears that Furna likes you."

Graen weighed my cheerful equivocation with his finely honed courtier's sensitivity and refused to press further. "Well, perhaps."

He changed the subject by rummaging through his purse, which he kept tied to his belt, opposite his sword. Out came bread and cheese wrapped in old green cloth, a few gold coins, some gems that Cathe had given him as a "gift from King Furna" that he intended to sew on his cap when he returned to Furnesse, some papers, and a ring. He put the ring on the papers and stared solemnly at the pile as if it were an altar before which he didn't know how to pray.

It was the Ring of Beauty that I'd given Aeren before I abdicated and went to the North Country. The ring that my sister Trenna showed me years ago in Sunnashiven and for which she was later executed when she used it to force Walworth to love her. The same ring that Isulde gave me after I escaped from Threle when Mirand changed history with the Wand of Surprises. Isulde said it was to replace my illusion ring, as if beauty replaces illusions. Wash it in rose water for three days and you can make anybody love you, but whether that love was magical illusion or real I never had cause to learn.

"Stormr gave me these." He placed his hand on the papers, his fingers not quite touching the ring. He looked hard at me. "I can't read them. They're in Sarana. They belonged to Queen Aeren." Then his face rested into open sadness, like an old actor going pale and solemn for sympathy, only the sadness was real. "After the dragon blast, you might remember that my servant removed the queen's belongings from her horse and placed them on mine. He then placed my weapons on the queen's horse, which I rode." His voice went dry. "Almost like pledging a troth."

"I didn't know." I wasn't aware of the custom. "My lord Graen. With all respect, you are grieving for somebody you hardly knew and with whom you didn't even share a language." I tried not to sound as annoyed as I felt.

"We shared a heart. She made me see myself as I truly am. No one else ever did that."

"I'm sorry." Actually, I was, and not entirely because of his history. I was also sorry that Aeren had created this mess, and that Graen was heartbroken over a fictional persona that she adopted in response to my fiction. I briefly considered telling him the truth. I knew that he would eventually read the trial records and piece together the truth for himself, because he would learn about Aeren's dragon form and guess that she was the dragon he saw in the sky after the blast. Then he would hate me for letting him mourn. But I considered how it might jeopardize our quest, affect our swordsman's new sense of himself, if he were to learn that Aeren had been as willing to blast him as anybody else in the party. I decided that was why nobody else cared to enlighten him. While I was considering what to say, Graen spoke again.

"You know Stormr helped himself to my horse after it wandered loose. So I asked him for her things." Graen hesitated, as if he didn't wish to offend. "He was gracious."

"So?"

"So I understand you are both aligned to evil gods and that you would both prefer to disguise your allegiance for the sake of the quest. Of course that doesn't concern me—I have great trust in King Furna's judgment. But it's obvious you don't like each other." He fidgeted slightly, unsure of my reaction. "Nevertheless there's something truly kind in Stormr's nature, a kind of deep virtue that is so extreme it almost terrifies."

I laughed.

"Yes, I know I'm not speaking sense. But when I spoke with him, it was easy to forget he's evil."

"So forget he's evil. I'd like to."

Graen laughed at my humor. "Sometimes it's easy to forget you're evil, too."

"I've heard that before."

"Master Zyren said the queen was upset enough to run away because of something you said. Stormr told me that Master Zyren lied."

"Master Zyren lied."

"Did he also lie when he translated that she said she would be performing in Threle to honor King Furna?"

"Aeren might have said that. King Furna didn't want any of us to know more about our quest than necessary and that would have been a logical cover story. *You* weren't told everything until we reached Hala."

Graen considered this. He appeared to accept it.

"Lew . . . you knew Aeren so well. What can you tell me about these papers, this ring? It feels like a magical weapon when I hold it."

"I gave her that ring when she became queen. It is magical. Under the right conditions it enhances one's beauty. I don't believe she ever wore it."

"Why didn't she wear it?"

"I don't know. She probably considered it cheating. Or something." Graen looked like he wanted to say more, but couldn't bring himself to speak. "As to the papers. Aeren *was* a storyteller. They might be tales she was writing. If you lend them to me, I will translate them for you." Of course I wanted to know what she was writing, particularly if Stormr had read them. But I also intended my offer as a kindness to Graen. I couldn't tell him the truth, but I could give him whatever I found in her words that might bring comfort.

He gratefully gave me the papers, but not before he kissed the foreign language like it was holy writ. I managed to look sympathetic as I stuffed them in my cloak.

"Why don't we send on a request to King Furna for another wizard?" We—meaning Cathe, Stormr, and myself—were standing impatiently in Cathe's apartments, where he had arranged a strategy meeting, and then, inexplicably, arranged for Graen to miss it. I knew I was asking for the obvious, but "obvious" was a fairly hypothetical concept lately.

It was an odd day—riddled with sourceless shadows like clouds crawling over the earth. Nature was burnt and bent, and this day appeared more warped than most. It was also the day after Graen gave me Aeren's papers to translate. They appeared to be tales, but I hadn't had an opportunity to do more than glance at a few of them the previous night. So I was annoyed by this unexpected meeting preventing me from satisfying my curiosity.

Cathe ignored my question by waving his hand at plates of stale fruit and pale cheese. I ignored his attempt to distract by ostentatiously taking out my battery of wands, except for the Wand of Surprises, to emphasize the excessive amount of power I was hauling about. "Why should I compromise my effectiveness by carrying an unnecessary energy drag into Loudes, when another wizard can better focus on wand work?" I slowly laid the wands side by side, deliberately arranging them to occupy as much space as possible on the small window shelf. They glowed in the strange passing shadows and went dull in the sun.

"Because another wizard . . . which *would* have been Zyren . . . was to have assisted and defended the queen, under the assumption that should it come to a magical battle, your attention would have been gloriously preoccupied." Cathe sounded like an officious steward brightly reassuring his master's guests of the great feast he had just contrived for them, while desperately pretending that the chaos they saw waving through the curtained corners was actually a flag for exquisite preparation. He then did his best to spin another distraction. "Of course, we hoped Aeren would take to training—Furna had great confidence in her—but she had limited magical experience."

"That depends on how you define magical experience."

Cathe passed breezily over my response. "Well, as it turns out, you *are* clearly the gods' choice. *King.*" His chirpy tone had an edge of impatience that told me he was afraid of something.

Stormr blanched. "It isn't clear what the Brother is, except maybe the gods' cursed. Aeren *was* Furna's first choice for killing the king."

"You don't appear to be Furna's first choice for anything."

Stormr also ignored me, but with less effort. He coolly glanced at the teaching wands, which were now mottled in the hour's strange light. "And yet for all anyone knows, the lady is Gondal's true ruler." He sounded bored, cutting, and quietly insistent. It was quite a trick.

Cathe smoothly bent his head in rapid agreement, an agreement he underscored by waving his arm in the general direction of the wands. "But had Aeren been necessary to the cause, she'd still be here." He leaned forward on his staff with both hands and briefly closed his eyes as if he cared, letting us savor his impeccable illogic. "And so would Zyren. That is my prayerful belief." Then he gazed seriously at both of us. "Unfortunately, she's now more of a liability than a few extra wands. Even if she were to return, we can't risk more chaos."

"Only if she isn't the true queen. If she is, then we need her. Whatever the risk." Stormr had a wonderful way of obliterating Cathe's aimless theatrics.

"Or we just . . . you know, remove all doubt." Cathe backed off a little, but only a little, from our disapproving stares.

"Or we just . . . you know, remove you." Stormr sounded utterly casual, which sharpened his mockery. He waited. So did I.

Cathe staved off our discomfiting silence by assuming an awful veneer of smiling confidence. "So." He nervously laid his staff against a pillar. Then he turned toward us and clapped his hands as if he were describing a fun new dance step. "Here's the short of it. If Aeren *was* to die, Brother Llewelyn here would be king without question."

"We don't know that," Stormr corrected. "And neither does anybody else."

"And we wouldn't have to concern ourselves with the nuisance of random dragon turnings, should she return." Cathe sounded somewhat desperate and somewhat sanguine. It was almost amusing.

"We don't have to concern ourselves with that particular nuisance now. There's a never-ending supply closer to hand." I spoke with less coolness than Stormr, mostly because I had no idea where Aeren was or whether she would return.

"So where is she?" asked Stormr sensibly.

"Damned if I know." Stormr didn't like me repeating his words. "Maybe she's researching the source of that first blast."

We waited for Cathe to speak. Not because we cared for him to continue, but because it was awkward and strange for Stormr and I to be on the same side of an argument. Cathe earnestly glanced at each of us in turn but got no response. "Simplicity is the better part of strategy, don't you think?"

Stormr casually took a soft pear from a plate, studied its speckled colors in the passing sun, and slowly ate a mouthful of its mush, just to make Cathe wait for his response. I did the same. The pear went tasteless and vague in my mouth. Stormr continued making a show of eating the squelchy fruit like he was silently critiquing Cathe's food preferences. He also made a deal out of staring into the air, as if he needed to think long and hard about choosing his words because Cathe hadn't understood him the first time. "If Aeren is the true queen, we're useless in Loudes without her and there's no point in proceeding. And even if anybody, including the Brother, could determine whether he embodies the Gondish wasteland as opposed to his wasteland of a heart, we still don't know if Aeren also embodies that wasteland—"

"My 'wasteland of a heart' says you're a bad poet."

"I speak truth, not poetry. We need both of you. Alive. If one of you dies, for all we know Gondal passes back to the elves and the world passes into something . . . else."

"That's your fault. The 'for all we know' part. We traveled together for weeks and nobody bothered to find out."

"Zyren bothered. He failed. Apparently Aeren's thoughts and feelings on the matter were too complicated to navigate into anything resembling truth—"

"You mean Aeren is complicated? And Zyren managed to figure that out? Without my blessed assistance?"

Stormr fumed. It was beautiful to crack his cool. "We don't know if she ever accepted your 'gift.' We don't know anything except that she couldn't keep the throne!"

"Well, I do know some things. I know how to call to her through our wizard bond. I also know how to talk to her, and possibly persuade her of her importance to . . . you know . . . everything. I mean, one 'wasteland heart' to another."

"Yes, and you spoke so well to her before that she killed Zyren and tried to kill us."

"That's Zyren's fault."

"It's also yours."

"Brothers." Cathe had nothing useful to say, so he raised his hand and spread his fingers as if to ask for silence. "This is why my original suggestion—"

Stormr ignored him. "We can't risk you angering her again by embarking on some new ill-conceived adventure in 'diplomacy.' And if she is the queen of Gondal, the world can't risk you angering her again."

"Then let's proceed to Loudes on our best guess, Brother. Or send somebody with no protection against her dragon form to look for her in the hope that no protection will be needed, preferably somebody with no wizard bond who can call to her, somebody who has no history with Aeren that might allow for something resembling an honest conversation. I mean, I'd offer myself for the job, but I understand you've got a better proposal."

"Well, then" —Cathe disrupted our engaging conversation with another cheery hand clap— "if there is another way to find the girl—"

"There isn't." Nobody liked this but nobody proposed a better idea. "Then tell me again why you're avoiding the topic of bringing on another wizard to carry these wands, and why they are necessary."

Cathe didn't like being pulled back to the original subject. "You see, it's like this. A spare wand or two of your choice is useful; a spare wizard is an unnecessary liability because you've got the gods' protection."

"Then I don't need these." I gestured toward the window ledge.

"All right, then, here's truth. Choose one or two to keep. Two that you have so aligned your energy with that they are extensions of your will. Leave the rest if you must, but when or if Aeren returns, you will need to train her on some of them, and so you will need to be adept with all of them."

"Which is of course why you insisted I practice with these wands long before this intriguing morning when you suggested it would be a convenience should she die. And why you've also said my weapons practice was for aiding me in improbably dangerous situations."

"I meant," sniffed Cathe, "should she return—"

"Then we'll need another wizard to spot her."

Cathe declared our meeting over. Whatever the real reason for my unnecessary wand training, he wasn't about to let me in on it. When I tried to read him I came away with dust and shadows, and the sickening image of Habundia-Christus kissing a flattened toad into powder, and then pressing that powder around Hecate's eyes and mouth. I had no idea what Cathe knew about my mandate, but it took all my concentration to avoid being overcome with nausea.

Stormr noticed that I was trembling. He offered his arm for support, which would have made him vulnerable to my entering his shield had I accepted his help. I remembered what Graen had said about Stormr, but far from being "almost terrified" by his unexpected show of kindness, I was intrigued at having provoked it. I refused his offer by slowly making my way to the window ledge as the two clerics intently watched. I then took all the wands and stuffed them in my cloak. Not because I wanted them, but because I suddenly decided I didn't want Cathe to have them. And then, for some reason, I bowed slightly to Stormr in acknowledgement of his gesture, and left.

That night, emboldened by my moon, I mumbled a half-remembered witch-working that Caethne taught me when I lived in Walworth's secret household in Helas. Through the witch-working, I held hands with the wind, or something like that, and slipped outside the king's residence. Nobody followed me. As I made my way through Hala's empty streets, I heard a woman sobbing in the distance. Sometimes her cries sounded like a lost raven's. Hecate's bird.

But mostly the city was dull with thick, unsteady night. Thick because the windows held no lanterns, and since I didn't want to call attention to myself by conjuring a light, structures were difficult to see. Unsteady because when I opened my wizard senses to better make my way through the dark, the night revealed those strange cracks and crevices that Furna said came from Mirand bending time to steal a victory for Threle. I encountered one of those strange sourceless shadows that I had remarked on earlier in the day. My witch-working had increased my sensitivity to nature, and so I heard the shadow crying as it spread into cloudy nonexistence. I watched it die. It thinned and dissipated over a windswept roof, now timeless as a barren grave.

I made my way out of the city, into the cleaner darkness of woods and fields. I found myself striding along a dead road and telling stories to the stars until the stars told me to stop. They were Aeren's stories, the ones I'd translated today, and I was telling them the way travelers do to pass time on a journey, or condemned prisoners do as a last offering to the hours, mixing my language with hers in preparation for my call. But my telling numbed as I remembered lying to her. Then the tales went awkward on my tongue and the stars stopped listening.

I walked in silence. For hours.

They used to say in Helas, by way of merchants' chatter, that on certain full moon nights, if you wandered away from a marketplace as it closed at day's end, and then away from the town, and then just away through fields and farms and woods and wilderness, the moon would "take you in" —that is, lure and trick you—and you would keep wandering forever. Or until dawn made you over into something new. You could find yourself in the next town, or the next duchy, or another country, or maybe even the North Country. But you have to carry the right energy with you, cede yourself to the night. Nobody ever did it, or did it right, because there was always business and supper and family at home, and more business pulling you into the next day. No one could just leave their life to go wandering. And so they told stories about it. Stories they spun out of Helan folk tales and childhood games that everyone laughed at but nobody knew how to disbelieve.

I do not know if the moon took me in. At some point, still in silence, I left the road and ambled through a haze of moonlight until I reached the crest of a hill. Then I lay upon the crest and willed myself into the spaces between the dull stars, trying to find a line where the world I knew ended and another reality began. Naturally, there was no such border, no way to escape my mandate. It was just another story to tell myself.

Then I rose and gathered random stones into a small ring. The air was cool and quiet, like an old dream, and the stones felt both familiar and unused, like magical items I'd learned wizardry on years ago and hadn't handled since. Which stars did they come from? I sat near the circle for a long time, sensing the differential between the everything without the circle's circumference, the distant hills and sky and dark night fields and more distant towns, and the hidden ways my life could have gone, and the empty spot of dirt within. Then I conjured a lonely black candle to mark the circle's center, lit it with wizard fire, and sent my call.

I called forever, like a wanderer "taken in" by the moon. For days, anyway, or until the moon waned into something I had no heart to work with. There was no response. Except once, upon a split of time, I thought I heard an answer. But it was only the rumbling shadow of the sunrise, which I heard through my heightened magical sensitivity, or the faint slide of color in the sky.

I returned to a hollow city. Maybe it was afternoon, but I was too exhausted from the previous night to mark the precise hour. Smoke rose from the wrong places and hung motionless over other wrong places. And then I realized that the smoke appeared "wrong" because it was coming from the open squares and markets while the house chimneys remained inactive. I briefly feared it was dragon smoke, but the wood fire scent indicated otherwise.

A cart rattled furtively across a side street, its rough clatter cutting through the peculiar silence that loomed throughout the city. The carter was hunched and focused on driving his donkeys as quickly as the animals allowed. He stared stiffly at the cobblestones passing under his reins. Then his cart lumbered past the corner and out of sight.

I saw no one else. Maybe I was dreaming Hala. Maybe Hala no longer existed and I was walking through an old story come to life. But as I entered yet another empty street, Cathe's guards marked reality by greeting me as if we were fast friends, tripping into chatter as if we'd just shared ale and gossip yesterday and didn't know better than to continue enjoying ourselves.

"Hey, Brother! Missed your robe for a few days."

"Well met, friends. Missed Hala's best."

The guards laughed and increased their stride, almost like happy folk dancers. "The king says you're out giving us a prayer. Hope you asked blessed Athena to shower us with gold." They laughed again and I couldn't help but laugh too. Damn Helas! Despite all, its heart remained.

Then one of the fellows went slightly serious. "Fighting in the marketplace, Brother. Some people burning stalls to protest whatever isn't liked today. Or yesterday. King's ordered everyone off the street."

Another added cautiously, "Sort of order never would have happened in the old Helas. The old duke, Walworth himself, King Mirand—no one restricted the people for anything before the southwest intruded where it wasn't wanted."

The guards fell into a silence that felt like agreement, so I did the same.

"You know Hala's in affray against itself?" one of the fellows offered carefully. "There's some as don't mind the southwest, and King Hathe."

"And others that do," said the other guard.

"Well, Threle's had experience with that sort of thing. Why not Helas?" The guards chuckled uneasily at my remark because none of them wanted to continue discussing politics. They quickly escorted me into the king's residence, where I just as quickly retired to my room and refused to see anybody. Within minutes there was a soft kick at the door. I opened it and saw an insistent servant standing there, holding a large basin of water.

"King Hathe sent me to—"

"Tell 'King Hathe' I intend to be in prayer for several hours." I took the basin. "Thank you. Oh, and tell the damn king I'll see him at my convenience."

She nodded nervously and left.

I threw a magical lock over the door and another one over the door that led to Cathe's apartments. Of course, Cathe could open my locks, but I wished to underscore my desire for solitude. When the basin water stopped sloshing, I splashed some on my face and chest, bathing in the simplicity of its stillness more than in the water itself.

Helan water. Holy water. Hala was burning. There was a time when I loved Helas and its people so much that my heart would have burned for and with the city. But now my heart was mercifully numb.

I stopped washing, and stared at the water as my numbness gave way to uncontrollable sadness, for I understood that I was now irrevocably estranged from the present. When I entered the city, I had briefly thought the smoke was dragonish, and Aeren's, before I forever understood that it wasn't. Aeren was dead. If she still lived, she would have answered my call. And so I killed her with a lie. And so the awful waves of mourning. And then something close to mourning, that is, knowing that the world twisted on, that Hala twisted on, but I would be alone, stumbling through everything like an invisible moon fallen upon an unknown world. Knowing that my past, my history, really did die with the dragon.

Mother. If Aeren yet was queen, I killed the Queen of Gondal with a lie. And so I am the King of Lies. I killed Aeren—my friend—isn't that enough to save a world? Must there be more? My prayer went to Hecate. First in thought, then in words I kept repeating like a spell I couldn't make happen. "I killed the Queen of Gondal with a lie. I killed my friend. I killed my friend."

For answer there was nothing but a pounding in my head, and then a pounding at the door, disrupting my words into shreds of useless energy.

I swayed a little, moved unsteadily toward the pounding, still muttering shreds of prayer for steadiness. I released my locks and opened the door. Lord Graen strode furiously into my room, each footfall a crash of anger.

"Uh, make yourself welcome, my lord."

His body was taut and shaking. White lines of wrath mottled his face, making it look more like a boiled parsnip than ever. "I heard you praying. *I heard your goddamned prayer!*"

"Graen—you heard a dream—a—"

Graen's sudden screaming obliterated my attempt to explain. "You liar! You lied to her! You lied to me! Zyren spoke truth!" He was so anger-mashed that the energy of his fury forced him to alternatively screech and crumple into gasps. "You killed Aeren! You told her a tale that sent her into the blast. *You told her a tale!* I heard you in your filthy prayer to your filthy goddess. And you call yourself her *friend?* And I thought you were mine?"

Graen lurched and grabbed a fistful of my cloak to slam my head against the nearest wall. He shrieked and fell as my moon waned his sword arm into something resembling a broken stick.

As I clumsily regained my breath and balance, Graen was writhing and cradling his new stump of withered flesh and cursing me and all the gods. "I hope you die in Threle. I hope you die like Aeren. I hope you lose the world and die friendless of your own evil." His words rose into breathless incoherent cries, like a dying animal losing its ability to move before losing its ability to feel.

I turned my back so he couldn't see the water in my eyes. Then I prayed. For both of us. Prayed for a healing that Hecate couldn't give, for a shining trick of wisdom that Hecate didn't own.

Ten

I continued praying for healing and wisdom, knowing that such things are not among Hecate's gifts, but hoping that some deity might respond. Graen spit, shuddered, and forced himself up off the floor. Unfortunately, the instant he righted himself, he keeled into the same wall he had tried to slam me against. At which point Cathe pranced through the door that I had always kept secured between our rooms.

"Why bother with wizard locks, Brother? I mean, between us?" Cathe's attention was immediately drawn to Graen, who had slid against the wall and was back on the floor, grasping at the useless tangle of flesh that used to be his sword arm. "A hit, is it?" The King of Helas sounded maddeningly unconcerned about his overking's best fighter.

Graen groaned a muddle of words to no one in particular. "A hit to murder. A loose story to strangle. Oh my heart, my heart."

"An accident," I mumbled to Cathe's slightly bent back. "Milord *misinterpreted—*"

Cathe gestured behind his back for me to stop talking. He then spoke heavily over Graen's gasp-ridden attempts to clarify his interesting situation. "You misinterpret much, milord. I hear *you* created a loose tale of havoc in my city yesterday, and now . . . this." Then he straightened and turned to me, ignoring the anguished mess that was now Graen. "Well. I suppose Stormr will heal him. If anybody can. Fetch the good Brother and see what he can do."

"I *can* walk," Graen protested. He clumsily placed his uninjured hand against the wall and pushed himself onto his knees. "No more clerics." And then, his body still trembling, he managed to draw Truthfinder from his cloak with that same hand and hold the weapon across his damaged sword arm as he huddled close to the floor. I watched his face stiffen with concentration before he turned his head toward the wall. Then I saw his shattered limb knit itself together, watched the flesh grow whole. I had to admire his mastery, although I felt somewhat chagrined at his weapons skill succeeding where my prayer failed.

Graen fainted from the energy he spent to restore his arm to what, in truth, his arm should be. But he recovered within seconds and stood unsteadily to face Cathe.

"My good King Hathe." Graen clutched the sword and swayed a little as he slowly regained just enough breath to continue speaking with hard effort. "Your cleric" —he jabbed Truthfinder in my general direction— "killed . . . the queen. I heard him confess it. I want justice, King."

Cathe's expression was so excessively grim that I knew he didn't give a fig for Graen's accusation. "You say *Llewelyn* killed Queen Aeren?"

"He told her some sort of terrible lie," Graen insisted. "And the lie killed her."

"You mean he killed the queen by *lying* to her? Oh, my. You are in a state now, aren't you?" Cathe's sing-song seriousness pricked Graen's courtier's sensibilities. Graen sputtered with helpless anger and jerked Truthfinder at nothing in particular.

"My good lord Graen." Cathe raised his hand as if to reassure. "I shall do all appropriate investigation into this curious matter." He looked dolefully in my direction and I played along by sighing and soberly staring at an empty corner, as if Graen's unfortunate accusation had given me much to consider. "But now you will retire to your room where we can speak privately. I'll follow shortly."

Graen sharply bowed his head to the king. Then he glared at me for several seconds with hostility so pure he could have bottled and sold it to a rejected demi-god. Then he left. Cathe waved his arm in annoyance as Graen's footsteps faded too slowly for his liking. After impatiently waiting for a minute or so, he softly closed the door. "This turn of affairs is richer than a pot of boiled leeches. Sometimes I think we should just tell the poor fellow the truth."

"What? And risk erupting his generous enthusiasm into uselessness?"

Cathe stared blandly through my tired sarcasm. "What did you learn in your travels? Where is she?"

"Aeren's dead." It was surprisingly hard for me to say this. It was even harder for me to say this to him.

Cathe leaned on his staff and studied me, clearly frustrated by his inability to read me through my moon. I let him wait impatiently for an explanation I had no intention of giving. He finally broke. "And that's all you care to say?"

"Yes." I could feel his frustration crawl through the spotted sunlight like a directionless snake. "Good day." He waited, irked at my simple dismissal, but equally unwilling to flash his vexation by begging my silence with unanswered questions. "I should like to return to prayer."

The high priest couldn't know whether to believe me. He smacked his lips in frustration as he felt his powerlessness peak like a fine poison. He sniffed. "Well. Then it seems you are Gondal's king. Perhaps we should honor Hecate by weaving you a crown of withered manuscripts." He smiled. The directionless snake suddenly scented a rotting hole. "Brother."

"I'm also tired."

"Yes, of course." But rather than leave, Cathe dropped himself into a chair and stared up at me plaintively. "We ... heads of state" —he flipped his hand dismissively— "have much to discuss."

I remained standing. "So discuss it. Or don't. Or leave."

Cathe sighed at my testiness. "Really, you might change that ridiculous Athenic garb."

"Really, you might get to the point of it."

"Hala burned last night." He spoke with such thick indifference I could barely distinguish the irritation it coated. Cathe cared less about the riots than about being bothered with them.

"Perhaps you need to do a better job kinging it around. Some people don't like you."

Cathe ignored my sarcasm. "Some are unhappy with my little kingdom, and would join Threle again. They've eaten their fill of Furnesse 'stealing their gold and gilding their troubles' as they like to say, and they see me as a client-king with no concern for anyone save Furna. Of course they're wrong. I've no concern for anyone."

"You'll make a fine god." I yawned and looked around.

"Actually I will, Habundia be blessed and be damned. Some of my people want me dead; most just want me gone to wherever I'm supposed to have come from. Others, not many now, still say that Helas properly belongs to the southwest, due to our shared language or some such, and that we should strengthen our ties with Furnesse. They look to get government positions and regard their promotion of Furna's taxes as an investment in their ambition, so they sit on sentiment to cover their real mark. But mostly they're happy to become anything but a Threlan duchy again."

"That's your problem."

"Yes, but it's a closer problem than anybody understood. Of course, there are always provocateurs accepting coin to torch words into destruction, but it seems our friend Graen can't help himself from causing civic disturbances. It's like the gods gave him a gift for that sort of thing without the wit to profit from it."

"And how did he grace your people with his divine gift this time?"

"Milord went to market wearing his accent and loudly praising Helas as the 'jewel of Furnesse.' I'm told that he declaimed to all within earshot, and then some, that his greatest boast was the service he would render in defense of the Helan people. Naturally, he did this in praise of himself."

"Naturally. And I suppose some of the Helan people weren't in a mood to indulge his pride?"

"Some cried, 'What? You mean defend us from your king?' Others took his unprovoked self-congratulation as a taunt to say that my poorly done kingship reduced this once gloriously independent duchy—the Helas once regarded as more Threlan than Threle—into a dismal bauble of a subject state in need of Furnessian protection. Which is true. That *was* the price of kingship."

I briefly calculated the merits of blasting Cathe back to Habundia Christus and calling it a day. But, given the landscape of my potential damnation, I decided not to kill him for damaging the former duchy I once held almost sacred, for killing the merchant songs I still loved. That was a test of Hecate's protection that I didn't care to make. The only defense evil clerics have against each other belongs to the gods—kill a brother or sister in evil and eternal damnation greets you like a glittering pageant. Perhaps my moon was a pass in this regard, but that wasn't clear. And blasting the king, the embodiment of Helas, of Helas's sadly splintered self-destruction, would of course judder through Furnesse, Threle, the world and beyond in ways that only the gods knew. But it was difficult to hold myself back. I had to focus on Graen to manage it. "A man who can stride unscathed through courtly society but reliably converts market banter into fire and ruin is a man we need to reassess."

"Yes, but I'm sure you can relate to that sort of thing and the wonder is *he's* clean. There's nothing in his mind that indicates he's anything but socially inept outside of a Furnessian court. Excellent swordsman, needs a minder. Don't know whether to bring charges against him for show or send him back to Furnesse as more trouble than treasure."

"Maybe you could make him a goodwill ambassador to the new world."

Cathe considered. "Not a bad idea. Furna wants to give him a kingdom once things are made right. Which needs to happen soon. It's time to send the party on to Loudes. But given Graen's present attitude, well, and the great difficulty replacing him, his training, his skill, and the risk of his tongue wagging all the way back to Furnesse—we do need to mollify him."

"So mollify him."

"Then we must offer some story concerning Aeren's death that won't cost us his loyalty." "That's Stormr's job if he'll have it. I don't have any stories."

Cathe sighed. "He's not likely to have it. Well . . . that's how fraught even innocence dresses lately. Best to avoid the world as it is." He clapped his hands. "Let us suffer into divinity if we can. It pleases the gods. But first, King," Cathe continued, suddenly pleasant. "I'd like you to kill somebody."

"Why?"

"I don't trust your heart and you won't let me read it. I mean, that is the short of it. We took some prisoners this morning for their role in the mayhem. Most of them for torching market stalls and throwing rocks, but one of them killed a guard and desperately needs to die for it. That is, I desperately need to know whether you'd kill a Threlan supporter upon my say so. Before we make some sort of peace with Graen and send you to Loudes to destroy Threle."

"And if I wouldn't?"

"Blessings, Brother! I know in prayer that you need us to fulfill your divine mandate as much as I need you to fulfill my divine ambition. You are treading Hecate's glory. You need to act like it." Cathe waited.

"And this prisoner was tried between yester eve and now?"

"I dispensed with all that. Really, why bother? This isn't Threle and there were enough witnesses to satisfy me. After all, justice is as justice does."

"I need some time in prayer."

"Undoubtedly. Why wouldn't you?" He rose. "Well. It needn't be a public execution. It would be cleaner to use one of your wands on the prisoner and let the guards remove what's left from the cell. I told them they could watch the performance, out of respect for their fallen comrade." He clapped his hands again. "So. Take your hours to rest and pray now. You must be clear-minded when you meet the condemned. I'll come for you at dawn."

I didn't care to pray. I no longer cared to rest, but I managed to sleep a little until nightfall. Dreams came like death's breath, fluttery and grainy. They unraveled like badly told tales. Then the moonlight hurdled through my windows. It licked my eyes like a hungry dog, waking me. I opened my palms in the moonlight, felt its coolness. *This too is Mother Hecate.*

The king's residence was flush with the kind of quiet one normally finds in nearly-empty inns, a sphere of near-silence contrasting with the noise and rush of the world's normal business, that is, if the world still held any normal business. But no outside noise strayed into my room. So I knew that Hala was also quiet after the day's destruction. Then I remembered how merry Helan towns used to be at night—drinking, dancing, jokes among friends.

I felt the soft hurt in my heart before I recognized that it hurt for Helas.

I didn't care for the prisoner, but I had no quarrel with the poor wretch. I'd done worse in my life than kill a guard, the crime for which this "Threlan supporter" had been condemned. For all I knew the guard had provoked the brawl. And yet I was to kill this stranger at Cathe's command, without the trial that would have once been the stranger's right. I was to kill without justice to satisfy the King of Helas that I would kill again to justify—to make right—the world. Not because Cathe cared for the world, but because he fancied becoming a god.

Something in me—either Aeren's influence or my own disordered history—wanted the prisoner's story. I needed to hear it before I did my job, as if this was still the Helas I remembered, still Threle, and it was my charge to understand the life I was taking. I sent my heart-hurt into the darkness and moonlight. I rambled like a mad animal through the king's residence. And then I descended like forgotten rain into the dirt of the dungeon.

I would know the lawbreaker I was supposed to kill.

The cells were underground and darker than the back of my heart. I conjured a candle. Wizard fire. I thought of Mirand teaching me to conjure. That was also in Helas, when he and Walworth made an invisible prison out of invented friendship and political expediency. Mirand apprenticed me, but only to keep me close so I wouldn't continue my travels and give away their location. Walworth conned me into believing we were friends and equals, and that I was essential to their secret plans to save Threle from invasion. Caethne taught me witchcraft while she called me "brother" and "twin." And so I came to see Helas as my home. Because it was then a Threlan duchy, I enthusiastically became a Threlan supporter. Like the prisoner I was to execute.

And now, by the light I had just conjured through Mirand's training, I saw Helans who had been arrested during the day's riots. Based on their quarreling, it appeared that some were Threlan loyalists, some still favored the southwest, others wanted Helan independence, and all of them had spent the day burning areas of Hala. Naturally, they all blamed each other for their present circumstances.

I felt a certain sympathy. None of them understood that they were imprisoned by the clash of their own political illusions with their new king's desperate dreams of divinity. Just as I hadn't understood when Walworth and Mirand caged me with my own illusions of brotherhood in order to safeguard Walworth's political ambitions.

Nobody appeared to be guarding the cells.

Some of the cells were empty. Some held prisoners in twos and threes. I approached each cell softly, like a wary beggar, but spoke like a king. "Show me the condemned."

Prisoners shrugged, cried, gestured, kicked the wall.

I moved on. "Show me the one who is to die."

"Show me Athena, Brother." "Give us a bless." "Heal poor Helas."

I encountered a cell that held a solitary hooded figure seated on the floor. "Are you the one who is to die?"

"Yes. Who wants to know?" The hood obscured the speaker's face and voice, revealing only a hint of steady gaze against my weak candlelight.

"A friend. If you'll have him."

I unlocked the cell with a simple spell and entered hooded, like the prisoner. And so we faced each other under the earth, on the damp dungeon floor, blind to each other's faces but open to each other's gaze. I reached out and pressed my moon-scarred palm against the condemned's hand, a hand which felt as cool and resolute as an old rock marking shifting ground.

It was long seconds before I spoke, long seconds of understanding and recognition as I read the prisoner I couldn't see, and even longer seconds to steady my voice once I realized who the prisoner was. "Do you know me, Aleta?" I dropped her hand and removed my hood. She slowly removed hers. Her eyes were slits of suspicion in the fitful light.

Aleta had always viewed me with the mistrust she reserved for all magic users. Including Mirand and Caethne, interestingly enough, despite Threle's longstanding alliance with her homeland, County Clio. We had worked together in Helas, united in our support of Walworth and his attempts to defend Threle against the southwest. And here she was in a Helan prison for her current support of Threle.

"I heard you died. I also heard you lived." Her tone was more exasperated than curious. The Countess of Clio was a fighter, and like all fighters, she hated ambiguity more than death. Then her tone slid seamlessly into a dash of anger. "At least that's the tale going about. And now you carry Athena and work for Cathe?"

"I'm here for you." I laughed a little when I said this, because our present situation was so odd.

She became contemptuous. "So *you're* going execute me? Now? Without a trial? Athena's broken scales"—Aleta always had a way with profanities— "but that's bloody fine. And you call me friend?"

"Justice is as justice does." I smiled involuntarily, the way one smiles when an unexpected cleverness pops like a garish puppet out of a disturbing jest. Then I felt myself stop smiling. "You saved my life once. Just before we crossed the border into Threle. Remember? Roguehan had invaded the southern duchies, and you rode with me out of a burning town in Medegard. A town that burned like Hala did today." Aleta was listening, but her face was now emotionless. "You were the only member of our party who worked through night and exhaustion to dig me out of a rock slide when it would have been easier to leave me to die. I've never forgotten that."

She stared briefly at her hand and looked dourly at me, as if spending a night chopping me out of an avalanche in the Sengan Mountains was nothing to her, something forgotten in the press of life. But then, Aleta was capable of being your friend without ever troubling herself to like you. It was one of her best qualities. "And so your life became such a bad job you want to get even for the favor."

"Eh. I see you've read the trial records."

Aleta ploughed over my attempt at humor like she was tilling salt into an enemy's field. "No. I just see you. The rest is obvious. Or just semantics." She spoke with her usual effortless honesty. "So let's get on with it then. I expect I'll die better than you did when Walworth sentenced you."

"I expect you will, Countess. But not tonight." I sounded oddly easy with myself, as if I were still putting it on for her the way I used to when I teased her about my magical studies in Helas. Aleta groaned in exasperation, covered her face in her hood, and threw herself on her side, facing the cell wall as if to say that our conversation was finished. She would have plain speaking, even from death himself, or she couldn't be bothered. I knelt on damp dirt and spoke cautiously to her back, my voice a stab against the dark between us, my words getting away from my understanding. And then my heart spoke in spite of itself. "Tonight you're going to be my second."

"Your second what?" Her voice shot sharply out of her huddle.

"My second prisoner," I said grandly. "Taken from Cathe on the eve of execution."

"What?" Aleta pushed herself part way up and turned a little toward me, as if to say that she would give me a half hearing. "Like that useless minstrel Ellisand, who nearly got us killed on the Threlan plains?"

"Like." This wasn't exactly true, but it was an honest enough answer to contain a partial truth. "If you didn't read the trial records, how do know Ellisand was my first prisoner?"

Aleta sat up and faced me again. "Because *after* Mirand saved Threle, and you disappeared from Walworth's castle, he wouldn't stop bragging about your great escape from Cathe and Kursen Monastery." I shrugged. "So why are you refusing Cathe's orders this time?"

"To honor our forgotten friendship." I spoke with less solemnity than I felt.

"To honor *what?*"

"All right, maybe I just like to annoy Cathe."

"You like to annoy everyone. What makes Cathe so special?"

"Countess. We'll discuss 'semantics,' as you put it, when I get you out of here."

"So get me out of here." She stood. Not because she believed me, but because her sudden show of readiness was the most efficient way to test mine.

I rose slowly. "I will. But there's something I need to do first."

"Naturally."

"I'm going to get you a weapon." I tried to lighten her skepticism by teasing her. "But it's magical, so I expect you'll be afraid to use it, and I doubt you'll be eager to learn how."

"Get me out of here and I'll learn any weapon of your choosing." Her voice was flat and dismissive, rebuking my teasing, my presumption, and on some level, my confidence. "And not only that, I'll use it ever at your service. Soldier's promise." A quick mind probe told me that her promise was sincere, even if she doubted me, or most likely, because she doubted me. It was a test of my honesty from someone who was still prepared to die.

It was also a piece of fine luck. I quickly pressed her hand, bringing down Hecate's force to tie poor Aleta to her freely given vow. "Then by Hecate I bind you to your promise." Poor Aleta. She would now fight in my service or die damned, unless I released her. She would feel compelled to fight for me, but she would not know of this binding or the cost of refusing to help me justify the world, unless I told her. But what to tell her, if anything, was another day's problem, after I'd had time to consider whether I'd just done something horrible or coldly necessary or merely sensible. If I was to leave Cathe and make my own way to Threle, I needed a fighter I could trust. The gods had provided one.

Aleta tilted her head and studied my face as if she were trying to eavesdrop on a dead language. I read her again. She didn't know if she knew me now; our past belonged to Threle and not to her. She gave me apples once in Sunnashiven, long before that business in the Sengan Mountains. We were accidental allies in Helas, the old Helas, but she blamed that one on Mirand and Caethne. She never considered us friends. She never considered us anything. She didn't care that I was evil—the problem was that she didn't trust me. But she admitted to herself that I'd never betrayed her, never harmed her, and had no quarrel with County Clio. I used to mock her fear of magic; I used to think more highly of myself than she thought I should. She remembered my role in saving Walworth at his trial, saving "that useless minstrel" and killing Cathe before his present existence.

Sometimes, in childhood, she loved the scent of Clion apples persisting in random places long after the apples were gone. It surprised her in lonely corners, in old unwashed bowls, in the cloth that covered the secret sword she kept in a hollow tree. It was all she ever needed to know of magic. Or of anything, really.

Then she simply recognized the oddness of our new encounter and the utility of her vow.

She firmly pressed my hand in agreement. "You're on it. By Hecate. And by anybody else you care to swear by."

It wasn't until I left the cell that I stumbled from the force of my newly renewed hatred of Cathe.

Cathe had chosen to reduce Helas, a place I once loved, to a weak, Furnessian subject state in exchange for kingship—a kingship he viewed as a convenient platform from which to destroy Threle, make the world right, and become a god. I would destroy Threle and turn Mirand because that was Hecate's mandate, and choice wasn't one of Her luxuries. Furna wanted Walworth and Mirand dead; I would do what was needed to avoid eternal torture, no more and no less, which meant that for my part their deaths were negotiable. Although given what I knew about Mirand, his was possibly less so. But I would not kill Aleta to set Cathe in confidence, and it was not on me to bounce Cathe into divinity.

I had the Wand of Surprises. I couldn't leave without pilfering Truthfinder from Graen. I had no idea how to teach Aleta to use it, but I did know that I couldn't leave it for Graen or anybody else to kill Mirand with by sending him into the death and defeat that should have happened from Roguehan's victory. I needed to change Mirand's alignment, and then I suppose I could listen to his story and kill him. Or something.

I went to my rooms and selected two wands, Aeren's stories, and a few necessities for travel. Then I made my way to Graen's room. I stopped. I opened myself to sense for magic. I knew Truthfinder was heavy with magic, I'd been around it enough. But I only felt a spot, like a prick of a spell. That could happen if the sword was shielded, if Stormr was keeping it protected when not in use and its power was wearing at the shield. I pulled at the dot of magic, the break in the shield, forcing with all my wizardry to manifest the object in my hands.

A small gold ring appeared on the scar in my palm—Aeren's Ring of Beauty. I assumed this meant that Graen was in his room, because he always carried her ring. But Graen had no right to it, despite Stormr's illicit generosity and my prior uneasy tolerance. The ring was mine. I had given it to Aeren to grace her status as Gondal's queen. And so, as Gondal's presumptive king, I pocketed the ring in my cloak. As to Truthfinder, if Graen still had Truthfinder, it was well shielded. Which had to be Stormr's work.

This was a difficult pass. It was almost dawn, almost time for Aleta's execution. Not light yet, but I knew it was the wide thicket of night that thins before it catches light. It was poor strategy to risk another confrontation with Graen if Truthfinder wasn't there, even if he couldn't harm me. But everything about tonight was poor strategy, and it was worse to leave the weapon here. I opened the door.

The first thing I saw as my eyes adjusted to the darkness was the outline of Truthfinder's hilt in the middle of the air. The second thing I saw was the pale glint of the blade, which was stuck into a dark mass on the floor. The mass resolved itself into a lump of clothes that resolved itself into the shape of a body. I thought it was shielded because I didn't sicken, but when I conjured a candle to see better, I discovered that the "body" was a sack of dust and corn husks wrapped in something that vaguely resembled an Athenic robe and that it was clearly meant to stand in for me. But the whole arrangement wasn't just about me. The blade also pierced a brown and blue tatter of a Helan flag that lay on top of the robe, and a piece of parchment that lay on top of the flag. I held the candle near the parchment to read the writing. A neat, angry hand proclaimed in Botha: "There is no truth in Helas."

Graen wasn't there. That meant he wasn't far, because I couldn't imagine him letting Aeren's ring out of his possession. I must have manifested it from his person, and there was no telling what kind of howl he'd raise when he found it missing. I pulled Truthfinder out of my stand-in on the floor and it instantly became obvious why I couldn't sense its power. Its blade was broken. Its magic had gone dead. I took it anyway.

So Graen had quit the quest and left fair notice of his intention toward me and the Helan king. Whatever. It wasn't like there was much he could do against either of us. Dawn was coming and I didn't have time to parse his political commentary beyond the obvious. I could think later.

But on my way to Aleta's cell, between listening for Graen's footsteps and outpacing the dawn, I caught myself mourning again for reasons I could helplessly analyze but couldn't forcefully name. King Furna's best swordsman had broken his sword, the weapon that had become an extension of himself. The ambitious courtier had scorched the status that meant so much to him. And he did this out of grief for Aeren, who had lost her status as queen and couldn't secure recognition, let alone status, as a bard. Graen didn't even recognize her as a storyteller, and yet he fell in love with her over a fiction and wanted to kill me over another. And kill Cathe for somehow facilitating the same. And Aeren herself had killed and died after learning the truth of the honest fiction I created for her. Perhaps she died angry, as she lived. Perhaps, in the end, she choked on something like a hard-willed innocence, her final excruciating effort to believe in herself before the awful betrayal.

When I got to Aleta's cell, I realized three things. One, that I had gotten so distracted I didn't have a weapon for her. Two, that I was feeling low on energy and needed to reserve some for our escape. Three, it was as near dawn as it was possible to be without breaking light.

Aleta stood as I entered the cell, but I wasn't focused on her because I was mostly aware of the minimal energy I expended to magically reopen the lock and conjure a faint reed light. "Where's my weapon?"

"Uh . . . "

"Where's this mysterious magical weapon that—"

"That's for later." She stared at me in disbelief through the rapidly weakening flicker. "We need to go. Now." She kept staring, kept distrusting. Against my better judgment, I conjured a small dagger and shoved it into her hand. "That's the best I can do right now."

"What do you expect me to with this?"

"Accept it. Take my hand, keep close, and my shield will protect you until we get some horses. Keep hooded. When we get someplace safe, I'll conjure a proper sword for you, but for now I'm conserving my wizardry."

Aleta was too sensible to argue.

"Actually—damn. Here." I used more wizardry than I felt comfortable with to transform her clothes into a monastic servant's, as I had Graen's when we escaped the riot. "You're my servant. Until we get clear of Helas."

"Understood."

Praise Hecate for Aleta's unfussy practicality! The reed sputtered into the dark and we left the cell. Aleta stayed gamely behind my left shoulder, holding to my hand and quietly letting me lead her up and out of the dungeon. I heard stirring in distant halls, real servants starting their work. But we didn't encounter anything except the night starting to bend before the inevitability of dawn. When we exited into a garden, it was lighter than it looked from inside. As we hurried instinctively past the rapidly sharpening outlines of bushes, I felt an odd sense of—not comfort exactly, but rightness. We knew how to work together.

When we got to the stables, Aleta glanced briefly at her servant's garb, sensibly saddled a small mare to match her disguise, and quickly led it out as I took a fine stallion. Nobody was there to stop us as we mounted and rode with the freedom of fallen birds out of Hala, out of darkness, out of wherever we were and into whatever adventure would have us.

Eleven

The Countess of Clio played monastic servant as well as she played life. Which is to say she hit the mark even when there wasn't one. She spoke no more and no less than appearances required, hiding her face from passing strangers in her best impression of pious humility. Keeping close as we rapidly made our way out of the city, she earnestly tricked the world.

But then, why wouldn't she convince as a cleric's servant? Truth is always in service to the gods, and Aleta had carried truth before she could carry a sword. That is, I'd never known her to be anything but truthful, as if plain speaking and acting were simply what she did because she couldn't be bothered with anything else. In some ways, she had been the gods' own servant all along.

We rode without fuss through sparse towns and desolate fields. Our sporadic exchanges merely underscored how easily we worked together, how much we agreed on strategy without having to say very much about it. We needed to get out of Helas. County Clio was our best option, and we both knew that the hidden forest paths west of Helas would eventually lead us there. We also sensed that when we spoke freely again it would be upon those buried paths.

This silent solidarity and our fast horses got us to the western border by day's end. The border was marked by a broken sign and a random wind stirring the meadow grass. An orange cat slowly pattered into the grass, attracted by the patterns the wind made. The cat did his best to ignore us. But maybe I only dreamed that part of the moment.

"End of Helas." I wasn't sure if I meant this as a greeting or a closing, or who I meant it for.

Aleta placed her hand above her eyes to block the evening sun. "Helas ended a long time ago. Day's nearly over." I took in the simple rightness in Aleta's natural, unadorned speech as I surveyed the wild meadow. The orange cat, if he ever really existed, had disappeared.

"Brother! Athena's fair son!" The speaker's loud voice startled me slightly more than it did Aleta, who pulled back on her mare to give the stranger space.

I looked down. "Yes, friend. What do you want?"

"Ah." His face was sad. It was made sadder by the excessive eagerness in his smile. But he didn't care to hide his fascination with my cleric's robes. "You here to leave, Brother?"

"We're here." There are some elderly men who don't feel right with themselves unless they screw up your day with good intentions. There is something both endearing and pitiable about that. Also, his eyes held old Helas the way old books hold forgotten history. That is why I waited for him to speak again.

He was breathless with the effort it had taken to approach our standing horses before we left Helas. He nodded to acknowledge my "servant" before turning again to look up at me. "Stay the night, sir? For a bless?"

Aleta stared at me with dutiful impatience. I slightly shook my head to acknowledge her concern before looking back at the old fellow. "We're on a spiritual quest. Praying to Athena's moon as she waxes and sets tonight." Aleta looked slightly mollified, but only slightly. "Here's your bless." I conjured a few gold coins to place in his hands. The man's face suddenly brightened into fiery gratitude. I couldn't watch. It's heartbreaking when old men look grateful, but it's heart shattering when old Helans do. Helans cherish their reputation as free traders; as such, they consider it shameful to be beholden to anyone. So being Helan, his gratitude quickly turned to a pride that bent and broke somewhere beyond heart shattering.

"Hey." He patted my horse. "I'll tell you what, Brother. Where are your supplies?" He indicated our barren saddles. "I've got cheese and bread. Good bread." His smile was suddenly desperate and earnest. It was a tenet of Helan mercantilism that he would earn his gold. "Wait." He ran to a mournful, shuttered shop a short distance behind us.

"We will need food," I cajoled Aleta, who was ready to kick her horse into motion. "And the fellow needs his pride."

She glanced impatiently in the direction of the shop. "Clio's three days at worst, and I know where there's forest ponds full of fish and fowl. If you can manage to conjure up a spear or a net, we'll be fine."

"And what will I eat?"

"Remainders from old Helas," sang out our new friend in his best merchant patter as he approached our horses, proudly shaking a large sack in each hand. Aleta resumed her quiet servant's demeanor as the man handed me a sack of foodstuff. "Cheese is from my daughter. She feeds her cows pure hay and lavender, as the seasons allow. With memories of sunshine for spice." His eyes twinkled a bit. "You won't find such flavored milk elsewhere in the world, or such flavorsome cheese."

"Thank you, friend."

He tied the second bag to my saddle as I inspected the first, and then he took the first back to tie to Aleta's horse. "And fine apple cider." A grin brightened his face as he produced a bottle from under his shirt. I gestured for him to give it to Aleta, knowing that apples were all her thing. "Pressed from my own recipe. Green Clion apples and a local variety from my house garden. With gold blossoms and verbena. Sweeter than snow." Aleta took the bottle, briefly smiled, and shoved it in her sack. Then she looked at me as if to say, "Let's go."

I nodded to the old merchant and kicked my horse into a trot out of Helas and into the early sunset woods on the other side of the meadow. Aleta's horse mirrored mine until we found ourselves surrounded by those woods. We had crossed the unmarked border. We were free. Free of Cathe, and free, in our forest solitude, to be ourselves.

"Take the lead!" I shouted merrily. "Servant no more. You know the paths."

She acknowledged my words by bounding ahead. I followed closely for an hour or two as the sun descended and the sky thickened into darker shades of blue. We rode in familiar silence as dusk slowly readied the forest for night.

When night began to displace day, Aleta stopped and dismounted. I did the same, leading my horse after hers through darkening gaps among old trees, over a small rise, and down into a hollow that was invisible from the path. We let the horses drink from a shallow stream, tied them to a pair of oaks, and removed the sacks, working easily as if we had been traveling together for years and couldn't be anything but comfortable with each other. Even the stream was keeping comfort in its way, holding the last suggestion of daylight under the gray of the setting moon. I cupped my scarred palm in the cold water, touched day and night. Drank.

"This is certainly convenient lodging, Countess."

"This part of the forest is full of these dells. The trick was riding as far as possible before stopping at one that's well hidden."

"An excellent choice. Shall we feast then, milady? With these 'remainders from old Helas' and the joyful waxing moon for company?" I mock danced a little.

"I don't care for the moon. But I would break bread with you." It was just night now.

"Fire." I conjured a small fire for light and made a dramatic flourish for fun. Aleta smiled a little, which amused me, considering that when we knew each other years ago she had no use for magic. Even though I should have been energy depleted by long hours of riding, I wasn't. There was something so right about this journey, about riding with an old comrade, I felt like I was drawing energy from the circumstance, from the adventure. "Here, allow me." I conjured a cloth for Aleta to place the food on and a pair of clean blankets for the night.

"Thanks. I can see better now." The countess produced a bunch of multi-colored carrots, a good, thick loaf of dark bread, and a wrapped cheese so large she needed both hands to place it on the cloth. Then came the cider bottle and a bag containing dried fruit and several small cakes. "Wine for cider; hearts grow wider." Aleta sounded exuberant and relieved as she chanted the merchants' patter. She cut into the bread and cheese with her dagger and cheerfully tossed fistfuls of food onto my end of the cloth. "Feast."

"Delighted." We ate, laughed, sang snatches of market songs. And then, I teased her in the dark like the old friend I wanted her to be. "And so, Countess, why have you been selling wares and indulging in swordfights like a common brawler around the kingdom's marketplaces? Nothing to do at home?"

Aleta sighed and poked at the fire. "I'm protecting my home."

"From Helas?"

"From the whole bloody southwest."

"I can appreciate that."

"And you?"

I ignored her question because I had no idea how to answer it. "I heard you drew your sword on a southwestern gentleman awhile back."

"Possibly I did. I've drawn my sword on a lot of people. What else did you hear?"

"I heard about an apple merchant with a Clion accent, who took offense to this same gentleman remarking that he wanted her apples to honor the dead."

"You mean, 'To honor the former ruler of Gondal.'" She laughed a little as she slightly mocked Graen's voice and manner. "Yes, now I remember. Some Furnessian fop started trouble with the locals, some of the locals went at each other, and I drew out of necessity. Some took 'former ruler of Gondal' as a reference to you. People haven't forgotten your role at Walworth's trial, when your testimony saved Walworth but got their former duke executed for treason. Also, there are rumors that you instigated the destruction of the Helan border camp during Roguehan's invasion of Threle."

I felt a sudden grief when she mentioned the border camp. Aleta noticed my demeanor change. She tried to jolly me. "You live on in Helas! Villain, hero, and one-time foreign king!" Aleta mock saluted with me with the cider bottle, then she went serious. "Do you know him?"

It wasn't like Aleta to be deliberately ambiguous, but I felt briefly that "him" could either refer to the "Furnessian fop" who prompted the marketplace melee, or to me as villain, hero and one-time king. I replied as straight as I was able. "To a point. We were traveling together."

"Why was he attempting to honor you with my apples?" Aleta wasn't Threlan, but there was something of the old Threle in her tone, which implied that Graen's antics were more remarkable than the fact of my former kingship, which was merely a given.

"Actually, he wasn't. Milord Graen was a bit confused."

"Is that why you were traveling together?" She laughed like we were old friends now. Or again. Or simply forever, and this was one of our meeting points in time.

"Eh. He was thinking of someone else. I left the throne to a friend after I abdicated. She didn't keep it long."

"I'd heard some marketplace banter that you kinged it around for a few moments in Arula. But then a queen?" Aleta sounded interested. "*That* I hadn't heard."

"Nobody has. That was sort of her problem. Aeren was both Gondish and unconnected to anyone who mattered in Gondal. So she could have set the sky on fire and scorched the earth for rabbits' gold and everybody would pretend they didn't notice, and nobody would hear anything about her. Or something." I was surprised by how angry I sounded.

"But this Graen fellow noticed when she lost the throne? You did say he wanted to honor her as Gondal's former ruler?"

"He knew her after. Before she died."

"I see." Aleta paused. "I'm sorry for your loss." Somewhere at or beyond the edge of the sky a faint star glided and disappeared behind a cloud. "So what are you doing here, King?"

"Protecting the world, milady."

"Aren't we all?" She shifted a little. "In some ways I'm protecting Threle as well as Clio. You know I was spying for Walworth? I suppose in some ways I still am." *Why didn't I catch this in her mind?*

"Doesn't he have people around him who can do that? Why ask you to leave your duties?"

"Of course he has people. But he doesn't have anybody he can trust *and* who knows this region as well as I do. And he doesn't ask me to do anything. I occasionally take it upon myself." *That's probably why I missed it. She probably wasn't always thinking of it, or wasn't thinking of it in the cell when she was focused on my unexpected visit and her vow.* "We have an understanding. Threle would defend Clio if necessary, and so, of course, it's in Clio's interest to share intelligence with Threle."

"You trust Threle to fight for Clio? If necessary?"

Aleta hesitated. She didn't like the question. I could tell by the way she looked away and sighed that she'd asked it of herself before. "I trust Walworth. Don't you?"

I was silent. And not solely because of my own experiences with Threle's king. I intended to use Aleta's fighting skills against Walworth. Her vow, and the bond I created through clerisy, would make that possible. But it would be easier on both of us if I could cultivate distrust against her old ally. By refusing to answer her question, I hoped to increase her doubts.

"Our countries' friendship runs older than the elves; so does our trading history."

"So? Threle would trade with anybody. You think a few apples, glorious as they are, would buy Threlan fighters willing to die for Clio?"

It was hard for Aleta to answer me. That is why she hesitated so long that I had time to watch the night clouds loosening and spreading themselves across bands of stars. "We have no other allies. If Threle betrays our ancient friendship, Clio is lost anyway. Sometimes you have to trust to what you have." She said the last sentence a bit sharply. She was referring to our escape as well as to Walworth.

"The gods help you, then."

"Right now we share an interest in knowing which way Helas leans." She sounded all confident soldier now, up for anything required of her. "Which is actually all ways, depending on the hour and the weather."

"Well, that's what makes Helas Helas. So how long have you been spying for—I mean making the best of trusting Clio's future to—Walworth?"

"Since Threle ended the war. When I sense it's advantageous to gather intelligence, I don merchant's garb and sell apples in Helas— you can learn more about the state of the world by spending a day in a Helan marketplace than you can by meeting with a dozen foreign advisors and their agendas."

"Agreed."

"And then I share with Threle whatever might be useful."

"Sure." I intentionally sounded unconvinced to bolster her uncertainty. She didn't respond. "Are you tired?" I asked this as if I wanted to avoid an unnecessary conflict by changing the subject. Let her think I was too politic to converse further on my misgivings.

She nodded. I magically extinguished the fire. I knew that Aleta would think through the night about the doubts I had voiced. The problem was that I would, too.

It was midmorning before I decided to proceed with my strategy. I had read Aleta when I woke at dawn, and occasionally as we rode. Her thoughts were ever present, mindful of her surroundings, and calm with practiced clarity. They did not include Walworth, except once, when I sensed her reminding herself that her choice to share intelligence with him was her choice, not his, and that it was still the right thing to do for her county. She had no control over whether Walworth would prove himself a reliable ally in the future, but he had been one in the past, and she did have control over the way she played the game. She was making the best decisions for Clio. That clarity allowed her to quietly enjoy the simple beauty of fresh sunlight, shimmering leaves, occasional birdsong, and the steady traipse of her horse.

So I kept present as well. "Hey, Countess, my highest lady of Clio, ruler of the world's best apple trees—are you bored yet of your poor servant's garb?" I had already changed my robe to Hecate's, but Aleta had not remarked on it, treating it entirely as my business.

"I hadn't thought of it." She glanced at her shift. "Something clean and practical then?"

"You're asking me to shower you with magic?" We fell to the warmth of a mutual smile. A little. "Of course." I transformed her servant's clothes to suit her request. "Oh, and I promised you a proper sword when I had the energy. Catch." I conjured a sword in her palm.

"Wooo!" Aleta brandished her new weapon in fun and rode ahead.

"When we get to Clio I'll teach you to use a magic one," I called after her.

"I know!" she shouted back.

We raced each other. Laughing at our stolen horses, embracing the sun and sky, and bantering. At one point we shared a few multicolored carrots that had escaped being eaten on the previous night, tossing them back and forth in a silly contest whose rules we kept changing. At another, while we let our tired horses drink from a stream, Aleta found a Clion apple in the bottom of her sack and sliced it through the middle with her new sword, splitting the halves between us like a mark of friendship.

"Brother Llewelyn. King of Gondal. Comrade in arms." The Countess of Clio intoned these honorifics with a light formality that hung somewhere between seriousness and play. "In recognition of our daring escape from Helas, of the service you rendered to me, know that you may always claim the protection and gratitude of County Clio, and that Clio will always recognize you as one of her own."

"My lady." I knelt briefly, made a theatrical flourish that I might have sort of meant to signal loyalty, and stood. "Forever in your service." Aleta didn't laugh. She barely smiled. I knew from her suddenly sober demeanor that she was entirely serious now. I also knew from my mind probe that her granting me Clio's protection and recognition was the highest gift she was capable of granting anyone. I made another bow. This time gravely. And in complete sincerity.

Then we ate the apple halves and laughed again. At ourselves. At everything. "Well," said Aleta, "the ceremony *was* required." She rubbed her hands together to dry the apple's stickiness. "But now you are a citizen of Clio, even should you ever resume the Gondish throne, and so it's done."

Now was the time for my strategy. "Then as your most loyal *servant*, Countess, and your friend, I offer you my service again. Let me be your emissary to Threle."

"Why?"

"If you've doubts about Walworth, what to share with him, whether and under what circumstances he would defend Clio, I can be of assistance. Also, I'm fluent in his birth tongue."

"He's also fluent in ours."

"Yes, but I can navigate Mirand's defenses. Purely in the interest of truth, of course. I will know what Threle is thinking and so will you, all so that you can make the best decisions for your land."

"Done."

I reached into the saddle bag the old man had tied to my horse. "Let's see what the old fellow gave me—perhaps some fine bread and cheese—to consecrate our new alliance." My new sovereign watched me intently as I emptied my bag near the stream, on a sweep of stones that looked untouched by anything save sunlight. There was packing straw and dried flowers. I knew those flowers grew wild throughout Helas and no place else. The locals call them "the tears of the dead" and use them to decorate tombs. I wondered if the fellow was using them to comment on the state of his homeland.

Finally, there was a faded purple cloth wrapped loosely around an indeterminable object. When I unwrapped the cloth, we both went still for a moment with surprise.

There were three jagged pieces of a broken crown.

It was not a particularly beautiful piece of work. In fact, it was utterly workmanlike, pedantic, and of some kind of inferior metal alloy—possibly lead and clay. The breaks weren't clean, and some of the crown had crumbled into dust. When we put the pieces together, a single scroll of indented line was its only ornamentation. I thought it might be a toy or a stage prop, except that there was writing engraved along the inside. The alphabet looked foreign and then it looked vaguely familiar, and then I realized it resembled the three scrolls I carried in the language I couldn't read, the scrolls I had originally stolen from Zelar's workshop, beneath Aeren's dragon cave.

"The crown of the world." Aleta spoke slowly. She looked vaguely puzzled but mostly amused, like she was trying on a joke. Although it wasn't the sort of joke I had ever heard from her.

"Perhaps the poor world needs a better crown." I had no idea what to make of it.

"Or whoever wrote the inscription did."

"*What?*" I stared at Aleta, clutching the broken pieces in both hands. "You were *reading* that?"

"Of course. That's Clioan, County Clio's original language. Everyone spoke it before my great grandparents adopted Botha to make trade with the southwest easier."

Why was Zelar writing his scrolls in Clioan? "Didn't you tell me when we first met in Sunnashiven, years ago, that Clio has its own language that nobody speaks? So this is it?"

"Well, yes, but I speak it. If only to myself. My father insisted I learn it, although I never appreciated it until after he died." She took one of the pieces from me and studied it. "It is odd to see it on a broken crown in your saddle bag."

"Aleta, how many people in the world do you think can read and write Clioan?"

"At least one."

"Of course, but how many others?"

"Maybe a few dozen older people. Maybe more. It's practically a dead language and I haven't heard it since my father died. Nobody conducts business in it anymore, but occasionally somebody has old documents that need translating. Sometimes that's fallen to me."

"You interrupt your duties to translate old documents?"

"If there's a legal necessity concerning my duties, I'll do it. Nobody else can." She spoke matter-of-factly as she gave me back the piece of clay and dust she was holding. "Here, King, take your crown. It's an interesting gift, but the day is getting ahead of us, and we can discuss Clioan on horseback as easily as here."

I wrapped the broken crown, shoved it in my saddlebag, and mounted. Then I kept hard to my lady's side as we rode the hidden forest paths to Clio.

Somewhere in our riding, in the late afternoon when the birdsong returned, I asked Aleta if she'd ever seen anything in County Clio like the "world crown," as we now called it. She hadn't. And she didn't recognize its inscription as having any particular significance in Clioan. "If it does, I'm not aware of it. I've never heard of the 'crown of the world.'"

We considered how the old fellow came by it and why he tied it to my horse, but we arrived at nothing. "Well, he uses your apples in his cider, why not use your county's ancient language on his crown?" Aleta smiled a little at my joke.

The crown itself gave me nothing when I tried to read its energy as we rode. It was a dead thing—it had none, not even a trace of the old fellow, which was odd. Since he had recently handled the crown, possibly made it, I should have been able to sense him in it.

"We'll get to Clio late tomorrow. Perhaps somebody there can help us out." Once Aleta decided this, there was no use discussing it further, not even in jest. The countess would not waste time in useless speculation.

This gave me the rest of the afternoon to consider whether I should ask Aleta to look at the scrolls. If their contents were useless—maybe Zelar was just amusing himself by housekeeping in a dead language—then I gained nothing by showing them. But if there was anything of interest there—such as directions to a weapons cache, or notes on designing unique magical tools—I preferred not to share that with anyone, particularly someone who could repeat it to Walworth long after any kind of binding spell would fade. And what if Mirand read it in her mind?

As to that, I knew that Aleta's freely given vow to use any weapon of my choice in my service would be as unreadable to Mirand as all clerisy was. Even another evil cleric would— at best—be able to read her vow but not my intent. But I was reluctant to risk Mirand discovering through Aleta what secrets Zelar's scrolls held. If there was anything in the scrolls I could use to help fulfill Hecate's mandate, it was best if Mirand didn't know about it.

And yet by day's end I decided it was better to learn the content of the scrolls than to not learn the content of the scrolls. Mostly because, for all I knew, Mirand already knew about them. After all, he was Zelar's former student. And if he did know about them, it was poor strategy for me to remain ignorant. Also, it was obvious that Zelar wrote them in a language that damn few people could read because he didn't want anybody else reading them, and that alone made their contents worth knowing. But I couldn't guess why he troubled himself with learning Clioan. Most wizards would just create their own code.

Then I refused to trouble myself. I just rode easily with Aleta until we stopped for the night.

Fire, moon, and as much light as I could conjure. We had taken care of the horses, made our camp, and quietly dined on the last of our bread and cheese. Our quiet was weighted. Almost sad. Almost holy. We both knew that we had been sacred with each other, that we were passing between two worlds. Not simply Helas to Clio, or Threle to the present, but from the grace between them and into the drift of the world to come. Our ramble in the woods would soon die into the rest of our lives. We had been friends. Soon we would only be friendly. That's the way of the world.

Aleta spoke. "We're close to Clio now, no more than another day's ride."

"It's been a fine adventure." I took the scrolls out of my cloak and tossed them in Aleta's lap as casually as if they were the multicolored carrots we'd tossed around earlier. "I found these in my travels. Can you read them?"

Aleta glanced over the first scroll and looked bewildered. "I suppose I could. They're definitely written in Clioan. But . . . " She laughed silently. "They're nonsense."

"I've had long acquaintance with nonsense."

"No doubt." Her smile faded a little as she focused on the scroll.

I sat next to her to better follow her reading. "An unvarnished literal translation would satisfy my curiosity, if you are so inclined."

She laughed again. "A literal translation to Botha would also be nonsense, but no worse than this." She placed her finger at the top of the scroll to underscore her reading. "Seven maybe squirrel she will have been they carry there is inside light for not a name."

"Thanks." I stopped her. "Literal is useless. I concede."

Aleta laughed. "Where did you find these?"

As I thought about how to answer, I remembered the scrolls that Aeren threw at me in Anda, the ones she said were Botha translations from elvish that Beotun had been working on. Something in the gibberish that Aleta just read made me think of them. I took one out of my cloak.

"I don't remember where I found this, but I kept it out of curiosity." I gave it to Aleta. "Does this look like a translation from Clioan to you?"

"Yes. I know this one. My father had me translate this same history, word for word. It's a common exercise for somebody learning Clioan. It's an ancient account of the Battle of Glecion."

"Is it a good translation?" I had no idea what to say, or why Beotun and Zelar had been troubling themselves with a demanding language like Clioan. It couldn't be a coincidence, Clioan was too obscure. Perhaps Mirand found it useful, given Threle's relationship with Clio? Beotun was Mirand's student, but Mirand had broken with Zelar years ago, long before Aeren killed him. And I couldn't parse why Mirand would bother learning such an unwieldly language when there are so many more effective and efficient ways to communicate secretly, if that was his purpose.

"There are no good translations from Clioan, if that's what you mean. It's accurate."

"I've got more." I gave Aleta the rest of Beotun's scrolls. "I thought these might be in elvish, but they look like Clioan."

"Yes, that's the battle text the translation is from."

I returned to Zelar's scroll, the one Aleta had read from. "What's the sense of it, if any, in Botha?"

"Something like—and this is really loose, somebody else might translate differently, but— 'One girl will have been bringing a nameless light.' Possibly 'nameless light' refers to a 'blank candle.' That's an idiom for an unlit candle or a dark fireplace or pretty much anything that could provide light but isn't doing so right now. It can even refer to a cloudy sky. So maybe . . . 'One girl will have been bringing an inside blank (unlit) candle.' 'Inside' could mean 'hidden' but that doesn't clarify anything."

"What about the seven squirrels?"

"It's more like a group of seven squirrel-like animals, or an indication that they are squirrels but their number is around seven. They are associated with the girl, the 'she.' So possibly, 'One girl will have been bringing an unlit candle to hide from the seven creatures that resemble squirrels.' Or, 'A group of maybe seven squirrels and one girl will have been bringing a hidden unlit candle.'" She looked up. "Old accounting records are easier. I give up."

"Please don't. I'm interested. And impressed." I never thought Aleta had the patience to learn a difficult dead language, and I was as fascinated with her ability to translate as I was with Clioan, not least because it was so unlike her. "Go on."

"Loose, then, into Botha. 'They will have been bringing the unlit candle to the moon for weeks, hoping to kiss the moon with dark or the candle with light. One day, after running as an enemy to the sky . . .' maybe 'against the sky'?"

"You tell me."

She did. She translated for several minutes through Zelar's scrolls before I began to understand that what she was reading was a bard's tale meant to amuse and another minute before I began to "hear" in Aleta's halting translation that the tale sounded very much like the sort of story Aeren used to tell. Why Zelar would have translated her stories from Sarana to Clioan was beyond me, but if I was indeed hearing in Botha a translation of a translation, I understood why it took me so long to recognize the tale as (most likely) Aeren's, and why Aleta's reading sounded particularly muddled. Sarana is a language that is so rich with poetry that it doesn't always translate well, which is why my Botha translations of Aeren's performance at Furna's feast failed so spectacularly. And Sarana to Clioan to Botha was even more difficult to follow.

Aleta paused again to puzzle a phrase that could have several nonsensical meanings, including "pumpkins smile at sad sunflowers" and "pumpkins and sunflowers smile over sadness."

"Thank you. Enough. You've become a surprisingly good scholar." I meant this. Clioan appeared to be a damnedly difficult language, and Aleta clearly put a lot of work into learning it.

"I'm not a scholar. I've just become a better warrior."

"Was that your father's influence?" I asked to give her something to talk about besides her necessarily awkward translation.

"No. Walworth's."

I didn't respond. I remembered how much Aleta had admired Walworth when I'd known her in Threle, how she aspired to be the sort of fighter he was, and how much Walworth valued the education he received from Mirand. "Well. You've become like him."

"Perhaps. Although I prefer to think I've become more like my-self."

"Eh. That's everyone's tragedy." I meant this as a joke, and Aleta did laugh in appreciation.

Later, I sat through the night by the "blank candle" of the extinguished fire. I tried to understand why Zelar had been translating Aeren's tales into Clioan, why an ambitious wizard like Beotun apparently had nothing better to do on his assassination mission than to learn Clioan, and why the old fellow gave me the "crown of the world" in Clioan. Letters from a dead language. Poems I can't read.

I had no answers. I had only the burden of my mandate, a broken crown, and the oncoming rush of the jagged world.

Twelve

Entering County Clio was like re-entering the world. Only more honest.

Orchards upon orchards. Sun. Apples running with colors like they just got drenched in your happiest dreams. The colors made me remember those dreams, which involved magic and friendship and a brilliant future in Threle. All of which made me remember who I was before Walworth's betrayal wrenched me into somebody else. Seeing those orchards, I understood why Graen wanted to honor Aeren with Clion apples when he caused that disturbance in Hala. When I pressed Graen about his odd attachment to Aeren, he had confided that she "made me see myself as I truly am." Aleta's land had a way of doing the same.

"To see Clion apples in all their glory is to know yourself," said Aleta, smiling as if she somehow knew my thoughts. Here and there an apple tree bent before the breeze, catching the sun out of the moment like it was catching Aleta's smile. The countess clearly embodied her homeland, which wasn't surprising. But something in Aleta's homeland embodied the world as the world was meant to be. Almost as if Threle's illicit victory hadn't happened.

And everything framed the sturdy cheerfulness of Aleta's people. Shopkeepers, farmers, artisans, soldiers—all of them moving and laughing and greeting each other with the quiet pleasure that purpose and native familiarity make possible. There were no strangers.

Clio was like a comfortable, close-knit household that somehow grew into a country. But a country that insisted on wearing the clothes it came with, a country that never outgrew its history. I knew from maps that Clio was roughly the combined size of Helas and Kant, but it felt smaller because wherever we rode, there was a sense that everybody either knew everybody else or knew people who knew everybody else. Therefore candor was not merely necessary. It wasn't even optional. It just was, like the cows and sheep and glistening corn and well-kept cottages and bright open gardens. Helas, and Threle generally, took pride in their traditions of free trade and free speech. Clio wasn't self-conscious enough to take pride in anything. It was too busy being itself.

"Countess. I'm proud to be a citizen of your fair county."

Aleta barely reacted. She was home now. My words were superfluous.

Sometimes people would wave and shout at Aleta like they were hailing a close friend that they only met occasionally and therefore were all the more excited to see. And then she would break her silence, grin, lean slightly forward on her weather-beaten mare, and hail them back as if she were riding Apollo's favorite sun horse straight from somewhere beyond the upper air. But there was no pretense here, simply a natural affection for her people that the countess wore like her apples wore sunlight.

"Season's strong, milady!"

"So are we," she'd call back to enthusiastic shouts.

Nobody remarked on her plain garb. And nobody appeared to care that my clerical robes marked me as evil. Aleta's border guards bantered easily with both of us as we rode through, trading well wishes. But the openhearted welcome I'd often found in Threle was absent. In its place was an endearing lack of curiosity that felt like a choked compliment. If Aleta was riding with me, then the people of Clio were too. It was that straightforward. It was also that qualified.

We rode slowly through evening countryside, tired now from traveling, and within sight of Aleta's castle. It sloped against the pitch of the next hill, its rocks glowing violet in the sunset's remains. We watched it fade until its towers became black shapes against the stars. Light wind. Night garden scents. Somewhere beyond the sound of our horses' hooves a rabbit chased a fragment of moon across a field. Tired though I was, I could feel the moon pulling me too with Hecate's breath.

The castle felt like it was part cottage, part ancient fortress, and entirely like the home of a close friend. We passed through intimate cook areas where servants were gathered near wide hearths. They shared bread and bowls of stew while chatting about the day's work. We trod narrow steps into a tower room where two guards nodded at the countess and continued perusing a map and discussing the day's watch. Aleta's castle reflected her personality: her love of home and her skill with war and how necessary one was to the other.

Aleta bid me good night and left me in a room that contained a neat hearth, sensible furnishings, and nothing else. *My lodgings are like the rest of Clio*, I thought. *There is nothing more nor less than needs to be here.* I sat on the firm bed. Too tired to move, I kept noticing the tight, symmetrical patterns of stonework that formed the hearth. I admired the clarity that informed everything in Aleta's domain, how her county was a kind of Truthfinder. Her people, her castle, and her land were entirely as the gods meant them to be. Here, the worst transgression was pretense. Perhaps it was the only one.

And then, as my thoughts faded into sleep, something close to perfect happened.

The rabbit returned. That is, the rabbit was still chasing the moon, and I found myself outside in the muted light watching the path that the rabbit made. Tall grass bent and waved with her passing. And I easily followed her path, or the moon, until the unsettled field folded into woods. And then there were old oaks and darker moonlight where the unseen rabbit ran.

I found myself standing in a bare circle formed by dead stumps and living woods. Out of the darkness, the fairy rabbit returned. She stood on a stump, punched at the air, and leaped into the arms of a shadow at the circle's edge whom I suddenly knew as Isulde. And then the rabbit was a moonbeam. And then she wasn't there.

"My poor pet's gone to light." Isulde entered the circle and pressed her palms against mine. "She only comes with the moon." Isulde lightly touched my moon charm. "Did you know you became a fairy prince while you chased her?"

"No. And what am I now?"

"You are yourself again. Complete." Isulde glanced outside the circle, where I heard heavy crackling, like somebody was out there trampling on twigs and leaves who didn't care whether or not anyone else heard. I followed her glance, but when I looked back, Isulde wasn't there either. There was only wind and night and a sense in my pulse that she had pulled me here only to pull this dream back to wherever it came from. I was alone with the world. If Isulde's visit had a point, it was this, although the point wasn't new and I had no idea what to do with it.

While I stood there deciding how best to find my way back to the castle, the crackling stopped and I got the sense of being watched, by the wood walker or the moon I couldn't tell. Then a blur of fury, like a recluse wounded by some unspeakable violation of his solitude, bolted out of the woods. The blur crossed the circle. The blur kicked me in the shin. And then it shouted a rage-filled greeting in perfect

Sarana. "That's for you." It took the time it takes to shift to one foot, grasp my injured leg, briefly hold off balance, and fall to realize that my attacker was Aeren. She kept ranting. "You're never around when it matters and now we meet in the dark of the gods-know-where?"

I felt far more surprise than pain as I tried to stand up and failed. "Do that again, buddy."

Aeren dropped to the ground so we were both at the same level, sitting in the dirt. "Why bother?"

"Well, one, because you're supposed to be dead."

"I am? And here I thought I'm never supposed to be anything."

"And two, because . . ." I stopped. This wasn't the first time Aeren had successfully injured me, however trivially, while I wore Hecate's moon. Its power had destroyed Graen's sword arm when he attacked me, but Aeren was unscathed. I needed to think about this, and about why Isulde had arranged this meeting, this circle cast by nature. "Never mind." I grabbed my leg, pretending to be distracted by pain so I could think. But I couldn't come up with anything convincing. "This is becoming a theme, the dead returning to keep me company. You. Stormr—" I decided it wasn't worth mentioning Cathe or adding Threle to the list, even as an unfinished metaphor.

"Yourself. Scorched if I know about your theme or why you're here." Aeren paused. Her anger now felt self-directed. Which was interesting. "You mean I *missed* Stormr?"

Something began to make sense. Not everything, and not a lot of sense, but more sense than previously. "You hit Zyren." Aeren wasn't mollified. She didn't care for half-measures. "But Stormr managed to imitate my shield and protect himself against your blast."

She looked like she wanted to blast him again. "Oh. So naturally you kept traveling with him?"

I took her question as a reproach for falling on the wrong side of her apparent dispute with Stormr, but her meaning wasn't that clear. What was clear was her ability to injure me without consequences, as if she was invisible to my moon. So I answered carefully. "Uh . . . not exactly. Aeren, I know you have a right to hate all of us, especially me, for giving you a lie."

"I hate whom I choose. It's easier that way." She suddenly looked confused. "What lie?" She waited for a response. I wasn't eager to provide one. "You mean when you lied about Beotun sending you a message to meet at Relyr's? Or when you lied about your wizard shields blocking each other despite apprenticing with the same wizard?"

I nodded. It seemed safest.

"And so we meet under new moon and nothing." She chanted this Sarana idiom in a tone of high frustration to show her annoyance at not understanding me. "You know what? I no longer care for your past intrigues with Threle." She didn't care for my lack of reaction, either, so she added sharply, "It takes energy to care. Maybe I no longer care because I lack discipline."

"I would never accuse you of that."

"So what if Threle was supporting your return to the Gondish throne without so much as a glance in my direction and then Helas tried to kill you? I expect as much from Threle. You didn't have to gild the story by lying about Beotun, but that's nothing to me now. I stopped thinking about your ridiculous lies about secret messages and wizard shields a long time ago, when King Furna made me his bard." She paused and rubbed her face as if she were cleaning off invisible shreds of old dragon scales, or rubbing moonlight into her skin. When she resumed speaking, her face was flushed and her tone stung. "And I'm still King Furna's bard." She looked away. That is how I knew she had just said something difficult.

"Aeren," I said sadly. "As far as I know, you are. But you killed his chief wizard and would have killed his chief priest. Your status now might be . . . somewhat unclear."

"They would have killed you." Her voice remained low and steady. "You know what? I risked my standing as King Furna's bard—as everything I ever wanted—to protect you." I was too astounded to speak. "I saw Stormr try to blast you."

I was no longer astounded. I was somewhere beyond astounded.

Aeren kept waiting for me to speak, to acknowledge what she had risked to protect me. But I had no words for that; only a poverty of silence. A silence that felt like a desecration to break.

When I did speak again, the words I had were hopelessly pointless. "So. Take me to the beginning, buddy."

"I just did."

"*I mean, what caused you to turn dragon?*" I wasn't exactly shouting at her, but I was shouting at something. Or shouting out of something in myself. Possibly out of the memories the orchards gave me.

Aeren hardened her face, at once mystified and taken aback by my sudden fervency. Then she just looked so uncomfortable and sad that I was immediately sorry at my unintentionally harsh tone. I forced myself to soften my voice into something more respectful. "I mean, I don't know what happened. I won't pry, I won't transgress into reading your thoughts." I was sincere about this, but only momentarily; I wasn't sure how long my sincerity would last.

"That's generous of you. Much obliged. So happy I can keep my thoughts private by telling you my story. What a gull's choice you give me. Broken fish or cracked beach."

"Aeren. Tell me whatever you want." I sounded dismissive without meaning to.

"I always do." Aeren sounded even more dismissive, but somehow that made me laugh, and that, unexpectedly, made her laugh.

"I consider you one of my last friends, possibly in my lifetime, and I'd really like to know what happened, *if* you decide to tell me. I called you once in Helas but you didn't respond. I thought you were dead. Did you hear me?"

"Yes. For several days."

"So why didn't you answer?"

"I wasn't ready."

Now I felt angry, and it was purely at her. "Why not? We all needed you."

"I was busy."

"Busy with *what*?"

"Busy with not feeling like responding." This was so like Aeren I had to laugh again, despite my irritation. "And I was still mostly dragon, at least in my heart, and quite far away when you called. I could barely hear you, and only when everything else was quiet. By the time I thought I *might* try to respond, your call stopped."

"Where the hell were you?"

She spoke like she was rebuking me. "Furnesse. That's where my dragon form flew. Where else does one go to touch the end of the world?"

"Inside one's heart?" I have no idea why I said this.

"Depends on what's in one's heart." She wasn't sure what to say next, so she paused and continued. "Where to begin? I went human. I asked to see King Furna. He invited me to tea. You know what he did when I told him what happened? He laughed so hard he broke the damn teapot and got sticky strawberry tea all over his hands and clothes. He never liked Zyren, and he had learned that Stormr was secretly working . . . wait for it . . . for your old friends in Threle. So I rid him of a problem, only to learn now that I actually didn't, because Stormr is still out there."

"Sure, but I'd like to know more about your meeting with Furna."

"My meeting with Furna, the King of Disguises. He was pretending to be an old woman, and a witch, and we agreed our simple tea was a magic brew. I was garbed as a young man. It was . . . comfortable. He appeared to forget himself as overking and so did I. I thought that if I believed in the gods, that meeting Zeus-All-Giver might be like this, a powerful overking disguised as one of an endless number of manifestations. Today an old witch-woman spilling tea on herself, tomorrow a dead cat. And then I suddenly felt sad—like the sadness I often get moments before I get the thought that the sadness is attached to." She stopped, waiting for me to say something. "Does that ever happen to you?"

"I don't know. I suppose it could."

She looked frustrated with my response. "Do you want to know why I felt sad?"

"Sure." I knew it was the only right answer, but Aeren appeared to be expecting me to say more.

"I thought, drinking tea with the overking, laughing with his assumed persona, that making tales should be like that. One day a witch-woman, one day a dead cat dreaming, one day a warrior betraying his comrades, and on that same day the force that motivated the warrior's betrayal and knowing how that force is a character too. Or a dying farmer's mixed feelings about an abundant harvest that fed his children while consuming his life. Or that damned proverbial broken fish. Or even the blessed overking himself. No limits. But for me it's like spilling tea on myself. I can imagine being those things—that's the tea—but I also know how self-important and pretentious that is. That's the tea spilling into a sticky mess. How easy to crush that way of being with reality—and how few bards can get away with it, even in secret."

"Did you say any of this to Furna?"

"I told his witch-woman character. Is that the same as telling him?"

I shrugged. "You tell me. So what did Furna say?"

"Something simple and beautiful. 'Pretend you're a bard.' And then he added, 'You have the overking's permission. I'll draw you a charter for a stage prop if you need one.' So here. He put in his charter" —she took out a small patch of paper— "that I am his royal bard and might imagine myself as I like. He then said I always was, but this was for me."

I read the charter—which was written in Botha and Sarana. I mostly felt relief. "Congratulations. Did he then spill tea on you?"

"He used the tea. He anointed my head with it. It was playful and serious. The way I imagine Zeus would be."

"So why are you here?"

She continued sadly and resentfully, although her resentment wasn't directed at me so much as at something out there that I didn't know about and couldn't guess. "Why weren't *you* there when I needed you?"

"I don't understand, Aeren. Needed me for what?"

"To tell people the scorch-be-damned truth. To put Zyren in his place."

"Uh . . . I thought you did that."

"You speak Botha, I don't. You're a wizard, I've barely got a bond."

"I still don't understand."

"Do you understand why I kicked you?"

"No. But I'm sure you have your reasons."

Aeren stared her anger into my heart. Then she finally spoke. "All right. Here's what happened. After you went heel nipping after Stormr the Cheerful, Lord Graen Whatever-His Job-Was asked me through Zyren what it was that I intended to do in Threle. Not that Zyren's Sarana was worth a goat's trick, but it was semi-passable when he thought it worth his effort to make it so. When I mentioned my mandate to be King Furna's bard, going to Threle to perform in Furna's honor, Zyren translated Graen's response as something like, 'You? A king's bard?'

"I had no idea if Graen actually said this, or said something like this, but Zyren was clearly enjoying the opportunity to dig at my heart. Graen did look surprised, which hurt, because I had to assume from his expression that nobody ever told him why we were going to Threle, and that made no sense to me.

"So I asked Zyren how it came that Graen didn't know. And Zyren said, in rather stilted, broken Sarana, I might add, that Graen didn't know much and that it wasn't clear why Graen was even here or why anyone was even here. And then he added, 'I thought you were here because nobody liked your stories in Gondal and you couldn't keep a throne. That's what I hear, maybe you've heard differently.' That hurt so much—it mirrored all the sarcasm I got in Gondal after I lost the throne and nobody believed I had saved Gondal in my dragon form. I went weeping away into the woods so nobody would see me. I wanted to find you. *I wanted you to set them straight with the truth!*" She shrieked these last words like a battle cry.

"And that's why you turned dragon?"

"In short, yes."

I couldn't even begin to parse this one out. "Tell me in long." I could understand the transformation happening in response to Roguehan's attack on Arula, but not in response to Zyren slapping her feelings. Then it dawned on me that maybe the two were equivalent, that an attack on Aeren's feelings, or rather, an attack on her sense of self, was an attack on Gondal, and that she did embody the land. I wondered if that meant that I didn't and how that affected my ability to fulfill Hecate's mandate.

Furna wanted me to execute Walworth with the Wand of Surprises and, in doing so, destroy Threle. According to Furna, if I was the "embodiment of the unyielding empty Gondish wasteland" I could "send Threle's stolen victory back to the cosmic wasteland of nonexistence." But if Aeren was Gondal and I wasn't, I needed to strategize how to train her to perform that execution, and how best to use her abilities along with Aleta's.

Aeren noticed that I had gone distracted with my thoughts. "Are you even listening to me?"

"Yes, yes. My queen, my bard—Furna's bard. Please go on."

"I felt profoundly ashamed that I had put on a charming bardic personality for Graen."

"So? I thought you had a charming bardic personality. When you choose to let it loose."

"I could only 'let it loose' because I believed I was Furna's bard. But Graen didn't even know I was a bard."

"That was enough to make you turn dragon?"

"The embarrassment of playing the bard for Graen was, of acting like I was some kind of court poet when he, a well-placed creature of that same court, had no idea of it. I told you the day we met Graen and his pompous peers that I could only be myself with them because Furna gave me that power. Without that power, that frame, I felt like a fraud. So I needed you to tell them the truth. To tell them *my* truth. But you were occupied with my lord high priest, the leading light of dour."

I remembered how Graen said that Aeren was weeping and sad when she left. It was Zyren that characterized her as showing "high displeasure."

It occurred to me that this was another indignity Aeren had suffered her entire life. Her real pain was the embarrassment of taking the risk of being herself, a self that was likely to get rejected without a platform that made her true self acceptable in other people's eyes. But she was barely "dead" before Zyren started to rewrite the story, tried to convince me and Stormr that poor Aeren had stalked off in anger and entitlement because her bardic abilities were unrecognized, that she was ripe with resentment and had too high an opinion of her own merits.

If Zyren's lies weren't the equivalent of murdering an unarmed person, they were close. I suddenly felt sorry that he was dead. I wanted to kill him.

"It felt awful, like I was, in Graen's eyes anyway, claiming a status I didn't have, like I had unwittingly become something I despise. Turning dragon was nothing to it."

"I understand."

"After everything I went through in Gondal, to add to the list, 'arrogant enough to act like she's a great creative bard' was intolerable. I needed you to explain—to Zyren, to everybody—why I was in the party. I was crying horribly."

"So I heard. That's what Graen told me."

She nodded. "So then I went dragon, or 'dragon' became me. I was hurt that badly. Because here I was, Furna's royal bard, and I couldn't get any more recognition than when I was Gondal's queen. And that's when I saw Stormr blast you. I don't think he saw me. I had wrapped my serpentine body around the oak trees like their roots were a treasure to be guarded. Their leaves cried to me in my dragon form, like a fall of rain against my dragon tears. I couldn't turn back into myself— my emotions were too strong, but I could watch you through the curtain of leaves. I willed you to see me but it didn't work. And then I willed anybody to see me through the dragon, but that didn't work either. And then, as far as I could tell from my distance, Stormr threw himself on you. And then there was a blast, I felt the ground tear up, so I assume it was him."

So Stormr, high priest of Habundia-Ceres, devotee of good, tried to blast me from inside my shield. Which makes sense, given that he was secretly working for Threle. And when my moon protected me, he learned that he couldn't hurt me. Damn! Stormr was the source of the first blast.

"All I saw was your body on the ground. What do I know? I thought Stormr had tried to kill you. At first I thought he had killed you, so I . . . slithered . . . onto the ground, still weeping. Then I saw you somehow survived, but you were arguing with Stormr and Zyren. I couldn't hear the argument. Then they walked away from you, and I blasted them and flew away to be alone. Because at that point I needed to be alone."

"Lord Graen told me he saw a dragon in the sky, dancing, although of course he didn't know the dragon was you."

"I might have been dancing. I might have been thinking." She paused. "I blasted him and Zyren when they were talking because Zyren lied and Stormr killed, or tried to kill. I knew your shield would protect you. But apparently Stormr stole your shield and lived. I don't know why Stormr tried to kill you. I don't know why he failed. I now know why I failed."

"But you saw me talking to both of them after Stormr's blast."

"Yes, but that doesn't mean you knew what you were doing."

I didn't respond. Then I felt so overwhelmed that I had to speak. "You sacrificed your status as Furna's bard to save me? And yet when we met in Gondal, you said you tried to kill me."

"That was in Gondal."

"Of course. That explains everything."

Aeren ignored my sarcasm. "I knew you had helped me with Furna. I also knew Stormr and Zyren hated both of us."

"How did you know that?"

"My powers of bardic observation." She continued to ignore my sarcasm by speaking without a hint of irony, which made me wonder if she was serious. "Sometimes I see more than wizards and clerics do, just by showing up. I didn't take Zyren's hatred personally at first, you can read in his face he had grown to hate everyone. That's fine, I can respect that. It's when he mocked me and pretended I wasn't a bard that I did take it personally because there's no other way to read that. But I didn't kill him until I saw him conspiring with Stormr. And I didn't attempt to kill Stormr until he tried to kill you. Without you my new position was clearly in danger."

"I see."

Aeren waited. "It wasn't selfish. I just felt that even though I have wanted kill you myself, whatever Stormr was doing wasn't justified."

"I see."

"And here's the best part. You wouldn't notice this, being a cleric and a wizard and everything, but when Stormr tried to kill you, I felt for the moment of the blast that he was also trying to kill me. Like in that moment we drew energy from the same source."

"We have a wizard bond."

"Not that. I knew . . . something else."

Well, that explains why Aeren can hurt me without consequences. Aeren did embody Gondal. I was right. An attack on her sense of self caused her to turn dragon just as an attack on Arula did. She sensed our energy came from the same source. When Isulde read my moon, she said, "You can only hurt yourself. Until you make the world go right." So Aeren, as my other self, could hurt me—with impunity.

"Aeren. That 'something else' is Gondal. We are both of us, together, its rightful ruler. Not one or the other but both. Together we are Gondal—together we are Gondal's monarch."

"So? I figured that out a long time ago. We still can't get past the Assembly."

"Why didn't you say anything? About us both being Gondal?"

She shrugged. "Because it sounds pretentious to say it after losing the throne, like I'm claiming a status I don't have. And because I thought you knew."

"So why didn't you make yourself known until now?"

"Because I stayed dragon for weeks. I don't know where I flew. Possibly Threle. Then Furnesse. Then the strawberry tea. Now I'm here—someplace else. I had a dream you were here, but it appears it wasn't entirely dream." She waited, obviously wanting to speak again but obviously unsure how to do so.

This was so unlike Aeren that I would wait hours if necessary for her to speak in her own time. I waited minutes.

"After the tea, after 'Zeus All-Giver' or the old witch-woman anointed me, Furna became himself. He half-teased and half-warned me, 'Careful, bard, when you follow the fairies, don't lose them again.' Something in the way he said this made me tear up. Then .. . that night, the next night, I don't know . . . there was a fairy. She led me here through a dream. Or maybe she was a dream. Sometimes I was a rabbit, like the face of the moon. Sometimes not, or maybe just the moonlight. The dream was something like that dark light passage I thought I might have conjured but probably didn't. I think the fairy was involved with that too." She stopped. "That's all I have."

Yes. And didn't Isulde sing in the hours, day and night, rushing and crashing as Roguehan approached Walworth's duchy the last time the world ended? She made that dark light passage, not the elves. She wanted us in Furnesse and now here.

"Surely there's more." I conjured a gold piece and dropped it in her hand. "Here, royal bard, I'll pay for the entire tale. Dream, fairy, rabbit—all of it. You've got me."

Aeren smiled and pocketed the coin. "All right. The entire tale. Just for you." She studied me the way old trees sometimes seem to study passing strangers. Then she spoke.

"Here, in this dry woodland circle, was a pond. And a fairy. The fairy said she once loved a pond and that her love for it still made her cry. So she gathered her tears in a raincloud to make this one. This pond loved the moon but the moon barely glanced at it. And so the pond exhausted itself to catch what moonlight it could.

"This poor fairy pond was weak. It caught little. Just enough pale moonlight to hurt. And then the fog would laugh at it. The cruel fog would mock the poor pond every morning, telling it, 'You missed. You know a captured moon never throws a circle large enough to bathe in. Go dry.' And then the ugly fog would burn away to please the sun.

"Anyway, this is what the fairy told me before she pulled me through the shimmer of the moon's reflection, into the dirty water. There was nothing clean here. Except the moon. The moon was clean but the fairy hid it. Putrid water held me under until my feet went bare and cold and simple like the dead. They churned ooze from the bottom. Ooze thickened the water. Dead things rose and nested in my hair. I was afraid to touch them, to untangle the horrors from my face and clothes, but the pond was all muck now and so it wouldn't wash them out. Then my body prickled like rotting water weeds as I drowned in the filth I could feel myself becoming. I still wanted the moon—for I was the pond now—but the fairy kept hiding it, like something you want to catch in a dream but the dream itself sends you elsewhere." She paused again. "Do you believe me?"

"Why not?"

Aeren looked like she thought I was teasing, but she continued her tale. "Then the fairy pulled me out or the pond went dry. Mostly some of both. Here, this circle, was a pond. Here, the moon did cleanse me, as if I bathed in her light like witches do. Here, the fairy gave me a gift. It's only a shimmer of a gift, but it *is* from the fairies. The way broken promises that bring unlooked for grace sometimes are."

Aeren waited for me to say something. I waited with her to find something to say. "So tell me of your gift. I paid for your tale."

"No, you gave me a conjured coin you didn't earn. But here's my gift. I can turn dragon now at will, or young man. Or both at once. But not like an illusionist can. It's softer and more mysterious than that. In the gift, I physically appear to others in my plain form. But if I choose, I can make a kind of dream in the air gather itself around me. So people feel the dragon around me and fear, or sense me as a young man and feel confused, even if I'm not in male garb."

"That was true before you went adventuring with the fairies."

"For you, perhaps. But now others can sense me as an animal or a star or a broken twig or a lost friendship or a mug of sticky strawberry tea. Or even King Furna himself. But it only works if I put it in a tale first. I mean, the dragon and the young man are always there, tale or no, I can make them happen, but the rest I have to create in words before I manifest their energy."

"Why is that?" I knew nothing of how bardic magic works, but I was fascinated.

"Because I'm not actually any of them, but once I imagine them, all of them are me. To use as I please. Also, I only get three a day. Fairies like threes." Aeren sounded almost jaunty; she was trying to make light of something she actually felt uncertain about. "The end."

I wasn't ready for her to end her tale. I also wasn't sure whether her tale had actually ended. "I don't know where we are in the night. Can you use one of your daily three now? I mean, you just told a tale about a pond, so . . . show me yourself as a pond."

"Not *a* pond—but this pond."

And then she did it. Nothing about Aeren changed. Except something around her suggested a scent of watery stagnation, although the air held only the scent of night woods. And her clothes were suddenly dank and fetid and sticking to her moist skin. Which kept making me think about a dead pond with dead things in it. Then it stopped.

And when it stopped, I felt like I'd just been jerked out of an intense imaginative experience and needed to adjust to reality.

"It's all right, bard. I believe you."

"Thank you."

"Here." I took the Ring of Beauty out of my cloak. "I also *believe* this is yours." I dropped it on her palm. It lay there plain as the waning moon that marked my own. "I managed to get hold of it after you went dragon." I saw no reason to mention pinching it from Graen.

Aeren shrugged and smiled. Then she shoved it in her cloak.

"Use it well, bard. Make the fairies proud."

Thirteen

We didn't do anything with the rest of the night. Maybe slept, maybe not. Aeren didn't bother to ask me where we were, which was just as well as I had no idea. We'd both been fairy-led here through a dream. That meant we could be anywhere, including Gondal.

When she did speak again, it was past dawn and something in the light felt old and difficult. Or perhaps I did. I had dug my hands in the dirt and leaves, trying to sense the ancient pond from Aeren's tale, trying to determine where Isulde had led us, and failing.

"I like this." Aeren cheerfully interrupted my clumsy attempt to know this place. "I like being out in the world. Tell me your stories, Wizard. Tell me about fairies and rabbits and how a dream can lead someplace real. I want to know everything. Like Zeus."

I didn't know what to say.

So I briefly told Aeren the facts of her new situation. That we might be in County Clio, that everyone spoke Botha and that few, if any, spoke Sarana. That I was friends with the countess and that I was sure she would welcome Aeren when we found our way back. "Also, I'm the countess's new envoy to Threle."

Aeren's playful demeanor dried. She glanced at the indentations my hands just made in the ground, and then at me. When she spoke again, she managed to sound inquisitive without admitting to curiosity. "Do you think the fairy led us to Threle?"

"I doubt it. I mean, I don't know. Maybe, but nothing here feels like Threle."

"Then you *do* think we're in County Clio?" She still sounded distant but also vaguely excited. "Does King Furna know?"

"Only if somebody tells him." I stood and surveyed the woodland around us. It was trackless. Even the sun gave nothing but random spaces between silent trees. "I don't know, buddy. Have you made any tales lately that involved calling fairies and asking for directions?"

"No. But I can offer them strawberry tea, since I spoke of tea in my tale. Although that would be my second transformation of the day, by my count." Then, before I could respond, Aeren stretched her arms in a mock wizard stance, swayed on one foot, and playfully chanted, "Pond into tea. Pond into tea. Dark into light and all things gray come above me. I am tea. For the fairies."

She did succeed in making me imagine a generous mess of spilled tea, ripe with the scent of old strawberries and spring mornings, staining up her hair and clothes. But it quickly faded into the woods around us.

"I was joking, Aeren. Fairies come when they come."

"So was I. Is there a better strategy for getting out of the woods?"

I wasn't used to this new, playful Aeren. I left the circle and looked around again, hoping to find something resembling a path.

This time, after the trees closed off all sight of Aeren, I heard light scratching in the brush, of the sort a large rabbit or a clumsy ground bird might make. Then I noticed furtive movement deep in the tree shadows, like an animal had scented the bardic strawberries and gotten itself confused when the promise of food suddenly disappeared. I kept listening for more movement, unable to see the movement's source. But I heard nothing, so I went into a light trance, trying again to know this place, to know where we needed to go.

The next thing I knew, there was a sharp pain in my shin where Aeren had kicked me, and I was roughly out of trance and on the ground with pain and surprise. Then more sounds of something scratching through brush. Closer now and somewhere behind me. But the moment I turned to look, a woodchuck plopped on my injured leg and waved its paws around in greeting.

"Pourra?" I could barely whisper the wood spirit's name. My hands shook from the heavy astonishment of seeing Caethne's familiar here, or else my hands remained steady and everything else shook as I took up his paws in greeting, mock dancing with him. "Naturally Hecate's charm has no effect on you, old fellow, no more than illusions do. Wood spirit privilege, eh? Nature is nature."

Pourra closed his eyes, rocked gently with my movements.

"I don't have any treats for you. Ask the forest." I put him back near my injured leg. He bowed and danced a little more, kicking against the forest floor, batting at vague sunbeams that kept suggesting themselves and disappearing. Because I couldn't probe a wood spirit's mind any more than I could probe a cloud's, I finally asked as he twirled around a broken stick, "Where's Caethne?"

Not that I expected an answer. Pourra let out a long contented sigh upon hearing the name of his mistress. He stretched himself in the mess he had just made and stared up at me, waiting. Then he gathered himself and lumbered off to eat some wild greens.

"Where's your witch?"

Pourra jumped a happy jump, shrugged, and kept pushing greens in his mouth.

While Pourra ignored me, I leaned back on my arms, scanned the forest, and did my best to figure out what I would even say to Caethne under these circumstances. I knew that Pourra wouldn't wander far from her. But I saw no indication of her presence in this mystery. Then, at the edge of my vision, I sensed a different movement in the tree shadows—that is, there was a barely perceptible stir out there that cut against the subdued shimmer of branches and leaves. The difference in the two kinds of motion drew my attention seconds before the stirring itself did. It was that subtle. I kept studying the forest, but only found a hint of a blur in the shadows, nothing more. And then, suddenly, a streak of blue and silver billowed like a falling storm between oak trees. And then nothing.

Except the hole in time I was now staring into, helplessly waiting for the hole to stare back. Because I knew with sudden clarity that I had just seen Mirand's robe.

I don't know how long I lost touch with all my physical senses except sight, but it was long enough for Pourra to crawl back from his morning feast, because the next thing I noticed was the wood spirit sitting near my injured leg and waving his paws around. The robe then wavered into sight again before disappearing into shadow, its wearer apparently taking no notice of the wood spirit. Or of me.

Weapons check. One broken Truthfinder. The Wand of Surprises. And the two wands I'd taken from Helas. I put up a clerical shield so Mirand couldn't sense their power. Then I quickly prayed to Hecate to take the pain from my shin. My hurt drained into the ground like dirty water.

Concealment was an advantage. Which is why I wasn't about to flag my location by reading him, because I knew he would sense that, even though he couldn't read me through my moon or my clerisy. I was also confident that he wouldn't be able to read a wood spirit any more than I could, but I decided it was better if Pourra stopped creating a commotion by brandishing his paws at the motionless willow behind us. The tree wasn't going to dance. It was dying.

So I conjured a fistful of verbena to attract Pourra's interest. "Mother's tears," I whispered Caethne's witch-name for verbena while I shook the bouquet in his face. Pourra instantly forgot his battle with the willow. He sucked the pale flowers until there were no more flowers, just melted colors on his face and tongue until he looked like he stuck his face in a rainbow. Then he hashed up the leaves with his teeth, devouring them faster than the forest greens he had just eaten. Then he stared at me expectantly, cupping his paws for more.

"You want more tears?" Pourra nodded. "Then come home to a bargain, old friend. One. Find the robe. Two. Bring its wearer to the willow." I glanced at the dying tree. "Three. This offer is a secret, like a secret poem between us." I had no idea how well Mirand and Pourra could understand each other, and I couldn't bind a wood spirit with magic. But I could buy his silence with treats. "Do this and I'll conjure more verbena for you. Whatever flavor you like and as much as you like." Pourra nodded so earnestly I would have laughed under other circumstances. As it was, I merely felt odd and sad. Not least because I assumed that Isulde had brought Mirand here, and that we both were lost.

Pourra finished what remained of the verbena and rubbed the remnants in his face. Then he wandered resolutely into a thicket, squealed, and violently jerked the branches of a lopsided bush, as if he were brandishing a flag. He waited while the bush stopped moving. When it finally went motionless, I felt a stillness that could only come from the depths beneath its hidden roots. I smiled a little. Pourra really wanted more verbena. I saw him bolt out of the thicket and disappear among the trees.

Then I slowly stood in the silence and hid behind the willow. I prayed. But my prayer kept breaking, as if Hecate was patiently crumpling the airy parchment my heart kept writing my prayer on. As if She was holding my drafts for future use.

And so I could only think. And what I thought solely concerned Mirand.

You want me dead. You sent Beotun to kill me. And then Stormr, or rather, you probably cultivated Stormr when you were pretending to be King of Helas. Or maybe when Furna gave your god-be-damned son, Cathe, your throne. And despite all you still wear Athena's colors in your robe, as if She smiles on your attempts to kill a former student. Or is that blue for Helas you wear?

I don't know the history. I don't even know your motive. I only know I could kill you and feel justified. But so what? What killer doesn't feel justified? Murder isn't my mandate. I am to turn you evil like myself. That is why Hecate used Isulde to bring me here, through some fairy path, armed with the Wand of Surprises. But She hasn't told me what to do with you after. Befriend you? Form an alliance? Clean up the mess? After all, at that point we would have both turned evil through circumstances beyond our control. Or perhaps I should just blast you to Hecate then and let Her sort it out.

My thoughts stopped. The silence thinned, as if somewhere beyond what I could sense, Mirand and Pourra were now approaching. I readied the Wand of Surprises.

But I think, mostly, I want your story.

Steady with the Wand. I glimpsed Pourra bounding through undergrowth and then blue and silver bounding behind him through brush.

Come closer, Master. I can't see your face for shadow, and I would see your face.

I drew my energy to balance the Wand's. Became one with the Wand. One with the moment. One with the world that Mirand broke. Aimed the Wand where the robe kept briefly showing itself. Focused on reversing Mirand's energy, on making it match my own and binding him to Hecate.

Pourra raced toward me. His companion emerged from the tree shadows, studied the dying willow, and stopped like sudden death at the point of my wand.

It was Caethne. She was wearing Mirand's robe.

Neither of us spoke to the other because, for several moments, neither of us understood how. But eventually Caethne spoke. Her voice bled energy like a damaged charm.

"And so." She darted her eyes from the Wand to my face. "Do you still hate me, Brother?" Caethne smiled the disheveled smile she often used to put me at ease when we lived in Helas. But fear mottled her expression the way truth mottles a hurtful joke.

I slowly lowered the Wand but kept it ready for use if needed. "Where's Mirand?"

"Dead."

Then I failed in my mandate and Hecate would grace me with eternal torture. So that is why my prayer in preparation for blasting Mirand felt unformed. I sickened so thoroughly I no longer knew myself. I only knew the willow's failing energy was pulsing into the ether as the sunlight hurt its leaves. And only that because I was falling against its slender trunk as if its suffering could replace mine.

Caethne remained fixated on the Wand. But she couldn't help noticing my reaction. She added absently, "Dead to me, anyway."

I heard her words before I understood them. First I felt the burning in my throat subside. My heart was still lurching, but it slowly became more regular. My breaths followed. Then my body gradually righted itself without the willow's support.

But I was still shaking, and I had lost my energy connection with the Wand, making it temporarily useless. "So why are you wearing his robe?"

"It amuses me. And I expect it would annoy him. If he knew." She sighed, slightly less terrified now that she understood that I wasn't going to blast her immediately, that the Wand remained lowered and so her words might save her life. "And I'm still his wife."

"So where is he?"

"I have no idea where he is. Or where anybody is. Or where we are." She glanced down at Pourra, who responded by tugging excitedly at her robe. She took him up and gently ruffled the fur on his head, comforting herself against this mystery that neither of us could parse. "Do you know where we are?"

"We're lost. Like everybody else in this blessed dirty world."

Caethne smiled again, this time with a spot of ease and sincerity. "Perhaps Sweetness knows." Pourra sighed and fell asleep against his mistress's chest. "And our old friend Isulde certainly does, but she's gone her own way." Caethne now appeared utterly unconcerned with this remarkable state of affairs. "These woods are not my woods."

More silence. Too much. Then I spoke. "Where's your tongue, witch? There was a time you couldn't wish the sun a good morning without telling every stick and twig about it."

Caethne closed her eyes and held Pourra closer, searching through the silence before opening them to study the willow again. She looked at me. "I've gone quieter, almost-brother." She hesitated. "I live alone now."

"So?"

"But I *would* speak to you. I asked Isulde to bring you to me—to my kingdom."

"Your what? You mean these woods that 'are not' your woods are some kind of witchdom you cooked up with Isulde?"

"No," said Caethne. But her simple "no" contained a trace of mirth, a touch of the old Caethne who used to tease me in fun. "She brought us here instead. Wherever here is." She set Pourra down.

"Your *kingdom*? *You* asked Isulde to bring us together? For what?" My impatience showed, but Caethne didn't seem to care. "Why don't you stop dropping colored pebbles to piece together and tell me what you know about all this?" I indicated the forest by jerking the Wand a little, to get her attention. "Unless you prefer that I just read your mind."

Caethne appeared to be more resigned now than afraid, and maybe slightly dismayed at her inability to resurrect our friendship.

"Read what you like, Brother. Here's what I know. I had a child who wasn't a child. That came from our killing Cathe, from my honoring my promise to deify you if you magically forced Mirand"—she spat the name— "to love me. The gods were so offended by my poor attempt to make you one of them that they punished me by using my womb to birth Cathe's spirit back into flesh." I winced a little as she continued. "Then my 'son' grew faster than a plague—as he always does, as he did when old Grana birthed him—and crawled his way to the Helan throne."

"I've heard. But you're not innocent. You were willing to use me to violate Mirand's free will."

"And you were willing to help me. Except I didn't have to violate anything. He very much offered himself. Remember?"

"I remember only one of us got charged for Cathe's murder. And only one of us got tried and condemned in the North Country for it. And that you also tried to wrench my alignment from evil to good without so much as a warning. Perhaps the gods were mostly offended by that."

"Well. That was an interesting night." Caethne smiled a little, looking briefly like the warm adopted sister that once charmed me. "The night the world changed into something else."

I wasn't about to get taken in. "You say you've gotten yourself a kingdom now? You mean your duchy wasn't enough for you to spin plots in?"

"My duchy is now my kingdom. The Kingdom of Caethne." She stopped speaking, waiting for me to respond to the hint of banter in her tone. "I suppose *I* changed the world in that way."

"And I suppose you're going to get around to telling me how that happened."

"How that happened is I informed my brother that his former duchy, which he left to me to run when he became king, is now under new management. Mine. In law as well as in fact. I then declared its independence from Threle."

"And Walworth simply took that in good humor?"

"I have no idea what humor he took that in. He never responded. I no longer concern myself with Loudes, Threle, or anything else. Threle betrayed me."

"There's a lot of that going around."

"Well, Mirand did, with Walworth's support. You know, I never saw Mirand after he offered himself to me in front of you, Walworth, and everybody else. So brave of him as Roguehan approached my castle. So strategic of him after Walworth abdicated as duke and made me "lord" of our land. All so Mirand could use the energy of our . . . encounter . . . to claim we were wed and assume his identity as my 'feminine' complement, as 'lady' of the land. All the better to embody the land and use that force through the Wand of Surprises to blast Roguehan. When Roguehan took on the kingship of Threle, it was only a matter of blasting Threle through him to reverse Threle's defeat into a victory that never happened."

"I know. I was there." I managed to sound bored.

Caethne looked like slightly offended, as she wanted me to say more. I had no intention of telling her that my own embodiment of Gondal's neutral wasteland, along with Aeren's, would help me restore balance when I blasted Threle back into defeat by blasting Walworth, Threle's king. When she realized I wasn't going speak, she said crossly, "Do you know that some actually accounted that clever work?" She waited for me to sympathize with her hurt, seeming to hope that by earning my sympathy she would gain my trust. When she realized that no sympathy, and no trust, was forthcoming, she added, "Well, no more of that. I was useful. I refuse to be so again. I refuse to involve myself in Walworth's affairs."

"Neutrality has its uses."

Caethne nodded agreement. "I brought our rapidly aging spawn, the product of that union, to Furnesse. Then I returned and informed the world that my duchy is now its own kingdom. And so is my heart."

"And what does all that have to do with you and Isulde?"

"Everything. We're friends," she cried. Then her voice went distant and more intense than I ever remembered Caethne's voice. "Sometimes. But then she brings me pebbles and shells and occasional dull afternoons when my tea goes sour and my magic doesn't work. And really then we're just" —Caethne suddenly seemed old, or at least weakened by all the wreckage in her life— "something different. Like strangers who also know each other in a different timeline. It's all become quite impossible with Isulde."

"Yes. But here we are because you asked her for a favor. So despite the uncertainty of your relationship, why did you ask her to arrange this meeting?"

"I need your help again, Brother. Isulde told me you left the North Country. And I thought she would bring you to me, the way I drew you to my castle in a trance in advance of Roguehan's arrival. You were cold to me then, but you did agree to help me with Mirand."

"Well, no more of that." I coolly repeated her words.

She ignored my tone because it was in her interest to do so. "Nature's torn at the edges now. Not in ways that everybody would notice, but I notice. And of course that's Mirand's fault. I've seen mushrooms splitting into wrinkled violets. The sun keeps going slightly wrong, but wrong enough to feel its shadows like mistakes. And so my witchcraft is also torn. And then, you *would* follow Isulde, but you might resist me, even if I did send another trance to you."

"Why should I help you do anything? The last time I did that you tried to change my alignment."

"You need a home."

"I'm a citizen of Clio. And possibly of Gondal if I decide to open that issue."

Caethne slightly raised her eyebrows before wrapping herself back in her uncharacteristic quiet. "I understand that Gondal barely exists now. As to Clio, I'll pay you more than whatever Aleta is paying you. Name your price."

"What makes you think Aleta is paying me? Do you think she was keeping some kind of Threlan bargain when she gave me citizenship? Or exchange of witch promises? What do you want, Caethne? Tell me what you need my help with, and I'll tell you what it costs." I had no intention of going in with Caethne on anything, but it was worth knowing what she wanted and why Isulde would bother herself with it.

"Protection."

"Protection from what? Is your brother going to invade your kingdom and take it back from you? Are we going to war?"

"And to set the world right again. And maybe to set you right."

"That would be a beggar's job."

"Perhaps. But when the world changed—I was briefly—my energy was briefly—" she hesitated, looking for words, which was very odd and very unlike the Caethne I remembered. She sighed and then her words streamed in a familiar tumble. "I *was* Duke of Walworth. And so when my brother abdicated I *was* King of Threle for a few moments, until Mirand obliterated those moments like so many old candles. So perhaps I should like to be 'king' again. Perhaps I should like to force Walworth to acknowledge my independence with something besides silence."

Something felt wrong. Caethne was never politically ambitious. "You've always despised politics, witch. And you said you've chosen a solitary life. Ruler of Threle hardly suits you."

"Destroyer of Threle does." She waited a long time for me to respond before she added in a tone of sincere respect, "Or do you prefer to work alone?"

"What makes you think I have any interest in destroying Threle?" I knew my sharp tone was a sloppy admission. So did Caethne. Which is why she gestured as if to embrace me and laughed like we were old friends conspiring to pull a prank on our comrades.

"What makes me think the truth? Honestly, Llewelyn, we have the same heart. And of course I read the trial transcript. After Isulde brought you back from the dead, you rejected my brother's offer of work, of protection. Then you left the North on your own, knowing what danger you were in from the rest of the world. If self-interest wasn't enough to bring you back to Threle, it isn't hard to guess how you feel about Threle. Not that I blame you. I haven't forgotten that after you risked all for us, my moon-damned brother told you to stay in Kursen."

"So did you. At least Walworth was honest about it."

"You offered to kill him so I could bathe Cathe in his blood, all to make Cathe a god. That was to be a piece of your revenge, until we decided to kill Cathe and make you a god instead. So of course you want to destroy Threle. And had you remained King of Gondal, I expect you would have tried."

"Caethne." I spoke with deliberate contempt. "Had I remained King of Gondal, I would have had better ways to occupy my attention than making war on Threle." I couldn't hold the contempt, though, because my thoughts wandered to the incredible elvish beauty of Arula and its destruction. I was suddenly distracted by a vision of deep sky forming colored birds in an ancient glass. And of the colors shading into something sacred each hour. So sacred I once chose eternal torture to save it, only for the bloody elves to scorch it all.

"So what 'better things' do you expect to occupy your attention in Clio?" Caethne asked sensibly.

The sound of someone approaching disrupted our argument. I grasped the Wand tighter, locking back on to its energy as Aeren came into sight, still wearing male garb. Pourra waved his paws in greeting. Then he playfully spit in Aeren's general direction and slapped his front paws on the ground a few times.

Aeren and Caethne stared at each other for long seconds, although it felt like Aeren did more staring, more perusing, than Caethne did.

"Welcome?" Caethne suddenly sounded warmly ironic and completely herself.

"Am I welcome? I don't know. Who are you?" Aeren glanced at both of us before addressing Caethne again. "You speak Sarana with a north Threlan accent. Are you and Llewelyn kin?"

"Yes," said Caethne. "But only in the ways that matter."

"No," I replied. "Except in ways that no longer matter."

"I see," responded Aeren. She kept staring at Caethne. Then she spoke again. "Well, kinship be whatever it may, sir. Your face was familiar when it was a woman's, but then I looked through you to see you are in truth a man."

"Uh . . . Aeren, this is Caethne. You once met her twin brother, Walworth the King of Threle."

"I know you," said Caethne gently. "I've read your story."

Aeren, who had no way of knowing that Caethne was referring to the trial transcript and not the sample that Walworth's official had once rejected, looked beyond confused. But then she decided, inexplicably, to play the charming bard. "You did look the lady when I approached, sir. But I see that you are a man, and that you now look nothing like Threle's king. His hair isn't peppered with gray against night. His eyes don't burn as yours do."

Aeren's playful words made the illusion of "Caethne" vanish. I suddenly found myself staring directly at Mirand, who was staring directly at me. I said a prayer and aimed the Wand, but my hands shook so badly I couldn't steady it. *"Get back, bard."*

"Why?"

"Just get behind me!"

"What if I don't?"

For the moment, I simply wanted to kill Aeren. "We'll argue philosophy later. *Move.*"

Mirand calmly assessed me while he addressed her. "Go, bard. I didn't come here for a tale. Or to see Llewelyn demonstrate a proof."

"What did you come here to see then, stranger? Llewelyn playing the rogue?" She quickly appraised my embarrassingly unstable stance. "Badly?"

"I came to see a willow die."

Aeren was still confused, and clearly as annoyed by Mirand's seeming non-answer as by me in general, but she did move away from him, glumly glaring at me for breaking up her show for no apparent reason. At least she had her priorities straight. Mirand quietly observed me, waiting for the inevitable without emotion and with a deep grace that was hard to watch.

Tableau for Hecate. One scattered bard who could see through illusions. That made sense, because now that she could create mild illusions from her tales, she had become a kind of illusionist. One master wizard wearing Athena's colors in his robe and offering himself to Hecate, disguised as a former friend and framed by an unknown wilderness. That made no sense, but who am I to argue? And me, the unwilling "Beloved of Hecate," working to restore the world to its former hell. All to escape eternal torture, bless be damned.

I supposed the elves would have done it up better.

I would get Mirand's story later, after I turned him. I would get everything later. "Drop your shield."

"Does it matter?" asked Mirand reasonably.

Actually, it didn't. We were physically close enough that if I handled the Wand correctly, it would reverse his energy through his shield. I immediately felt foolish, as if I had just proclaimed a lack of skill by asking Mirand to help me out by making himself an easier target than he already was. It didn't help that my hands were still shaking.

"I am for you, Wizard." And I dropped my clerical shield and blasted and blasted and wrenched and tore his heart's energy until it subsided and crested and frothed over into the same direction as my own. And I felt Hecate hold it there, smoothing it into ripples and bones until it felt like Mirand's actual bones had been removed from his skin, blackened, and replaced. He trembled like the earth was shaking, which scattered patches of it now were.

This was messy. I wasn't here to break the world like he did, just to break him. This was a merely personal penance imposed by Hecate, to balance turning El to good. Destroying Threle by killing Walworth was supposed to re-align the world. But I had blasted more energy than necessary, and so the ground shuddered like it was catching its breath. Not a lot more energy, not enough to change a country's defeat to victory and incur the gods' wrath, but enough to reveal that my heart was too unfocused to make a clean kill of his. I felt exposed. But whether Mirand noticed, and whether he was still trembling with a terrible new emotion or the newness of his reversed energy, I couldn't tell.

Pourra shrieked and ran for the nearest bush.

"Why did you kill the owl?" Aeren's voice was heavy with annoyance.

Damn! So "Pourra" was also illusion. Mirand had been carrying Athena's bird. But Aeren appeared to be less distressed by the poor owl flapping its death throes among the greenery than about her frustration at both of us for failing to disrupt our encounter to explain to her what was going on.

I had no idea what to say so I continued to ignore Aeren's frustrated sighs while Mirand continued shuddering and vomiting and clutching at the ground. I also had no idea how long it would take the wizard to recover, or if he ever would, or what to do next.

I prayed again and felt my moon sting like a dying wasp. I had a vision of myself as the dying wasp. The wasp died into the flattened toad. The toad then bloated to life as a mildewed book, rotting and unread into eternity. And then I understood that I had accomplished half of my mandate and that Hecate was pleased. But that's all I understood.

I spoke. "And so you shall wear Hecate's dust like a crown. As I do."

"Yes," choked Mirand. "The crown of the world."

As I considered this unexpected response, and while Mirand and I were both still recovering from a magical reunion that felt so weirdly sacred that neither of us was ready to discuss it, the master wizard pushed himself to his knees and stuck his hand in his robe as if he was reaching for a wand. And Aeren, who had already had her fill of being left out of this fascinating get-together, decided she needed to force the issue by turning dragon.

And somewhere in the rushing violence of her blast, I also instinctively blasted, even though had I been thinking clearly I would have remembered that my wand wasn't made to kill him and that his weapon couldn't hurt me or the dragon. But now, thanks to Aeren, there was thunder leaping into chaos and the earth melted around us into a patch of newly-seared dirt. I was rocking against the ground and cradling what was left of the Wand of Surprises, which had extended far enough outside my sphere of safety to catch part of her blast. It now resembled a burnt stick. Mirand was also holding himself close to the ground, but he appeared unhurt.

And Aeren was back in human form and screaming at him. "Who the scorch *are* you and why aren't you dead?"

And then Mirand laughed. For a long time. For longer than anybody should ever laugh. "My wizard-shield is proof against your dragon blasts. Didn't Llewelyn tell you I studied wizardry with Zelar before Llewelyn studied with me? We both carry Zelar's energy in our wizard-shields, and since Zelar made his own shield impervious to your blasts, ours are, too."

Aeren was so angry she didn't pause for breath. "Well, isn't that bloody fine? Then maybe you shouldn't play with wands. Because didn't Llewelyn tell *you* I killed Zelar with a wand blast?"

"Aeren, this is my former master, Walworth's chief wizard, Mirand."

Aeren didn't give a scorch. "I still killed your master with a wand blast."

"I know. But you had considerable help from Llewelyn. I read the trial records." Even though I had changed his energy, I apparently hadn't changed him. Mirand always had a way of being so bland with the truth that his response felt like a rebuke.

Naturally, Aeren took it as one. "*Help?* Llewelyn and I are one. Go scorch yourself."

"Yes," said Mirand, "I felt that 'oneness' in your blasts. And so did my illusion charm. Your combined reverberations made it fall outside my shield when I reached for it."

I noticed a mangled piece of trash on the ground, but not wanting to drop my attention, I asked Aeren to bring it to me. Surprisingly, she obliged without arguing, although it was nothing but ashes by the time she came back. She rubbed the dead charm's ashes from her palms and into the still air.

"Why did you reach for the charm?"

"Protection. It's more difficult to change an illusion than a truth. Even with a Wand of Surprises."

"Protection? I changed your energy *before* you tried to grab it."

"Perhaps I wanted to stain the moment with an illusion. The way some people use their own illusions to stain their lives."

His words hurt, because I knew he was critiquing me. But then so did the whole situation. I stood and leaned against the willow as the dust swirled and settled in the air. I was suddenly divided between wanting to put distance between me and Mirand and desperately wanting to know what he was doing here disguised as Caethne and why he wanted me dead and why Isulde was involved and all the rest. Then I considered how much of Mirand's life I had just taken from him, and I felt something like sympathetic respect for a fallen enemy. But maybe with less grace than such respect should carry. "Stand."

Mirand stood, physically recovered now. He nodded slightly, so slightly it felt utterly sincere and utterly devastating, as if he was both acknowledging my victory and questioning whether I had a point. I ignored what felt like a fair slight. Whether or not Mirand knew about my moon, he knew that his wizardry would do little through any clerical shield I might have up. And he also knew that I could still easily destroy or torture him by bringing down Hecate's force, just as I had destroyed his would-be assassin Beotun. With the added feature of now sending him to the wrong end of the gods. So he did the reasonable thing. He waited for my orders.

"Open your robe. Show us what other weapons you're carrying."

He did so. There weren't any. I told Aeren to rummage through his clothing to make sure. There still weren't any.

I then attempted to read him, but the moment I sensed his newly-reversed energy, I stopped. And not just because our wizard-shields were identical, and so reading him through his shield reminded me viscerally of our wizard bond. It was mostly because I felt so sad that I couldn't bring myself to do it. Not now, anyway. It violated decency, although I would have trouble explaining why. Except that Mirand first taught me how to use wizardry to read thoughts, and that I had once esteemed him as a demi-god.

And then I was grateful that he couldn't read me through my moon. "So *did* Isulde tell you where we are?" It was dreadful having to ask him, to admit again that I didn't know, but the day was getting on, and he had already acknowledged as Caethne that he was lost, too. Perhaps he had more to say now.

He didn't. "No."

Aeren clattered over Mirand's response like a crow with a gold piece. "I know how to get out."

"How?" Mirand and I spoke in unison without meaning to. It felt for an instant like we were working together in Threle again, and that made me feel a pit of mourning in my chest.

Aeren looked at me, ignoring Mirand. "Do you want him to know? Is he with us now?"

"Yes, I suppose he has to be." Aeren didn't question me, which was just as well. I didn't feel like explaining that Mirand and I now shared an alignment, and in that sense, he had no choice but to be "with" me. "Where are we, Aeren?"

"After you left me this morning, I turned dragon and flew around on a morning adventure. There is a rise west of here, and on the other side is a large farm, and beyond that a town." Aeren looked proud of her discovery. "There's no path, but I'm sure I can get us there in a few hours."

And so we followed the bard. Through the pathless choke of trees, like the detritus of dead history. The air felt remarkably clean between us, like mornings in late winter sometimes do. We walked in silence, slouching toward someplace known and nameless.

Fourteen

I walked with Mirand in awkward silence. Then we walked in odd silence. Then we just walked.

I kept my mind full of the challenge of breaking a path through a forest that had no paths. This tangle of tree branches, that fence of bush. And two stolen wands from Helas to clear all. We made our way in will and wizardry, sharing nothing but our mutual distance, following Aeren because there was nothing else to follow.

When we stood on the rise above the farm that Aeren had seen in her dragon form, we went even more distant. Because we no longer had to slog through woody undergrowth, we had to find another way to guardedly ignore each other. So we waited on the rise, waited for some sign from Aeren that we should enter the scene before us.

It was early evening now, and evening comfort was rising in the sky and coloring the rooftops in the town beyond the farm. We caught the moment evening fell; saw it nestle among the neat lines of cabbages and onions holding the field. That was something of a fresh distraction. It allowed us to continue revealing nothing to each other. We simply had to descend. And then we simply had to pretend that we weren't charmed by the homely loveliness of wherever we were, lest that show something of our hearts.

Except for Aeren, who stood near me, saw through my pretense, and remarked, "Yes, this *is* beautiful. But . . . that's as far as I know." She glanced over at Mirand, who was calmly assessing the view, as if to ask me, "What about him?"

I shrugged. Mirand couldn't read me through my moon, and I wasn't up for reading him yet. But now my reluctance wasn't solely due to respect for our former relationship. Of course Mirand would know if I probed his mind, but worse, he would know that I had to work through several of his defenses to do it, that I cared enough about his recent history to work for it. That was poor strategy, until I figured out what *was* my strategy. And strategizing was impossible until I decided how Mirand might now assist me in Threle's destruction. And thinking of us possibly playing the same coin on that one was like stumbling on wind.

Crossing the field made me slightly less uncomfortable for a few moments, because it was like crossing an untried reality that nobody had bothered to complicate yet. But when I finally spoke it was to Mirand, in Botha, and to Aeren's visible annoyance. "I'm sorry about your owl."

"Why?" Mirand's tone of simple curiosity surprised me, although I don't know what I was expecting.

"I didn't mean to kill her . . . Athena's bird."

"You didn't. The owl was a wood spirit. There was no 'Athena' about her." *So that's why the owl was able to kick me.* "You destroyed the illusion charm buried in her feathers, but she would have survived your blast." There was something vaguely sad about the owl not being Pourra and yet being a wood spirit like Pourra. Like seeing a dead friend in a stranger's face.

But Mirand's voice was so factual, so academic, that his response was almost a relief. As if we were still teacher and student, and working out elegant solutions to magical problems was the highest form of communication. So high it transcended everything else.

I kept myself steady, almost managing to sound cheerful. "Well. You won't be needing Athenic trappings anymore. And I suppose I now have a duty to teach . . . ." I struggled for the right word. "Obviously, we'll need to find a place to freely discuss your new relationship to the universe. It wouldn't be right for me to reverse your energy and leave you alone with the consequences." *Also, I had much to ask him in private.*

Mirand was silent, the silence of agreement.

"Although I'm sure you *can* find your way on your own," I added respectfully. We were leaving the field and entering the town now.

We moved aimlessly through random streets. Actually, I walked aimlessly and the others followed, which made everything worse. Aeren was eagerly enjoying her adventure. Mirand was eagerly watching me demonstrate that I had no idea what to do next.

Sometimes Aeren would saunter through the quiet evening as if she were a young lord looking for a fight. Which was easy to do as most of the townspeople were probably eating dinner, so the streets only had a scattering of other people. But she made the most of the scattering by smiling and nodding at unimpressed strangers, seeming to measure her heart by everyone she met.

"Bardic practice." She didn't need to explain, but she clearly wanted to change the conversation back to Sarana.

"Really? I thought you were just trying to be annoying."

"Really? I thought that was your job."

Mirand smiled a little at our banter. And then, as we approached a familiar field at the town's edge, I saw Aleta's castle in the distance, overlooking her land and catching the evening light. I didn't recognize the town because Aleta had brought me to her castle from the opposite direction.

"That's my friend's castle," I said quietly to Aeren. "We're home." I spoke as if this had been my plan all along.

"Then why did you take the long way?" asked Mirand reasonably, in Sarana, so Aeren would appreciate his implication that I didn't know my friends very well, or myself in relation to my friends.

She did. She giggled.

When we got to the castle, I told my fellow travelers to wait near an enclosure of apple trees. They seated themselves on a low stone wall. We formed an odd triad—a thoughtful, quiet wizard in an Athenic robe he no longer had any business wearing, a young bard in her male disguise who could appear to be anything she put in a tale, and me.

But whatever I was in the moment, I couldn't find it.

"What is your will?" asked Aeren playfully.

"To sing to the moon. And if the fairy shows, to ask her in for strawberry tea."

It didn't take me long to find Aleta. A servant led me to an unfurnished chamber, where milady was kneeling on a rough stone floor among an array of swords and other weapons. She was rubbing oil on them with a plain white cloth and wiping the excess with another. The oil held a faint scent of pine, although that could have been the pine logs on the hearth. More weapons leaned against a wall, glinting and drying. So flawless and deadly that had they been slightly less perfect they would have been high art.

"Countess."

Aleta looked up. "I wondered where you went. Nobody's seen you all day." She sounded more mystified than angry. Rising, she placed a sword against the wall and selected a dagger from over the hearth; her weapons work was clearly her priority right now.

"I . . . I was out performing my sacred duty to you."

"And?" She made a genially dismissive gesture with one hand to indicate that "sacred duty" was not a concept she had much use for. She then carefully balanced the dagger on her other palm as she bent closer to the fire to better examine the blade.

"I went to pray. And I had a . . . a kind of dream, a vision maybe, last night."

She rose and placed the dagger on a ledge near the hearth. Then she faced me, semi-interested but mostly impatient to get on with it. "And?"

"And I followed it."

"Naturally."

"And I found . . . two people stomping through your woods. Walworth's chief wizard, Mirand—" Aleta gasped in surprise. She was now entirely interested. "And . . . somebody I thought was dead. My friend Aeren, the one-time queen of Gondal."

Aleta stared hard at me for a few seconds. "You found them together? What is Mirand doing here in secret? What is anybody doing here in secret?"

"What is anybody doing in Clio, milady?" I spoke dolefully, with more than a touch of concern in my voice. "Mirand came disguised as Caethne. I had to tell him to put on proper attire." Aleta glowered. She had always despised Caethne, which is precisely why I mentioned her. Anything to raise her doubts concerning Threle's alliance with Clio. "It's passing odd, and I *can* assure you that Queen Aeren and Mirand don't know each other. They weren't wandering together and they still aren't, except that they're now wandering with me. I had to introduce them."

"Yet they both happen to be running around in my woods. And you *did* tell me your friend Aeren was dead."

I nodded. "Obviously I was mistaken. The queen has always had bardic aspirations. She apparently left Gondal to travel disguised as a male bard, telling stories on the road." I didn't want to tell Aleta about Aeren's sojourn in Furna, at least not yet, because I hoped to persuade them to work together with me against Threle. Furnesse had supported Roguehan's conquest of Threle, and whatever doubts Aleta now had concerning Walworth, I knew she considered Furnesse an aggressor, a potential enemy. Also, the Countess of Clio, who valued authenticity as much as her people did, was likely to disdain King Furna's proclivity for roleplaying and disguise, and therefore likely to be suspicious of Aeren's Furnessian ties.

She was suspicious of Aeren anyway. "You mean she gave up a kingdom to tell tales for applause?"

"Not exactly. Maybe. I don't know everything yet."

"And they *both* happen to be disguised." Aleta went quiet, trying to parse this out.

"As were you, recently. Sometimes pretense is the sister of necessity."

"And sometimes pretense is the sister of pretentiousness. Or worse. What was the nature of this . . . dream?"

"It was a fairy sending. Isulde . . . for purposes that still aren't clear, brought the three of us together. Here. In your woods. Although Mirand indicated that he might have instigated that."

I expected Aleta would be less than enthusiastic about this information, but I was wrong. She stared thoughtfully at the hearth. "I remember Isulde. I remember her presence when Roguehan arrived in Walworth's duchy and almost destroyed Threle." Aleta then simply looked sad. "And now *she's* here, too?"

"Well, not anymore. But Mirand and Aeren are. I would suggest inviting them to stay. So I might speak privately with them."

I read Aleta. She was torn between wanting to believe Mirand was here with friendly intentions and the suspicions I'd raised in her during our escape. Which was perfect. I wanted Mirand in the castle, where we could speak privately, but I also wanted Aleta to distrust him.

"I'd prefer not to offend the King of Threle's chief wizard, but the last time I saw Isulde, a country almost died and an empire actually did. And then the seasons went strange." She picked up a sword and studied it as if she were a wizard reading a tracking crystal, measuring how the blade reflected ruddy flames against the hearth's dark stones. "This one kills with light. It takes practice to use." She placed it on the ledge with the dagger. "Somebody saw a dragon this morning. Looming over the town. A lot of people are avoiding open areas." Aleta gestured at the weapons against the wall, as if to say the dragon sighting was why she was cleaning them. Of course, Aleta's not having read the trial records meant she could have no idea of the dragon's connection to Aeren. I saw no reason to enlighten her. "It's best if you did speak with Mirand. Alone. Use whatever means you have to find out why he came here disguised, in secret, with Isulde's help. Learn what he knows about dragons. As my new ambassador to Threle, it's your job to discover what Threle's intentions are. Of course Mirand may lodge with you, to make that easier."

"Of course. And the queen? She needs a translator. Her knowledge of Botha is limited."

"Ah, yes, like everything else in Gondal—your friend keeps to her own world. Well, my knowledge of Sarana remains limited. Would her presence be disruptive to your interrogation?" She didn't hesitate to use the word "interrogation" concerning Mirand, but she didn't like using it.

"Yes. Probably."

"Then she may stay in the room across from yours, next to yours, or wherever you find convenient, as you might need to interrogate her, too. We'll speak again when you know more."

Aleta took up a cloth and resumed her work. I left to resume mine.

A servant brought Mirand to my room. I wasn't ready to talk to him alone. And I wasn't eager to share a room like we once did as teacher and student, even if that would make questioning him "easier." I needed time; I needed clarity. So I procrastinated by bringing Aeren to an unused chamber some distance down the hall.

I lit the small hearth with a spot of wizard fire and touched a few candles to the flame, placing them on a table in the corner. The room was sparser than mine, almost martial in its austerity, but it lacked nothing needful. "Wash basin." I conjured some water for a plain copper basin near the hearth. "Table. Chair. Candles. And we're home, buddy." Aeren plopped herself on a bone-colored blanket that was stretched tightly across a narrow bed. She looked vaguely perplexed and sharply tired in the firelight. She also appeared utterly uninterested in my attempt at geniality. So I went serious. "But don't turn here. Somebody saw you this morning. The countess is now preparing her armory against" —I then tried to sound more playful than I felt— "some sort of mystery dragon that appeared in the sky and threatened her town."

"Does she know it was me?"

"No. But let's keep it that way. Here" —I conjured some paper and writing implements— "your job is to write some tales, to write some splendid things for you to become as you will." If I couldn't lighten her mood, at least I could distract her. "If you need anything, call on me and I will translate for you."

Aeren looked thoroughly unhappy with my offer to translate.

"You're among friends here, bard. And it's fine that you don't speak much Botha. Nobody in Clio speaks much Sarana. Really it's an even deal." I turned to go.

"Why are you lodging with that strange wizard, your former master, after we tried to kill him?"

So that's why she was upset. "Countess's orders. Besides, I'd like to know why the three of us are here, so I need his story. This arrangement allows me to get it." Aeren looked unsettled. "I mean, while . . . I eagerly await yours." I gestured at the paper I had just created for her and turned again to leave.

"I'd like his story, too."

"Why?"

"Because I tried to kill him." Now it was my turn to look confused. She helped me out. "I mean, he is the Threlan king's wizard. Isn't that how they do things in Threle? After a prisoner is condemned in a Threlan court, isn't he allowed to tell his story—his life—before he dies?"

I slowly turned to leave for the final time. "No. In Threle they usually get the story first."

To the story. My room was bright. It was pulsing with the energy of the wizard fire that Mirand must have drawn to the hearth. But Mirand wasn't there. When I examined the hearth, I realized that it opened into the next room. Then I saw light from his side spilling into a darker corner of mine through a dull wooden door that was slightly ajar. I hadn't noticed this door last night, but then last night I was barely there before I wasn't.

I decided that there was something "right" about this arrangement—in that although Mirand and I had separated our lives in every way possible, we were once again sharing quarters as we did when I was his apprentice. I thought ruefully that our wizard bond resembled the shared hearth, a semi-secret tunnel through rough stones that was dangerous to traverse but impossible to avoid.

And then I remembered how I saved his life in Loudes when he and Walworth stood trial for treason, when their only "crime" was secretly attempting to defend Helas and Threle. And how after risking my own life to gather the evidence that saved theirs, they abandoned me in Kursen Monastery. A betrayal that greatly encouraged me, over time, to align myself to Hecate. I reminded myself that there was justice in my pleasing Hecate by forcing Mirand to become evil like me. I couldn't care about his loss, but in my youthful naivety I never imagined we would end up here.

I entered the adjoining room without knocking. Mirand looked up with mild interest. He was seated on the far side of the hearth, and my entrance had disrupted his reading. He lowered the scroll he had been studying and waited to see what I was going to do.

"So you're still here." I surprised myself by sounding both inhospitable and welcoming.

"Why wouldn't I be?"

I sat on a bench near the fire, opposite him. "You *are* free to leave. Free to return to Loudes or wherever you please. Free to stay in town or country tonight if that dresses your desire. Clio is friendly and you speak Botha as well as I do. Why are you *choosing* to remain here?"

"You promised me a lesson in evil. I'm here to collect." He playfully tossed the scroll into a wall recess that contained several other scrolls. Then he looked at me expectantly, as if he were testing me.

"A lesson in evil." I suddenly felt self-conscious and silly, which of course was his intent. I tried to find something to say that would be new to this highly experienced scholar; something that wouldn't sound like I was somehow disparaging his considerable learning. I paused to think. Mirand kept waiting with such a deliberately non-judgmental air that it felt like a reproach. And then—because the silence between us was worse than anything I could fill it with—I decided to simply speak. To him, to the fire, to the night—my discomfort with it all be damned.

"Your life energy now flows in opposition to your past, in opposition to how you were meant to be at your beginning. You won't seem different, although clerics will certainly be able to sense your new alignment. I did. And you won't feel differently about anything in your life. That may be the worst of it. Being evil doesn't mean you no longer love Athena, or learning, or teaching, or Threle, or your friends, or wizardry, or anything else that mattered to you before the change. But now you can no longer love those things without sickening from your new spiritual distance from them." I was starting to sound apologetic, so I stopped myself.

"Yes." Mirand spoke with a touch of impatience. He knew all this. I was wasting his time.

"So . . . you might decide to live in solitude, to avoid the things that now cause you pain. And . . . you might learn that it's possible to live in solitude even as you twist through the political trash of being a king's chief wizard in a bent world. A solitude of the heart. You refuse attachments. You bond yourself to nothing and no one. You sludge through your work and sometimes you go home, and if the gods are kind, for maybe a moment, you can hold something beautiful without hurting—a magical incantation, a poem, a snatch of music that floats and disappears on an affectionate breeze. And then the universe spins rapidly on and those same things torture you again. And then, one day, mercifully, you die.

"But not everyone can manage it. Such a life will rapidly deplete your personal energy. So much so that when you die, it will be early and sudden—like that wood fragment that just went to ashes in your wizard fire. But a solitary life does offer a kind of secret tryst with the world without having to wear the mess that goes with it. It's an attractive option for some."

"It's not my option. Go on."

"Or, of course, you could learn to preserve your energy through clerisy. If you are inclined, you can slip the world, enter a monastery, attach yourself to a high priest, and petition an appropriate deity for protection. Perhaps Hecate—if you can bear the burden of taking on Athena's opposition."

"I took on history's when I used magic to change Threle's defeat to victory. I can take on Hers." The ease with which he admitted his role in breaking the world was so disarming it took me a moment to resume.

"So. You petition Hecate. You burn your most beloved books, and pray that She accepts your sacrifice. And if She accepts you, you will experience your love of scholarship shrivel into the tedium of rote learning. And you can go far enough with rote learning to see how beautiful the best scholarship is, but you will always be in separation from it. And everything you write will read like an offense against it. You see, scholars like us reject Athena for Hecate, not out of love for Hecate—although something *like* that could happen—

but because we now experience Athena's pure brilliance as unremitting torture. The thing you loved is now deadly to you. So you have to stay dark, deep in Hecate's womb, to live—until Hecate is all you know, and all you . . . I would say take comfort in, but it's really all you have to avoid discomfort in."

"The gods no longer concern me. I only wish to do what's right."

"Perhaps. But your conjuring a victory for Threle where none was meant to exist concerns them."

Mirand contemplated the fire, which was dying a little. "Fair as is." He spoke with a quiet conviction that was devastating, because its brevity rebuked my previous speech. Also, I somehow knew without reading him that he respected my clerical knowledge without necessarily respecting how I came by it. "I see you've done well with rote learning." There was a slight tease in his voice, or maybe I just imagined it.

To disguise my difficulty with speaking further, I threw some logs on the hearth and drew down my own wizard fire. When my flames combined with his, they briefly showed blue and brown, like the Helan flag, before going pale yellow and red. Mirand and I smiled a little at the accidental symbolism. All of our past since my apprenticeship briefly disappeared.

Then I spoke. "There is a third option. You might, without even realizing it, find a middle way, a back door in. The back paths will keep you at a distance from what you care about—you get see the curl of the beloved's hair but not the beloved, if you will—so it limits damage to yourself. Over time it gets tolerable, if not ever entirely painless.

"Best, you can tread these paths alongside whatever else you choose, solitude or clerisy, so long as you don't mind tripping on your own heels as you move. Because the things you love and your energy now repel each other. Or rather, those things now torment you as much as their opposites once did, but your heart keeps remembering differently. I know those paths. Here's a map.

"Scholarship flattens into rote learning. Friendship segues into strategic relationships with whoever you can use. Patriotism gets traded for personal glory. Love of nature's beauty becomes the sickening longing to rot and ooze into nature's underside—that's Cathe, your cyclic son."

Mirand winced.

"We do not necessarily destroy the things we love. Our lack of access to those things destroys us. And in the aftermath we become distortions of ourselves. I suppose I could help you. I suppose I could be your guide through some of the worst of it. You're not a cleric—you won't suffer dietary changes, and you won't suffer as intensely as I did when Cathe wrenched me deeper into evil than my own choices ever could, but it still takes practice living this way."

Mirand raised his hand. "Enough. I prefer to study the process, not the mask."

"So I've heard." I remembered seeing those words in Mirand's handwriting, rebuking Beotun for noting on my essay that he had "problems with the sincerity of these arguments." I considered asking him about Beotun, but my words went elsewhere. "They say that evil is a choice. It was for me—at first—before Cathe, when I lost everything I cared about. And oddly enough it was for you; you didn't resist when I blasted you. Why?"

"I've sacrificed myself for Threle before. This is no different."

"Do you plan to return? To Threle?"

"If I can. If Threle will have me." He spoke with a hint of self-deprecating humor and more than a hint that he was lightly commenting on my lecture.

We laughed. A little. And for the space of that laughter, we were colleagues again. "So." I conjured two mugs of warm ale. "I'll drink to Threle with you." Mirand smiled a melancholy smile and lifted his mug in a silent toast. It was a kindly gesture, but neither of us drank more than a sip. "Why and how did you persuade Isulde to bring the three of us to a fairy meeting?"

"The *three* of us was not supposed to happen. Isulde took it upon herself to include Aeren." Mirand set his nearly-full mug near the scrolls in the recess beside him. I set mine on my bench. If we weren't going to drink like comrades, then we weren't going to drink. "I don't know what fairy-business Isulde has with the world right now, or why she wants Aeren in it."

"Neither do I." I spoke with more ease than I felt, and Mirand seemed somewhat nonplussed by my tone. "You can't read a fairy. It's all a smear of rainbows, except when it isn't." He didn't smile at my attempt at humor. "What *is* your business with the world? And why did you seek me out disguised as Caethne, in the company of fairies, to pursue it?"

"Isn't it obvious?"

"No, it's merely dodgy."

"I learned from my own sources that you were in Hala, with Cathe. I wanted to know your intentions toward Threle." Mirand spoke with the disarming frankness that often unsettled me when I was his student.

"So why not just ask?"

"How?" Mirand's exasperation was obvious, but whether it was directed at me or himself wasn't clear.

"Send a wizard call through our bond? Invite me up to Loudes for tea?"

"You know your clerical shield would have blocked my call, even if it could reach you. And I didn't care to risk being heard by any other . . . *former* apprentice." His exasperation remained steady. "So I begged Isulde for the favor. I carved her name in raindrops to amuse her with my wizardry, gave her pretty toys to play with that I conjured from ancient tales, whatever she wanted."

"And it worked? You made a trade deal with a fairy?" I was sort of impressed. "That's . . . extremely Threlan of you."

"If I did, it failed. In the end, Isulde brought me to you on her own terms. Hence Aeren."

"Why did you come disguised as Caethne?"

"I didn't expect you to speak truth to me. I was wrong." Thus Mirand simply and eloquently conveyed his appreciation of my lesson. Something about this understated compliment cut a little. It reminded me of when I was his apprentice, before I turned evil.

"So you assumed that you couldn't read my intentions if we met?" It was worth knowing what Mirand knew about my defenses.

"Yes. You know your clerisy would prevent that. I tried anyway. You're well protected."

"Hecate loves me." I spoke with mock seriousness and saluted him with my still full mug. A little of my conjured ale spilled on the bench, like an accidental libation.

"Well, somebody does. Given that you survived that encounter with my former student in Anda."

"About that. Why have you been trying to kill me?"

"Don't flatter yourself. I haven't." Mirand stopped speaking, as if he was so offended he had nothing more to say on the subject. Then his anger cracked through his silence. "I didn't know you were back in Gondal until you blasted Beotun through the tracking crystal he stole from me. I did know you were potentially a king. I had no more idea of your intentions toward Threle than a cave has an idea of the moon. Also, you had just paid for your crimes against the state, so Threle had no further interest in you. And you were nowhere near Threle. So tell me. Why *would* I send an assassin to you?"

I read him. He knew I was reading him, because he dropped his defenses to let me. I sensed the evil current that I had created around him, and then I sensed, beyond that, that he was speaking truth. And then I stopped. Truth was enough. "So what was Beotun's problem?" "Helas. He knew your history from the trial records; he insisted on discussing it with me often enough. He wanted to avenge your destruction of the Helan military camp on Kant's border, that you undertook from the safety of Kursen Monastery. Beotun's brother died in the fire you caused. He guessed you'd show up in Anda, looking for Aeren, because where else would you go?"

I shrugged. "I'm used to being unpopular."

"If it's any consolation, he tried to kill me, too. He was at the trial in Loudes when I confessed to my role in destroying the Helan border town. He resented my escaping execution on a legal technicality." Mirand had argued at the trial that he had already paid for his role in destroying the town because he had died in the explosion and then been revived. But the slight emphasis he placed on "legal technicality" indicated that he was also referencing my death and return at my North Country trial. Mirand was implying that our common love of Threle, and our separate crimes against her, and our similar experiences of redemption, was a bond deeper than wizardry.

I had no idea yet what he wanted, but whatever it was, he wanted desperately.

"You made a brilliant argument." I spoke as Mirand often did; intensifying the compliment by speaking as if I were merely stating a fact.

He didn't care. "I argued the law, not justice. Beotun understood that, which is why I refused to condemn him after I navigated my way to the Helan throne. He repaid me by helping Cathe convince Furna to end my brief reign by promising to keep Helas aligned to the southwest. He tried to kill you while making it look like he had my blessing. If he couldn't kill me, he could frame me as abusing my power as a Helan king by assassinating somebody I had no legal right to kill. It was his way of spitting on Walworth and your North Country trial."

"Do you know why he was claiming to be studying elvish while actually studying Clioan?"

"No."

"And your spy Stormr? Did he try to blast me because he's a secret Helan loyalist, too?"

"Stormr no longer works for Threle." Mirand spoke with a touch of defensiveness. "How did you know he once did?"

"It's a guess in the dark. I mean, he did try to kill me." I had no intention of discussing Aeren's visit to Furna with him.

Mirand nodded and rolled his eyes in annoyance. When he spoke, it was partly out of curiosity and partly out of disbelief. "You mean you bested Stormr in a clerical battle?"

"I survived the battle. So did he. Why did your *former* spy want me dead?"

Mirand considered. "I don't know. Stormr was a bad match. He's not a loyalist to anything except flattery, and then only flattery of a certain kind."

"He does enjoy his high priest status."

"Yes. Unfortunately nobody else does." We laughed a little at Mirand's unexpected turn at humor. "I suppose he's back being Furna's problem now."

"Actually, he's Cathe's." Something about that made us both laugh again.

Then Mirand went serious. "Beotun tried to kill you for politics. Stormr probably tried to kill you for religion. See what comes with the crown of the world?"

"What is the crown of the world? You used that expression when I . . . changed you." I didn't ask about the crumbled crown that the old merchant gave me. I didn't want Mirand to ask why Aleta and I were running from Helas a few days ago.

"It's why I'm here, unfortunately, and why Isulde concerned herself at all. You embody Gondal's neutrality. Having experienced your joint blast with Aeren, I now know that you both do. You also, in some sense, carry something of the world. A citizen of Sunna by birth, Threle by adoption, Gondal by fate and now County Clio by seeming chance, you carry the world's energy, it's crown." Mirand didn't sound particularly happy about any of this. "That is why Walworth would support any ambitions you *might* have to replace Cathe as King of Helas."

"The last time a wizard offered to make me king of a country the elves destroyed it."

"That was your fault."

"And Walworth's. From what I understand."

"After your trial, Walworth would have proposed having you rule Helas as a client king of Threle. You didn't want to work with him so the job fell to me."

"Why couldn't you keep it?"

Mirand suddenly looked very old and very sad. "I broke the world when I wrenched Threle's victory out of history. The gods won't let me heal Threle because I damaged the world, their world, to save Threle. That is why I couldn't keep the Helan throne, and why Furna was successful in deposing me. I was to heal Threle by reuniting Helas with her proper homeland."

"And you think *I* can do that?"

"Well, it's a backward path, as you put it. A distance from the beloved. But yes – given what you carry, you could heal, if you chose. You could reunite them and make Threle whole again."

I considered for a long time. I read him; he was and had been speaking truth, which made everything more difficult than it already was. Mirand was offering something like redemption, a way of bridging my spiritual distance from Threle, a country I still loved, despite my evil alignment. But I still had a mandate to fulfill, and it was in direct opposition to Walworth's offer. "Evil clerics aren't skilled at healing."

"Then what are you skilled at?" Mirand's temper flash shook me a little, but his outburst quickly subsided. "Of course Aeren—the dragon—would be queen. Otherwise what you carry of Gondal would be incomplete. Eventually the two of you could use Threle's resources to take back Gondal, and rule together there. To that end—is the dragon now your wife?"

"No."

"Sister? Like you once considered Caethne?"

"No. I've had ill luck with sisters."

"What is she to you then?"

"She's my friend. Something you and Walworth wouldn't understand." Mirand showed mild exasperation by shuffling in his chair, which was more of a reaction than I expected. "But I would meet with Walworth. Here or in Loudes. Let me know his pleasure."

"I'll let you know his will."

Fifteen

When I entered Mirand's room again, I was carrying a basket of Clion apples that someone had left near my door. The apples sparkled like a pile of weeping jewels. They sought comfort in a sturdy blanket of plain bread. I smiled to think I was holding an honest basket of County Clio and that Mirand and I were about to share it.

But Mirand wasn't there. I set the basket on the bench. Our untouched mugs were cold now, and my conjured ale smelled stale and looked like dried syrup in the clear morning light. I then observed that he had carefully laid his robe on his unused bed. Next to his robe was a knotted cord of shattered illusion charms. I stared at the broken charms for a few seconds before I grabbed the robe inside my shields to read its energy.

Which flashed so Athenic, so lawful good, that I sickened and staggered with its force. The damned charms had read evil, not him! I searched through the robe for further magical items but found none. That meant that the force of the robe came solely from Mirand's personal energy, from a level of wizardry to which I'd once aspired. It also meant he really was being truthful behind his mask.

As I threw the robe on the floor I noticed a note on his chair. It read:

> Study the process. After you changed my energy to evil, the combined blast of you and the dragon, the force of Gondal between you, changed me back to what I was. I can't read you. Your skill with clerisy protects you well. But your lesson taught me everything I needed to know about you. The robe is payment for same.

I had no intention of wrapping myself in Athenic energy. I burned the damned robe to oblivion in the hearth with Hecate's force and kept reading.

> The "crown of the world" I gave you when you left Helas with the Countess of Clio disguised as your "servant" was a gesture of good will that you apparently can't read. You might benefit from asking the dragon to interpret that one for you. My own spying on the ground taught me that the Helan people lean toward returning to their homeland. I hope you do, too.

> -M-

And so. Mirand was playing with illusion charms in Helas, too. On the border of Helas and the secret forest paths. Like a poem. For a wizard who never studied illusion, he was having a time of it with the damn charms. Hope he enjoyed his little game.

I sat in Mirand's chair and contemplated the burning robe. I did fulfill Hecate's mandate to turn Mirand. But only by the thinnest of definitions, and only because Hecate is nothing if not excruciatingly legalistic. Something like this had happened before. When Hecate told me to destroy Gondal or enter the North Country and die in a state of eternal damnation, I chose to die damned. Rather than destroy the elvish Beauty that Gondal held, the artefacts in my castle, I rode to what I believed was certain death. The North was supposed to kill me. I carried a death ban against entering that part of the world.

So what happened? Walworth interfered and so I died and came back. And because I failed to fulfill Her mandate through no fault of my own, or barely fulfilled it in a sideways sort of way, the elves saved their art but razed Arula. I still had no idea, under the circumstances, if Gondal was saved. Perhaps it merely remained. And now Aeren and I embodied what remained, but Gondal wouldn't have us. But that was like another poem.

Backward paths.

Was there a way to . . . I don't know, just barely kill Walworth and just barely destroy Threle and so avoid eternal damnation once more on a technicality?

If there was, I didn't see how becoming king of a fractious former Threlan duchy like Helas would get me there. And healing Threle was dangerous work while I carried Hecate's mandate to destroy Threle. I wasn't going to risk damnation a second time. I'd risked my life once for Threle and here I was still suffering the consequences. Think again.

As the last scrap of robe smoldered into gray smoke, the sound of somebody stamping around in my room lurched me out of my thoughts. When I entered my room, I saw an impatient Aeren pacing near the shared hearth as the smoke dissipated. "Did you get the basket of apples I left you? They were near my door. I don't want them."

"Yes." I gestured confusedly at the open door behind me. "They're in Mirand's room."

"He won't want them, either. He's leaving."

"I know. So why don't *you* want them?"

"I'm leaving, too." She threw herself on the edge of my bed and grinned like an old fox. Then she sprung back to her feet as if keeping still was impossible.

"Why? You just got here. You haven't even met the countess."

"Your former master, the Chief Wizard of Threle, offered me bard work in Loudes." The fox grin got bigger. She pranced a little. Then she stretched her arms and swayed a little more because the damned prancing wasn't enough to release all of her energy. She was awkward and graceful by turns and utterly thoughtless with enthusiasm. It was all highly annoying. I wanted her to stop.

"You tried to kill him yesterday and now you're his traveling companion?"

"I tried to kill you once and we're still friends."

"Apparently there's a lot of that going around."

The prancing slid into a clumsy scuffle and stopped. The swaying also stopped, and the fox smile disappeared. "Why shouldn't I go where King Furna was sending me? I'm still his emissary to Threle. Mirand says they love good stories in Loudes, and obviously King Walworth's court attracts many people from the northern duchies who speak Sarana."

"Walworth's court official rejected your bard work. Remember?"

"Well . . . not anymore." She smiled again, but there was no fox about it. It was softer and more self-deprecating now, almost embarrassed. Then she closed her eyes and sighed, as if she was remembering herself while resenting having to do so. Then she came back to the sad, angry Aeren I used to know. "I suppose I could," she responded carefully, "but I don't have to. Thanks for the reminder. Buddy." She was now thoroughly irritated.

"You called him a 'strange wizard' last night and questioned why I'm staying with him. Now you want to travel with him?"

"I thought it was odd for *you* to stay with him, considering how you greeted him yesterday. How does your personal history with him concern me?"

"You dragon blasted him!"

Aeren dragon-glowered in response. "I followed you out of loyalty. I also said last night that I wanted his story." She stopped glowering. She didn't want to argue; she merely wanted to convince. "The most esteemed Master Wizard Mirand *is* a strange wizard, but he's also brilliant and I love his sense of humor. You know, he joked with me about my dragon blast. He's actually a lot of fun to talk to when you get to know him."

I groaned. "And when did you accomplish that feat? Get to know him I mean?"

"Last night. When we were waiting for you by the apple trees. We were watching the moon rise over the field, and Mirand said that he respected my decision to blast Zelar, because Zelar had destroyed my life by using my tales against me to trap me in a dragon form. He also confided that there were times when he had considered blasting him. So we have that in common. I had asked him about the trial records he mentioned yesterday, and he knew all about Zelar turning me into a dragon to guard his wizard lair, and you showing up there and freeing me, and our adventure in Gondal. He also told me all about your trial in the North Country and everything you told King Walworth about me."

Anybody else would have condemned me, or Walworth, or both. But Aeren merely added with an easy carelessness I still wasn't used to, "I learned a lot."

"I'm sure."

"So. I told him I was King Furna's bard now and that I had been traveling with you to Threle to perform on Furna's behalf before we got separated. He did ask me how that happened."

"I hope you didn't tell him."

"Why would I? I suppose he can read me." Then she spoke seriously. "I said I got lost in the world."

"I suppose that's true."

"Does it matter if it's true? That's when he offered me work in Loudes."

Damn Mirand! And damn Aeren, too! Promise a bard a stage and she'll follow you to hell. And pay you for the privilege. And the worst of it was that Mirand was absolutely sincere. He'd arrange some position in Walworth's court to fulfill his promise and keep her happy. Nothing about this arrangement would be illicit, except that he knew that even if I changed my mind about meeting with Walworth, I would follow Aeren because I called her friend. And then, after buying Aeren's loyalty with bard work, he would try to persuade both of us to rule Helas and heal Threle. And Aeren, full of her newfound bardic success, would eat that up like the old fox she sort of resembled this morning would devour a nest of fallen birds and beg for more. Damn both of them! Mirand for a manipulator and Aeren for . . . what? For finally feeling free to be herself?

Furna needed both of us to destroy Threle because, for all he knew, we were both Gondal's rightful rulers, and as such, the joint embodiment of Gondal's isolation and neutrality. As it turned out, he was right. Furna wanted us to destroy Walworth by focusing that neutrality through the Wand of Surprises. As king, Walworth embodied Threle, the Threle that now existed through Mirand's stolen victory, and neutrality was needed to restore the world to balance. But Aeren's dragon blast had destroyed the Wand, so we needed a new strategy.

Yet even without the Wand, Gondal's ancient neutrality mattered, because Mirand needed both of us to heal Threle. Our combined blast "healed" him from my damage. I needed to keep Gondal, that is Aeren, with me, because our combined ability to embody that force was a weapon that both Furna and Mirand wanted to use, and that made it valuable.

"Don't you have anything to say about my working with your former master?"

"Yes. They used to say in Helas, 'Promise a bard a stage and she'll follow you to hell. And pay you for the privilege.'" I sounded slightly colder than I wanted to and far colder than I meant.

Aeren's voice stiffened with hurt. "You think I'm vain."

"I think Mirand is playing with you for his own purposes. The way his master Zelar did."

"You think I'm vain."

Damn, but I had to proceed carefully through her sensitivities. "Mirand wants to separate us."

"Separate us from what?"

"He wants to encourage me to come to Loudes."

"Why do you need 'encouragement' to come to Loudes? Can't you just go? You go everywhere else."

"Aeren," I said with all the jagged candor I could force into my voice, "I don't think you're vain." She looked straight at me; she was forcing back tears, but she was listening. "I think you're the opposite, and that's the problem. Mirand promised me something . . . extraordinary last night, too. Something close to my heart. Something nobody would reject. And yet I did." She wasn't convinced. "It involved Helas, but given that Mirand recently ruled Helas and supports Threle, I was skeptical." She still wasn't convinced, but she kept listening to me to the exclusion of everything else the universe was throwing into this awkward morning. "Don't trust him, buddy. Remember, he was Zelar's student, and whatever he tells you he thinks of his old master now, he was once close to him. The last time you took up a wizard's offer—"

"That's the second time you've reminded me of something I'd rather forget!" The dragon temper was back. *Excellent!*

"You bear fairy gifts now, but you lack a sense of what that means or how badly a powerful wizard might covet them. Why do you think Mirand wanted to leave with you and not with me? If he has so much influence over who performs at court, why did some know-nothing official reject your tale after Arula was razed? You were still the putative queen, even if you were working in an inn. Or do you really believe the Threlan court was unaware that the presumed queen of Gondal petitioned them? And now, an evening's chat with a 'strange wizard' under rising moon and apple trees and you're suddenly that same chief wizard's favorite storyteller? Step right up bard, here's your stage?"

Aeren was as silent as a dragon hovering in a desolate sky. She spoke quietly, almost tearfully, to the ashes in the hearth. "You do think I'm vain."

"No, bard, I think you've been given a precious gift. I also think you're being used for it."

She looked up.

"Why isn't he even giving you time to meet the countess?"

She shrugged.

"You know, I spoke with him at length last night. I'm not prepared right now to repeat everything he said, but you need to think hard about Threle's relationship with your patron, King Furna, before you just decide to follow Zelar's former student there, *by yourself*, on a whim. This isn't what Furna intended when he set you up with a traveling party and you know it's not what he intended. Furna was supporting you after Threle rejected you, and you would repay him by taking up a position in Walworth's court on the word of a 'strange wizard' you just met? A position that may or may not exist?"

Aeren stared at me in abject silence. I knew my mentioning Zelar scared her, but the rest actually shamed her. "You mean you don't think I should go?"

"I'm not going. And I've had experience with Mirand. Of course, that may change, and if it does, you can travel with me and a proper traveling party."

The worst thing about my argument wasn't my attempt to out manipulate Mirand. The worst thing was that every statement I made was true but didn't add up to the truth, while every statement Mirand made was simply true.

But I won. Aeren agreed to stay in Clio. I called for a servant and scribbled a note in Sarana that said, "The Queen of Gondal desires to stay with me until I receive word from your king. – L." Aeren nodded and signed it to indicate that she agreed. Then I told the servant to bring it to Mirand.

Aeren sat heavily in my chair and glumly stared at the floor. She was embarrassed, and I felt miserable for her.

"Hey, buddy, I've got something to show you. I don't understand what it is, but maybe you can help me out." Mirand had told me to ask the dragon about the crown, so I gingerly took it out of one of my travel bags. She gasped in recognition when she saw the pieces.

"Where did you get this?"

"An old Helan merchant gave it to me. Someone who clearly had no use for it."

"It's mine." She took the pieces from me, but the poor crown went to dust and rubble between her fingers until there was nothing left. "I made it. From mud and clay and a broken pot. It used to have a piece of colored glass for a jewel."

"For your coronation, queen?"

"No. This is what I sent to Threle to call attention to my tale. The one they rejected. It was called 'The Crown of the World.'"

Now it was my turn to stare in silence while Aeren clumsily wiped crown dust from her traveling clothes. "Well." I watched her fingers makes streaks of gray on her cloak. "It appears that Walworth's official had no use for the crown of the world, either. It ended up on the Helas border." Aeren wrenched her mouth into a semi-smile, as if she found that both funny and infuriating. "Was it Beotun that inscribed the crown with a Clioan phrase?" She had told me Beotun's Clioan scrolls were in elvish. I was curious as to whether he lied to her or she lied to me.

"No. Scorch Beotun. *I* wrote the phrase in the clay." She didn't want to talk about this, but she also didn't want to credit anybody else with her crown. Pride got the upper hand, as it usually does. "Not that it matters, but I taught myself Clioan from an old book I found in a pile of tavern trash. That was before I met Zelar, before I met you, and long before I met Beotun."

"Why?"

"Because I did. I felt hidden in Anda . . . so buried by my inability to cut through the social order and find a spot from which to draw an audience. So I decided to translate some of my tales into a language that nobody can read."

"That's sensible."

"You speak sarcastically, but actually it was. Just not in a way that anybody else could understand—which was the point. It was pure and personal—to make my stories over in a secret language, so that no matter what happened in the real world, my stories lived in an invisible one that nobody could destroy and that only I could understand. Because who speaks Clioan anymore? Particularly in Gondal? Of course Zelar took my translations underground into his workshop where I didn't have access to them in my dragon form. I'd give anything to have those back."

"Then, bard, here's my gift to you." I produced all of the Clioan scrolls from my cloak. Aeren eagerly grabbed them out of my hands. "I've been carrying them ever since we left the inn, without knowing they were yours. You told me that some of them were written by Beotun. In elvish. So you were guarding your treasures, Stormdragon?"

"I assumed you wouldn't recognize elvish if it covered you in spit. Or Clioan." Aeren shook one of the scrolls excitedly. "This is the tale I called 'The Crown of the World.' I sent the original version, in Sarana, to Loudes, where it got rejected. But even in that version I used Clioan for the 'crown of the world' phrase."

"Why?"

"Because Clioan is like a hidden language and the crown of the world is hidden. It's the confluence of all the forces in the world, it makes things right, but the one who bears it may not even know it. *It's all about the secret justice of the heart!*" She was bouncing a little now.

"So the crown of the world is kind of like a poem you can't read." I spoke these words, but I said them without thinking. Then I remembered how I couldn't read the crown, how it lacked energy, and that Isulde had told me that my moon was a poem I can't read.

Aeren went still. "Do you read Clioan?"

"Not exactly."

She didn't believe me. "I described the crown of the world as a poem you can't read. How would you know that?"

"I didn't." I spoke wearily. "Wizardry, fairies, residual magic, lucky guess maybe. I carried your scrolls near my heart and your crown found its way to me. Maybe some of your language did, too?" She still didn't believe me. "I don't read Clioan, but I am skilled at reading hidden things."

She gathered her scrolls as if I had violated her heart. She stomped toward the door.

"Aeren. What little I know—the nothing I know—of Clioan is from Aleta. I showed one of the scrolls to her—I forget which one—along with the crown. She translated a few random lines and that had to be where I heard it." I didn't want to tell Aeren that Isulde had described my moon that way, because I didn't want her to know about my mandate. Not yet, anyway, and maybe not ever.

"Sure." Aeren spoke harshly and quietly. She didn't like anybody knowing Clioan, even Aleta, who had more right to the damn language than Aeren did.

"I do know the Countess of Clio will be very impressed with you, with your knowledge of her county's ancient tongue. You and she are among the very few people in the world keeping Clioan alive. Perhaps the only people."

The bard smiled. But only a little and without sincerity. "Then I should like to meet her. To keep the language alive."

I arranged to meet Aleta privately. I also arranged to move Aeren into Mirand's abandoned room. As Aleta wasn't proficient in Sarana and Aeren barely understood a few Bothan phrases, I knew I would be their only translator, so proximity would be a convenience. I had no idea of either's conversational skills in Clioan but I assumed they were minimal, as neither had had anybody to speak it with and the language itself appeared to be an exceptionally convoluted affair.

Perhaps they could pass notes. Which would be charming the first time and cumbersome ever after.

Anyway, Aleta approved of the arrangement. We were in her private chamber, a neat, unfussy room whose walls were as bare as Aleta's habitual honesty. The room held what I can only describe as a comfortable severity. The walls caught the sun, showing its light like they existed to reveal whatever truth was hidden in each moment. When the light found the dishes that Aleta kept above the hearth, I noticed they were painted with realistic scenes of well-maintained farms and abundant apple harvests. A bench that resembled the one I had used the previous night held a colorfully embroidered blanket. The embroidery depicted an old farmer leading an old dog toward home and sunset. The home was a tidy, welcoming cottage whose door vaguely resembled the main entrance of Aleta's castle. Behind the farmer was an overturned apple basket.

"My mother made that before I was born." When Aleta said this, she sounded nostalgic, reverent, and matter of fact. "They say she knew my birth would kill her." It occurred to me that Aleta's chamber was very much an extension of her—plain spoken with spots of warmth. Except Aleta's warmth was so genuine that you always felt it more keenly than anybody else's.

While I was still taking in the pleasant austerity of the room, the countess told me to sit. As I settled myself at a sturdy table bearing neatly arranged swords, she asked me to tell her everything I had learned about Mirand last night. Which I did. Sort of.

Meaning that once again I was truth*ful* without actually trafficking in truth. Which felt like a necessary desecration of Aleta's hospitality. But a desecration nevertheless.

"Milady. This what I know. Master Mirand came here holding more illusion charms against me than you can hold swords against a dragon. But as Mirand isn't an illusionist, I have to believe that somebody in Threle made those charms and worked with him on how to use them. Possibly somebody close to Walworth. I mean, I can't imagine Mirand acting without the king's consent. Can you?"

"No. But I also can't imagine Mirand coming here disguised. As anybody. Let alone as Caethne, whom he barely sees. I understand she's closeted herself in her duchy and is refusing to involve herself with Threle or with the rest of the world."

This was interesting, because Mirand had said the same when he appeared as Caethne. Aleta's corroboration made me think he was speaking truth. "Well, perhaps that's why he chose her image to project. He—or Walworth—knew that if Caethne has separated herself from the world, she wouldn't be likely to know or object. Anyway, the charms did more than create his oddly chosen disguise. Whenever I read him last night, and I did try more than once, they prevented me from seeing him as he truly is. Here." I laid the cord of broken charms on the table. "These charms are designed to obscure, to present their wearer in any way he chooses."

Aleta picked up the charms and dropped them in disgust. I quickly probed her mind. Even though she had willingly accepted my use of wizardry to disguise her as a servant during our escape, she loathed Mirand's use of illusion to disguise who he truly was. The former was for self-preservation. The latter was a lie that emerged from an unknown motive. "How did you know that he had these? If you couldn't read him, I mean?"

"At some point, I discovered that I wasn't reading him accurately. And, well . . . the charms are now destroyed." I smiled with a touch of at-your-service grandeur, to imply that I had destroyed the charms. This elicited an appreciative nod. The countess liked my "work." So far. "And the now the charmless master wizard is gone and I've moved Aeren into his room, as you know." Aleta nodded again. "Did you know that when he left he didn't say so much as a by-your-leave to me?"

"He didn't speak to me, either."

"But he did speak—at length—to the Queen of Gondal, who is still somewhat distraught by the experience." Knowing that Aleta had never been completely at ease around Mirand, I knew this would intrigue her.

"I can understand." She spoke slowly, weighting each word. "I've never gotten accustomed to Mirand's . . . intensity . . . myself. I've always preferred to deal with Walworth."

"Agreed. But even though I'm getting ahead of my story, here's what Aeren told me this morning. Mirand promised her anything and everything she ever wanted, including a bard position in Walworth's court, if she would leave Clio immediately and accompany him to Loudes. She refused."

Aleta's skepticism was so thick that I could feel it without reading her, but another quick probe of her mind told me her doubt concerned Aeren's refusal, not Mirand's offer. "Let me understand this. Your friend supposedly disappears to bard it around in whatever hidden corner she can whisper her tales in, yet she refuses a court position doing the same?"

"Yes."

"I don't believe you." There was nothing accusatory in her voice except the weight of experience. "No bard, musician, would-be actor or professional fool, no matter how useless, refuses the promise of fame. It's like a law of nature. Only far less interesting and far more dreary."

"You'd like Aeren." I spoke gently, but that only increased Aleta's disbelief. "She's had some bad experiences with wizards, including a horrific experience with Mirand's former master, who once promised her something similar. That alone made her hesitate."

"Merely hesitate?" Aleta laughed. "What else did she need to come to an outright refusal?"

"I can't say. But she was brought here by Isulde in a kind of fairy trance. I know she hasn't made sense of that experience yet and she's still profoundly affected by it. And of course since Mirand did say he arranged that without providing her with further explanation . . . " I let Aleta come to her own conclusion about Aeren's mistrust of Mirand.

"As far as anyone can arrange what a fairy does. Did he even pretend to be truthful when he said this?"

"Pretend? I don't know. Every time I read him, I got a strong sense of truth. Everything else was obscured."

"Did he tell you why he was here under such remarkable circumstances?"

"Yes. But I found what he said so . . . disturbing, so mystifying . . . well, the short of it is, Countess, is that he also promised me something close to my heart, which I also refused. Something that would have consequences for the world, which probably explains why Isulde arranged our encounter, with or without Mirand's help."

"So that's why he was here. Isulde led him to you . . . disguised . . . so he could make this offer. And took her own interest in your friend." Aleta didn't exactly believe me, but I could read that she was afraid to disbelieve me. "What was it he offered you?"

I hesitated for effect. Studied the light spreading across the wall. Looked at the newly-washed floor, sighed once, and then looked solemnly at Aleta's hard expression. "He offered Threle's support in making me king of Helas, with the understanding that I would then reunite Helas with Threle. Obviously I refused."

"Why? That's almost as strange as your friend's refusal. Why wouldn't you want to rule Helas?"

"Because . . . " This would be delicate business, but clerisy is wonderfully persuasive. "I have my own doubts. Helas is a small

Botha-speaking duchy . . . kingdom . . . whatever it happens to be this week. And Threle is apparently in a mood to . . . *unite* . . . is the word Mirand used . . . with any Botha-speaking territories it can as a bulwark against the Botha-speaking southwest."

"He said this?"

"No. My impressions and experience said this. He didn't have to."

"So you . . . think . . . he wants County Clio?"

"Yes. Eventually. Anyway, I think that enough to not want to involve myself in the intrigue. I'm tired of intrigue. However, I did agree to speak with Walworth directly at some point, but only to test my impressions. Naturally, I would like you to be there, Countess."

"Naturally." Aleta fell very quiet and very angry. "I should insist on being there."

"So King Walworth will send for me—for us. But before that happens, I have a plan. A way to protect your . . . *our* county, as I may now call Clio my homeland, thanks to your generosity."

I removed the Truthfinder from my cloak and laid it gingerly on the table. Aleta studied the broken sword with something approaching awe. She looked at it long enough for the light to move across the walls. "May I?"

"Of course, Countess. This is the weapon I promised you." Aleta carefully, and then firmly, grasped the hilt. "This is also the weapon I choose for you to use in my service, that is, the service of our county. As you promised." Her vow, my clerisy, held strong as I knew it would. I could feel our bond. "But first we need to repair the blade." I smiled confidently. "So it's magic will sing again."

"Can't you? With all your knowledge of magic?"

Damn! The wielder of a Truthfinder will destroy himself if he carries duplicity. Most likely my moon would simply destroy the weapon, but I wasn't the right person to "heal" this sword.

"Milady. It's your weapon. Heal it in truth, your truth, and you shall carry it well. I remain your humble adviser, but the healing must come from the one who carries it. Yourself."

She set it down.

"Master it and we'll bring it with us to Loudes. 'Show' it to Walworth. It restores things to their true forms, to what should be, so perhaps you can use it to satisfy yourself as to what his true intentions are."

"True forms." Aleta was intrigued.

"If he is being honest, if he truly is Clio's friend, the sword won't reveal him to be anything else. If he's lying, you have the right to defend your county."

"It's poor strategy to go there."

"He won't come here." Aleta considered this. I spoke again. "I believe that Isulde brought Mirand and me together, not at Mirand's request, but because she decided to let us know, through fairy play, what's afoot. I believe she brought Aeren because we once shared Gondal's throne, and the Gondish land we embody is so neutral and keeps so much to itself that the gods want to use it to help County Clio maintain its historic neutrality. If Aeren was brought here for any reason, it's for that, to keep the energy of Gondal together, so together we can be of service to Clio. Here."

Aleta crossed the room and sat on the bench. She stroked her dead mother's handiwork, thinking.

"There's more." I spoke as the countess looked up from the blanket. "Gondal's queen is a great admirer of your history. Did you know she taught herself Clioan, and out of respect for Clio's history, has composed secret stories in it? That was one of her tales you translated for me." Aleta tilted her head to the side, utterly fascinated. "That crazy crown was her handiwork, although it still isn't clear how it found its way to the Helan border. But Aeren has 'barded it around' a good deal, as you put it. I had no idea of her passion for Clioan, because she lacks a typical bard's pride and keeps her passions private, but it makes sense. Who better in the world to help save Clio from Threle's duplicity?"

Aleta rose, paced away from the bench, and stopped to briefly shut out the world. I watched her back and shoulders tighten. She was thinking physically, the way old soldiers do in the heat of a difficult battle, when logic is a deadly burden and only divine frenzy protects. Then she stretched her sword arm toward the hearth. She was making a supplication, but her gesture had nothing to do with the gods.

"We will repair the Truthfinder. I will learn to use it to the best of my ability. We will go to Loudes when Walworth sends for you. The Queen of Gondal is my honored guest for as long as need be."

"So be it, Countess. I am your servant. And your friend."

Sixteen

Running bright with truth. That was County Clio's motto. I saw it everywhere. I saw it forever. Neatly carved over shop doors. Painted like holy writ on devoutly unadorned walls. Emblazoned in clear black thread against the sunrays that held the center of Clio's flag. Sometimes the words invaded my dreams until I swear I began to read them minutes before I woke. I never heard anybody speak the motto, but I heard "truth running bright" through the way Aleta's people spoke everything.

Aeren heard it too. Without even knowing the language, she remarked on the clarity and confidence of the voices around her. "Nobody hesitates before they speak. There's no hint of hesitation while they speak. And then, when they stop speaking, they stop with conviction. Like they carry some weird faith that they've said everything that can be said. For always and ever. Is everybody as casually candid as they sound?"

"Probably."

"But is truth ever that easily granted?" I could almost feel Aeren playing with the idea.

"It is if you believe it is. Maybe it is here."

Anyway, the streets and markets were soaked in these cadences. Which quickly ran from refreshing to wearisome. Nobody understood honesty as a strategy, or even as a choice. So after a while all conversations were so predictable that they almost weren't worth having. But then, neither puffery nor slander had become an acquired skill. Those who attempted either did so clumsily and to much disdain. And when praise or calumny was given, it was sincerely meant and sincerely earned.

Aleta's fellow citizens were fine people, but Clioan culture occasionally grated. Clioans had traded poetry for a limited version of reality that could be known and measured and accurately described only as far as hard description went. And in making this trade they lived in a reality more artificial than anything they shunned. It's impressive how much truth you can speak when you exclude everything interesting. It's equally impressive how little you actually end up saying. Once you reduce anything to a sheath of inarguable facts, you inevitably miss everything that matters.

County Clio may have run bright with truth, but for the next several weeks, everything existed in translation. That is, I kept remembering something Mirand used to say when I was his apprentice: "We can *only* know truth in translation, and only in free translation at best." Well, here was "free translation" in abundance.

First, the obvious. Aleta wasn't interested in the awkwardness of conversing with Aeren through Clioan notes. Although at their first meeting she did accommodate with a brief written greeting in response to a much longer letter that Aeren presented to her. Aeren looked slightly disappointed with the brevity of Aleta's response. I then translated the following exchange.

"Also," said Aleta in a tone that was half cheerful and half rebuke, which made her words sound entirely like a rebuke and only underscored the brevity of her written response, "instead of dressing like a wandering actor for attention, you might want to dress in a way that shows people who you are."

"This is how I am. In my heart." Aeren said this quietly and sincerely, with a subtle intensity that made me proud of her. She then spoke as if she was giving Aleta a high compliment. "What is the difference between me dressing like a male bard and you dressing like a highly skilled fighter?"

"I *am* a fighter." Aleta took less notice of Aeren's hurt expression than she took of Aeren's attempt to charm. "You may dress as you wish, but in Clio people won't take you seriously if you show yourself around dressed like something you're not. I'll provide you with more appropriate clothes if you want them."

I tried to mollify Aleta. "I'll conjure something for the queen to wear." Aeren had no idea what I had just said, so she nodded cautiously in my direction, managing to unwittingly snub the countess.

Aleta then suggested that Aeren make herself useful by translating old Clioan documents into Sarana. "It's not a necessary job, but I understand it's something you can do. I've translated many of them into Botha, but preserving them, and Clioan history, in a second living language is something I've thought about for a while." Aleta waited with a touch of impatience for me to translate; she spoke again before Aeren could respond. "Of course, you don't have to do anything, and you may stay as long as you wish. Although I can't imagine *why* you are here aside from being my chief advisor's friend."

Because Aleta was running brighter with truth than necessary today, I translated to Aeren that she was, of course, free to do as she liked and that she was quite welcome to stay as a fellow head of state.

Aeren quietly expressed insincere gratitude and agreed to translation duties with equally insincere enthusiasm. Aleta's curt disparagement of her bardic identity had left a mark that wasn't going to fade. We left soon after, with the understanding that I would show Aeren to the library, even though I had no idea where it was.

Secondly, the not so obvious. Meaning that there was also something like "free translation" going about like an open secret in a closed court. A secret that Mirand had dropped.

As it went, the scrolls in the wall recess in Aeren's room were blank. I learned this because Aeren was making use of them to write tales and to translate Clioan history. She would carry them back and forth to Aleta's small but tolerably appointed library, where she spent most of her time working and avoiding Aleta. It fell to me to present her translations to the countess, who had no way of assessing them but was vaguely pleased that Aeren was doing something vaguely useful. She said nothing further about Aeren's bardic garb.

A few days after I took on the role of go between, Aeren called me into her room and handed me a scroll. "Is this yours?"

The scroll was littered with Sarana text written in Mirand's tight, insistent hand.

It was a transcript of our conversation, which he had obviously manifested and left for me to find. Across the top he had written, "Copy for you. I'm taking mine to Loudes."

Naturally. I was so annoyed I forgot Aeren was there. I mostly, in that moment, simply wanted to free myself by fulfilling the rest of my mandate and retiring to an isolated cottage somewhere. The world could die without me in it. Then the feeling passed into something more complicated.

"Did you really say all these things? About evil, I mean? And about friendship?"

"Sure." I managed to sound nonchalant. "And Mirand managed to copy them."

"Oh." Aeren paused. "Well. Leaving aside that Mirand apparently has nothing to say on his own concerning friendship, you made *your* relationship with 'evil' sound like some pseudo-intellectual prattle that wouldn't convince a dry bone to stay dead. But it was quite a show."

"The problem with pseudo-intellectual prattle is that sometimes it's true."

"No, the problem with pseudo-intellectual prattle is that it's always true. Or true enough but incomplete. Like everything else. Zelar's evil was nothing like yours. Yours is apparently nothing like anybody's."

"Apparently." I really wanted to change horses. Fortunately, Aeren did that for me.

"So. Threle wants us to rule Helas? And then Gondal? And that's the offer 'close to your heart' that you refused for both of us?"

"Since you read the scroll, you know I'm willing to talk to King Walworth. And I did say you could travel with me if I do go to Threle. If we speak with Walworth, we will speak as Gondal, not as one or the other. And then we will, when we have all the facts . . . evaluate our options."

"You warned me against trusting Mirand. If you don't trust him, why talk to his king?"

"Because there's a reason Threle is tempting us with offers. And there's no reason to refuse to learn why."

"Of course. One should never refuse to learn anything." She might have been mocking me, but I didn't care. And by the time I did care enough to speak again, she had left for the library.

Third, the not at all obvious. There was "free translation" running bright through my daily interactions with Aleta and Aeren, aside from those sparse occasions when I translated for them. Aleta and I needed to repair the Truthfinder. Aleta assigned that task to me, due to my training and experience in magic. I didn't want to tell my new sovereign that my strategic use of duplicity meant that I was not the best candidate for repairing the sword. So I decided to use her library to research how to go about repairing such a weapon, thinking maybe I could guide milady through whatever needed to be done.

I found nothing useful. However, Aeren found a Clioan book devoted to magic weapons and agreed to translate sections of it for me without telling the countess, whom she barely spoke to anyway. Which meant I was able to derive what needed to be done and able to direct Aleta to do it. "Since you will wield this sword, milady, *you* must repair it." This wasn't true, but to borrow a phrase from Aeren, it was "true enough." Aleta believed me. And under my direction, she did get it working. Which was impressive.

I also managed to do weapons training with Aeren. I still had the two wands I pinched from Helas, and my bard was delighted to learn how to use them. Working through our admittedly tenuous wizard-bond, I taught Aeren how to match her energy to her wand and how to blast objects together. "As Gondal, when we attack, we attack with the force of our land, with the neutrality of the wasteland. There may be situations in which it's useful to defend ourselves without you turning dragon." I didn't tell her it may be useful for both of us to blast Walworth and so destroy Threle, because I didn't know that yet myself. But I certainly wanted the option.

After several weeks of weapons training and navigating the awkwardness of Aeren and Aleta limiting their mutual contact, I received word from Walworth that he desired to meet with me . . . and the Queen of Gondal. As soon as convenient.

Aeren and I were in the library when the message arrived. Maybe it was morning. Possibly it was another dream running bright with truth. But I looked up from a matter I was researching for Aleta to see a bottle of Krygon ale on my table, perched among some old books as if it had always been there. Which it hadn't. And, as I held the bottle, idly questioning whether it fell out of an old dream and whether to acknowledge it as the old joke it referenced, my old illusionist comrade, Baniff the Gnome, playfully swaggered out of invisibility and presented me with Walworth's terse message. Which was a masterful touch. Mirand had conveyed my thoughts on friendship to Walworth, so Walworth had sent the first "friend" I ever made in Threle. I read the note. Then I warily studied the illusionist.

"Lad! And how goes ye now this many a day? Many a year, is it? Thought ye might be missin' a bit of the old Krygon about now." Baniff had almost always addressed me in Botha. His informal use of Sarana was painful and practiced, because while Sarana is often an intimate language, it is never familiar. He was obviously speaking to and for Aeren, but his attempt to charm failed splendidly.

"What's a Krygon? Isn't that some kind of ale gone bad?" Aeren was remembering Zyren's harsh joke about Krygon ale, and her voice conveyed her clear irritation at Baniff's chatter interrupting her work. Which was convenient, because it saved me from having to respond.

"Why milord lass." Baniff playfully gestured at the ale bottle, skillfully including Aeren in the sudden camaraderie he was trying to coin out of nothing. Damn, Mirand had trained him well. "Didn't you know that Krygon is the finest ale squealed out of sunshine and dead swamp in fair Sunnashiven, the lad's own birth city? Don't be fooled by the sludge. I promise ye it looks better 'n it tastes."

"Fair what?" Aeren wasn't taken in by the show. She didn't know much about the world beyond Gondal, but she had somehow acquired an accurate impression of Sunnashiven. "Last I heard, Llewelyn was from northern Threle." She looked at me and shook her head slightly, as if to say "Who's this?" Getting no response, she turned her attention back to the gnome. "And why are you referring to a pile of books as a 'sludge' after you've stood there staring up at them for the last several minutes as if you couldn't figure out what they're for?"

"I was staring at the lad here." Baniff's face told me that he was surprised that Aeren could see through his illusion spells, but he masked his expression with a good-natured tease, as if we were the best of friends and had just seen each other yesterday. "Tryin' to figure out what *he's* for."

The gnome's sally made Aeren laugh a little in spite of herself. I spoke over her laughter. "Baniff. Buddy. The Queen of Gondal commands enough bardic magic to see through your illusion spells and into your last drunk. Your fake bottle and recent invisibility are nothing to her."

Baniff made a deep bow and a triple flourish with his weather-beaten hat. "Well, lads, illusion doesn't affect everyone." I took this as a veiled reference to my getting taken in by Mirand's use of illusion charms. His gesture also annoyed. If he was entirely insincere, it would have felt belittling. But he was sincerely trying to show courtesy to Aeren, so the gesture felt mocking, but only in the way a warm joke between close friends does. That is, he didn't mean the gesture but he managed to indicate that he meant the respect it referenced.

This confusion of meaning and message worked. Aeren returned his bow. And with as much elaboration. "You speak Sarana with .. . a curiously delightful accent."

"Well, milord, it's said we gnomes do three things well. Live long, drink long, and . . . speak Sarana with a curiously delightful accent." Aeren laughed again, louder and more easily this time. "Shall I recite some poetry for ye?" The gnome waved his hat again and began to shuffle himself into an improvised dance as a prelude to a poem.

Now I laughed, momentarily forgetting how easily Walworth's circle had once enticed me, at a much more naïve stage in my life, into an illusion of friendship. Then I made myself sound needlessly formal. "No poetry, Baniff. But you may tell the King of Threle that the King and Queen of Gondal will meet with him . . . as soon as convenient. To us. And that we plan to travel with the Countess of Clio, whose favor we very much cherish." Aeren scowled a little. "When are you returning?"

Baniff adopted my formal demeanor as another friendly tease. "We leave at once. The king awaits your response."

"We?"

"Ah, yes. My traveling companion. Six illusion spells and the threat of gifting him free casks of Krygon for life couldn't stop him from inviting himself—I mean *complementing* my journey. He wants to see the lassie so badly. Fancies himself an old friend of the queen's."

I could see Aeren desperately puzzling over who this old friend could be, which was difficult because she had as many old friends as

I did, which is to say, none. Then she smiled and gasped with genuine excitement. "Is it King Furna? Is he here? Yes, of course I must see him." As she rose with the litheness of a new dancer eager to impress, an equally excited figure stumbled over himself into the library and fell like a wounded cow, clutching and kissing Aeren's cloak in an embarrassing display of . . . not emotion, but of a well-trained ability to display emotion. The show was apparently intended as some sort of tribute, because he placed at her feet a tangle of over-blown roses and a small, blunt sword that was painted like a garish puppet's toy. I think the too-wide "blade" had a badly-done image of some sort of . . . animal with bleeding roots for limbs, maybe? . . . or a tree grinning in pain? Some oddness that didn't exist in nature and thankfully didn't need to. I know the hilt bore stripes of bewildering colors, as if the artisan had insisted on inventing his own. Aiming to damn nature twice, he hit the mark both times.

And then the wounded cow kissed the sword. More than once. With great ostentation. Which simply made everything worse.

The cow was Lord Graen. He also managed to knock over Aeren's table of carefully organized books, disrupting her morning's work and earning disfavor so thick you could wear it in a winter storm. Although it wasn't clear that he noticed.

Graen addressed her in rapid, breathless, botched-up southwestern Botha. In fact, his speech was so rushed and scurried with bovine-like lowing that even I had difficulty following him. But as Aeren kept staring indignantly at him and at me, I did my best to translate without laughing at him or smacking off his head to make the nonsense stop.

"My queen yet lives. My queen. I thought you dead." Untranslatable cow-lowing. Or something. "I imagined you gracing the gods with your presence, making the stars jealous by living among them." Aeren angrily narrowed her eyes; I knew she felt like Graen was mocking her, or that maybe I was. The problem was, he wasn't. "I watched for you in the night, in every night, by every candle, by every light of life itself—" Then I stopped translating because it was too ridiculous. And because Baniff, who understood Botha as well as I did, caught my eye and made a subtle hand gesture and a face that broke through my caution and made me laugh against my resolve. He'd clearly had his fill of Graen, too.

So I let him ramble in a language that Aeren couldn't understand until my latent sense of decent incivility interrupted him. "You're done. You want to have another go?"

"Another what?" Graen knew I was referring to our last encounter in Hala, but his political instinct made him feign surprise. "My *friend*. The queen of my heart lives. And so all is forgiven." He opened his arms as if to embrace me like a brother. I stood with mine folded, to Baniff's obvious amusement.

"I'm not your friend."

Graen glanced at a comically unhelpful Baniff. Then he noticed that his "queen" had disappeared with whatever work she could salvage from the toppled table, leaving the unhappy nest of flowers and the toy sword among the remaining scattered books. I knew she had slipped out of a door that was partially hidden by the bookshelves, but I wasn't going to enlighten Graen. I also knew she would be ranting for days about this disruption. "Where did she go?"

"I don't know," said Baniff affably. "Maybe she doesn't like you."

Graen looked sadly at his rejected gifts. As he slowly bent to retrieve the ridiculous sword, I spoke inquisitorially to his back in a way that was calculated to change the mood and take advantage of his confusion. "So. You abandoned Helas and made your way to Threle. Why didn't you return to Furnesse?" Since Mirand saw me leaving Helas, and Graen would have told Baniff I was recently there, I decided I had no reason to avoid giving away my recent stay by asking Graen why he left.

Graen stood, looking more useless than the sword-shaped bauble in his hand. He did manage to make eye contact with me, but he couldn't hold it. He spoke stiffly. "King Furna sent me to Helas to work with his cousin. Helas was not satisfactory . . . for many reasons. So I decided to seek my fortune elsewhere."

"One of those reasons is apparently no longer valid." He knew I was commenting on his recent enmity toward me in Hala having suddenly swerved into friendship.

"Yes! Thank the gods! But I also developed a strong dislike to Furna's cousin . . . 'King' *Cathe*" —he emphasized the name to show both his disgust and his knowledge of Cathe's real name— "who apparently has his own interesting past, and little need for my service, given his habit of excluding me from important decisions. When he refused to take my . . . admittedly premature view of the queen's fate seriously—"

"Even though your view turned out to be wrong?"

"Yes, but Cathe didn't know that. Just as he blamed me for causing a civil disturbance in Hala without knowing the facts."

"Didn't you?"

Graen thickened up his practiced courtier's blandness. "That depends on what you call a disturbance." Baniff looked with mock seriousness at the mess Graen had just caused, which made it more difficult to suppress my laughter. "As to the queen." Graen took a long breath. "I admit I was wrong about you."

"Well, given the facts," I spoke while indicating the spot near the overturned table where Aeren had been standing moments ago, "what else can you do?"

"Well, *given the facts* when I left Hala, I thought Threle might be interested in what I knew; in what you and I trained as brothers-in-arms for. Me for Chief Wizard Mirand and you for King Walworth, was it not?"

Of course Graen's tongue would make things more challenging on that end than they already were. But I managed to mirror his blandness. "So you've turned the shoe for Threle. Well done."

"And I hear you've done the same now for County Clio, Brother. And I also hear that Threle would be happy to have you back but is pleased that you are supporting an old and cherished ally." He glanced at Baniff for confirmation.

Baniff looked noncommittal. Then the gnome picked up an inexplicably streaked rose, pretended to study it for effect, and dropped it, looking impeccably underwhelmed. "Threle would be fair with ye, lad." The illusionist's voice was tinged with a sad sincerity I couldn't let myself believe in.

"Fair is as fair does." So was mine.

Baniff left immediately after our encounter. Graen refused to leave at all. He was resolutely cleaning up his mess in the library when I went to inform Aleta about the morning's events.

The countess wasn't happy. When I told Aleta about Baniff's brief visit and Walworth's message, she irritably remarked that I should have learned more from him before he left, even though reading through layers of illusion would have brought up nothing useful. She also expressed annoyance at him finding his way through her castle without an invitation, when she was out scouting the sky for more dragon sightings. "Mirand shows up in disguise and tries to manipulate you into joining Threle in its fantasy of uniting my land with his. And now Baniff shows up—*invisibly*—and without so much as delivering a plain good greeting to me, delivers Walworth's message to you. Neither of them found it in their interest to approach me directly."

"True."

I waited while Aleta considered the facts. She didn't like the inference she was forced to make, but her highest annoyance was reserved for Graen. "Isn't he the same Furnessian fighter I chased out of the Helan marketplace?"

"Yes."

"I remember you mentioning his name. So he's traveling with Baniff now?"

"Well, not now. He's still here."

Aleta briefly closed her eyes, slightly shook her head, and sighed. "To spy?"

"Possibly."

"Keep him here. Read him, if you can. That is, if Threle hasn't made that impossible. Find out what *he* knows. We will visit Walworth at our convenience, to show that we owe him friendship but not prompt obedience."

"Agreed. See any dragons this morning?"

"No."

"Perhaps they're hiding."

Graen was easy to read. The problem was, predictably, that he didn't know anything useful. Whatever Walworth really wanted, he hadn't shared with him. And so Graen knew no more than Threle decided he needed to know. Which was nothing. I learned that Graen blew into Threle like a furious wind, spilled what he knew regarding Helas, and earned himself a place swording it around in Walworth's orbit. When Mirand returned to Loudes and revealed that Aeren was in Clio, Graen invited himself on Baniff's excursion. Now he was once again my problem.

Aleta decided it was prudent to limit her contact with him, lest she inadvertently reveal something to Threle's new "spy." She also didn't want to chance being recognized from the marketplace incident. So my days were devoted to weapons practice and playing translator for Aeren and her exasperating Furnessian cow.

Which turned out to be another sort of weapons practice, because both of them behaved badly.

Graen wouldn't stop his pestering and Aeren liked feeling her power. And since I had convinced her to reject Mirand's offer, she also liked to underscore for me, her humble translator, how strong her bardic power was, making sure I couldn't fail to appreciate how much I made her give up. A conceit that quickly put me out of patience and often made me wish she'd gone to Threle with Mirand.

So here's what happened.

Graen kept stealing strange multi-colored roses from people's gardens and leaving them at our door. I caught him once. He playfully bowed, swirling his new cap to the floor, but with such easy good humor I was surprised by a rush of vaguely friendly feelings that I quickly put aside. "Queen Aeren once noticed my sensitivity to flowers in a way that made me aware of my sensitivity to everything. These are for her." His ridiculous cap was adorned with violets. I remembered the cap he wore in Furnesse with its mess of embroidery and trinkets. Now, instead of an image of a garden, he was wearing the real thing.

"I'll let her know. Again."

Graen laughed a little. Then he laughed a lot. "Yes, my little gifts are a daily offering now. I once feared that my love of colorful, blooming, springing *life* would be perceived as weakness in a swordsman like myself. So I hid it." He put his hands to his eyes and lurched in a mock gesture to indicate secrecy. Then he laughed again. And I laughed, because his gesture was so comically natural while being completely unlike Graen the politic courtier that it did amuse. "But when I'm with Aeren I could wear gardens in my cloak and care nothing for other people's opinions."

"Uh . . . that's good. I guess."

"And when can I see my queen today?"

"Later. When we're both up for it."

"Ah, yes, my lord translator." Graen pressed some coins in my hand. "Eternally grateful for your service. And for you."

I felt bad for the guy, but only in the way I sometimes I feel bad for fools.

I then made the mistake of teasing Aeren about these daily offerings when I brought them into her room. "Looks like milord is now committing morning larcenies to please you. Can't you make it stop before Aleta finds out and has him thrown in a cell?"

Aeren didn't like the tease. "You mean before Aleta charges him with being himself? Or with displaying a self she doesn't happen to believe in? Which one carries a higher penalty?"

"Stealing from the neighbors."

Aeren lectured me. "Lord Graen is the consummate swordsman who can kill demi-gods with his weapon and yet swoons like a moonstruck maid before a lilac bush. I watched him do it. Swoon before a bush, that is."

"So did I, bard." When I begged off translating it wasn't worth the commotion from either of them so I got to see everything.

"Maybe that makes him more vulnerable than he needs to be. And not one to play with."

"Maybe that makes him interesting. Like an unexpectedly complex character. And in case you haven't noticed, I'm *playing* with Aleta. She doesn't care for me showing my true self either." Unfortunately, whatever point Aeren was using Graen to impress on Aleta was clearly getting missed as truth's own votary kept her distance from both of them. "Besides, I've no control over milord. What would you like me to do? Go to Threle?"

"You've got a Ring of Beauty. Why don't you wash it in rose water and see if Graen jumps over the moon at your bidding? Then tell him how ridiculous he's behaving and maybe he'll stop." I could tell that my sarcasm hurt more than I intended it to.

She ignored my tone. "I don't want the damn ring. I don't want to look like somebody else."

"Then Graen's got more courage than you do."

And so it went.

And then, soon after, she washed the damn ring in rose water. Whether to spite me or play with her new bardic powers or make some obscure new point wasn't clear, but her decision didn't appear to have anything to do with Graen or Aleta. Which I decided was remarkably insensitive on her part and clumsy on mine for taunting her to do it. Especially since poor Graen would have jumped over the moon, sun, and stars if he knew how. What happened is by combining the ring's power with her own limited gift of bardic illusion, she looked . . . well, not conventionally beautiful, but like a much more intense and compelling version of herself. She appeared simultaneously like the attractive young man she always insisted she was, and like her plain female person, and there was no contradiction between the two. It was just there. You noticed it in a way you couldn't point to and yet couldn't miss. Sometimes it was odd, like the streaked roses she made the water from, but the result was utterly fascinating. If I hadn't known her so long and wasn't a priest of Hecate, I might have been taken in. Graen didn't have a chance.

But he stopped filching roses. He turned from cow to goose, following her everywhere. And when Aeren insisted on privacy, he followed me because I was connected to her. "She puts me in her stories."

"I know. She puts everybody in her stories."

"But she puts *me!* She told me if I'm not careful, I could kill a demi-god with my sword." He smiled like he had just learned how. "A demi-god!"

"I know. I was there."

And so it continued to go.

Until one morning I found myself with Aeren in the field near Aleta's castle, the same field we had crossed with Mirand on the evening after our fairy encounter. We were blasting stumps and stones and dimming sunbeams with our wands for fun. We were friends again, and of course we were arguing about everything for more fun. It was as if Graen had never happened.

"You appear to have run out of rose water." Aeren looked like her former self, and I meant this as a compliment. "Maybe that's why your wand work is getting better."

"I ran out of roses." She blasted a mound of dirt. Without my guidance.

"You'd never know it from Graen. Are you done now?"

"Done with what?"

"With whatever point you're using him to make?"

Aeren took aim with her wand and lowered it without blasting. "He does what he does. If he likes my tales and wordplay, how does that concern me?"

"You know who you remind me of lately?"

"No."

"Ellisand. Remember him?"

Aeren shrugged. "Yes. The minstrel who tried to outmaneuver me from the royal bard position you promised me before you abdicated. How the scorch do I remind you of him?"

"He could be difficult, too. He liked to pretend his music was just a job and that he had no idea of anything else."

"Maybe it was."

"Or maybe he liked pretending it was. Aeren, your bardship *is* a job, but you like pretending it isn't."

Aeren lifted her wand again and blasted another dirt pile. She didn't give a damn. "You mean I get paid?"

"No. I mean since Furna and the fairies gifted you, you need to use those gifts responsibly. And you should use them to . . . I don't know, show people ways to become their true selves, show them paths to be who they should have been before their lives mangled them into something else. Only a few will take those paths, but a lot of people like knowing the paths are there."

"Didn't you tell Mirand all about paths?"

"I told Mirand a lot of things. What you don't do is turn a swordsman into a mewling lamb as a show of power to the countess."

"What if he *is* a mewling lamb? Or something. Maybe I did my 'job' or maybe I was just there when it happened. Or maybe this is one more turning of not being accepted even with a charter from King Furna and a blessing from the scorch-be-damned fairies. I understand your friend Ellisand creates all kinds of 'paths' with a lyre and gets praised for it. I get unasked for advice. Is that because my male garb isn't convincing enough today?"

"No, it's because you shouldn't encourage Graen to be a fool. He's identified so much with one of the characters in your tales that people are laughing at him behind his back."

"So what do you want me to do? Go to Threle? Furnesse? Sweep floors in Gondal?"

"Stop treating him like a character instead of a real person. He loves flowers too much. Show him something ugly for balance. Give him the whole world, not half. A true bard should hold up a mirror, not a flattering portrait. Maybe he needs to remember he's also a fighter and that pain exists, too."

Aeren considered this. And while she was considering, Graen showed up to augment our chat into something truly uncomfortable, because really what else was he good for?

"My heart. You are so perfect."

Aeren looked at me with something that wasn't quite agreement and wasn't quite remorse and wasn't quite pride, but was freely touching hands with all of them. Then she turned her attention to Graen.

"My lord. I once knew a dragon that only" —she stopped, waited without expression because I was hesitating in my translation, and then continued— "that only a swordsman with soft flowers in his heart and hard truth in his eyes could approach and live."

I spoke the words in Botha and nodded approval. Graen remained still and smiling. A bunch of delicate flowers trembled in his hand, nodding drunkenly in the morning light.

"One day, such a swordsman decided to try his fate by regaling the poor creature with gifts. He brought her his childhood toys, hidden in a box that only he could see. He brought her his most precious wishes, locked in a language that only he could speak. He brought her golden bowls to drink his dreams from."

This wasn't one of her better tales, but Graen was transfixed.

"He brought her his secrets to share like a raisin cake."

"Did he live?" Graen was gone. Into the story and gone.

"I don't know." Aeren continued sadly. "The dragon tore the gifts in half. She promised to guard one half in her cave with the rest of her treasure. The other half she kissed with fire and returned. This half was now so bright from her kiss that the swordsman couldn't look at them without burning his eyes. So he carried them on top of his cap, for all to see. But they burned the eyes of all who saw them. And so the townspeople hated the swordsman, because he hurt everyone with the joy he felt from the dragon's kiss."

"What happened to the other half?"

"They became shadows in her keeping."

Aeren stopped speaking for a long time. She stared at the ground.

"Is there more to the story?"

"Yes. One day, to guard the swordsman against the world's mockery and to keep him whole, the dragon returned the rest of his gifts, unasked."

And then Aeren turned dragon.

Graen didn't scream. Maybe he couldn't scream because a world died in his heart. And then his heart died as he kept staring at the dragon, who slyly picked up the fallen flowers and devoured them as Graen helplessly watched. And then he ran. Just ran. But I knew he wasn't running from the dragon, he was running from the moment when the dragon devoured his flowers, for he had no weapon for that. That is how I somehow knew that he was running somewhere to die.

"Satisfied?" Aeren was her not-no-simple-self again.

As I tried to parse whether I, Aeren, or Graen was to blame for this new disaster, Aeren coldly reached into her cloak, took out the Ring of Beauty, and smashed it.

Seventeen

Aeren disappeared for days. Three days. Six days. Nine. Like a timeline from an old folk tale. And of course she ignored my wizard calls.

Aleta expressed impatience, as she now wanted to travel to Loudes. When I told her that Graen had also left with no explanation, she said she was tired of Walworth's people coming and going as they pleased. Of course I withheld what actually happened. She then ordered that preparations be made for us to leave, with or without Aeren. Which meant that I wouldn't be able to embody or manifest Gondal, if needed.

And then, on the morning we were making ready to start our journey, Aeren showed up.

"Are you coming with us?" I spoke flatly, without interest, although her answer obviously mattered. I just couldn't bring myself to ask where she went.

Aeren shrugged. Her voice was just as flat and unenthusiastic. "I suppose."

"Then get yourself a horse." I spoke without emotion as I turned my back to load supplies on mine. Much as I wanted Aeren by my side when I met Walworth, so as to meet Threle as Gondal, I was done translating for her.

She spoke harshly to my back. "I flew three days until I found his body. He died of a broken heart, like a prince from an old story. I made him a grave and put flowers on it, for rebirth, so that he might come again through the flowers. I also broke my wand and buried it with him, because he was a fighter and it was my only weapon."

Damn! By destroying her wand in some mad gesture of respect for Graen, Aeren had compromised our ability to take out Walworth. I was suddenly so angry I had to remind myself that I never told Aeren about my real motives for training her in wand work and bringing her to Loudes. So I didn't respond. I mounted my horse.

"And then I flew to Furnesse. Maybe you'd like to know what King Furna told me."

Actually, I did, but I didn't want to make it easier for her. I looked down from my saddle, shrugged. "I suppose you'll tell me." I started to leave.

"Stormr left Helas. He went back to Furnesse and Furna arrested him as a spy for Threle. Furna is deciding whether to execute him. He left Helas because Threle showed up there with an army and King Cathe went into hiding in a monastery where Threle can't touch him. So right now Helas belongs to Threle again but it doesn't have an actual ruler of its own. Maybe Walworth really does intend to set us up there."

This was interesting information, but I still wasn't in the mood to show I cared. So I rode off to join Aleta's party the instant before Aeren finished speaking.

Our route took us northeast through secluded forest paths. We traveled in silence and so there was nothing to translate. Everyone merely understood that we had nothing to say. I rode between Aleta and Aeren, speaking only as necessary, which was mostly not at all. Aleta's servants did their jobs.

At one point, thinking I could always blast without a wand but that Aeren couldn't, I reluctantly gave her my mine. We were now in a Threlan duchy on the west side of the country, somewhere west of the Duchy of Glamisson, having crossed the unmarked border into Threle without remarking on the crossing. We had gotten separated from Aleta and the servants, and I leaned over from my horse and placed the wand across her saddle, speaking directly to Aeren for the first time on our journey. "Don't lose it." She avoided looking at me, as if she preferred whatever distance she could create. This was her way with me since I stopped speaking to her, but she did take the weapon. I knew at some point we would need to communicate, and I felt glum about my silence widening the rift, so I tried to soften things a little by attempting to open a conversation. "What's the end of the story with Stormr?"

Aeren stared straight ahead, looked down at her horse's neck, and responded quietly and carefully. "I don't know. Ask Furna. Ask Zeus." She looked sad and tense and confused, and I knew without reading her that all of that came from her not being able to communicate with the party, not wanting to communicate with me to ask to communicate with the party, and her chagrin at me suddenly giving her my weapon because it reminded her of what she did with hers. And then she said something that was clearly meant as some kind of offering to me. But it only made everything worse by coming across as an insincere acknowledgement of a wrong. And because she bravely thought it was the right thing to say and not because she meant it. She put the wand in her cloak and looked ahead at Aleta's back, who was a long distance ahead of us.

"I should give up tales."

"That's your choice, but you'll be miserable if you do."

"I'll be miserable if I don't."

"Everyone's miserable. You're not special."

Aeren kept staring at her horse, kept refusing to look at me. "So I've heard. About not being special, I mean."

And then we returned to silence.

Sometime that night, Aeren disappeared with the wand. When her absence was noted the next day, Aleta told the servants to spend exactly one morning looking for her in the nearby field and town, which I suppose was harsh but necessary. One of them returned with pieces of my wand, smashed as if it had dropped from a great height. Another reported that the townspeople spoke a language that none of us understood, but that they excitedly indicated through drawings that a dragon had been seen flying due west at dawn.

Whatever. So Aeren was retreating to Furnesse. Maybe she could keep Stormr company. I couldn't care. When Aleta suggested that Aeren had been taken by the dragon, I didn't argue.

And so we continued. We entered Glamisson in the early evening and took lodging in a comfortable town. I remembered traveling through Glamisson years ago as a clerical student, when I was secretly planning to save Walworth and Mirand at their trial. In those days, I heard the singing streets and buildings, caught the energy of the story of the wizard who built singing streets and walls in each town as a tribute to his wife's beautiful voice. Now I heard nothing but what was there for everybody to hear—crowd chatter, horses, merchants ringing bells. Beautiful in its own way, as Threle always is, but not as beautiful as it truly was in its deepest self.

"Glamisson doesn't sing anymore."

Aleta half smiled at what she considered my nonsense. "It never did."

Two days later, the Duchy of Sengan welcomed us with its traditional acorn and a kiss, tokens of the deep contrasts that marked the duchy's land. The countess accepted her welcome graciously, lightly kissing our greeter's cheek in turn. I merely assented to the custom and rode on as if Sengan didn't touch me. Except it secretly did. Sengan was still hard like an acorn and soft like a kiss, still an improbable huddle of opposing extremes manifesting themselves in jagged mountains and gentle valleys. Only the valleys I remembered that once held snow like bowls of fleece were now bare and burned. When I traveled through Sengan on my way to the trial, I had remarked how those extremes marked the difference between what I truly felt and the mask I had to wear to survive and carry out my plan. And now those same extremes marked another difference—between what I truly felt about my mandate to restore the world and what I . . . well, truly felt about my mandate to restore the world. Meaning Sengan's division still mirrored my own, Threle and all its charms be blessed.

And then, as we were just about to pass out of the Sengan Mountains and enter the vast Threlan plains, the Truthfinder broke. I have no idea how, but Aleta was practicing with it, challenging herself by trying to find something she could restore to its true form. Her Clion servants, being as true to themselves as all her people, were happy to let the countess wave the sword at them. They laughed, but none of them changed. The Sengan Mountains weren't changing, either—a few rocks turned to slightly different colors, that was it. Although that might have been the turn of the sun as much as the sword. But that's when the sword broke.

And, naturally, given the nature of my own relationship with truth and our limited resources, I was of no use to repair it.

Which led to Aleta making her usual sort of sensible, logical decision. "There's no reason to continue to Loudes without the sword, because I no longer have the ability to use it to satisfy myself of Walworth's true intentions."

"I can read him."

"If you were unable to read Mirand, you can expect Walworth will be too protected for you to read him." *I knew she was right.* "Given the dragon sighting in Glamisson and the recent sighting in Clio, I'm returning to Clio where I can be more useful. I will await your report on the meeting."

"You made a soldier's vow to me. You carry other weapons."

Aleta looked thoughtful. She spoke judiciously. "I promised to learn any weapon of your choosing and use it ever at your service. I learned the weapon of your choosing, I was willingly using it in your service and my people's, and would have continued to do so. But the weapon broke, so my vow is fulfilled." Damn Aleta's patient logic. I tried to sense our bond, the clerical bond I established through Hecate to bind her to that promise. The bond was also broken. So her promise was fulfilled.

"The gods keep you home." That was all I could say to it. Aleta nodded in appreciation. Then she left with her servants.

And so. I left the Sengan Mountains and entered the Threlan plains alone. Without art, without truth, without even the ability to embody Gondal—weaponless.

I hadn't remarked on the mountains when I crossed them with Aleta and our party. But once they were behind me, I turned to them. I looked at them for minutes the way one looks at familiar things with the sudden realization that, despite that familiarity, you've never truly known them. The Sengans are black, rocky mounds holding blinding white snow tops to the sky, and they mark oppositions like everything else in Sengan. I kissed the acorn in a helpless gesture of uniting extremes and threw the acorn toward the mountains like an offering. Then I turned my horse and proceeded to cross the plains.

There is something about the midland plains of Threle that feels like the outer limits of eternity. You sometimes cease to know yourself because the ground and sky are endless and impersonal, and at times their claim to reality simply overwhelms your own. You lose your idea of yourself as separate from all else. And then you lose yourself. But the plains don't take you in. Nor do they reject you.

They just don't exist with you. And so they don't acknowledge you. And after a few days immersion in their vastness, there's the gods own work to be done acknowledging yourself.

This was my third crossing. Once with El, to Loudes, to Walworth's trial, taking the same path I rode now. And then, following Caethne's witch call to Walworth's duchy in the north, when I rode across the plains to her castle, where Threle stole victory by breaking the world. And here I was again. Same sky, same unchanging expanse, same view of Threlanche.

I did not stop in Threlanche. But due to my distance and perspective across the flat terrain, I saw it forever as I rode. The city was always there, like something both ill-defined and endless that had no way to leave and so left me no way to ignore. So much so that when I finally couldn't see it anymore, nor even see the suggestion of its towers in the haze of faraway air currents, I felt like I was not so much alone again as abandoned.

And still I rode. Through an expanse of Threle that no longer felt like Threle, or like anything. The days resembled eternity—timeless, frozen, as if I were the only movement, a mindless, goalless movement, like a number "moving" through a mathematical proof or a vector in a physical description of a magical formula. And then I merely knew myself as a physical line of force describing Hecate's will. And then not even that.

My awareness of myself lurched out of whoever I was, and I no longer existed in separation from anything. There was only horse, and long, flat brown plain, and unnamed plants and wind—and I was like oil or blood or rain smeared over all of them and then I was—if I was at all, but words don't reach the mark here—all of it. Like a flash of Hecate's dream.

I think I stopped by night.

When the red towers of Loudes rose in the distance, I knew I had ridden two days from Threlanche. I also slowly returned to myself, remembering in time—not all-at-once time but mundane time—where I was. But my riding still bore a resemblance to my journey through the North Country, where everything bends and changes as soon as you think you know it, where multiple suns birth moons and smile themselves into fairy toys.

And when, perhaps a day or so before I saw the red towers, I saw swathes of spring violets nodding among the fully ripened corn, and the once pure sky shredding into patches of olive green and dark blue, I understood that Threle was responsible. Loudes was Threle's capital. Loudes was the king's home. In the rest of the world, nature frayed in barely-seen spots, and at a distance, as in Gondal, in unseen unsensed ways—here, near the source, it was florid and unmistakable. This was the result of Mirand and Walworth's stolen victory.

Why would Walworth not want to fix this? I chose death to save Arula, and Walworth chose to do nothing to save the world. He could abdicate, he could work with the best wizards and clerics in the world, and he refuses to clean up his blotch on history.

This understanding made me sadder than my mandate, but it clarified things.

And then I knew that I had entered Loudes without realizing it, the way one enters Threle. Not because Loudes fails to mark its limits like Threle fails to mark its borders, but because my thoughts were a kind of unmarked border that distracted me from realizing I was in the city now. And then, I felt an overwhelming desire to visit the courtroom where I had risked everything to save Walworth and Mirand's lives. The courtroom where King Thoren, who then ruled Threle, accepted my testimony but decided under Threlan law that I had to return to Kursen Monastery. The courtroom that led me back to Kursen, where I learned of Walworth's betrayal and, as a result, tendered myself to Hecate.

The courtroom was empty now, and smaller than I remembered. If there were officials about, I didn't see any. The sunlit squares on the wooden benches looked clean and cold and the benches looked long unused, as if the court was taking an extended break—not just from legal business—but from its place in the world.

And so I opened my mind to Mother Hecate, because Her energy manifests itself in all legalities that strangle and limit lives, and because the intersection of my life with this dead court was a crossroads that led directly to Her. She came to me. She kissed me cold.

"Bird and wingless. I remove your moon but not your duty."

"Mother Dark. Shall I finish this journey unprotected?"

"Yes."

"But the fairy . . . Isulde . . . told me the moon will break when I restore balance, and then" —I choked, barely forming the prayer— "to go to Mother's heart."

'My will is my own. My moon brought you here, but you shall make the balance solely out of yourself and your own power. With your heart alone or not at all. The line of scar in your body reminds you of your future if you fail."

"Will my magic be enough?"

"Your wizardry was earned. Your level of clerisy was given to you through Cathe's interference. I now withhold it. When you destroy Threle and restore the world, you must work from what is yours and nothing else." Hecate ended my prayer.

I rose shakily, absorbing the court's emptiness into my own. My moon was gone. My scar line, earned under divine torture, chafed when I leaned on a bench for support. I don't know how long I stood there before I left, or whose time to measure it by.

And then, with only my wizard shield to protect me, I found the king's residence.

"What do you seek, traveler?" The guard was friendly, as Threlans usually are. He addressed me in Sarana, the king's language.

"Safe lodging. And a meeting with King Walworth."

"And who are you, friend?"

"Llewelyn. Of County Clio."

"Would you prefer Botha then?"

"No. I prefer solitude."

"I'll send a message."

Again I missed time. There *was* time—there were unexpected changes in the afternoon light, and clouds coating rooftops with soft cloud shadows, and unfamiliar languages emerging and vanishing into casual knots of passing people. But none of it touched me.

And then a quiet servant led me to a cluster of richly appointed rooms. "Be home."

"I will."

I locked the door and sat lightly on the floor, throwing myself into a trance that would no longer come, praying to Hecate, feeling the weight of history curl around me. Hecate did not respond.

Of course I would have to wizard blast Walworth, as I had no other means of attack. And I would have to drop my wizard shield to do it. And even now, it was possible that Mirand was reading me through my shield . . . through *our* shield, through our wizard bond. I didn't sense him reading me, but there was no longer anything to stop him. And why wouldn't Walworth be protected against wizard blasts and against mine in particular?

And yet there was no way to destroy Threle without destroying the one who embodied it, no way for me alone to obliterate the entire country save through killing its king. Walworth had damned the world to save Threle. If I failed to make that right, we would be damned together. And if I succeeded, well then the king could explain himself to the gods. That wasn't my concern. If my motive was the selfish one of avoiding my own damnation, wasn't his also selfish? Didn't he really damn the world to save himself?

There is no right. There is no wrong. There is only motive. And when you find that motive, it's often ugly and not worth the quest.

A rap on the door interrupted my thoughts. The quiet servant had returned.

"The king will see you now."

Pale and trembling, I followed her through a blur of palace and then through a hall of dirty windows. I could see through the sullied windows that the sky was checkered now. Light and shade made random patterns under my feet. I was grateful that I didn't need to speak.

And then I was alone and just inside the doorway of what could have been the throne room. That is, there was a throne, carved with swords and dragons and sun and moon. And a line to divide all. But the chamber was too small for royal audiences and held little else, and so I couldn't tell if the real throne was elsewhere. There was an unlit candle on each side of the throne, one black and one white, and an exceedingly bright, white canopy above and behind, framed in black.

I waited uneasily near the door, wizard shielded and just inside the room. The servant had gone her way. The room was unoccupied save for myself and the shadow of myself that the happenstance light from the hall cast on to the canopy. That is, above the throne.

I am the shadow king. I am the poem you can't read.

I moved to the right corner on the same side of the wall as the doorway and waited for Walworth to enter. My shadow moved with me, leaving the canopy. I didn't sense anybody trying to read me through my shield, but that could change at any time. I supposed I would drop my shield and blast him. I also supposed he was so well protected that my blast would only serve as a last-minute argument for divine mercy until whatever wizards protecting him returned fire, which wouldn't take long. And then I would go back to Hecate—as rotting unread book or unwilling son. So be whatever may.

Hecate said I could only work out of myself, out of what was mine. And what was mine was . . . what? My childhood in Sunnashiven, my early loyalty to Walworth's cause, my sincere and improbable love for sincerely improbable Helas, that damned orange cat, Caethne's witch songs, my youthful experience of intense friendship and learning, risking everything for Threle at the trial, my dedication to Hecate, Isulde's dreams, Ellisand's music and my role in saving it, turning El against his heart's longing, the death of poor Devon whose friendship I forced, my first meeting with Aeren in her dragon form, becoming King of Gondal, my trial in the North Country . . . always the damned North Country. And now here. Here to close. And then to open. Everything.

Yes, Mother, all is motive. But what motive now is mine?

Would we be damned together? I supposed we were both shadow kings. His wound on history and my binding to Hecate—is there a difference? Hecate said my level of clerisy was not from myself. But Walworth's kingship over a country that should have been defeated was not meant to be—therefore it was not his own. Hecate had withdrawn my shadow, my clerisy. Walworth's victory was also a shadow. And didn't his twin, Caethne, sometimes call me her twin? Didn't that make me Walworth's?

Caethne once taught me an old principle of witchcraft, of nature itself, in which like stands in for like. A doll for a person, a green candle for new plants, a piece of bark for a roughened heart. It is not mere substitution. The trick is seeing the like as the like—relating to the bark as if it, somewhere in the mind of the gods, *is* also a roughened heart, and perhaps the roughened heart of someone you know. It makes a path.

Behold the shadow of the country that razed the world. Behold the shadow on the throne, the king's mark against the gods. Behold another backward path. See it. Know it. And kill it.

And then I noticed, that sometime in my thoughts, or somewhere within them, a shadow had usurped part of the white canopy. I knew the shadow was Walworth's. He was waiting in the hall outside the door, where the uneven light threw his image on the blankness that guarded the empty throne. Waiting for what, wasn't clear. Of course the room would appear empty to him, so perhaps he was waiting for me. Or he knew I was there in the unseen corner and was simply somehow waiting for my thoughts to clear.

I dropped my shield. I flattened myself further into the corner, knowing I was now defenseless and liable to be blasted into damnation at any moment by any wizard reading my thoughts, and that Walworth would be shielded and guarded. I studied his shadow as if it were a process, not a mask, the way Mirand had advised Beotun to study my essays. That is, the shadow did not obscure like a mask; it revealed its source. But what it revealed was ephemeral, a point in Walworth's life, a life in process as mine was.

So I drew on the witchcraft that Caethne, Walworth's twin, once taught me, and saw the shadow on the throne as like to mine.

And then I saw the shadow as his life—as Threle—gone wrong.

And then I saw myself as shadowless, as Mother had left me.

And, then risking everything—knowing I could get blasted first—I wizard blasted his shadow on the throne—as a like to his life, and to wronged Threle—with the intent of restoring the world to what it should be. With the intent of writing a poem you can't read. If Walworth embodied Threle, then, considered in the right way, his shadow embodied a shadow Threle; the illegitimate Threle that Mirand's wand blast plundered out of history. And so by blasting the shadow, I intended to destroy that shadow Threle. And by destroying the shadow Threle, I intended to restore the world to what it should be. Without killing Walworth himself. Just as Walworth had apparently fulfilled Threlan law by letting me die but not interfering when Isulde revived me.

And buried in the magical poem I had just created, in its divine structure, I saw the back of Mother Hecate's skirts as she faded into dying stars. And I also saw, perhaps as one sees like for like, the face of Her opposition, Athena, smiling soft approval. And then the vision ended, and I was back in Loudes.

Naturally, I destroyed the throne. And the room. And the hall. And, based on the rubble, a reasonable area of the palace. I was laying on rubble, unshielded and somehow unhurt, as reverberations from my blast continued to run in all directions as if someone had thrown a stone in a cosmic pond.

Then I noticed my scar line had disappeared. And just as I knew that Hecate had placed it there to remind me of the tortures that awaited should I fail in my mandate, I now knew that I had undone Mirand's damage and balanced the world. The waning moon scarred into my left palm had also disappeared. And then I looked up and saw the patchwork sky had now gone blue and clean, and it held light the way I remembered it was supposed to. I had assumed that Walworth and his wizards would be well-shielded and therefore survive the blast, but I tried to open my clerical senses to discover if anyone had died. I couldn't do it. My bond to Hecate was broken. In fact, I was bonded to no one.

When the reverberations stopped, I searched around but found nobody. I might have heard Walworth's voice in the distance, but he was hidden by the ruins.

I expected the results would be more dramatic. When Walworth participated in tearing open the universe, I felt like I ran through a divine cataclysm to escape the results. Now, setting things right, there was damage, but not nearly so much. Forces go where they want to go, and when you open a path, they go about their business with comparatively little fuss. But whether Threle was now somehow a defeated country embodied by Furna or had just been pummeled back into balance with the world and newly restored nature, I couldn't guess. And then I thought of Athena and Hecate again and decided that if Furna was a stand-in for Zeus All-Giver, it could easily be both.

And then I got tired of thinking.

Somewhere in an undamaged part of the king's residence, I found the quiet servant clutching a pillar for comfort. I approached her as if it were all just another day. "Two messages." I conjured two pieces of sealed parchment and two gold coins. "Favor me by sending this one to King Furna and his Royal Bard in Furnesse at the end of the world. And this one to Countess Aleta of County Clio." The servant nodded and took the coins and parchments. Inside Furna and Aeren's, I manifested in Sarana, "All is well." Inside Aleta's I manifested in Botha, "My report on the meeting: All is well."

And then I returned to the ruined throne.

I heard Walworth's voice in the distance again, but I had no desire to approach him. I conjured a bottle of Krygon Ale and poured the ale on the wreckage as a libation to everything. Then I conjured a note inside the empty bottle and left it to catch sunlight on the blasted throne.

The note was addressed to Walworth and Mirand. It read in Botha and Sarana, "Job's done."

ABOUT THE AUTHOR

Karen Michalson writes literary fiction disguised as genre fantasy. She is a criminal defense attorney and former English professor. She studied law at Western New England College (now University) and has a Ph.D. in English from the University of Massachusetts at Amherst. She lives in Massachusetts. Visit her online at http://www.karenmichalson.com.